# GUARDIANS OF DAWN

# YULI

## S. JAE-JONES

**TITAN** BOOKS

Guardians of Dawn: Yuli
Print edition ISBN: 9781835415610
E-book edition ISBN: 9781835415627

Published by Titan Books
A division of Titan Publishing Group Ltd
144 Southwark Street, London SE1 0UP
www.titanbooks.com

First edition: August 2025
10 9 8 7 6 5 4 3 2 1

This is a work of fiction. All of the characters, organizations, and events portrayed in this novel are either products of the author's imagination or are used fictitiously. Any resemblance to actual persons, living or dead (except for satirical purposes), is entirely coincidental.



A CIP catalogue record for this title is available from the British Library.

EU RP (for authorities only)
eucomply OÜ, Pärnu mnt. 139b-14, 11317 Tallinn, Estonia
hello@eucompliancepartner.com, +3375690241

Printed and bound by CPI Group (UK) Ltd, Croydon, CR0 4YY.

For all the besties
who take things seriously,
but in an unserious manner

# PART

THE WAKING DREAMERS

Princess Yulana had a problem.

Well, it was more like seven smaller issues combined into one much larger one, which was the matter of coordinating a rescue effort with the Bangtan Brothers.

And the problem was too much visibility.

From her vantage point on the edge of the town square, Yuli looked with amazement and dismay at the screaming hordes of people that chanted the members' names as the boys passed through the streets of Urghud. Just the week prior, a somber hush—along with the chill of winter—had settled over the northern capital in the days following the Warlord's funeral. White banners were still draped over the canopies of every storefront, flapping like ghosts in the ever-present wind, but a festive atmosphere had descended over the city ever since the Bangtan Brothers docked in Urghud's harbor.

It was going to make this rescue operation that much more difficult.

"By the Great Bear." Yuli scowled, observing a handful

of youths fawning over the eldest, Bohyun, on the edge of the crowd. "They're just a bunch of *boys*."

Good-looking boys, she had to admit, even if their looks did nothing for her. Of them all, it was sly-eyed Taeri who was her favorite, because his slinking grace brought to mind the dancers of Zanhei's pleasure district. Although it was Sungho who played the feminine roles in their plays, Taeri reminded Yuli of the courtesan-poetess Huang Jiyi with his heavy-lidded eyes and pouty lips.

"They haven't been in Urghud in two years," said Auncle Mongke beside her. "Why should the rest of the Morning Realms enjoy their talents while the north languishes unloved and forgotten?"

Yuli rolled her eyes. Several players and performers traveled through the northern capital on a regular basis throughout the year, although none had been quite so eagerly anticipated as the Bangtan Brothers. In the weeks leading up to their presence in the city, paper posters with their likenesses had been plastered on wooden walls all over the marketplace. They had always been popular, but now it seemed as though everyone—*everyone*—knew of them, and some even went so far as to exchange little tokens carved with the boys' names and iconography with one another in their own sort of black market.

"Focus," she said to the shaman. "We need to be in place when Junseo gives the signal."

She met the Bangtan leader's eyes across the square, where an enormous pyre had been built. Despite the chaos and consternation caused by the presence of the performance troupe in their midst, the crowd was rather subdued, and an uneasy air hung over the proceedings. It had been several years since the last public execution of a magician in Urghud, and the pile of kindling in the center was a stark reminder of the uncertain times through which they were all living. Rumors of abominations in the south, the undead to the west, and the Heralds of Glorious Justice on their front steps, bringing with them hundreds of refugees from the steppe villages and the possibility of civil war. Magic was returning to the Morning Realms, twenty years after the north thought it eradicated during the Just War.

And for the first time in two years, a magician had been found in their midst.

"Here." Auncle Mongke surreptitiously handed their niece a bright red hood, a few shades lighter than her distinctive ruddy hair. "Don't forget to put it on when the time comes."

"I won't." Yuli tucked the hood into her coat and rearranged the dull brown scarf covering her face and hair. "But it won't do us any good if no one's paying attention to me because of the Bangtan Brothers."

It appeared as though the northern chapter of the Guardians of Dawn had underestimated the Bangtan Brothers' popularity. Junseo and the other boys had experience in smuggling magicians to safety in other parts of the empire, but no one had taken into account their growing fame when organizing this rescue mission. The plan was to hide a few of the members among the crowd until the right moment, when the prisoner was being led to the pyre, before setting off a series of distractions, during which Yuli—dressed in her bright red hood—would grab the victim and run. Junseo, Sungho, Taeri, and Yoochun would then put on and take off their own red hoods in the crowd to act as decoys, while Bohyun, Mihoon, and Alyosha would continue raising mayhem with magic.

A classic bit of misdirection, Sungho had said. One of the oldest tricks of the stage.

But the members weren't exactly going unnoticed, especially Bohyun, whose handsome face might have been his greatest asset onstage but was his greatest liability when trying to mingle.

Which brought Yuli back to her original problem: visibility.

"The Huntsmen have arrived!" a crier shouted, and the crowd's attention was momentarily diverted from the Bangtan Brothers to the cadre of riders galloping through Urghud's eastern gate. Yuli drew her scarf tighter about her face as the wolf-helmed rider at the head of the column bore down on the square—Maltak Ogodei, son of the Falconer and his father's proxy while the Kestrels held the imperial city against the encroaching force of the Heralds and their allies down south.

"Citizens!" Ogodei called from atop his restless mount. "Rejoice, for today we rid the north of a pernicious evil!"

Yuli rolled her eyes. The Huntsmen were little more than a rowdy rabble of raucous university students, more concerned with personal glory than with protecting the people from the threat of magic. In the Falconer's absence, Ogodei had taken up the Kestrels' charge to hunt down and pass judgment on anyone with even the most tenuous connection to treason, harassing and terrorizing the populace in the name of order and safety. Neither he nor any of the Huntsmen had ever faced down true evil—not a single abomination or revenant or even a member of the Heralds of Glorious Justice.

Until today.

The crowd gave a wary, half-hearted cheer. Executions of magicians and their sympathizers were meant to be public, to act as both a deterrent and entertainment for the audience, but there were more than a few—Yuli included—who did not have the stomach for it.

"Come, mimi," Ogodei said, gesturing to the small, plump figure on a docile mare beside him. "Bring forth the abomination!"

Yuli stiffened as Maltak Kho, First Daughter of the Maltak Kang, urged her horse forward. Draped over the pommel of her saddle was a slight figure, bound and blindfolded. For a moment, Yuli saw another figure lying there—redheaded and all too familiar—before she blinked away the memory. The last time she'd faced Maltak Kho had been at an occasion much like this two years before, when it had been her cousin, Jochi, facing the pyre. As though sensing Yuli's stare, Kho frowned and scanned the crowd from atop her mount, her dark, long-lashed eyes immediately catching on Yuli's as though they were the only two in the square.

The force of Kho's gaze shot through Yuli like an arrow—barbed and hooked, catching on all the soft, tender parts of her soul. For a long moment, the girls stared at each other, two years of regret and resentment hanging heavy between them.

"Mimi," Ogodei hissed. "The prisoner."

Kho startled at the sound of her brother's voice, breaking the spell between them. Yuli pulled her scarf tighter over her hair and face, trying to disappear back into the crowd. Her pulse pounded in her ears, and she could feel her cheeks glowing nearly as bright as her hair. Kho dismounted and gently lifted the prisoner off her horse, setting them awkwardly on their feet. Beside her, Yuli heard her auncle suck in a sharp breath, the bells of their pointed, twin-tailed shaman cap jingling uneasily as shocked murmurs rose all around them.

"Behold!" Ogodei called triumphantly. "The abomination to be purged!"

The abomination in question was a child, no older than seven or eight. The crowd shifted uneasily on their feet; it was one thing to cheer for the execution of hardened criminals, but a child was another matter altogether. Yuli reached into her coat for the red hood, looking around for the Bangtan Brothers. The mission had grown even more urgent, but none of the boys were in a position to set off the distractions.

She had to take matters into her own hands.

The Council of Shamans had gathered around the pyre and begun singing, a low, thrumming drone that resounded throughout the square as they prepared to sing the child's soul to the eternal blue skies. Slowly, smoothly, Yuli reached into her sleeve to pull out her brush, just enough to hold it between her left thumb and forefinger, palming the rest from view. Her mind grasped for character for *fire,* one of the first spells she had ever learned from *The Thousand-Character Classic,* although she had had little occasion to practice or use it. She quickly surveyed her surroundings; no one was watching. Taking a deep breath, she lifted her left hand and quickly sketched the spell before her, drawing on the void as the Guardians of Dawn had taught her. A glowing white-gold glyph shimmered in the air, and Yuli carefully, surreptitiously maneuvered the magic through the crowd with slight gestures. She wove the spell in and around their legs and feet, toward the pile of dried yak dung and kindling.

"Come on, come on," she murmured, willing the pyre to catch fire as Kho walked the child up to the stake. A bead of sweat rolled down her hairline, but no one seemed to have noticed her strange behavior. No one, save a youth in ragged furs on the other side of the square.

Anxiety drove a sharp spike of cold through her middle as she caught their gaze. What had they seen? How much had they seen? Had they even understood whatever it was they saw? The youth said nothing and raised no alarms, merely tilting their head so that their curls glinted with a hint of auburn. Yuli's hand strayed to her own auburn tresses hidden beneath her scarf in disbelief, wondering if she had seen a ghost.

"Jochi?"

*Whoosh!* The entire pyre suddenly went up in a blaze, sending a blast of hot air rippling over those closest to the conflagration. Kho threw up her hands in surprise, releasing her hold on the child. Yuli immediately swapped her dull brown scarf for her bright red hood and ran forward, sweeping up the little magician in her arms.

"The Heralds!" came a cry from the crowd. Yuli thought she recognized Alyosha's deep baritone. Thank the Great Bear the boys knew how to improvise. "The Heralds of Glorious Justice are here!"

At once the audience broke into pandemonium, shouts of panic and terror as the people scrambled for shelter. The Heralds had been harrying the northern boundaries for weeks now, and the fear topmost on every citizen's mind was the possibility of a guerrilla fighter in their midst. *Bam!* A minor explosion of dirt and debris went off on the far side of the square, and the crowd roiled, scattering in all directions and churning up clouds of dust that covered everything in a faint haze.

"The abomination!" Ogodei shouted over the chaos. "Don't let them escape, you fools!"

Junseo materialized by her side, his own red hood at the ready. She immediately traded hers for her brown scarf as the Bangtan leader donned his cap, acting as a decoy. He disappeared into the crowd, his tall height an easy target for the riders on horseback.

"There!" Ogodei called, pointing in his direction. "Follow that red hood!"

*Bam!* Another explosion, and more shrieks of surprise. Several of the Huntsmen's mounts spooked, bucking and rearing, causing even more mayhem in the crowd. Another red hood popped up several yards away, and Ogodei roared, unable to turn his horse and maneuver through the throng. In the midst of the tumult, no one noticed Yuli slip toward the mercantile district with a suspiciously child-shaped bundle in her arms, a bundle that was growing heavier and more unwieldy with each passing moment.

All save one.

"You!" came Kho's voice from atop her horse. "Halt!" She frowned. "Yuli?"

"Mother of Demons," Yuli swore. She could feel her scarf slipping off her head, revealing her distinctive hair. She let the child down on their feet and rearranged her head covering, scanning the crowd for a member of the Bangtan Brothers. She spied a bright red hood in the distance, drawing the attention of the other Huntsmen, but Kho stared her down, her long-lashed eyes narrowed with both suspicion and disbelief. Reaching for the knife in her boot, Yuli swiftly cut the child's bonds and removed the blindfold from their face. The little magician looked frightened and bewildered, but there was no time to explain. "Can you run?" she asked.

They blinked in confusion but nodded.

"Then run!" Yuli grabbed the child's hand and half dragged, half carried them toward the mercantile district.

"Where are we going?" they cried.

"Not now," she gritted out. The Guardians of Dawn safe house was a run-down secondhand bookshop at far end of the marketplace. "Just keep up."

Behind them, Kho struggled with her horse in the crowd before giving up and dismounting to pursue them on foot. Yuli was taller, faster, but burdened with a prisoner she was trying to help escape. It wouldn't be long before Kho caught up to them, and while Yuli was reasonably sure she could overpower the other girl if necessary, the last thing she needed was to be definitively outed as a magician sympathizer. Her best bet would be to try to lose Kho in the myriad turns and alleyways of the mercantile district.

"This way!"

Left, then right, then right again. At least the child was quick. They might have been small and frail, but they were swift and agile, leaping over carts and barrels, bobbing and weaving around various obstacles as well as any competitor during the summer sporting events on the steppes. They were quick but not quick enough, and soon, Yuli could hear Kho's voice shouting clearly over the din of the crowd.

"You there! Halt! I command you to stop!"

Suddenly, the auburn-haired youth from the square appeared before them, gesturing frantically down a darkened passageway. Yuli did not question their appearance nor their aid, immediately ducking down the space to find a narrow path running along the back of several storefronts and a low boundary wall, which stretched to both the left and the right. She could hear Kho's booted footsteps crunching along the gravel and dirt behind them and took a gamble, turning left and squeezing through rancid piles of refuse and rubbish, taking advantage of the shadows and obstacles that hid them from view.

The footsteps stopped.

Yuli chanced a glance over her shoulder. Kho stood at the crossroads, craning her head this way and that for a glimpse of her quarry. Yuli pressed herself flat against the building, holding her hand out to shield the child and to keep them from sight. There was a flicker of movement at the other end of passageway, a glint of auburn, and Kho immediately turned and followed that specter in the opposite direction.

It was a long moment before Yuli allowed herself to relax and catch her breath. Whoever—whatever—that youth was, they had just saved their lives, or at least given them a bit of a reprieve.

"Who are you?" the child asked in a trembling voice.

Their eyes were overlarge in their pinched face, the hollows too sunken, the cheekbones and chin too sharp. Up close, the little magician was older than she had initially thought; their malnourished body gave the impression that they were quite young, but there was a weariness in their expression that spoke to years of hard living. Ten, or perhaps even older. Ogodei had called them a *pernicious evil,* but they were hardly a threat to anyone, despite the magic in their veins.

"I am," Yuli said, remembering to tuck stray strands of her red hair back into her scarf, "a member of the Guardians of Dawn."

To her surprise, instead of gratitude—or even relief—the child's shoulders slumped with what seemed like disappointment. "Not the Heralds of Glorious Justice?"

"No." Yuli frowned. "Is that who you were expecting?"

They shrugged. "The Guardians of Dawn haven't done a single thing for the magicians of the Morning Realms," they said. "But the Heralds are out there fighting for our freedom. I thought you had come to recruit me."

"Recruit you?" Yuli raised her brows. "No, we came to rescue you."

"From what?" the child scoffed.

She gestured back toward the square. "From being burned alive?"

They shrugged again, and Yuli did not know what disturbed her more: the indifference in the gesture or the resignation in their expression.

"Come on," she said, holding out her hand. "We need to get you to safety."

"And where's that?"

"Tarkhun's bookshop," she said. "You know it?"

They nodded. "At the end of the Street of the Spear."

"Good, because that's where I want you to go in case we get separated."

"What if the Huntsmen catch me?"

"I won't allow that to happen."

The little magician eyed her warily. "How can I trust you?"

Yuli resisted the urge to stamp her feet with frustration, swallowing down her impatience. They were only a child, after all. "Because I'm a magician too."

"Prove it."

They didn't have time for this, but Yuli removed one of her mittens and held out her bare hand to the little magician. They took her fingers in theirs, and the hum of bone-deep recognition rose at their touch, the chaos in their blood resonating. The child relaxed.

"Can we go now?" Yuli glanced worriedly around them. At the far end of the narrow passageway, she could see the shadows of people still fleeing the square, chased by the deafening hooves of Ogodei's Huntsmen. They would have to find some way of blending in with the crowd. Yuli fingered the red hood hidden in her coat sleeve, then looked down at the child shivering in their thin woolen tunic and trousers. "Here," she said, removing her dull brown scarf and wrapping it around their head. "We need to change our appearance. Be ready to run when I tell you."

They made their way to the street entrance, and Yuli carefully leaned out to survey their surroundings. The majority of the commotion seemed to have subsided, but a Huntsman on horseback slowly patrolled the street on the far side, blocking the way to the Street of the Spear. She stiffened at the sight of the wolf helm; it was not just any Huntsman, but Ogodei. Yuli cursed beneath her breath.

"Stay where you are," she whispered to the child, pulling her red hood out from her coat sleeve. "I'll distract the Huntsman. Once the way is clear, run straight for Tarkhun's bookshop and don't look back."

The child nodded. Yuli slipped on the bright red hood over her own auburn hair and stepped out into the street.

"Hoi!" she shouted, waving her arms about. "Over here!"

At the sight of red, Ogodei whirled his mount around, kicking into a gallop. Yuli ran in the opposite direction as fast as her long legs could carry her.

*Now!* she cried, touching her mind to the child's. The ability to communicate mind-to-mind was one of the Guardian of Wind's gifts, and the only useful one as far as Yuli was concerned. The little magician took off without a second thought, leaving her alone with the Maltak Huntsman on her heels.

The breath burned in Yuli's chest as she pumped her arms and legs as hard as she could. She was fast, but not even she could outrun a galloping horse. But she didn't need to outrun the Maltak Huntsman for long—only long enough for her to duck and hide somewhere.

Then she would give Ogodei a *real* hunt.

Leaping over barrels and burlap bags filled with foodstuffs, Yuli quickly turned down a narrow alleyway and crouched down behind stacks of supplies. She could hear the horse's hooves thundering ever closer, but stopped to close her eyes and take a deep breath.

And exhaled her spirit.

The instant sensation of weightlessness, of freedom, pure, expansive potential. She was formless, shapeless, in the air and everywhere, and for a moment, Yuli allowed her ki to float free, reveling in exhilaration. Spirit-walking was the Guardian of Wind's other gift, and while it was not always the most practical, it had always been the most exciting.

Concentrating, she pulled the image of herself together—tall, broad-shouldered, freckled, and wearing a red hood—and launched her spirit from her hiding place. She ran past Ogodei and his horse in the opposite direction in a blur of speed, and she could sense his shout of surprise as his mount startled and reared.

Once more that sense of exhilaration ran through her. No longer imprisoned by the earthly burden of flesh, Yuli could duck, weave, dart, and fly without the constraints of exhaustion or fatigue. The Maltak Huntsman was no match for her speed, not when she no longer had to concern herself with such mundane matters as breath and weight and limbs. Every few moments she paused and waited for Ogodei to catch up, laughing as she dodged his grasping hands, which passed through her spirit form like air. She was getting reckless, but she couldn't help but needle him. Play with him. Toy with him. So often as a child, Yuli had trailed confusion and chaos in her wake, playing pranks on her elders and peers, crowing with triumph as they failed to catch her. What she loved best about being free of her body was that she could run and run and run for days without slowing, without tiring, without worrying about injury or obstacles or anything but the open skies. She could do this forever. She wanted to do this forever.

"What is this devilry?" Ogodei cried. "What is this abomination?"

And suddenly it wasn't a game anymore. Yuli felt the cord tethering her spirit to her vessel snap tight with anxiety, and she resisted the inexorable pull back to her body. She had been more than reckless; she had been a fool, brazenly flaunting her magic and her abilities without a second thought to the consequences. If Ogodei got a good look at her spirit form, if he caught a glimpse of the red hair beneath the hood, he would recognize her as the First Daughter of the Gommun Kang, as the granddaughter of the late Warlord, as—

Yuli returned to her body with a gasp.

"Another abomination walks among us!" Ogodei cried. "Huntsmen, rally to me! To me!"

There was a clattering of hooves against dirt as the other riders came from all corners of the marketplace.

"We muster at Maltak Manor tonight," the wolf-helmed warrior said. "And tomorrow at dawn, the hunt for the red hood begins. Search every home, every residence, every business. Be on your guard; there may be more than one."

The thumping of fists against shoulders in salute. Yuli held her breath, crouched down in her hiding place behind piles of grain and other foodstuffs. "Hail!" the Huntsmen shouted as one. "Tomorrow at dawn!"

Tomorrow at dawn. Yuli thought of the safe house at the end of the Street of the Spear and closed her eyes. The Guardians of Dawn might have rescued the little magician from the pyre, but the child was in just as much danger as before. They all were.

She felt the prickling tickle of someone's gaze at the back of her neck. Yuli opened her eyes in alarm and looked up to catch the same auburn-haired youth—the one from the square, the one who had helped them—staring back at her. She could not quite decipher the expression in their dark copper eyes, but when she blinked, they were gone.

The road from Kalantze to the bitterest north was haunted.

Zhara had always been rather ambivalent about ghosts. Growing up, she had read tales of vengeful spooks and woebegone spirits but had preferred her little romance novels borrowed from Master Cao's bookshop in the Pits. According to the stories, ghosts lingered where there was unfinished business—an injustice unaddressed, a sin unpunished, or a generational curse unbroken. Although she had lost her own parents at a young age, the proper rites had been observed and their ki sent on to the cauldron of the universe by the death nuns of the Azure Isles to be reborn and remade anew. She had never had anything to worry about from lost souls except for the occasional thrill from a horror novel that kept her up at night.

But after the past ten days, she was no longer so sure of her convictions.

"Stop fiddling with those," Gaden gently reprimanded Ami as she continuously, furiously wiped at her glasses with a corner of the scarf wrapped around her neck. "You'll only make it worse."

"This constant condensation is driving me to the brink," Ami complained as she replaced her spectacles on her face, whereupon they instantly fogged up again. "I can't *see* anything."

"It's because it's cold," said Gaden kindly.

"I *know* that," Ami said irritably. "I just wish I could figure out a way to stop it."

"You're a magician," Han pointed out. "Surely you can find a spell that prevents your glasses from misting up in the first place."

"I would if I could see *through* them," she muttered. By habit, she reached for the fragments of *Songs of Order and Chaos* she carried tucked into her sash at all times. "And if my fingertips weren't in danger of freezing off."

The hardships of the road had taken a toll on all of them—Zhara, Ami, Gaden, Okonwe, and even Han, whose good cheer had carried him all the way from Zanhei to the outermost west but had withered in the face of such brutal cold. Zhara had never been more miserable in her entire life, and she had spent most of it sleeping on the dirt floor of her stepmother's kitchen. Born and raised in the southern climes, she was unused to the bone-slicing chill, and the exhaustion of her body left her even more vulnerable to the plunging temperatures. Not even the warmth of Sajah's cat form around her shoulders could stave off the bite of winter.

The strange emptiness of the towns on the way to the Sweet Sea did not help matters.

"Another one," Han muttered as they passed yet another abandoned village on their route—animal pens empty, wooden buildings hollow. "Is there anyone left on the northern road?"

"Another victim of the Heralds of Glorious Justice, I

bet," Gaden said bitterly. Many of the smaller villages and outposts along the way had been claimed in the name of magician liberation, their residents vanished—either fled to Urghud or joined to the Heralds' cause.

"I don't know," Han said with a frown. "I don't see the banner of the Four-Winged Dragon anywhere."

It felt as though they had been on the trail of the Heralds for weeks now. Zhara knew that the more militant wing of the Guardians of Dawn was on the march toward the imperial city, but beyond that, news had been scarce to nonexistent. Many of the Guardians' safe houses farther south had begun to sympathize with the Heralds of Glorious Justice, believing magicians and their allies should rise up to seize power for themselves in the wake of the Warlord's death. But there were other forces in the empire that would resist such a rebellion, and the Morning Realms teetered on the edge of civil war.

Okonwe shook his head and pulled a battered map from his sash, spreading it atop their cart pulled by a pair of long-suffering yak. "We're ten days out from Dafeng," he said, pointing to the northernmost city in the Middle Kingdom of the empire. "It's likely the Heralds would have turned west toward the imperial city from there."

"Then what happened here?" Ami asked, squinting over the tops of her spectacles at their surroundings. The skeletal remains of tents and more permanent structures looked ghoulish in the fading light, canvas and fur flapping in the bitter breeze, the movement reminding Zhara of ghosts.

"A raiding party?" Han asked.

Okonwe looked uncertain. "Perhaps," he said. "Although I feel there would be other signs of violence. Broken arrows, churned turf, marks of a skirmish." He furrowed his brow. "It seems as though the people here just . . . left."

Zhara shuddered. The eerie, haunted sensation rose

up around her again, pressing on her ears, making the hairs at the back of her neck stand on end. "Let's move on," she said. "I'd rather not camp here for the night, if you all don't mind."

"We still have an hour or so of light left," Okonwe said. "We can press on for a little while. I'd rather not linger myself," he admitted. "There's something . . . unnerving about this place."

"We're all jumping at ghosts," Ami said quietly.

*Ghosts.* The word fell over the party like a blanket of snow, and shivers arose from them all that had nothing to do with the cold. Zhara pulled out the crystal encased in glass at her throat, the stone she had taken from the caves beneath Mount Llangposa. The crystal was made of magic, glowing in its presence and dimming before demonic energy. It gave off a faint rosy-gold light, reassuring her that all was well.

For now.

"Then it's settled," she said. "Let's get moving."

A strange, keening draft picked up in the last hour of twilight, an eldritch, voiced wind that sang as it swirled around them. It brought with it the dry, icy scent of snow and—Zhara wrinkled her nose—a curious emptiness that reminded her of the nothingness of death. They had all fallen silent as they walked, huddled together for warmth and comfort. Their way was lit by the softly glowing horn of Rinqi, the Unicorn of the West, and Zhara and Ami held aloft the illuminated magic crystals from the caverns beneath Mount Llangposa to keep the shadows at bay.

"Maybe we should have stopped at that abandoned village after all," Han said beneath his breath. "It's even creepier out here than it was back there."

Zhara couldn't disagree, slightly regretting their decision. "Just a little while longer," she said. "At least until this wind dies down and we can start a fire."

"There are people up ahead," Ami said quietly, pressing her glasses up her nose. The enchanted spectacles Zhara had given her granted her friend the ability to see the threads of ki woven throughout the world, just as they would appear to the girls in their Guardian forms.

Okonwe's hand strayed to the broadax strapped to his back. "People?"

She nodded. "Two," she said, a furrow appearing between her brows. "I think . . . I think one of them is a magician. But their ki is . . . different."

The big, black-skinned man lowered his hand, although he did not relax. "Tread carefully," he warned. "Magician or no, we don't know where their allegiances lie."

Zhara nervously glanced at the blade stashed with their supplies in the back of the yak-drawn cart. They had not come across any bandits, abominations, or undead on the road, nor had they come across any Heralds in the course of their journey, but their ever-present threat had hung over their heads the entire time. Although she had faced down greater demons and monsters before, Zhara thought she would be perfectly content if she never had to raise her hand in battle ever again.

The others prepared themselves for the encounter; Han readied a staff while Gaden put on a mask to obscure their scars. Ami brought out a horned headdress from the cart and fitted it over Rinqi's head to disguise her horn, as well as blankets and saddles to cover her distinctive body. Unlike Sajah, the Unicorn of the West could not change her form to hide her true nature, and the farther they ventured into northern territory, the more hostile—physically and politically—the landscape would become.

As they drew closer, Zhara could make out the dark silhouette of a lonely circular tent made of felt and fur.

"A message waypost," Okonwe said with relief.

"How can you tell?" Han asked.

The big man nodded at the few horses in a nearby paddock, short, stocky, and hardy-looking, their coats fuzzy instead of smooth. "Our four-legged messengers."

They had seen a few wayposts along their journey, and had sheltered at more than a few. Zhara's spirits lifted at the prospect of having a potential place to stay for the night, in the company of other humans instead of haunts.

"Hail!" Okonwe boomed in his deep, bass voice. "Any room for a party of travelers?"

The tent flap opened and a small figure with a long, thin mustache emerged. "Hail, travelers," they said cautiously. "What brings them to my ger at this late an hour?"

The party turned to Han, who cleared his throat. "*Summer, fall, winter, spring,*" he sang, singing the Guardians of Dawn password phrase. Of them all, he had the most pleasant voice.

The postmaster blinked and stared in bewilderment. "Bit touched, are we?"

The group exchanged wary glances. Not a safe house, despite the presence of a magician.

"Just overtired," Okonwe supplied. "We could use a place to rest. We've come all the way from Dafeng, and there have been precious few places to stay on the road."

The postmaster peered at them in the dark, taking in the big man's complexion, Gaden's masked face, and the strange assortment of animals by the cart. Zhara looked to Ami, who gave a slight shake of her head. Not a magician. The other must be inside.

After a long moment, the postmaster relented. "Come in," they said, pushing the flap open wider. "It does no good to dwell in the open after nightfall. It is the hour when haunts and hungry ghosts roam the roads, after all."

"Hungry ghosts?" Zhara asked.

"Ganshi," the postmaster said. "Disembodied spirits who will try to suck out your ki and possess your empty vessel."

Like demons. Zhara caught Ami's eye, and she could see the same thought had crossed the scrivener's mind. They followed the postmaster inside the ger after securing the yak and Rinqi in the paddock with the horses. Sajah refused to dirty his paws with the livestock and transformed himself into a little mouse to hide up Zhara's sleeve.

From the outside, the tent had not appeared like much, but the interior was spacious, comfortable, clean, and *warm*. The space was partitioned off with hanging hides to cleverly create the illusion of rooms, and at the center of the ger was a lit brazier, the smoke escaping through a small hole in the middle of the roof. Over the flames was a large cast-iron wok, and the sizzling smell of onions and fried meat filled the air. Beside it was a pot of what looked to be gruel of some kind.

"Sorry, I was just preparing dinner." The postmaster cleared some room on the floor around the brazier. "Sit, sit, make yourselves at home, friends," they said, eschewing formalities in the northern fashion. "My name is Basho, and I offer my sincere apologies for being such an inadequate host."

"All will be forgiven," Han said, practically drooling as he stared at the food, "for a plate of whatever is cooking there."

"Just a quick pheasant stir-fry, nothing fancy," Basho replied. "But you are welcome to partake of what I have."

"We have rations we can share," Okonwe offered. "Dried meats and tsampa."

"Respectfully, I would decline the tsampa," Gaden

said. "One can only eat it so many days in a row before the tongue yearns for something with flavor."

They all sat down on the clean dirt floor as Basho passed around bowls filled with gruel, topped with steaming meat and vegetables. Everyone tucked in with gusto, their hunger a greater spice than any their food had been seasoned with. Everyone except Ami, who was looking around the ger in confusion.

"Where is the other person?"

Basho stiffened mid-bite. "Other person?"

Zhara gave her friend a warning glance.

"I, er, I just thought there was someone else here," the scrivener stammered.

The postmaster narrowed their eyes. "There is," they said cautiously. "My brother, Nurden." They tilted their head toward one of the partitions draped at the back of the tent. "But he is ill with the waking dreamer sickness."

Gaden frowned. "The waking dreamer sickness?"

"Have you not heard?" Basho resumed eating. "I've passed along many messages from people all over the north about a mysterious plague afflicting parts of the empire."

Zhara thought of the abandoned village they had passed before arriving at Basho's ger. A plague. She thought of the outbreak of abomination that had riddled Zanhei and the undead infection that had swept through the west. She slid a glance to Ami, who was blinking rapidly with either excitement or anxiety. Perhaps both. If Basho wasn't the magician, then it must be Nurden, hiding behind the partition.

Okonwe shook his head. "As I've said, we've been on the road a good while. Most of the places we've seen have been abandoned, their inhabitants gone. We've assumed most had fled the coming war or joined the rebels."

Basho studied them all closely. "The Heralds of Glorious Justice?"

Tension filled the tent and Zhara straightened in her seat.

"Yes," Okonwe said carefully. "I believe that's what they're called."

The postmaster looked grim. "Aye," they said. "They've not come this way, although I hear stories of them from the travelers fleeing north to Urghud." They gave them all a considering look. "Are you refugees yourself?"

Zhara looked to the big man, who shook his head again. "We're couriers on our way to meet a shipment of goods coming in from the Azure Isles at Arkhevet."

"I see." Another pregnant pause. "Strange times, these," Basho murmured. "Abominations to the south, the undead to the west, and now the waking dreamer sickness on our thresholds. To say nothing of the coming war."

"When the world is out of balance, the Guardians of Dawn are reborn," Ami said quietly.

Sajah started in Zhara's sleeve, but the postmaster did not appear alarmed. "Aye," they said again. "I've heard too of these tales. Legendary warriors walk the Morning Realms once more, as they did over a millennia before to seal the Mother of Ten Thousand Demons back into her realm."

"Do you believe it?" Han asked in a guarded tone.

Basho met his gaze, then shrugged. "The matter of magic is beyond my concern," they said. "I have messages to deliver and an ailing younger brother to care for."

Zhara relaxed and looked toward the partition at the back of the tent. "May I ask what happened to Nurden?" She could feel Ami's eyes boring into the side of her face, silently communicating something she did not quite understand.

"I don't know." Basho refilled their empty bowl and rose to their feet, moving to the partition and drawing it back. On the other side was a young man lying supine on a pile of furs. A jagged scar cut from the corner of his right lip to his temple, long healed but wicked. His wind-darkened complexion was ashen and wan, his eyes were half-lidded and staring into nothing, and if it weren't for the slow, scarcely perceptible rise and fall of his chest, Zhara might have thought he was dead. "But one day he lay down and never got up again."

"Waking dreamer," Ami murmured, fingers twitching, eyes distant. Zhara knew she itched to pull out her notes on *Songs of Order and Chaos.* "I've heard that phrase before, but I'm not sure I know of a waking dreamer *sickness.*"

Basho pulled up a stool and sat beside their brother, balancing the bowl precariously on their lap as they leaned over to angle Nurden's head toward them for food. Ami sucked in a sharp breath.

"Here, let me help," Zhara said softly, kneeling beside Basho and angling her arms beneath the young man's back. She could feel Sajah squirming with discomfort against her wrist.

"Thank you," the postmaster said. "I'm sorry. I shouldn't trouble you like this."

"Zhara," Ami began, then paused. There was something approaching fear in the scrivener's face, but Zhara could not understand why.

The postmaster gently tipped the bowl of gruel against their brother's lips, and Nurden swallowed reflexively. Zhara's hands trembled slightly as she supported the young man, her fingers mere inches away from the bare skin of his neck. Ami could see the world as though with Guardian eyes at all times through her enchanted spectacles, but Zhara—like any other magician—could sense another magician by touch, and she was dying of curiosity to see whether Nurden was one of them.

"What was your brother like?" Han asked gently. Zhara knew he was thinking of his own little brother, Anyang, back at the palace in Zanhei.

Basho looked down at Nurden's scarred face and sighed. "Sensitive. Empathetic. Prone to strange fits sometimes. We didn't realize he had the Taint until he had a run-in with the Kestrels when he was a small child."

"The Taint?" Zhara asked, her fingers creeping ever closer to the skin of Nurden's neck, curiosity warring with propriety.

"When is a magician not a magician?" Basho said softly. "When they have the affliction but not the ability."

Silence blanketed the ger, the word *magician* falling like a thud to the ground.

Han studied the unconscious young man. "Your brother is an anti-magician?" he asked carefully.

"Is that what they call it?" The postmaster picked up the bowl of gruel again. "Here in the north, we call it the Taint. Or have, ever since the Just War. The Kestrels can identify a magician or one tainted by magic by touch, and those with the affliction but not the ability were not executed but taken away to serve the Falconer in his corps of hunters." Basho closed their eyes. "My family had always been sympathetic to magicians, but my brother's Taint brought too much scrutiny. We fled the city that night."

"That's it!" Ami said excitedly. Five heads turned to look at her in surprise. "*Waking dreamer* is the old word for *anti-magician*."

"Waking dreamer is so much better than anti-magician," Han grumbled. "I'm going to call myself that from now on."

"Why are you telling us this?" Okonwe asked in a low voice. "How do you know you can trust us?"

The postmaster shrugged. "Who would you tell?" they asked reasonably. "There's no one around for miles. In a city, surrounded by hundreds of others, everyone is suspect, whether or not you were a magician or an ally. But out here"—they gestured to the darkness outside—

"survival is a different matter. As I've said, the matter of magic is beyond my concern."

"Basho," Ami said hesitantly. "Do you—do you know your brother is . . . empty?"

Zhara looked up in surprise. The fear had not left Ami's face, and whatever the scrivener saw through her enchanted spectacles was enough to give Zhara pause.

"Empty?" Basho was taken aback. "I suppose you could describe someone afflicted with the waking dreamer sickness that way. Asleep, awake, and neither. As though the spirit were gone, even though the body still lives."

*The body still lives.* Zhara thought of the undead, their vessels empty of ki. How could one be devoid of essence but still be alive? She brought her bare hand to rest against the back of Nurden's neck, curiosity having finally won.

She didn't know what she had expected. Ami had said he was empty, but Nurden was not empty the way a bowl was empty; he was hollowed out the way a creature would leave tracks in the sand. She could sense the impression of who he had been, the muted magical resonance of the ki that should have been there, but there was nothing. An impression of the person he was had been left behind, and Zhara felt that absence like an ache.

And yet.

Something stirred in that absence, that void waiting to be filled. Something dark and familiar, something that reminded Zhara of coming upon the tombs of captured magicians beneath the slopes of Mount Zanhei. Zhara gasped.

"What?" Basho asked. "What is it?"

She immediately drew away and met Ami's gaze. She knew now what it was that the scrivener had seen.

Demon.

Yuli stared at the poster advertising the Bangtan Brothers hanging outside the bookshop on the Street of the Spear. The seven figures depicted on the flyer looked nothing like the members, having been drawn from vague descriptions, but she was surprised she could recognize them individually anyway. Tall and lanky would be Junseo, slim and cheery would be Sungho, small and scrappy Mihoon, big and puppyish Yoochun, curly-haired Alyosha, sly-eyed Taeri, and—to her everlasting amusement—handsome Bohyun, whom the artist had decided to portray as a heroic warrior, the ultimate portrait of northern beauty.

And there, next to their poster, another broadsheet with a crudely sketched portrait of a figure wearing a red hood was pasted on the wall.

WANTED, the sign read. FOR AIDING AND ABETTING IN THE ESCAPE OF A KNOWN MAGICIAN. PLEASE RELAY ANY INTELLIGENCE ABOUT THEIR POTENTIAL WHEREABOUTS TO THE HUNTSMEN, AS WELL AS ANY SUSPICION OF THE PRESENCE OF THE HERALDS OF GLORIOUS JUSTICE IN

The image of a wolf was stamped on the paper, the sigil of the Maltak Kang.

*Well,* Yuli thought, *that was fast.* Not two days had passed since the Guardians of Dawn had rescued the magician child from the pyre, and already there were posters with her likeness plastered everywhere. She had mostly stayed home since the escapade—an arduous punishment, considering the constant trafficking and politicking about the imperial succession crisis going on at the Gommun Manor—and pretended to study for the university entrance exam. Now that her engagement to Prince Rice Cake had fallen through, Uncle Bayar had insisted she at least make the attempt to matriculate.

"You just want me out of the way so you can establish yourself as leader of the Gommun Kang," Yuli had growled at her uncle.

"I *am* the leader of the Gommun Kang," Uncle Bayar had growled in return. "And going to the university would do a wayward young woman like yourself a world of good."

Yuli would have preferred to ride with the Golden Horde, as her mother and Aunt Görte had done before her. But it didn't matter that women were also warriors in the north; Uncle Bayar was determined to turn Yuli into a political pawn for the good of the Gommun Kang. If not as a wife, then as a diplomat or some sort of ambassador.

She could not think of anyone less suited to those roles.

"State your business," came a gruff voice behind her. "It's getting late."

Yuli turned to face one of the Huntsmen, easily

recognizable by the wolf pelt they wore around their shoulders. "Just stopping by to get some books," she said, awkwardly rearranging the texts in her arms. "University entrance exams are in a few weeks, as you know."

The rider squinted at her. "Your Highness?"

Yuli squirmed, wishing she had remembered to cover up her red hair. As the First Daughter of the Gommun Kang, she was rarely questioned about her comings and goings throughout the city, but she had forgotten how nosy all the nobles and children of the Five Golden Families could be. "What?" she asked shortly.

The rider shrugged. "Nothing," they said. "Just surprised to see you by a bookshop, is all." They smirked. "Carry on, Your Highness."

Yuli scowled. "You have something to say to me?"

They lifted their hands. "I would not dare," they said, the smirk never leaving their face. "I've seen you fight in the winter games."

"Good," Yuli snarled. "Now be on your way and leave me to my business."

"As you wish." The Huntsman sidled away, but not without casting a snide glance over their shoulder.

Grumbling, Yuli slid the door to the bookshop open. "Tarkhun!" she called as she entered the small, dark, and cramped space. "Have you—"

To her surprise, Tarkhun was not alone. The bookseller gave her a wide-eyed warning glance, nodding and smiling pleasantly at the customer standing before them at the counter—a short figure in a tight-fitting black woolen tunic embroidered with gold at the neck, cuffs, and hem. Their silken black hair braided into two plaits, wound with amber beads and yellow ribbons.

"I'm afraid not," Tarkhun was saying with an air of regret. "We don't carry such titles here."

"What sort of bookshop doesn't have the works of Xiri

Joqaar?" the customer muttered. "They write some of the best horror stories around."

"If you are looking for popular books," Tarkhun offered, "we do have the latest installment of *The Maiden Who Was Loved by Death* available."

"You, and everyone else in town." The customer sighed. "You wouldn't happen to have anything by Huang Jiyi?"

Yuli's ears perked at the mention of Huang Jiyi. She had not been in contact with the courtesan since she left Zanhei all those months ago, but she did still occasionally fondly recall the manner in which they parted. "If you're looking for *Tales from the Downy Delta*," she said, "I can direct to you to some other establishments that peddle that sort of literature."

"I've already read it," the customer said grumpily as they turned around to face her. "I was looking for something more recent."

Yuli stiffened.

Maltak Kho.

The other girl froze. For a moment, the two of them stared at each other, taking in the changes their time apart had wrought in the other. It was the first time in two years either of them had been so close to each other's presence, the first time since Jochi's exile. Yuli shifted, suddenly too aware of her enormous hands and broad shoulders taking up too much space in Tarkhun's cramped little shop. It had been too much to hope that time had not been kind to Maltak Kho, but instead her former best friend was prettier than ever—those coltish angles giving way to plump curves, her exaggerated doll-like features softened by newfound flesh.

*Different,* Yuli told herself. Not prettier, just different. Something fluttered about her rib cage at the sight of those dark, long-lashed eyes, which had remained unchanged since she was a little girl.

"Gommun Yulana." Maltak Kho inclined her head in greeting. Even her voice seemed more graceful, more elegant, and more mature.

Yuli swallowed. "Maltak Kho," she returned thickly. Suddenly the collar of her fur-lined coat was too tight, and the close, constricting quarters of the shop were unbearably stuffy. She cleared her throat, willing indifference into her tone. "What are you doing here?"

The other girl raised a brow. "I could ask the same of you," she said, crossing her arms. "You were never much of a reader, as I recall. Although"—her full lips quirked—"it seems you have developed a taste for poetry. *Tales from the Downy Delta*?"

The shop grew even warmer. "People change," Yuli said shortly. She felt tongue-tied and awkward, stymied by her inability to charm or tease her way through her discomfort. Kho was not like other girls; she had known her too long, yet not long enough at the same time.

"Evidently." Kho's gaze fell to the pile of books in Yuli's arms. "*Indigenous Worship Practices of the Steppe*," she read aloud. "*A Complete History of the Five Golden Families. The Analects of Bashur Khring*." She raised her eyes. "You really have changed."

Yuli wrapped her arms tighter around the texts. "I'm studying for the university entrance exam."

"You? University?" Kho gave an astonished laugh. "I thought your grandfather believed university was for bureaucrats."

The Warlord had never cared much for what he considered the soft southern way of governance, with all the officials and ministers and politicking that accompanied it. Northerners had always been ruled by the Law of Might, where anyone—regardless of blood, birth, gender, or education—could prove themselves capable to lead through trial and opportunity. It was why Uncle

Bayar had been Obaji's last choice to lead the Gommun Kang when he had still been alive; her uncle had never ridden with the Golden Horde.

Yuli shrugged. *"A true warrior keeps their wits as honed sharp as their blade,"* she quoted.

*"For one never knows when one must wield either,"* Kho finished. She fiddled with a wolf tooth hanging from a chain around her neck. "From *The Analects of Bashur Khring*. I am impressed."

Yuli had actually gotten the line from Junseo, but she wasn't surprised by the source. The leader of the Bangtan Brothers was astonishingly well-read. "Yes, well, I'm more than just a pretty face, you know," she quipped before remembering to whom she was speaking.

Kho's lips twitched again, and for a moment, it was as though no time had passed and Yuli felt a twinge in her chest. "Then perhaps I will see you and your pretty face in classes next spring."

Yuli colored. She had forgotten Kho attended university. The other girl had always been bookish, preferring reading to racing the other children out on the steppes. Of the Five Golden Families, the Maltak had always produced the most diplomats, courtiers, and scholars, and Kho's mother, the Lady of Wild Things, had served as the Warlord's liaison to the Azure Isles during his reign. As First Daughter of the Maltak Kang, Kho was certain to follow in her mother's footsteps, perhaps even serving in the imperial court whenever the succession crisis was resolved.

If it ever was going to be resolved.

"I thought you had finished your studies," Yuli said, flinching inwardly at how awkward she sounded. Kho had been the youngest person to ever matriculate at the University of Urghud two years ago, when she had just turned fourteen. Just before Jochi, just before their friendship had been irreparably broken.

"I'm taking extra courses on the Azurean dialect and alphabet and will assist with teaching," Kho said. "But depending on the outcome of . . . well, depending on how things turn out, I may be leaving school sooner."

The Conclave. The gathering of all the leaders of the various provinces of the Morning Realms to crown the next emperor and swear fealty on the Star of Radiance. At the moment, there was no clear successor for the Sunburst Throne; although the rest of the empire abided by the rule of primogeniture, in which the oldest child of the sovereign inherited the title, the north did not hold with such notions. Heirs were chosen from the most worthy of one's children, and the Warlord had died before naming his successor.

"You mean the potential civil war?" Yuli studied the other girl closely. "I can't imagine you ever fighting in the Golden Horde."

Kho flushed then. "We may yet avert civil war," she said primly. "If we install a strong candidate on the Sunburst Throne."

Yuli scoffed. "You speak of the Lady of Wild Things."

Kho lifted her chin. "And if I do? My mother was one of your grandfather's most trusted advisors, and far more acquainted with imperial politics than anyone in the Gommun Kang."

"Your mother has never ridden to war," Yuli said disdainfully.

"Might is not enough to establish order." Kho shrugged. "Governance is not the same thing as winning battles."

Yuli had no response to that. She hated politicking almost as much as she hated studying; the games of power and influence were her uncle's purview. She had inherited Obaji's disdain for bureaucracy as well as his reactionary disposition; the Warlord had believed places like the university bred nothing but softness, fit only to be buried beneath piles of paperwork.

"Loyal to your kang as always," Yuli said softly. "How well my cousin and I learned that lesson all those years ago."

Kho's nostrils flared. "What happened to Jochi was not my fault."

"Friends, friends," Tarkhun said nervously. "It is growing dark, and I am afraid I must be closing up shop soon."

Kho's eyes flitted to the windows of the bookshop, then to the bookseller. "My apologies," she said. "We'll be going."

"Speak for yourself." Yuli dumped her stack of books on Tarkhun's counter. "I still have business to conduct."

The other girl inclined her head. "Fine. I'll take my leave, *Your Highness*." She thumped her right fist to her left shoulder, the salute seeming all the more sarcastic for the honorific.

Yuli's lashes fluttered. Kho had never addressed her by her title before; she had always been Yuli. Just Yuli. The gulf between them seemed even wider than it had been when they were yelling at each other. She hated that Kho had won this encounter, that she had drawn first blood. Yuli had never been a gracious loser at anything, not even a conversation. She declined to return the salute and Kho exited the bookshop without further fanfare.

"You couldn't have treated these texts with a little more care?" Tarkhun grumbled as he took stock of the returned titles.

"Why does it matter?" Yuli asked. "This shop is only a front anyway."

Tarkhun shushed her anxiously. "We still do regular business," he said in a lower voice. "And our resources are not so unlimited that I can procure new stock so readily." He tilted his head toward the door. "Do you mind?"

Yuli pulled a brush from her sleeve and quickly sketched the spell for *silence* around the cracks. "Nothing new from the Paper Wolf?" she asked.

The bookseller shook his head. "I sent them a message about the folio last week but haven't heard anything since."

The Paper Wolf was the Guardians' black market contact, trading in rare and illicit texts. Not all they provided were books of magic, but the Guardians had hoped they would be able to track down the remaining parts of *Songs of Order and Chaos*. They had been the one to direct Yuli to the palace at Zanhei for the southern fragment, giving her a reason to agree to her engagement with the Royal Heir.

All in all, that debacle hadn't ended all *that* badly, she supposed.

"What of the magician child?" Yuli asked. "They made it to you safely . . . didn't they?"

Tarkhun smiled. Reaching beneath the counter, he pulled aside a thatched rug, revealing a hidden trapdoor. "It's clear, Crackle," he called down into the basement. "You can come on up now."

"Crackle?"

A small child peered up through the trapdoor at them. "Hail," they said shyly. They took in her pointed hat and the wisps of curly red hair escaping her braid. "Oh, it's you."

"Your name is Crackle?"

The little magician shrugged. "Don't have any parents, so I never had a name. Crackle is what I call"—they lifted their hands, which glowed softly with a bright turquoise light—"*this*."

Their magic.

"I've reached out to the Bangtan Brothers," Tarkhun said quietly. "And we've decided it's best if the child leaves with them in the next week or so."

Unexpected disappointment twisted in Yuli's gut. "But the boys just got here," she said.

"I know," the bookseller groused. "I had hoped to catch a performance before they left." He glanced at the poster hanging inside his bookshop. "Unfortunately it's hardly been a festive atmosphere out there at the moment."

The Huntsmen had cast a pall over the city with their unannounced raids on homes and businesses. People dared not venture out of their homes for long, to say nothing of congregating in public spaces to watch an entire play.

"I want to see the Bangtan Brothers," Crackle piped up from their hiding spot behind the counter. "I didn't know who they were the last time they were here."

"If you're lucky, you'll be traveling with them," Tarkhun said. "They smuggle magicians to safety all the time."

Excitement and disdain warred in the little magician's face at the word *safety*. "Oh," they said with disappointment.

Yuli was half amused, half irritated. "I would think you would be ecstatic to get away from here."

Crackle made a face. "What makes you think that?" they said scornfully. "Why would I want to go somewhere I don't know anyone, don't know the right places to sleep, the right places to steal from, or the right places to hide? The north is home."

"If you go with the Bangtan Brothers you won't have to hide anymore," Tarkhun said. "The Qirin Tulku—"

They snorted. "The last I heard, the Qirin Tulku was dead." They were surprisingly well-informed for a child of the streets.

"The Guardians of Dawn are still committed to the safety of every magician in the land," the bookseller said, but the words sounded uncertain, even to Yuli's ears.

"Safety," the little magician scoffed. "I would rather freedom than safety."

A soft flutter brushed at Yuli's heart. Crackle was only a child; they shouldn't need to worry about things like *freedom* or *safety*. They should have both. They shouldn't have to choose. In a post–Just War world, children like Crackle, like Yuli herself, had had to grow up far too fast. "I know," she said quietly. "But we can't be free until all of us are safe."

The little magician stared at her disbelievingly. Their eyes were dark, and despite the difference in age between them, Yuli felt very young and inexperienced before that knowing gaze. "You have it all wrong," they said fiercely. "We can't be safe until all of us are free. Anything else would just be running away. Like a coward."

Yuli was at a loss for words. Crackle had more conviction in their tiny body than she felt she had had her entire life.

"We need not finalize all our plans tonight," Tarkhun said soothingly. "We can discuss matters when we reconvene with the Bangtan Brothers. Safety, freedom, it doesn't matter when we are all fighting on the same side."

"Are we?" Crackle's gaze was hard. "Because as far as I can see, only one side is fighting at all. When it comes to the Guardians or Justice, I would rather the latter."

"We all believe in the same cause," Yuli said. "Even if we don't agree on the means."

The child snorted. "Soft," they said, and Yuli could see the same disdain her grandfather possessed reflected in the little magician's eyes. "You lot will keep running and running and running to somewhere safe. But what happens when there's nowhere left to run?"

# 4

What Ami really needed was a reference system. Now that she understood just how the fragments of *Songs of Order and Chaos* were supposed to go together, it was easier to understand what parts of the old demonology text were missing and how to translate what she already had. But *finding* information in a sea of words was more difficult than she expected, and she couldn't decide if she needed an index referencing page numbers or something closer to an encyclopedia.

Either way, she needed more supplies than she currently had.

Ami pulled her glasses off her face and pinched the bridge of her nose. The enchanted spectacles might have given her the ability to see the world as though she were in Guardian form, but sometimes they gave her a headache. A lot of things gave her a headache—too-loud noises, scratchy textures, the way certain foods felt in her mouth, the lack of sleep. Basho's ger was full of things that overwhelmed her, and she wished she could just wrap herself up in a cocoon of darkness and rest. The others had fallen asleep shortly after supper, and while Ami had retired to bed with the rest of them, she had spent a rather restless night. That eerie wind had howled through the tent all night, singing with a high-pitched and keening voice that had nearly been human in its sound. Ami had tossed and turned on the pallet she shared with Zhara, unable to sleep for the stiffness of dread in her muscles, clenched so tight she ached with anxiety. She had read the phrase *ill wind* before, and until that moment, had not understood what it had meant. The howling was the antithesis of a lullaby; instead of soothing her to slumber, it drove her mind to sharpness and dark thoughts, and she could have sworn she heard a whispering in her ear, eldritch words she could almost make out, if only she had the courage to listen.

So finally, in the early hours of the morning, when the barest sliver of gray cracked the unrelenting black of night, Ami got herself out of bed and did what she had always done in times of sleeplessness: read a book. Or more specifically, she had gone through her translation of *Songs of Order and Chaos* over and over again, trying to remember what it had said about waking dreamers.

She had been haunted by more than an ill wind all night.

On the far side of the ger, on the other side of the opposite partition, a young man empty of his ki slumbered in a state between sleeping and waking.

It was that emptiness that troubled her more than anything else. Ami had encountered both abominations and the undead before, and there was something of the quality of emptiness within Nurden's body that had tugged at her Guardian senses. She knew Zhara had been equally disturbed, although neither of them had been willing to tell Basho of their concerns. The poor postmaster had enough on their mind, and Ami didn't want to add *potential demonic energy* to their burdens. She toyed with the crystal from the caverns beneath Mount Llangposa in its golden cage about her neck. She couldn't tell, but she thought the light within—the light that blazed in the presence of magic—seemed dimmer than before.

*Prrrrt?* came a soft voice behind her. Sajah emerged from behind the partition, questioning why half his warm bedding had disappeared, his fur puffed out in alarm.

"Shh, little lion," Ami whispered, pressing a fingertip to her lips. "Don't wake the others."

The cat gave her a slow blink of acknowledgment, his golden eyes glowing in the dim light, but his fur did not settle. Instead, he seemed even more agitated than before, tail lashing, ears pricked upright.

"Can't sleep either?" Ami beckoned and Sajah slid into her lap, body tense and muscles coiled. She ran her hand over his raised ruff, but he gave a hiss of disapproval. It was a moment before she realized the cat was not scowling at her, but at something over her shoulder. With a start, she saw the shadow of a person behind her, standing so still and so silent she had not noticed their presence. Someone slight, almost frail in frame.

Someone with a scar that ran from lip to temple.

"Nurden?" Ami breathed, her hands trembling in Sajah's fur. The cat dug his claws into her calves, preventing her from standing up to greet the sick youth. Without her spectacles, the young man's silhouette was slightly blurred, almost transparent. Slowly, hesitantly, Ami lifted her spectacles back to her face.

Sajah hissed again.

"Ami?" came a hoarse voice from the other side of the ger. Ami glanced up to see Gaden poking their head around the curtains. "Is everything all right?"

"Yes," she said in hushed tones. "Go back to bed. I'm sorry if I woke you." She looked over her shoulder back at Nurden, but to her shock there was no one there. It had been a long, sleepless night. Perhaps she had simply imagined it, although she couldn't quite shake off the sensation of having seen a ghost.

"No, I've been awake for a while." Gaden emerged from behind the screen to sit beside Ami before the fire. "Can't sleep. Too many thoughts in my head, not enough silence."

Ami made a sympathetic sound. "About what?"

"Civil war," they said darkly. "I can't stop seeing those battle flags planted by the Heralds of Glorious Justice in all those abandoned towns we've passed." Gaden looked down at the scars covering their left hand. "It feels like it's all my fault."

Ami said nothing. Gaden had been raised by the Heralds of Glorious Justice, who had rescued them as a baby from the imperial palace in the hopes that they would grow up to reclaim the Sunburst Throne in the name of magician liberation. But Gaden had rejected that destiny along with the identity of Mugung heir, the surviving scion of the last ruling dynasty, wanting nothing to do with the Sunburst Throne.

"If I had remained Princess Weifeng," they went on, "if I had taken leadership of the Heralds as my auntie Lee-Lee had wanted, would the Morning Realms be in such chaos today?"

"The Warlord still would have died," Ami said gently. "And the empire would have found itself in the midst of a succession crisis anyway."

"Would it?" Gaden lifted their gaze to meet hers. The burn scars running down the left side of their face were pale and silvery, a map of constellations scattered across their cheek. Ami had always found them beautiful. "There is so much I could do," they said, placing their hand on their chest. "When Auntie Lee-Lee told me I had power,

I thought she meant political power. But now I know she meant the Star of Radiance."

For the longest time, the people of the Morning Realms had believed the Star of Radiance to be an imperial gem, an heirloom passed down from generation to generation that conferred the divine right to rule. But the Star of Radiance was not a jewel; it was a person. A person with the power to compel anyone to do their will.

And that person was Gaden.

"Sometimes," they said softly, "I wonder if I did the right thing, walking away from the Heralds."

Ami was taken aback. "What do you mean?"

"Abominations, the undead, greater demons," Gaden murmured. "Perhaps it's my fault the world is out of balance. The Star of Radiance is meant to protect the land." They looked away. "One drop of will gifted from every person in the Morning Realms to the Sunburst Warrior so that they may seal the Mother of Ten Thousand Demons back in her realm."

Ami tilted her head as she studied them. "Do you believe you should sit on the Sunburst Throne?"

Gaden was quiet. "I don't know," they said. "I don't know if I believe in a world with princes and princesses, emperors and conquerors. Power concentrated in the hands of too few leads to strife. I think too often we look to someone to save us, when we must learn to save ourselves." They reached out for Ami's hand, and she twined her fingers with theirs. "But then again, maybe I'm just a coward. I could *use* this power, the Star of Radiance, for good. But I'm scared," they whispered, laying their head against Ami's shoulder. "Because I'm afraid that means I have to be someone I'm not."

Ami brought up her other hand to stroke their hair. "You are Gaden," she said. "No matter what you choose, that is who you truly are."

They laughed. "You make it sound so simple."

Ami was confused. "Is it not?"

The two sat in companionable silence for a while, watching the glow of the fire wax and wane. Despite the quiet, Sajah had not fallen back asleep, his golden eyes fixed on a point in the ger as though watching an invisible intruder. Outside, the yak began an anxious lowing from their pens, the horses snorting and whinnying in distress.

"Something's disturbed the animals." Gaden rose to their feet. "I'll go take a look."

"Wait." Ami laid a hand on their arm. "Let me go with you." She patted herself down for her brush case before remembering she had left it by the pallet she had been sharing with Zhara. The other girl was still sound asleep, so Ami took care not to disturb her as she rooted through their things.

Something moved out of the corner of her vision, just beyond the edges of her spectacles. Startled, she lifted her hand to the crystal at her throat, but it had gone dark.

The hairs stood up on the back of her neck.

Near where Nurden's body lay between sleeping and waking was another figure kneeling by his side. "Basho?" she called.

"Basho's asleep." Gaden, fully dressed in furs and armed with a small bone knife, pulled back the hide partition that separated the sleeping quarters from the rest of the tent. "Is something the matter?"

When Ami looked again, the figure was gone. She bit her lip. "I don't know," she said uncertainly. "But something feels . . . off. Let's go check on the animals." She grabbed her coat and hastily threw it on, heading into the bitter night.

It was bitingly cold outside. The skies were clear, and the wind was howling even louder than ever. The unobscured moon shed its weak light over the proceedings, lining the frost-bitten world in silver. The horses jostled and pawed the frozen ground, and in the distance, Ami could make out the faint glow of Rinqi's horn, pulsing and unsteady, as though she were afraid. With a flourish, she quickly drew the character for *light* with her brush, holding her hand up high to chase away the shadows.

There was someone standing beside the animals in their pen.

Ami halted. The figure's silhouette was blurred and indistinct, and she cursed the constant fogging of her spectacles.

"What is it?" Gaden asked.

"There's a person standing by the paddocks," she whispered, pointing in their direction with her brush.

Gaden squinted in the green-gold light. "I don't see anyone."

The figure started walking toward them, drawn toward the light like a moth to flame. The blurriness of their outline remained as they moved, and Ami resisted the urge to clean her glasses. There was something strange about their movements, as though unhindered by the buffeting of the wind through the tall, dead grasses. Their clothes did not flutter, their hair did not ruffle, they moved through the world as though completely unaffected by it. On a hunch, she pushed her glasses down the bridge of her nose and peered over the rims. The world without her corrective lenses was hazy and indistinct, but the shadow she expected to see standing before them was gone. She could make out the looming heads of the horses and the low bulk of the yak huddled in the paddock, but of the stranger themself, there was nothing but a vague wisp. She pushed her spectacles back up her nose and the figure reappeared, no less translucent and wavering than before.

A chill that had nothing to do with the killing wind sliced through Ami's bones.

"A ghost," she breathed. A being of pure spirit, pure ki, unattached to any body. More and more details of the figure grew clear as they stepped into the circle of Ami's light. Their hair was dressed in the shorn sides and horse-tail plait of the northern peoples, although their garments remained shapeless, formless, more like rags than discrete articles of clothing. Their mouth opened and shut, opened and shut as though trying to speak. The ghost was close enough now that Ami could see a distinctive scar curving down the side of their left cheek, permanently extending their lip in a cruel imitation of a smile. She went still. She recognized that face. She recognized that scar. "Nurden?" she asked in disbelief.

Gaden briefly turned their head over their shoulder. "Where?"

She thought back to that brief, unsettling encounter before Gaden had gotten out of bed, of that unshakable feeling that she had somehow seen the young man standing behind her. But Nurden was still lying on the cot in Basho's tent, caught between sleeping and waking.

His body. His spirit.

Separated.

"Gaden," she said in a low voice, "go fetch Basho and the others."

"And leave you here alone?"

She shook her head. "I'm not helpless; I'm the Guardian of Wood." Her hand shook as she held out her brush. "Besides, the worst thing a disembodied spirit can do is inhabit our bodies like a vessel, according to *Songs of Order and Chaos*."

"Is that supposed to make me feel better?" Gaden muttered.

"Go," she said quietly. "I'll speak with the ghost."

And then they were gone, leaving Ami alone with the spirit. His lips had not stopped moving throughout the entire exchange, mouthing the same silent words over and over again.

*Help me. Help me. Help me.*

"Tell me how I can help you." She reached her hand out to the ghost, but her fingers passed through his as though he were no more substantial than smoke. She thought of Yuli then, of how she could touch and hold the other girl's ki, but it appeared as though ordinary spirits were another matter.

At that, Nurden's expression changed. It was strange watching the features of a ghost shift as though animated by flesh and bones. There was something uncanny about it, the muscles moving both too smoothly and not smoothly enough, as though the spirit struggled to remember the body when untethered from it. Nurden's eyes went wide with what looked like fear, before the shape of his mouth changed, the words different than they had been before. It took Ami a long while before she thought she understood what he was trying to say.

*Demon. Demon. Demon.*

A sudden, liquid cry, and the flapping of wings. Something whistled past Ami's ear—something dark and pulsing, something that made her ears pop with a drop in pressure. Then a bright silver figure dropped from the sky, colliding with Ami and sending her tumbling to the ground as an explosion of ice and frozen mud burst from where she had been standing just the moment before. Beside her, an enormous silver bird folded its four wings, throwing its head back to trill another warning cry. Temur, the Eagle of the North, and Yuli's celestial companion.

"Ami!" Gaden's voice.

Whirling around, she saw a slim figure outlined by moonlight moving toward her, a silhouette she did not recognize. The figure raised their hand, and a dark corona appeared around their fingers. The light wavered around them, as though struggling to escape a vortex, wreathing the figure in shadow. With a gesture, the figure thrust the gathered darkness at Ami, a billowing cloud of wrongness and malice.

Magic.

Dark magic.

With another cry, Temur rushed in front of her, all four wings outspread to shield her from the attack. The cloud struck the Eagle in the chest, enveloping the creature, but Temur brushed off the shadows as though they were no more than rags, shaking her feathered head and screeching.

A blaze of blinding light as a column of fire roared into life. Zhara, transformed into a living girl of flame, the Guardian of Fire in all her glory. The night briefly brightened into day, throwing into stark relief the features of the figure in shadow—blackened eyes, a gleeful expression, and a wicked scar that ran from temple to teeth.

Nurden.

Ami scrambled to her feet, looking in amazement from the body of Nurden standing to her left to the ki of the same person to her right. There was an agonized expression on the ghost's face—not of physical pain but a spiritual one. Her vision swam; through her enchanted spectacles, Ami could see an endless abyss beneath the living skin and bone of the embodied Nurden, the emptiness transformed into a dark ki.

Demon.

"Halt!" Zhara cried, brandishing a glowing blade at the young man. "I order you to stop!"

"Don't hurt him!" Basho burst from the tent, waving their arms in panic and confusion. "Please!"

Zhara hesitated and Nurden snarled, lashing out with another bolt of darkness from his hands. She cried out as the demonic magic struck her in her sword arm, flames flickering to reveal human skin beneath her Guardian form. Zhara dropped her blade and fell to one knee, her other hand clasped over the wound.

*Thwack! Thud! Smack!*

With a roar, Han came running out of the tent swinging a bo staff, which struck Nurden across the torso, shoulder, and the back of the head in a series of quick movements. Nurden stumbled but swiftly regained his footing, reaching out to catch the next blow in the palm of his hand. He wrapped his fingers around Han's weapon and the staff shivered, squirmed, then transformed into a serpent. Han gave a shout of surprise as his bo turned on him, sinking fangs deep into his arm. Gaden ran forward, throwing their arm around Han's shoulders and dragging him back to safety.

A high-pitched yowl deepened into a roar as a small orange cat leaped from the tent, its shape growing, lengthening, broadening until an enormous feline chimera landed atop the young man, peacock tail lashing furiously. Sajah opened his enormous jaws and the tiny silver horns on his brow crackled and sizzled with lightning, thunder rumbling ominous across the cloudless skies. But Nurden pressed his palms against the Lion's head, and the lightning faded from Sajah's horns, his glowing eyes darkening as shadows wreathed them both.

"Sajah!" Zhara struggled to her feet, her flames unsteady.

Darkness bloomed where the cat and the young man struggled, pressure rippling out in all directions. Ami clapped her hands over her ears in pain as Sajah's body went flying, landing with a thud several feet away. Zhara rushed to her companion's side, sobbing in terror as the light flickered in his lantern eyes. From her pen, Rinqi screamed, sharp hooves bashing the paddock gate, the light in her healing horn incandescent with rage. The ground buckled and roiled, deep fissures appearing in the frozen earth, shaking Ami from her stupor.

She had to help. But her mind was a terrifying blank, wiped clean by the fear that overwhelmed all rational thought. Ami tried to gather herself, to become the Guardian of Wood, but she had never been good at battle —too nervous, too stiff, too unable to think on her feet.

Nurden shook himself off and rose to his feet, easily avoiding and swiping aside the broad swings of Okonwe's ax with a wave of his hand. Ami closed her eyes and found the seed of glowing green-gold light within her, letting it flourish and blossom around her. She placed her palms on the icy ground, reaching out with her power to grab the threads of ki that wound through the world.

At once the ground shifted beneath Nurden's feet, turning liquid, trapping him up to his hips in mud. Ami shaped the earth to her command, fashioning manacles of rock and gravel, chaining his arms to his side. The young man struggled and fought against his bonds, but without the use of his hands, he could do no more dark magic.

"Zhara!" Ami gasped. "Now!"

Zhara tore herself from Sajah's side and clapped her fiery palms on either side of Nurden's head, closing her eyes in concentration.

Silence fell over the clearing.

Then Nurden began to laugh, the sound doubled, as though another voice sounded through his vocal cords.

"Think you can turn me back into a human, Guardian of Fire?" he said gleefully. "But I am already human."

Zhara's flames wavered, and she met Ami's gaze. She could turn abominations back into humans with her Guardian powers, but Nurden was right; he was not a monster. He was simply a demon wearing human flesh. "Ami?" she asked uncertainly.

Reflexively, Ami reached for the fragments of *Songs of Order and Chaos* tucked into the back of her sash, but her notes and the text were back in the ger. "I don't know," she said. "I don't know what is going on." She glanced down at her hands, the green-gold light of her magic shining through her skin. As the Guardian of Wood, she could give life where there was none, but Nurden was not dead. He was separated from his ki. Ami glanced at the ghost hovering on the edges of the proceedings, then back at the young man trapped in the mud.

Nurden laughed again. "Guardian of Wood," he sneered. "No power of yours could banish me. My master, the Moth Demon, is greater than the both of you."

And then he began to sing.

His voice was high-pitched and dissonant, a cacophony of pitches that grated and keened at the ear. An ill wind, an ailing wail. Han cried out at the sound, writhing as he collapsed to the ground. To Ami's horror, she could see the muted royal blue ki of her cousin shivering and quivering within his body, his eyes bulging as his soul tried to escape the bounds of his flesh.

"Stop!" Gaden shouted over the eldritch melody. "I command you to stop!"

Their words rang with the force of the Star of Radiance, compelling everyone around them to freeze. White light radiated from their chest, encasing Nurden's body with a sheen of power. The demon stilled, their song silenced.

"I banish you," Gaden said softly from Han's side, and even Ami could feel the force of pure will leveled at the darkness within Nurden. "I banish you back to the realms from whence you came."

The demon within the young man shrank, shrieking as it shriveled smaller and smaller and smaller, until there was nothing left but a pinprick of black, which disappeared in a blink. Nurden slumped in his bonds, his body an empty vessel once more.

"Didi!" Basho ran forward to catch their brother as the mud around him crumbled away. Ami and Zhara returned to their human forms, the cold and the dark descending once more as Zhara's flames dissipated. "Nurden!" The postmaster shook the young man, trying to rouse him. "Bring him back!" they said, wild-eyed and desperate. "Bring him back!"

The girls exchanged glances. "I'm sorry, Basho," Zhara said gently. "I don't—"

"You, who can turn yourself into living flame? And you"—the postmaster turned to Ami—"who can command the very earth to dance? Neither of you can bring my brother back to me?" They gave a despairing laugh. "Who are you? *What* are you?"

"We are," Zhara said quietly, "the Guardians of Dawn."

Basho looked at each of them one by one. At the enormous four-winged bird; the Unicorn placing her healing horn on the peacock-tailed Lion; the big black-skinned man; the young man nursing a snakebite; the scarred youth at his side; and the two girls—ordinary once more after a night of extraordinary events.

"I have said the matter of magic is beyond my concern," the postmaster said heavily. "And I shall stand by my word. But on the morrow I want you all gone."

Ami and the others said nothing as Basho gathered up their brother and carried him back into the tent. The postmaster did not turn around to give them a second glance, but neither would they have been able to see the ghost trailing in their wake, still mouthing—

*Help me, help me, help me.*

*A folio*, the message read. *With a taikhut.*

Maltak Kho fingered the message, which had been accompanied by a crude drawing of a bisected circle— one half dark with a drop of light, the other half light with a drop of dark. She could have sworn she had seen this symbol—this *taikhut*—before, but she could not recall where. Surely she would have made note of it if she had come across it while cataloging titles for the university library. When Kho first started working for the head librarian organizing the archives, she had had fantasies of finding long-lost texts, important academic studies, or even—she thought with a frisson of guilty excitement—a forbidden book on magic that had slipped through the Warlord's grasp. Alas, most of the so-called *dangerous* works had already been purged years before; what few titles Kho had been able to rescue were not particularly significant—treatises on indigenous rituals and practices, magicians' commonplace books that had fallen through the cracks, collections of errata and other notes on reference texts long since burned.

"A romance novel, eh? I never knew you were the type, Kho-yah."

Kho shoved the note beneath her copy of *The Maiden Who Was Loved by Death*, looking up to catch the head librarian of the university, Teacher Alani, smiling down at her.

"Now, now, there's no shame in reading romance," the librarian said, her eyes twinkling. "I have plenty of titles by Jae Hyun I can recommend if you'd like, although I'm afraid you won't find many on the shelves in here."

Kho fiddled with the yellow ribbons at the ends of her plaits. "Just taking a brief break. I'll get back to work in a bit."

Teacher Alani waved her off. "Go on, enjoy yourself. There will always be work tomorrow, and you are still young. Why don't you go join your friends down at the taverns for a change?"

Friends. The briefest image of red hair flitted through her mind before she chased it off with force of will. Kho gave the librarian a tight smile. "You know I'm not much for company, Teacher."

"You used to be." The librarian studied her closely, her iron-gray hair haloed by the weak winter sunlight streaming in through the high windows behind her. "There was a time I constantly had to chase your companions from these study halls. Whatever happened to them?"

One was in exile—likely dead—and the other had barely had a civil exchange with her in two years. The encounter in the bookshop with Yuli—Princess Yulana— returned to Kho with a wash of something resembling shame, if shame could somehow feel akin to pleasure. "People grow and change," was all she said.

Teacher Alani pursed her lips. "Mmm," she said noncommittally. "Well, I worry about you, Maltak Kho."

Kho raised her brows. "Worry about *me*?"

"Aye." The librarian nodded. "It must not be easy," she murmured, "being the First Daughter of your kang. The well-being and reputation of an entire bloodline is a heavy responsibility to place on anyone's shoulders, let alone a girl not yet the age of majority."

Kho felt the weight of the wolf fang about her neck. "It is an honor to be named my mother's heir."

"Is it?" Teacher Alani's eyes were hard. "To be the heir of the Lady of Wild Things must be a terrible burden."

It was. Her mother was the head of the Maltak Kang and one of the most powerful figures among the Five Golden Families. The Maltak were second only to the Gommun in terms of wealth and influence, a position Kho had been made acutely aware of since birth. As it was when she had participated in the youth games, those who came in second knew better than anyone just what it took to be first. The Lady of Wild Things had always been ambitious, and her children had only ever been pawns in her political games.

"I am loyal to my kang," Kho said. It was the simplest response, if not entirely the most truthful.

"Oh you Maltak are loyal, all right," the librarian said. "Live and die by your watchwords, you do. But there are many kinds of loyalty. Loyalty to yourself. Loyalty to a greater ideal."

Kho frowned. "Why are you telling me this?"

Teacher Alani sighed. "Because I am fond of you, child. And because I want you to become your own person. You've always been an obedient, dutiful daughter; you even entered university to follow in your mother's footsteps as court liaison to the Azure Isles. But what is it you really *want*?"

Kho blinked. All her life, her destiny had been subsumed by the good of her kang. *For the greater good,* her mother would say. Always for the greater good. Her desires did not matter if they did not serve her family, so she had never learned how to want.

"I don't know," she answered honestly. "I suppose I've never really thought about it."

"Well," Teacher Alani said with a sad smile, "then perhaps it's time you do."

Kho fingered the pages of *The Maiden Who Was Loved by Death*. In the book, Lord Death was always telling Little Flame that to be selfless was to be selfish. Kho didn't consider herself selfless, but she had never once given thought to what it meant to be selfish.

"I will," she said quietly. "Thank you, Teacher."

The librarian's smile broadened. "Good. Now, why don't you take the rest of the evening off? Maybe find your brother, eat a good meal, have some fun. Ogodei knows how to enjoy himself; I hear he didn't show up for his classes again today."

Kho shook her head. Ever since their father and his Kestrels had left to hold the imperial city against any claimants to the Sunburst Throne until the Conclave, Ogodei had taken his role as proxy Falconer to heart. He was likely terrorizing the citizens of Urghud with the rest of his Huntsmen, turning out families in search of magicians in their midst.

"I'll look for him," Kho promised. More than likely, he would be down at the Eagle's Nest, raising a ruckus with his companions as he was wont to do after a successful— or unsuccessful—hunt.

She gathered her things and headed out of the library through the frozen university courtyard, the light already fading. Nights were long this time of year in the north, bringing with them the bitter winds from the Frozen Wastes. There hadn't yet been any snow; instead, a thick mist seemed to linger here and there, unusual for this time of year. She hurried through the streets of Urghud's pleasure district, where raucous sounds of merriment spilled over into the evening air from the various inns and taverns lining the streets. Kho made her way toward the Eagle's Nest, one of the more disreputable establishments in the city and one of Ogodei's favorite haunts to drink and dice. University students looking for cheap rice wine and even cheaper thrills gravitated toward the tavern, along with a rather more unsavory clientele—the mercenaries, bandits, and pirates who preferred to conduct business there.

The first things Kho noticed the instant she stepped foot over the threshold and into the open-air courtyard of the Eagle's Nest were the overturned seating platforms and the clusters of people groaning and nursing bruised heads and battered limbs. It looked as though a storm had ripped through the tavern—signs and wooden menus were ripped off walls, several decks of playing cards and Sparrow tiles were scattered about the ground like leaves, and bits and shards of smashed pottery were absolutely everywhere. At the back of the courtyard, Kho could see that not even the small building containing private rooms for more clandestine encounters had escaped the damage, its paper-shuttered doors torn and hanging off their hinges.

And in the middle of it all were the Huntsmen, singing and shouting and generally making nuisances of themselves. At least they hadn't brought their horses. She couldn't see her brother anywhere, but she had no doubt he had started the entire fracas.

"Hoi, Maltak Kho!" The tavern owner hailed her from across the ruined courtyard. "We have a score to settle, your kang and me."

Kho surveyed the damage and swallowed down her irritation. "How much?" she sighed.

The tavern owner eyed her fine-combed woolen coat and the wolf pelt lining her cuffs and collar.

With another sigh, Kho reached for her purse of silver and placed the entire thing on the counter. "I trust this will suffice," she said.

The owner snatched up the money, weighing it expertly in his palm. "Aye, this will do," they said gruffly. "For now."

Damages settled, Kho picked her way through the wreckage, looking for her brother amid the chaos.

"Mimi!" It was Tuyaa, the only female member of the Huntsmen. "Where have you been? You've missed out on a roaring good time." She was drunk; Kho could smell the stink of fermentation on her breath.

"At the university," Kho said shortly. "Working." She crossed her arms. "Unlike some of you, I have a job and responsibilities to fulfill."

Tuyaa shook her head. "So serious, for one so young!"

The bulk of the Huntsmen were her brother's age cohort, having just gained their majority. Most of them had chosen not to attend the university when they became adults, electing to ride with the Golden Horde instead. None of them possessed the Taint, and were therefore unqualified to join the most coveted wing of the Horde— the Black, also known as the Kestrels—but joining Ogodei's unsanctioned cadre had given them all a chance to earn some glory in the Falconer's absence. Although Kho was not an official member of the Huntsmen, she frequently rode with them, mostly to keep an eye on her brother's antics as First Daughter of the Maltak Kang.

"Where's Ogodei?" she asked wearily.

Tuyaa gestured to the back rooms. "Probably sleeping off a massive headache. We had a run-in with some refugees down by the docks."

"A run-in?" The raids conducted by the Heralds of

Glorious Justice had displaced many to the south, most of whom had fled to Urghud to find sanctuary from the increasing magician threat. No one quite knew what to do with the refugees; none of the heads of the Five Golden Families could agree on a course of action, and the slums were growing more and more crowded by the day. "What were you doing down there?"

Tuyaa shrugged. "Someone tipped us off about strange magic being used among the arrivals," she said. "And your brother went to investigate."

Of the Huntsmen, only Ogodei possessed the Taint, which allowed him to sense a magician by touch. Had he been anyone other than the eldest child of the Lady of Wild Things, he would have joined the Kestrels under his father's leadership. But the Lady of Wild Things had greater plans for her children than a mere position in the Golden Horde.

Kho stiffened. "And?"

Tuyaa shrugged again. "We didn't find anything. The refugees weren't exactly cooperative either—they claim there is sickness among them—but they always say things like that when they're hiding something."

Kho closed her eyes. Ogodei had a propensity to be brutal in his zeal to find and root out traitors, and the only reason she rode with the Huntsmen at all was to mitigate her brother's worst impulses. The capture and sentencing of Gommun Jochi two years prior still haunted her, and she had wished every day since then that she had spoken out.

"Did you see evidence of sickness?" she asked the older girl.

Tuyaa snorted. "If there's any disease among the refugees, it's a plague of laziness," she said. "They could sleep through anything, these newcomers, even through a dozen Huntsmen bursting down their doors. They called it"—she tapped her teeth, swaying a little on her feet as she tried to think—"what was it? The waking dreamer sickness." She scoffed. "Never heard of it. Likely made-up."

Kho frowned. If there was indeed illness breaking out in the refugee population, it was a problem the heads of the Five Golden Families could not ignore. Disease spread quickly in quarters as close and as cramped as Urghud, and winter would only make the spread of sickness worse. She shook her head. "I'll tell my mother," she said. "Perhaps she can call the Grassmoot." The Grassmoot was a gathering of not just the Five Golden Families but all the people of the steppes to confer and gather on matters of governance.

"The Lady of Wild Things to the rescue again, lah?" Tuyaa laughed. "Your mother should be the one to sit on the Sunburst Throne, not any of those Gommun brats."

Kho said nothing. That was precisely her mother's intention, but to say so aloud felt somehow . . . indecent. Instead she merely inclined her head at the older girl, excusing herself from the conversation. "I'll go find Ogodei," Kho said. "And take him home."

"Good luck rousing him." Tuyaa grinned. "He's had several bowls of the barkeep's special brew."

Kho headed toward the back rooms, where she found her brother prone on the floor of one of the private apartments, surrounded by the detritus of the Huntsmen's revels. Wrinkling her nose in distaste, she nudged him with the tip of her boot.

"Wake up, gogo," she said. "It's time to go home."

No response. She wondered how much he had had to drink. Depending on the number of bowls of the barkeep's special brew he had had, it could be a long while before she could get him on his feet.

"Gogo," she said again, reaching down to shake his shoulder. "Gogo, come on."

Again, no response, not even a moan.

With a grunt, Kho rolled Ogodei over. His limbs flopped as his face was revealed, and Kho was taken aback. His eyes were half-lidded and rolled back into his head, his features slack and empty. For a moment, she did not recognize him; the skin sat oddly on his bones, more like an ill-fitting mask than a person. She had dragged her unconscious brother home more times than she cared to count, and she was familiar with the way he looked when deep in the throes of an alcohol-induced slumber. Her arms prickled with goose pimples that had nothing to do with the chill wind rising in the courtyard outside; there was something uncanny about the stillness of his face. There was no discomfort, no peace, just . . . nothing. She had seen dead bodies before, and she was reminded of how they resembled the people they had been in life as much as a painting did of a landscape in reality. A good facsimile, but only a pale imitation.

"Ogodei." She ripped off her glove and placed two fingers against his neck. His flesh was still warm and his pulse fluttered faintly beneath her touch. Alive. But he felt curiously weightless beneath her hand, an empty rag doll bereft of stuffing. "Ogodei?"

*The waking dreamer sickness,* Tuyaa had said.

Kho had never heard of the disease either, but she thought there was some truth to the refugees' claims.

The wind whistling through the holes in the doors keened at a high, nigh-unbearable pitch. Ogodei gasped.

"Gogo?"

Her brother sat up and turned to face her. The color had returned to his face, but there was still something lacking about his expression. His dark eyes were flat, and they looked on her as though she were a total stranger.

"Gogo?" she repeated.

He blinked several times. "Mimi?"

She punched his arm. "Were you toying with me?" she demanded. She punched him again. "Why didn't you wake up?"

There was something glassy about his red-rimmed gaze, but despite the evidence of his revels, he did not seem drunk. "I was tired," he said.

His voice was affectless, neither teasing nor defensive. Like any big brother, Ogodei liked to needle his little sister and get beneath her skin, and despite his best efforts, he could never entirely disguise when he was being playful. He always had a little smirk to his lips that he could never quite control.

The smirk wasn't there.

But there wasn't anything else there either.

"Is everything all right?" Kho asked hesitantly. "Did something happen? With . . . with Mama?"

If Kho found it difficult to be the First Daughter of the Maltak Kang, she knew it must be even more difficult to be the disfavored child of the Lady of Wild Things. Ogodei was prone to dark moods when it came to matters of family, moods that frequently turned him sullen, mulish, and occasionally cruel.

"No," he said simply. "I was just tired." He shook his head, looking down at his hands and flexing his fingers over and over again. "Let's go home."

Bemused, Kho got to her feet and reached out to help her brother up, but he refused her offered hand. She watched as he made his way through the courtyard, ignoring the hoots and calls of his Huntsmen as though he did not know them. Unease threaded through Kho's limbs; her brother had ever been loud and boisterous, beloved by his companions for his sociability. To callously ignore them was unlike him, even if he was as tired as he claimed.

At the threshold, Ogodei turned to look over his shoulder at her. "Are you coming, mimi?"

She followed him wordlessly through the gates and up the street toward Maltak Manor in the distance. The wind had not ceased its howling, and now brought with it the scent of something almost putrid. Foul. An ill wind, as the elders would have said. A killing wind, one that left livestock frozen in their pens. Darkness had fallen completely, and Kho hurried home after her brother, unable to shake the sensation that the shadows were somehow alive and watching their progress.

Before long, they arrived at Maltak Manor, greeted at the gates by a pair of ever-present guards. Ogodei moved past them without a word, up to his quarters at the top floor of their four-story house. Kho exchanged worried glances with them before retiring to her own rooms. It would be a long time before she would be able to fall asleep, haunted by the blankness in her brother's eyes.

And outside, the wind continued to sing.

Arkhevet was a lot more glum than Yuli remembered.

It had been a long while since she had gone spirit-walking, and an even longer time since she had visited the port city across the Sweet Sea from Urghud. The last time she had set foot in Arkhevet had been before her mother died, and before she discovered her magic. She had been enchanted by the various sights and sounds of a new city, filled to the brim with people from all over the Morning Realms. There had been caravans of goods from as far west as the Dzungri basin and as far south as the Five Sisters in the Shining Sea, as well as sweet melon-squash from the Azure Isles and luxurious silks from the Middle Kingdom.

All that was left now was a pathetic little fish market.

Yuli wandered through the streets of Arkhevet in spirit form, trying to reconcile her memories of a thriving, bustling city with the dismal, dour ghost town it had become. Windows shuttered, storefronts abandoned, streets empty, it was as though she had wandered into the aftermath of a battle instead of a trading port.

And everywhere she went, there were signs of a coming civil war.

What had been restaurants, eateries, and livestock trading squares had all been transformed into forges, smithies, and armories producing arms and weapons, the constant ring of metal against metal having replaced the mellifluous voices and accents of merchants and sailors. No customers, but she could guess where the supplies were being shipped to—either on to Urghud or down the Infinite River toward the imperial city.

If she were still in her body, it would have gone cold with dread.

The emptiness of the streets left Yuli feeling vulnerable and exposed. With no crowds to blend into, her spirit form was too noticeable, and if anyone looked too closely, they would realize that the edges of her body were translucent and blurred, the colors of her coat and hair not quite natural or right. She was only holding the idea of herself together with the recollection of what she looked like in the mirror, and with each passing moment, she grew less and less certain of how well she knew her own body. Was she even this tall? Did she remember her freckles correctly? Yuli had never thought this hard about how she existed as a physical being before—how she looked, how she took up space, how she moved through the world. Even her athleticism was thoughtless, taken for granted, centered only on how movement made her feel in the spirit rather than in the flesh. Powerful. Unrestrained. Free.

The only time Yuli was ever conscious of her body was in the proximity of pretty girls, when it was impossible to ignore the flutter in her stomach or the warmth suffusing her limbs. She thought of Kho in Tarkhun's bookshop and the way her former best friend made her *feel* every beat of her heart, every breath from her lungs, the undeniable tangibility of skin and lips and hair. It had been a long time since anyone had made her feel that way, but then again, Kho had always had a way of making her feel grounded.

Yuli wrenched her thoughts away from Kho, flinching from the memory like a wound. She could sense the tug on the tether that connected her spirit back to her vessel as her stomach clenched. Even when she wasn't around, Kho made her acutely aware of her body, and Yuli wasn't sure what to think about that. So she wouldn't. She was good at not thinking about things that made her uncomfortable. Yuli had lived a charmed life; the ability to vacate her vessel at the slightest bit of discomfort or inconvenient feeling had not adequately equipped her to face the reality of the coming war. Growing up, she had never given a thought to what would happen to the Morning Realms after her grandfather was gone. That was a matter of politics, and politics were the purview of her uncle Bayar. She had always expected to ride with the Golden Horde once she reached her majority, and perhaps even fight for the title of Grand Kang someday during the Grand Game. She had always been the most comfortable riding and fighting; it had been her cousin, Jochi, who had been the thoughtful one. Jochi, whom she had always assumed would sit on the Sunburst Throne. Jochi, who could have changed the course of the Morning Realms. Jochi, who had been so wise, so kindhearted, and a magician.

Jochi, accused of treason by the Maltak and exiled to the Frozen Wastes.

Who would sit on the Sunburst Throne now?

Yuli shook her head. One thing at a time. If she thought too hard about the future, she found herself paralyzed by indecision. She was here to coordinate the rescue of Crackle to safer parts of the empire. The Bangtan Brothers would need to secure passage from Urghud to Arkhevet, at which point the Guardians of Dawn would help the little magician disappear.

She spied the safe house at the end of the docks—the harbormaster's residence. It had been one of the first safe houses Auncle Mongke had told Yuli about when she was a little girl, when the shaman first discovered their niece's magic. Yuli had been fortunate that it had been her auncle who had discovered her abilities and not anyone else; the shamans believed that magic was a connection between the mundane world and the spirits. Or they used to, before Obaji overthrew the Council. The new Council of Shamans were mostly comprised of members from the Five Golden Families who did not have the courage to ride with the Golden Horde nor the wit to attend university.

Candlelight lit the windows the harbormaster's residence, but it was the light of the magicians inside that drew her attention. The ordinary living appeared to Yuli's magical sight as beings of ordinary dullness, but the ki of magicians and anti-magicians was bright with colors, and there were two shades sitting inside that she recognized instantly: rose-gold and green-gold.

Zhara and Ami.

Again, if she had been in her body, her heart would have soared.

"—no word from the Bangtan Brothers," Zhara was saying as Yuli materialized in the room beside them. "I had hoped they would leave some message behind."

"No message, but a messenger," she quipped. "I'm faster and more secure."

Zhara gave a slight shriek of surprise, dropping what looked like a letter to the floor. Recovering quickly, the other girl threw her arms around Yuli's ghost, and it never failed to amaze Yuli that she could *feel* the Guardian of Fire's touch as though it were a physical sensation, even though her body lay leagues away in Urghud.

"Hullo, Bubbles," she said, returning the hug. "About time you showed up." She winked at Ami. "You too, beauty."

Zhara pouted. "It's a long way from Kalantze to here, and unlike you, we had to make the entire journey on foot." She lightly punched Yuli in the arm. "You couldn't have bothered to check in on us once in a while?"

"Aiyo!" Yuli rubbed her shoulder. The punch hadn't hurt, but the fact that she could feel it at all was still startling. "Temur was with you the whole time! Besides, I was busy."

"With what?"

Yuli crossed her arms. "Oh nothing much, just rescuing magicians and tracking down the northern fragment of *Songs of Order and Chaos* like you asked."

"Yah," Han complained. "No greetings for me?"

Yuli turned to face the Royal Heir. "Good to see you, Prince Rice Cake." She grinned. She nodded at the others. "Gaden. And—forgive me, but I don't think—"

"Okonwe," rumbled the big warrior beside Gaden. "An honor, Your Highness."

A shiver ran down the thread connecting Yuli's soul to her body, and she could feel herself stiffen on the other end. It was one thing to be the Warlord's granddaughter in Urghud, where Obaji's name gave her a measure of protection from prying eyes. It was something else in the presence of other magicians and their allies, where Obaji's name was synonymous with genocide.

"Have you found *Songs of Order and Chaos*?" Ami asked, pushing her spectacles up her nose. The scrivener was surrounded by piles of paper on the floor, two crumbling leather folios open beside her containing pieces of the ancient text on demonology.

Yuli shook her head. "Not yet. We've been in touch with the Paper Wolf, our black market contact, for any potential leads, but nothing so far."

"The Paper Wolf?" Gaden asked.

"That's what they call themselves." Yuli wrinkled her nose. "I've never met them, but they like to communicate via cryptic messages with the Guardians' safe house in Urghud."

"Talk about cryptic messages," Zhara said, riffling through several crumpled messages in her hands. "I can't make heads nor tails of any of these. *Spell to cure warts. Batu's cousin. Why am I always sweating around this one person, do they have magic—* Oh!" She blinked in surprise, then handed a slim bamboo tube to Han. "This one's for you."

"Me?" Han's eyes widened.

"It says WONHU HAN," Zhara said, pointing to the label wrapped around the tube.

Han accepted the missive in bewilderment, pulling the wax stopper at one end and fishing out the paper.

"Some of these letters are so old," Zhara remarked. "Why did they never get delivered?"

"Because," Okonwe said heavily, "the Kestrels got to the recipients before they could be sent."

A silence fell over the room.

"So," Yuli said awkwardly. She would have cleared her throat if she could. "What news on the road from Kalantze?"

"Temur didn't tell you?" Ami asked.

She shook her head. "Temur doesn't speak to me, or at least not like that. I can see what she sees when our minds are connected. It's how I knew you lot had arrived in Arkhevet."

Zhara and Ami exchanged glances. "What do you know of the waking dreamer sickness?" the Guardian of Fire asked.

Yuli frowned. "I haven't heard much about it," she said. "What is it?"

Ami nervously fiddled with the crumbling leather strings of the folios containing *Songs of Order and Chaos*. "We think—I think—it might be some sort of demonic affliction."

Distantly, on the other side of that connecting thread, Yuli felt dread settle its cold weight over her shoulders. "Demonic affliction?"

Zhara nodded and relayed what had happened to them shortly before they arrived in Arkhevet. Yuli went pale.

"So you're saying," she said slowly, "that demons can somehow . . . possess and control the bodies of anti-magicians?"

"Yes," Ami said. "Although the vessel must be empty of its original ki first."

Yuli looked down at her hands. No, they weren't her hands—not her *real* hands—they were merely the idea of a part of her body she had fashioned into a physical likeness.

"How?" she whispered. Again, she felt that invisible tether connecting her spirit to her vessel twinge with discomfort. She had never thought of her gifts as the Guardian of Wind as anything spectacular, unlike the Guardian of Fire with her power of transformation or the Guardian of Wood with her ability to give life where there was none. Yuli's powers had seemed more like a fancy party trick without many practical applications; she had never given much consideration to what happened to her body when she went spirit-walking. The idea of her body lying back in Urghud, empty and waiting to be filled by a foreign essence—she would have shivered if she could.

"I don't know," Zhara said quietly. "But we do know there is a greater demon out in the world who can pull the souls of people from their bodies."

"The Moth Demon," Yuli said. "One of the Lords of Tiyok."

"Yes," Ami said, sorting through her notes. "It's mentioned here, somewhere." She continued searching for a while before giving up with a grunt. "What I really need is some sort of reference system," she muttered to Gaden, who was helpfully organizing the papers to the best of their ability.

"We think this must be the demon of the northern portal," Zhara said. "And the source of this waking dreamer sickness."

A greater demon. Yuli thought of the Chancellor of Zanhei, who had been the Frog Demon of Poison and Pestilence in disguise for years. "That means," she said with dawning horror, "that there is a Lord of Tiyok walking among the northerners."

Ami nodded. "A magician," she said. "Only magicians can be possessed by a demon."

"And the dead," Zhara added.

"And the dead," Ami amended. "Oh, and I suppose anti-magicians too now." She shook her head. "There is so much we don't know of demonology," she moaned, pressing her notes to her chest. "Let's hope the Paper Wolf can deliver on *Songs of Order and Chaos*."

"An anti-magician," Yuli mused. Those with the Taint had been conscripted as Kestrels for their unique ability to sense other magicians with a touch. It was why the purges had been so devastatingly efficient all those years ago. "There are many anti-magicians in the north," she said slowly. "Those with the affliction but not the ability were spared the pyre. The Moth Demon could be anyone, really. How do we find their identity and defeat them?"

"By closing the northern portal," Ami said. "It was how Zhara defeated the Frog Demon, and it was how Gaden and I destroyed the Locust Demon."

"Do you know where it is?" Yuli asked.

"At the Singing Skies," the scrivener said.

Yuli frowned. "I've never heard of that before."

Ami shook her stack of papers. "This is why we need that northern fragment of *Songs of Order and Chaos.*"

"What do you propose we do?" Yuli asked. Both she and Ami looked to Zhara for guidance.

The Guardian of Fire seemed troubled. "It's clear we need more information than we have," she said slowly. "And we won't find that in Arkhevet. But Urghud . . . ?" She lifted her gaze to Yuli. "Is the Guardians of Dawn's presence much larger there?"

Yuli wouldn't necessarily say it was *larger,* although she had to admit there were more resources. "Not by much, but we would have access to more literature at Tarkhun's bookshop," she said. "But it would be dangerous. The rest of the empire may be slowly opening up to the presence of magicians, but it's still not safe in the north. The Guardians of Dawn in the city are more focused on smuggling magicians *out* of the city, rather than in. Speaking of which"—she looked around the room—"I need to speak with the harbormaster about ships and schedules. There's a magician child we need to find passage for."

"A rescue mission?" Zhara sat up. "I've never partaken of one before." She seemed excited, which Yuli found both worrisome and adorable.

"What would we be doing?" Ami asked. "Take them all the way back to the outermost west? It seems like a waste, especially now that we're here."

"Not you," Yuli said. "The Bangtan Brothers. We have a portal to find and a Moth Demon to defeat."

"The boys won't be staying in Urghud?" Zhara asked with disappointment. "I had hoped to see them."

"Taking the magician all the way to the outermost west seems unnecessary," Gaden remarked. "Magic has returned to the Morning Realms and there is no denying it anymore. Surely there are safe havens closer than Kalantze."

"They can go to Zanhei," Han said quietly.

Five heads turned in surprise. "Are you sure?" Zhara asked.

Han nodded. "Once we defeated the Chancellor—I mean, the Frog Demon—my father allowed magicians to exist openly in the city." He turned the piece of paper in his hand over and over again. The letter was short, only a few lines long, written in a delicate, elegant hand. "I will make sure that continues."

"You?" Zhara frowned. "What do you mean?"

He closed his eyes and handed his letter to the others. "It's from Xu," he said heavily. "My father has died. I am to return to Zanhei to take my place as sovereign."

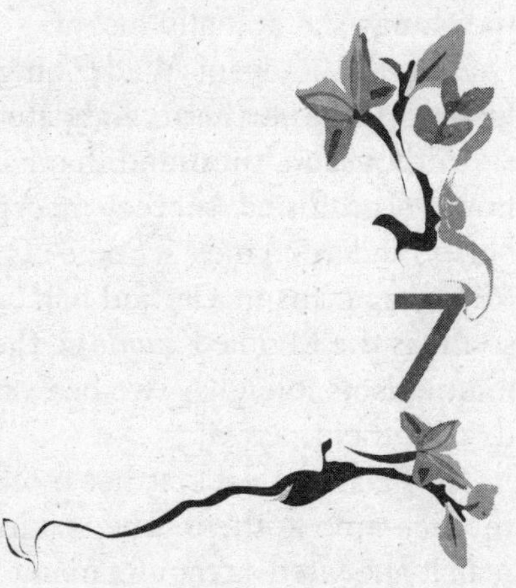

It had been a long time since anyone had called the Grassmoot.

Kho wandered with her mother through the refugee slums of Urghud, distributing food and medicines to the needy. Word of the upcoming gathering had already spread to the farthermost reaches of the city, and even the newcomers were abuzz with the news. The last time the Grassmoot had been called, the Warlord had declared war on the magicians and the Mugung Dynasty, sweeping south with the Golden Horde to claim the imperial city and install himself on the Sunburst Throne.

And soon they would assemble to decide the next emperor of the Morning Realms.

Of course, that was not the Lady of Wild Things' express intent when she summoned the Grassmoot. It was a matter of public good, she had said. Of figuring out ways to provide for the most needy among them, especially the refugees. But Kho had learned long ago that the things her mother said did not always align with the things she actually meant.

And the Lady of Wild Things meant to put herself forward as the northern candidate for the Sunburst Throne.

"A thousand, thousand thanks," a refugee said to Kho, bowing profusely as they accepted gifts of flatbread, barley, and dried meats. Some of those claiming sanctuary from magicians in Urghud had come from regions as far south as the Middle Kingdom, their accents strange, their mannerisms foreign. "Two heavenly maidens have graced us with their mercy!"

Kho glanced back at her mother, who was tending to the sick among them. The waking dreamer sickness was real; it appeared as though many of the refugees had been afflicted by some strange disorder that caused them to lie in a state between dreaming and waking, unable to be roused. The Lady of Wild Things graciously visited each of these sickbeds, speaking to the ill in her melodious voice, offering encouragement and words of comfort to the family members.

"I'm so sorry," she was heard saying over and over again. "Please let the Maltak Kang know what can be done for you."

"Maltak! Maltak!" the refugees would chant, as though the name were a sort of benediction. "Maltak! Maltak!"

The Lady of Wild Things would then lower her lashes demurely, humbly waving off the adoration of the people.

Then the chorus of begging. "Lady, Lady," the people would sob, "a blessing for our children!"

The Lady of Wild Things hesitated, fiddling with the black stone amulet at her throat. "I'm no shaman," she demurred politely.

But the refugees would not be deterred. After an appropriate amount of self-effacing humility, the Lady allowed herself to be drawn into makeshift shanties and lean-tos to lay her hands on those afflicted with the waking dreamer sickness.

It made Kho's skin crawl with discomfort. Her mother cut a glamorous figure among the rag-ridden, downtrodden populace in her coat of shining white wool, the neck and sleeves trimmed with silvery-gray wolf fur, echoing the streaks of silver in her own dark hair. The Lady of Wild Things knew the importance of a good image, and her stroll through the docks of Urghud was as much for the citizens of Urghud to witness her magnanimity and generosity as it was to benefit the needy. Kho had seen the myriad eyes peering at them through cracks in doorways and windows as the Maltak Kang made their way down to slums with wagons and carts loaded with supplies, the children pointing and murmuring with admiration at the show of compassion.

Ever scheming, ever politicking.

"We will stand for you, Lady Maltak!" came the adoring cries from the crowd. "Empress of the Morning Realms!"

The Lady of Wild Things said nothing, merely giving her audience a cryptic smile. She and Kho continued on toward a dining establishment near the water to break for their midday meal, having dispensed of their good deeds for the day. As a diplomat's daughter, Kho knew the value of relationships when it came to amassing power, although she was surprised at her mother's efforts to charm the refugees. By law, all those living within northern borders were eligible to have a say at the Grassmoot, and while the refugees were becoming a significant population within Urghud, Kho didn't think there were enough of them to sway the outcome.

"Many seeds make a fruitful harvest," the Lady of Wild Things said. "It does no good to discount support from any quarter, no matter how small. Remember that when it is your turn to wear the fangs of the Maltak Kang." She toyed with her necklace, a long rope of wolf fangs woven together with leather and thread. A large black stone hung from the center, its surface smooth and polished as a mirror. As a child, Kho remembered playing with the amulet as it dangled from her mother's neck, fascinated by how it seemed to absorb light rather than reflect it.

"Yes, Mother," Kho said, feeling exhaustion overcome her. The expectations of being First Daughter were a heavy burden to bear at all times, but she was especially conscious of the weight in her mother's presence.

"For the greater good," the Lady said.

"For the greater good," Kho repeated. *Loyalty* was the watchword of their family, but sometimes Kho thought it should be *for the greater good*. The greater good was the reason any of the Maltak ever took action, whether it be for the good of their kang or for the good of the empire. She thought of Teacher Alani's words in the university library. *There are many kinds of loyalty. Loyalty to yourself. Loyalty to a greater ideal.*

For her entire life, her mother had been loyal to ambition. The Maltak had never produced many warriors of great renown, although their family was rife with scholars, politicians, and courtiers. Theirs was the wealthiest of the Five Golden Families, their influence cultivated through diplomacy and coin over several generations. Others looked on them with suspicion for their cosmopolitan ways, but the Lady of Wild Things had been indispensable to the Warlord during his reign for her relations with the Azure Isles and had won a not inconsiderable amount of power for their kang.

But that had not been enough.

She wanted the whole of the Morning Realms.

"What of the other heads of the Five Golden Families?" Kho asked. "Do we know how they will stand at the Grassmoot?"

The Lady of Wild Things stroked her amulet thoughtfully. "The Nuwage and the Tzorig will stand for us," she said. "We are bound by marriage to the Tzorig through your father, and the Nuwage owe us their allegiance for resolving the matter of Azurean pirates in the Bay of Dragons. The Shulgin lack the numbers and the will to counter us; they will choose our side over the Gommun."

"The Gommun still have the Golden Horde," Kho said.

In many ways, the military force was the most powerful political faction in the north. The Golden Horde was comprised of members of every family, every kang, including many of the nomads living farther out on the steppes. In times of war, the greater good superseded the internecine squabbles of the Five Golden Families, and the people would set aside bloodlines for battle, fighting together under the direction of the Grand Kang. The Warlord had been Grand Kang during the Just War, and now his daughter, Yuli's aunt Görte, was the leader of the Horde.

The Lady pursed her lips. "It is true our strength has never been in arms," she said. "And we will need the Golden Horde at our backs when we claim the imperial city from the Heralds of Glorious Justice." She smiled, and Kho flinched. The Lady of Wild Things had never been an especially beautiful woman, and she was even more terrifying when she smiled, her sharp, lupine features lengthening menacingly. "But the Gommun are weak. The Grand Kang is ill."

"The Grand Kang is ill?" Kho was taken aback.

Her mother nodded. "With the same waking dreamer sickness that is plaguing the refugees down by the docks."

Kho thought of the afflicted in the slums. It had been more like walking through a slaughterhouse than a sick house, bodies on the ground, still and unmoving. Many even had their eyes open and stared into nothing, with only the shallow rise and fall of their chests to indicate they were still alive. She had been reminded of the night she tried to rouse Ogodei from the Eagle's Nest, the way his skin had fallen slack over his bones and the terrifying emptiness of his expression. The Lady of Wild Things had taken the time to bless them all.

"Is there a cure?" Kho asked. There had been a few in the slums who had awoken from the disease, but no one could say why or how. They all possessed the same haunted look—eyes empty, countenance blank. Waking dreamers, indeed. She thought uneasily of Ogodei. Although he had fully recovered from his raucous night out with the Huntsmen, there was something about him that seemed . . . changed.

Her mother shrugged. "No one in the refugee camps seems to have died of it. Perhaps it is merely a sickness that will run its course."

"So the Grand Kang may yet recover."

"Perhaps," the Lady of Wild Things conceded, fiddling with her necklace once more. "But not, I think, in time for the Grassmoot."

Kho frowned. "How can you be certain?"

Her mother's smile widened. "I can't, of course. But whether or not the Grand Kang recovers in time is immaterial. The fact of the matter remains: the Golden Horde is leaderless, and the time has never been more ripe for a coup."

"A coup?" A chill ran down Kho's spine.

"Yes." The Lady of Wild Things held her gaze. She shared her daughter's eyes—long-lashed, dark, and intense. "The time has come for the Grand Game."

Kho closed her eyes. She had known this day would arrive ever since word arrived of the Warlord's death— the day her mother would finally use her in her political games. Kho had spent most of her life waiting for this moment, diligently studying languages and history at university in order to prepare for whatever it was the Lady of Wild Things would require of her daughter. "You would declare the Grand Game at the Grassmoot," she said. "To challenge Gommun Görte for the title of Grand Kang of the Golden Horde."

"Not me," the Lady of Wild Things said sweetly. "But my champion."

Dread settled in the pit of Kho's stomach. "Ogodei?" she asked hopefully, though she already knew the answer.

"I have other plans for your brother," her mother said. "But you, my child, are the First Daughter of the Maltak Kang, my heir, and my champion."

Kho shook her head. "I'm no warrior," she said in a small voice. The Grand Game consisted of three competitions—the Trial of Strength, the Trial of Wits, and the Trial of the Soul. Kho, like every other child of the steppes, was a decent enough horsewoman, but she had never once ridden away with any accolades during the youth games held every year. That had been Yuli—the best archer, the best fencer, and the best fighter of their generation.

"A great leader is more than the strength of their arms," the Lady said.

"*A true warrior keeps their wits as honed sharp as their blade,*" Kho whispered. It was true that a challenger could lose the Trial of Strength and still become Grand Kang if they won the other two. But northerners respected might; Kho could win the Grand Game on a technicality, but would the Golden Horde honor her victory? "What happens if we lose?" she asked.

The Lady's eyes glinted. "That's where your brother comes in."

Kho didn't know whether to be relieved or upset that her mother had other plans. Of course the Lady of Wild

Things would not rely on a single outcome to further her goals. "What do you mean?"

"The Golden Horde is not the only formidable fighting force in the Morning Realms," her mother said. "The Azureans possess an equally powerful navy."

Kho sucked in a sharp breath. "And you think the Fleet Queen would lend her ships to our cause?"

"In exchange for a favor, yes."

A favor. The political situation in the Azure Isles was an even thornier mess than the succession crisis embroiling the mainland. The Azureans had always maintained a level of independence from the rest of the Morning Realms, although they had thrown their support behind the Warlord during the Just War. The Lady of Wild Things had maintained these relations throughout the Warlord's reign, and now she was capitalizing on years of hard work.

"What sort of favor?" Kho asked.

"Just a matter of local politics." The Lady waved her hand dismissively. "But we must wait until spring when the Strait is clear. Until then, we carry on in the north."

Sometimes her mother's concept of time amazed Kho. Spring was months away, and she was already putting her plans into motion. Many seeds make for a fruitful harvest indeed. The gathering of the Golden Horde, the Azurean fleet, the support of the people of the steppes, an alliance of the Five Golden Families—the Lady of Wild Things had been moving pieces into place for a long, long time.

"And then what?" Kho asked in a soft voice.

Her mother looked down at her black stone amulet, stroking its edges contemplatively. "We go to war," she said simply.

Outside their dining establishment, Kho could hear faint shouts in the distance, a low, droning chant almost akin to the throat-songs of the shamans. With a frown, she slid the window shutters aside and peered out onto the street. A brisk wind blew in from the water, bringing with it the scent of ice from the tundra. A crowd from the slums was gathered around the establishment, their voices raised in a cheer.

"Maltak! Maltak! Maltak!"

The Lady of Wild Things slid aside her own shutters to gaze down on the adoring refugees.

"A miracle, a miracle!" they shouted. "The afflicted have awakened!"

Kho clearly recognized the faces of the newly wakened dreamers scattered throughout the assembly, their eyes hollow, their expressions blank. Their gazes were fixed on the Lady of Wild Things, and the intensity of their focus made all the hairs on the back of Kho's neck stand on end. Unease churned the food in her stomach when she realized they were all blinking in unison. One movement. One entity. For a brief moment, she felt as though she were staring into the face of a myriad-eyed bug, and her skin crawled in revulsion.

"Maltak! Maltak! Maltak!"

Their lips formed the same word, their voices merged into a singular dissonant sound. The Lady of Wild Things basked in their praise before raising her hand to quiet their chants.

Silence fell at once.

"My friends," she called, her sweet voice carrying on the breeze. "I am unworthy of your gratitude. But be assured that you will always have a staunch advocate in the Maltak Kang to be your voice when you feel unheard. I am honored by your trust, and hope I will always live up to your expectations."

A cheer, and the crowd broke out in chants once more. Kho slid the shutters closed and returned to her meal as the droning hum of voices rose ever louder outside.

*Maltak! Maltak! Maltak!*

8

The docks at Urghud's harbor were haunted, but not with ghosts.

The skies were clear down by the waters of the Sweet Sea, a thin rime of ice already forming where the water met the shore. A strange fog had settled over the harbor, coating everything in an icy slick. Yuli's eyes caught shadows where there weren't any, and more than once, she thought she saw a shape dart just beyond the edges of her vision—a spirit, a specter, a stranger. In the depths of winter, when the winds blew wispy drifts of snow hither and thither, some of the elders of Urghud would call it *ghost's breath* or a false fog, but this mist was nothing like that. It lingered, for one, sitting low on the ground, still and unmoving.

It also stank of death.

There was a particular smell Yuli associated with the burial mounds at the Hills of the Dead, a smell like burnt metal, only sharper and bitterer. Auncle Mongke used to tell her it was all in her head, that the Hills of the Dead smelled like nothing more than dirt and the decaying remains of food offerings and incense. Nevertheless, the stink persisted, if not in her physical nose, then in what Yuli supposed was the spiritual equivalent of the sense of smell.

And the harbor was rotten with it.

"Is it just me," Sungho muttered, "or does anyone else find this fog . . . creepy?"

There were mutters of agreement from the others.

"I would have thought it got too cold and dry during the winter here for mist," Mihoon remarked, huddling with the others for warmth around a small brazier. The Bangtan Brothers waited with Yuli by the docks for the boat that would bring Zhara and Ami, the very same ship that would bear them from Urghud to Zanhei with Crackle in tow. The harbor was abandoned, empty even of the hopeful refugees who hung around looking to pick up odd jobs loading and unloading ships arriving after midnight.

"It's too cold for *anything*," Yoochun said, cuddling against Bohyun. "I don't know how you northerners can bear to live like this."

"We don't," Yuli said, burying her nose in the fur lining of her coat. "It's probably why your devoted followers aren't out here to wish you farewell."

She was honestly surprised there wasn't a small crowd in the harbor to see the boys off. Sometimes Yuli thought they ought to recruit some of the Bangtan Brothers' more dedicated enthusiasts into the Guardians of Dawn for their unparalleled ability to uncover every little detail about them—their favorite foods, their hobbies, their interests. Not even the Warlord's spy network could compare with the level of organization and information sharing among the members' most ardent supporters.

"We asked them not to come," Taeri said simply. "Our followers respect our wishes."

Yuli thought of the roaring throngs that had gathered for every single one of the boys' performances in the city and found it difficult to believe, and yet here they were, completely and utterly alone. But she supposed she wouldn't have wanted to be out on a night like this either. Northerner born and bred she might have been, but even she would have preferred a nice warm bed to standing out near the open water.

"Just be grateful you won't have to attend the Grassmoot tomorrow." Yuli shivered. "Waiting for hours in the cold while people drone on and on about the dullest things imaginable? No, thank you."

"Do you know why the Grassmoot has been called?" Junseo asked, holding his mittened hands up to the brazier.

Yuli shrugged. "Something about how to handle the matter of the refugees," she said, glancing at the stragglers around them. "But anyone with a grievance to air can strike the Drum of Sorrows for the chance to speak."

An official Grassmoot had not been held for as long as Yuli could remember. Northerners were fairly egalitarian in principle, with anyone having the right to voice their opinion at any time, but mundane matters of daily governance were mostly handled by the heads of the Five Golden Families. Which the issue of the refugees ought to have been. Yuli couldn't fathom why the Lady of Wild Things had called for all the peoples of the steppes to muster, unless she had some ulterior motive. Which Yuli suspected she did. The Maltak were always scheming, always conniving. Although the Lady of Wild Things had enjoyed a high position in the imperial court, Obaji had never fully trusted her, citing the Maltaks' disposition toward soft southern tendencies like bureaucracy and civil etiquette. The Warlord had ever been brutally efficient, preferring the straightforward outcomes of war to the torturous dance of politics.

Which had made Yuli's friendship with Kho all the more foolhardy, although she didn't know it then.

It hadn't been easy to make true friends as the favorite grandchild of the Warlord. As the daughter of the liaison to the Azure Isles, Kho was the only other person she could consider a peer. Yuli had always been a social child, never wanting for attention, but her magic and her position as a member of the new imperial family had ever kept her at a slight distance from others her age. Except Jochi, but Jochi was blood. It was one thing to be wholly herself with family; it was another to be wholly herself with friends. She had never had a close confidante, nor anyone to whom she could go when she wanted to be Yuli—just Yuli—and not a princess.

Until Kho.

"I wish we could have done more for the Guardians of Dawn before we left," Junseo fretted. "We never did find that northern fragment of *Songs of Order and Chaos.*"

"That's not your fault," Yuli said. "We are at the whims of the Paper Wolf."

"Who *is* the Paper Wolf?" Mihoon asked. "I hadn't realized there was a black market for magical artifacts here in Urghud as well."

Yuli pulled her cap down to cover her ears. "There isn't," she said. "We don't know who the Paper Wolf is. The Guardians of Dawn have only been in contact with them for the past two years."

Mihoon frowned. "Why the past two years?"

She thought again of Jochi. His trial had been two years ago, the last time a magician had been publicly sentenced for their crimes. "I don't know," she said. "But they won't join our organization openly. Whoever they are, I suppose it's been safer to keep their identity secret."

"There it is," Alyosha called from atop their covered wagon. "The ship."

The second youngest had the keenest eyes of the group, for it took the others a while longer before they spotted the silhouette of a large junk headed toward the harbor through the mist. In the distance, they could hear the voices of the sailors calling to one another as they guided the craft to the pier. Yuli strained her eyes against the weak light of the crescent moon, startling for a moment to see the silhouette of a figure standing by the unlit lantern at the end of the dock. Unlike the other spectral shadows wreathing the harbor, this shade was distinctly person-shaped, with a hand raised in greeting.

They were gone within the next blink, leaving Yuli feeling colder and more unsettled than ever.

"Hoi!" a voice called out from the ship. "Is there anyone there who can lend us a hand?"

"Hoi!" Junseo called back. "What do you need?"

"A light! Something to show us the way through this cursed fog!"

There was no one standing by the unlit lantern now. With some trepidation, Yuli retrieved it and tipped it toward the brazier, lighting the wick inside with the coals. A corresponding light blazed from the prow of the ship, and Yuli walked down between the docks to guide the vessel toward shore.

"Yuli!"

A petite young woman with a mass of wavy black hair raced down the gangplank. An enormous smile split Yuli's face as she opened her arms wide and Zhara threw herself into her embrace.

"Oof," Yuli grunted as she stumbled back a little. "You're stronger than you look."

The reality of hugging Zhara was nothing like hugging her in spirit form. The solid weight and heft of another person in her arms was a revelation—the sensation of Zhara's hair tickling her chin, her strength as she squeezed, the inescapably embodied *existence* of someone she cared about that she could experience with her whole self, not just a part of it. Yuli found herself unexpectedly tearing up. She had not felt like this in a long, long time.

Zhara pinched her.

"Aiyo!" Yuli yelped. "What was that for?"

An impish grin crossed the other girl's face. "I've always wanted to do that in person."

Yuli rolled her eyes. "It's good to see you too, Bubbles." She glanced behind her at a short-haired, bespectacled scrivener descending the gangplank. "And you, beauty."

Ami shyly inclined her head in acknowledgment. Unlike Zhara, she was far more reticent in person, lingering apart from the others uncertainly as the Bangtan Brothers surrounded them, chattering excitedly.

"Nene!" Yoochun cried. The youngest member wrapped his arms around both Zhara and Yuli, lifting them both off their feet. "I've missed you!"

"I've missed you too, didi," Zhara managed, laughing between breaths. She reached up to ruffle his hair. "What are they feeding you?" she asked in amazement. "You've grown so much!"

"I wish you were coming with us," the boy said tearily. "The seven of us, you, and Han-gogo like it was on the road to Kalantze."

Zhara gave him a watery smile. "I wish I could go with you too," she said.

"Hoi!" One of the ship's crew called down to them. "Can anyone lend a hand?"

The sailors were unloading shipments of goods from Arkhevet and beyond: sacks of grain, spices, produce, and—Yuli noted with a sinking heart—crates upon crates of weapons. A chilling reminder of the impending civil war. She thought uneasily of the upcoming Grassmoot and the vacant Sunburst Throne. The last time the

Grassmoot had been declared, her grandfather had overthrown the Mugung Dynasty. Only this time, there was no emperor to depose, but an empire to gain. The Heralds of Glorious Justice claimed they were marching to the imperial city in the name of magician liberation, but who would they install on the throne if they won? Yuli blinked as she realized the north had no answer either. Her grandfather had named no heir. Who would the north support in the war of succession?

It was the Lady of Wild Things who had summoned the Grassmoot.

Dread stiffened Yuli's limbs.

The Bangtan Brothers scrambled to help the sailors unload the cargo, and Yuli scanned the deck for other passengers. "Where are Gaden and the others?" she asked Ami.

The scrivener pushed her spectacles up her nose. "They decided to travel to Zanhei with Han," she said softly. Her gaze flickered over Yuli's shoulder, staring at something in the darkness behind her.

Yuli was surprised. "Why?"

Ami's expression was obscured by her glasses in the moonlight. "Our duties diverged," she said simply. "They thought they could do more good in the southern provinces with Han than helping me and Zhara with the northern portal." Again her eyes kept going to a point over Yuli's shoulder before darting away again.

Yuli peered at the scrivener. "Are you all right?" she asked.

Ami frowned. "I'm just uncomfortable with all these people standing about."

"People?" Zhara whirled around. "But there's no one else here."

Yuli narrowed her eyes. In the light of the lantern, she thought she caught a glimpse of that stranger's silhouette once more, standing even closer than before.

Ami went still. "You can't see them?"

"See who?" Zhara asked in a bewildered voice.

Ami shot a glance to Yuli. "The ghosts."

Ghosts. Yuli thought of all the scary stories she and Kho used to tell each other in the dark, giggling together under the covers of each other's beds. Stories of those who hadn't had their souls sung to the eternal blue skies by the shamans, doomed to linger on this earth until released by last rites. To be cut off from the cycle of rebirth was a tragedy, and the lack of closure often turned these spirits mournful or vengeful, haunting or cursing those who were unfortunate enough to cross their path.

Zhara sucked in a sharp breath. "You mean . . ." She trailed off, running her hands through the mist in wonder.

Yuli squinted into the fog at the lone figure she could see. It was difficult to make out their features in the dim light, but she thought she caught a glimpse of red in their hair. She stiffened, remembering the glimmer of auburn she had seen the day she rescued Crackle from the clutches of the Huntsmen. The youth who had saved them.

"Jochi?" she breathed.

At the sound of her cousin's name, the figure started.

"You can see them too?" Ami asked in amazement.

Yuli stepped forward, hand outstretched. "Jochi?" she asked, her tone brimming with hope. Two years before, he had been exiled to the Frozen Wastes for the crime of being a magician. Exiled, not executed. Cold comfort, quite literally, that her favorite relative had been spared the ire of the Falconer's pyre, even though the punishment was practically a death sentence for a fourteen-year-old boy. But perhaps he had survived. Perhaps he had somehow made it back to Urghud, hiding among the refugees, returned to sort out this succession crisis.

The redheaded youth gave her a sad smile, their mouth forming words she could not hear.

"Can you not see the others?" Ami asked.

The mist grew thick around them, slithering around as though with a mind of its own. "I only see *him*," Yuli said in a choked voice. "My cousin, Jochi."

"Do you not see the other disembodied spirits?" Zhara asked.

Yuli was taken aback. "Disembodied spirits?"

"Yes," Ami said. "Ghosts of the living, those untethered from their physical vessels."

The word *living* sent a further jolt of hope down Yuli's spine. She looked longingly at the form of Jochi before her, but he continued to mouth something at her. "Talk to me, cousin," she said softly. "What is it you want to say?"

"Here." Zhara took Yuli's mittened hand in her own and placed something small, hard, and round in her palm. Yuli glanced down to see a necklace set with a clear stone the size of a robin's egg. "It's a crystal from the caves beneath Mount Llangposa," Zhara continued. "It's made of pure magical ki. It glows at our touch and goes dark in the presence of demons. We haven't discovered all its properties yet, but I thought you should have one."

Yuli removed her mitten and wrapped her bare fingers around the stone. It felt almost warm in her hand, as though it were alive, resonant with the same vibrations she felt when she touched another magician. At once, a bright white-gold light filled the harbor, cutting through the fog surrounding them.

There were faces in the mist. Yuli nearly dropped her crystal. Faces, so many faces mingled with parts of an arm, a hand, a shoulder, a leg. A writhing, wreathing mass of ghosts, visible beneath the light of her stone. Beside her, Zhara let out a quiet yelp of terror, clinging to Ami. Ghosts of the living. The disembodied ki of those afflicted with the waking dreamer sickness. Each of their empty bodies a potential host for a demon.

"So many," Yuli murmured.

There were hundreds, if not more. The horror of it all threatened to overwhelm her, her skin crawling with revulsion. A potential demon army, right in the city of Urghud itself. The ghostly mist wrapping the harbor also crawled up the streets, flowing down tiny alleys, dead ends, passageways. Every corner was thick with another face, another countenance, another mouth, all twisted in the same silent plea.

"Help me," Ami said quietly. "That's what they're saying. *Help me, help me, help me.*"

"How?" Yuli looked to Jochi. Unlike the others, he was whole and himself, his expression clear and present. Was his body also lying somewhere in the Frozen Wastes, bereft of his spirit?

Her cousin reached out to touch his fingers to her chest. She didn't feel the weight of a body against her, but she *felt* his touch the way she felt an emotion—fear, joy, dread, apprehension. She couldn't hear his voice, but she could understand his words.

*You,* he said. *You can help them.*

"How?" she repeated helplessly.

*The Guardian of Wind,* he said, *can tether and untether souls from their vessels.*

Yuli went still. She had always thought of her Guardian powers as being spectacularly useless, limited to her own spirit, her own ki. Spirit-walking and communicating mind-to-mind were nothing like being able to transform lead into gold like Zhara or bring rocks to life like Ami. But if she could affect others with her abilities . . . that changed things. The enormity of possibility frightened her.

"Jochi," she said, unable to keep the tears from her voice. "Where are you? Why are you here? Come back to me. Come home."

He gave her a soft, enigmatic smile as his edges

blurred. He was dissipating, disappearing, and she could not hold on to him. His lips moved but she could no longer understand.

"Jochi? Jochi?"

She struggled to decipher the shape of his mouth, to grasp his last words to her.

"He's saying *beware*," Ami said slowly, squinting at the redheaded ghost. *"Beware the . . ."*

Jochi was fading fast, and he took on a desperate, pleading expression. His eyes were the last to vanish, holding on to Yuli's gaze long after he was gone.

*"Beware the Sleepers,"* said Ami, *"for they wake."*

# PART

## THE GRAND GAME

It was the morning of the Grassmoot and Ogodei was nowhere to be found.

Ogodei had never been much of an early riser, but when Kho climbed up to the third floor of Maltak Manor, she found her brother's quarters empty.

The rest of the household had been up before dawn getting ready for the Grassmoot—preparing ceremonial foods to offer the ancestors, cleaning and polishing armor and tack, arranging gifts, and putting on their finest colors. The Grassmoot might be a political affair, but it was also an opportunity for people to meet and mingle with friends and family they had not seen in a long time, as roving bands of nomads from the steppes headed toward the Tower of Offerings outside the city. There was nearly a festival atmosphere to the proceedings, as the Maltak household made dishes to bring and share, as well as gifts of jewelry, furs, and yak wool to exchange with other kangs.

Kho fingered a small bracelet about her wrist, beaded

with turquoise and decorated with white tassels. There had been a time when she stayed up late with the other women of the household, making necklaces and jewelry to give away to loved ones. She had given a matching bracelet just like this to Yuli once, right before the youth games two winters before. Now she had no one to exchange tokens with.

"Gogo?" Kho called as she approached her brother's room. Unlike many of the other old manors in Urghud, the Maltak home had been built more like a castle than an estate. It was one of the tallest edifices in Urghud, four stories tall, with thick walls made of brick and stone and small windows to keep out the cold. Ogodei had the topmost floor entirely to himself, a private tower for the prince of the Maltak Kang, accessible only by a ladder to be dropped down by its occupant. Kho had made the journey from her rooms to her brother's so many times as a little girl, longing for company whenever she had scared herself reading horror stories in the dark. While he always made fun of her, he also never turned her away, a habit he maintained even though they were no longer children. His had been the shoulder she had cried on when Yuli had turned away, had abjured their friendship. His had been the teasing and laughter she endured afterward.

To her surprise, the door was already open and the ladder lowered, but when she climbed through the entrance, Ogodei wasn't there. "Gogo?"

His quarters were in shambles—bed unmade, cupboard doors open, clothes strewn about the floor. There were books and papers scattered everywhere and atop every surface—the floor, the low table, the rug, the couch, and even the bed. The emptiness of his rooms did not shock her; more than once, she had come up to see her brother, only to find he had either sneaked out with his friends or not yet returned from his exploits. No, it was the books. Ogodei had never been the most enthusiastic student, often finding it difficult to read even though he knew how.

*The words twist and crawl all over the place,* he would say.

What few things he did like to read were illustrated adventure serials, his favorite when he was young being one about a boy who wanted to grow up to be the greatest pirate baron of the Azure Isles and then, when he was older, naughty stories with racy prints sold between plain covers at street vendors just outside the university. But the texts laid out in disarray in his room were neither of those things; they weren't even novels. As far as she could tell, most of them were dense, scholarly works of some sort, filled with such small, tight handwriting that even her eyes strained to read it.

Ogodei hadn't been out in the streets with the other Huntsmen much since that night she found him collapsed at the Eagle's Nest, shutting himself up in his rooms, muttering to himself. Sometimes in the middle of the night, Kho thought she could hear an eldritch whispering that sounded almost like the chanting of prayers coming from his quarters. But she had assumed he was merely in one of his dark moods where he slept all day and barely ate. Those moods generally passed with enough time and space, at which point he would once again be carousing in the taverns with the Huntsmen.

But her brother hadn't been spending his time lying abed.

He had been reading. Studying, even.

But what he had been studying was incomprehensible. Kho picked up a loose sheet of paper, trying to make sense of the nonsense scribbled there. She couldn't recognize the writing system; the letters were more like symbols or glyphs, with no repeating patterns that she could see. Not a phonetic alphabet or a syllabary. Some sort of code?

She dropped the page in realization.

Kho was looking at the Language of Flowers.

She knew of the magicians' writing system, which used logograms to represent words or ideas, although she had never seen an example of it. Any and all books of magic were burned during the purges following the Just War, the knowledge smoke in people's memory. A small burn of jealousy kindled in her stomach. Ever since Jochi's exile, she had spent the past two years mired in the university archives in search of any scrap—any hint of magical writing—she could preserve, knowing she was sifting through ash for remains. Where had her brother found these texts? What was he doing with them?

Then she noticed a smear of black on her palm. Rubbing at it with her finger, Kho gave it a tentative sniff. Ink?

Ogodei wasn't just studying the Language of Flowers; he was *writing* in it.

Her hands shook, her fingertips and face going numb. So many questions without any answers, and she didn't know what to feel or think. Her first thought, ridiculously, was that this was not her brother's hand. His calligraphy had always been atrocious, uncontrolled and uneven, the letters twisted and backward. Perhaps the writing did not belong to him, did not represent a descent into madness, or worse—treason.

But everywhere she looked she saw evidence to the contrary. The carelessly discarded brushes on his desk, the half-dried dish of ink, the sheets of paper covered with scrawls and mistakes.

Kho then thought of her father, the Falconer, far away in the imperial city with his legions of Kestrels. He had been the Warlord's head magic-hunter, the emperor's most devoted enforcer of anti-magic policy. It was bad enough that Ogodei had the Taint, but to be discovered *studying* magic? There was little room for mercy in her father's conservative heart; he would expect Kho to turn in her own brother to the authorities.

Wildly, she started gathering up the loose papers, casting about for some place to hide them. Her father might believe in the law, but she was a Maltak first and foremost: *loyalty* was her watchword. If anyone else came up here, if someone else saw—

"Kho-yah!" came a voice from downstairs. "Where are you?"

She glanced through the windows at the growing light. The kang would be headed off to the Tower of Offerings soon, which stood a league outside Urghud's eastern gates.

"Mimi!" the voice came again. Ogodei. "If you don't come down, we're going to leave without you!"

Kho stopped what she was doing, suddenly realizing the consequences of her actions. She was trespassing in her brother's quarters, and she realized with some unease that she wasn't sure of how he would react if he found out she had discovered his secret. No, the wiser course of action would be to confront Ogodei in private, ask him about his illicit activities, and plan accordingly. If her brother were truly sympathetic to the magician cause, then perhaps they could work together. Kho's heart lifted. As children, they had been close—she and Yuli and Ogodei and Jochi—but ever since Jochi was exiled to the Frozen Wastes, distance had come between them all. Jochi was a festering wound they all shared and maybe this was her brother's attempt to heal. To make peace with betrayal, just as she was trying to.

She could hope.

"Kho!"

"Coming!" she called. She scattered the pages of writing over Ogodei's room again, and her glance fell on his unmade pallet, where a leather folio of pages had been left open. The pages atop his bedclothes were written in a different hand, the ink faded with age. Frowning, Kho picked up the leather cover and turned it over.

On its face was etched a symbol—a bisected circle, one half filled, the other blank, each with a drop of the opposite contained within.

All the hairs stood up on the back of Kho's neck.

*A folio,* the message had read. *With a taikhut.*

She didn't know the symbol's significance but sensed its power nonetheless. There was power in imagery; Kho knew that from both her studies at the university and her own life. In the north, the Five Golden Families differentiated themselves by sigil and color—a yellow wolf for the Maltak, a red bear for the Gommun, a green horse for the Nuwage, a blue eagle for the Tzorig, and a white spear for the Shulgin. During the reign of the Mugungs, they had identified themselves by the symbol of the sunburst, which had in turn been taken from the eight-spoked wheel of the faith of the Great Wheel. Farther south, the Heralds of Glorious Justice rode to the imperial city under the banner of the Four-Winged Dragon, the previous dynasty's battle standard, signaling their intent to declare war. This *taikhut* reminded Kho a bit of the talismans of the Way the priestesses of Do wore around their throats, the dark and light spirals representing the constant flow between order and chaos, chaos and order.

A cold stillness overcame Kho.

She knew what the book was. It was the most forbidden book of magic in all the Morning Realms. A book of demons and dark magic, so evil that even the Mugung Emperor had ordered it destroyed.

"Kho!"

"I'm coming!" she called again. Picking up a brush from Ogodei's desk, she scribbled a quick note, leaving it unsigned. Shoving the note into her coat, she climbed down the ladder to join the rest of her kang on the grounds. It would be good to get an early start on the Grassmoot.

Because she had a stop she needed to make first.

# 10

*Beware the Sleepers, for they wake.*

Ami sat in the cellar of Tarkhun's bookshop, working on her encyclopedia for *Songs of Order and Chaos*. After much agonizing and deliberating, she had decided that her notes would be best organized in a system of journals, with an index book referencing her work. Tarkhun had blinked in astonishment when she had asked for a stack of ten journals to use, but had provided them without any complaint.

Working at Tarkhun's bookshop was entirely unlike transcribing light romance novels for Master Cao back in Zanhei. It had animals, for one, and not just Sajah and Rinqi, who had already made themselves at home with the chickens and lonely yak out back. The shop was more of a shack with an attached stall than a proper store, more like Tarkhun's home than a place of business. Indeed, the bookseller lived at the shop, sleeping in a hay-filled loft above his wares. The safe house for the Guardians of Dawn was in the cellar, which was less a basement than a crude dugout stocked with a few pallets along with Tarkhun's food stores. The cellar was freezing, but the bookseller had provided them with a brazier and coals, which Sajah, Zhara, and Ami had slept near, as close as they dared, the night they arrived. Thankfully Tarkhun had provided them with plenty of furs, but Ami found it difficult to work down there with her ink constantly icing over.

But she preferred the cellar to the warmth upstairs. It was more comfortable, at any rate, than Zhara's silence.

Ever since the two of them had set sail across the Sweet Sea, and ever since they parted ways with Han, Gaden, and Okonwe, Ami found herself held at arm's length, not by Zhara's quiet grief but by her own discomfort. She was sharply reminded of what her life had been like before she found Zhara and the others, that feeling of apartness and aloneness that had been a constant backdrop to her childhood. Her two older half-sisters had married and left the house before Ami had been old enough to form intimate relationships with them, but even if they hadn't, neither of them had been much inclined toward her mother, whom they considered a *foreign interloper* in the family. And once her mother had died, Ami had become so preoccupied with managing her father's madness that she was both unsure of and disinclined to manage anyone else.

She realized on some level that this was unfair. Zhara did not place the weight of her sorrow on anyone else's shoulders, and a part of Ami understood that friends shared each other's burdens. But she had never had friends growing up save for the plants in her mother's garden, and they asked for so little in return. It wasn't as though Ami didn't want to give; it was mostly that she didn't know how. She had never grown up knowing the right actions to perform nor the right words to say, and she was mostly afraid of getting things wrong.

When Han had announced his need to return home, the first thing Zhara had done was cry.

That had been expected.

What she hadn't expected was for Gaden to cry as well.

It had taken a lot of arguing and bargaining, but in the end, it was decided that Han would not travel alone. Although Gaden possessed the Star of Radiance, both Zhara and Ami could seal demonic portals on their own, so Gaden's presence was not necessary in Urghud. Han's intention with his return to Zanhei was to gather an alliance of the southern city-states in support of the pro-magic cause, and to potentially reach out to Pang Lok and the Heralds of Glorious Justice ahead of the Conclave in the spring. Gaden's presence would be infinitely more useful to Han than to either Zhara or Ami, so it was decided they and Okonwe would accompany him south.

It was at this point that tears began glistening along Gaden's lower lashes.

Their plans made sense. As sorry as Ami would be to be parted from Gaden, and no matter how much she would miss them, it was the most logical course of action to take.

She supposed she hadn't taken into account how feelings did not follow logic.

On the morning of Han, Gaden, and Okonwe's departure, Han and Zhara said their private goodbyes, while Gaden bade farewell to Ami.

"I wish I were going with you," they said softly, gently tucking an errant strand of her hair behind her ear.

She didn't have her glasses on. But sometimes she preferred looking at Gaden this way—without magic, without any artificial barrier between them. It made their beauty easier to behold when it was blurred around the edges; the clarity of their features would hurt that much more in the moments before they were parted.

Without her glasses, the roughness of Gaden's scarred cheek smoothed in a silvery-pink sheen on their skin, and the intensity of their expression was easier to bear. Although she had difficulty meeting anyone's eyes on her best days, Ami made sure to keep her gaze focused on Gaden's, to hold her face close enough to bring them into focus. Up close, the world dissolved into vague colors, leaving only the exact shade of rich earthen brown she had grown to love.

"We're both needed elsewhere," Ami said.

They gave a soft laugh. "Will you miss me?"

"Of course." She was almost affronted they had to ask. "Why wouldn't I?"

One side of their lips twisted higher than the other. "I know, it's just . . . I needed to hear it." They touched a gentle fingertip to her chin. "You say so much with those beautiful eyes of yours, but very rarely do the words ever escape your lips."

Ami touched her own fingers to her lips then. "Why should I, when you know how to read their expression?"

"Ami," they said in a low voice, "would you . . . would you still care for me if I were no longer Gaden?"

Echoes of their earlier conversation rang in her ears. *The Star of Radiance is meant to protect the land. I could use this power for good. I'm afraid that means I have to be someone I'm not.*

Ami knew they wanted what was best for the people. But she wanted what was best for them.

"You will always be Gaden," she whispered. "No matter what else the world calls you. You will always be Gaden to me."

They shut their eyes and pressed their forehead to hers. "Thank you."

She closed the distance between them, their lips meeting, then parting in farewell.

That had been five days ago, and the last time Ami had had any meaningful contact with another person.

So she had made the best of her time by working on her encyclopedia of *Songs of Order and Chaos*. Ami had decided to use one journal as a master index and numbered the others one through nine. She knew she would keep track of the topics and page numbers in the master index, but waffled on whether to spread the topics out a few per book or to simply start transcribing chronologically. In the end, she decided to work chronologically, just as she had in her initial translation work with her father.

*Before the creation of the cosmos, there was consciousnes. When consciousnes awoke, it gave itself a name, and in doing so, it gave itself life.*

Ami cursed her frozen ink, which left blots on the first page, causing her to misspell *consciousness*. It was easier to be messy with loose sheets of paper; she didn't feel as compelled to keep things neat and pristine. She supposed it was a blessing in disguise to have started her encyclopedia with a mistake—it relieved the pressure to be perfect.

Halfway through writing about the emergence of Do and the principles of Jun and Yan, the manifestations of Order and Chaos, Ami was suddenly overcome with doubt about the entire endeavor. Was this the most practical use of her new journals? Perhaps she should have started with the most relevant and important information to their quest—the last battle between the Guardians of Dawn and the Mother of Ten Thousand Demons, the resting places of the four celestial companions, and how to seal Tiyok back into her realm with the Star of Radiance. Perhaps then it would make it easier to tally the pieces of information they were missing and what they ought to be looking for in the last two fragments of *Songs of Order and Chaos*. And what of this waking dreamer sickness? And what was it Yuli's cousin had said? Something about Sleepers?

In that moment she missed Gaden dreadfully. They had a way of setting her mind to rights, of smoothing and soothing her rambling thoughts into some semblance of order by simply allowing her to talk at them until things started to make sense. Zhara was good at many things, especially for making sense of the thorny tangle of emotions that Ami did not always understand, but sometimes she found conversing with Zhara a little overwhelming. Ami was good at listening, and she was good at talking, but what she could not reconcile was the mix of both. Zhara seemed to combine the two activities with some rhyme or reason Ami could not quite grasp, and it sometimes left her struggling to find her bearings.

The door to the cellar opened, bringing in a rush of warm air that sent the pages of Ami's notes flying.

"Pardon, pardon, a thousand pardons!" Zhara fell to her hands and knees, scrambling to gather the loose scraps together.

"It's all right," Ami said awkwardly.

Zhara silently handed her the pages and then turned with what sounded suspiciously like a huff. Ami tensed, anticipating some sort of chastisement or a word of reprimand, but none came. Instead, the other girl merely retreated to the pallet they shared with a book instead of huddling around the brazier for heat. Another light romance novel by Jae Hyun, an older one, not *The Maiden Who Was Loved by Death*. Ami remembered finding it rather middling.

The silence that followed was not comfortable. Ami had never thought much about the quality of silences before, whether they were easy or awkward or fraught. For her, silence was often merely silence, but she sensed something was bothering Zhara, and that something wasn't her parting from Han. In fact, Ami suspected it had to do with her instead.

"Is everything all right?" she ventured.

Zhara lifted her eyes from her book before returning them to the page. "Yes."

Ami nodded and returned to her own work.

"Actually, no."

Ami met Zhara's gaze across their cramped quarters and, to her surprise, found the glimmer of unshed tears in the other girl's eyes. Concerned, she immediately dropped her work and knelt by her friend's side. "What's wrong?"

To Ami's alarm, Zhara immediately burst out crying. "I'm sorry," the other girl said, snuffling into her sleeve.

"What for?" Ami was more confused than ever.

"It's just . . ." Zhara sighed, regaining control of her composure. "I suppose I've been feeling hurt that you haven't asked me how I was doing before when I clearly wasn't doing so well, what with leaving the others and all."

Ami squirmed. She had clearly done the wrong thing again. "I'm sorry," she said. "I . . . I didn't think—I didn't know how to ask."

"It's all right." Zhara wiped at her eyes with the back of her hand. "How are you? Are you doing all right, being apart from Gaden?"

Once again, Ami felt herself at a loss. She had thought they were going to talk about Zhara's feelings now. "I'm fine," she said. "I miss them, but it is what it is."

"Is it?" Zhara sighed again. "I know all this makes *sense*; the others deal with the impending civil war, and we deal with the matter of Tiyok and sealing the demon portals. It's just . . . after all we had been through, I had thought Han and I would . . . see things through to the end together, I suppose." She turned the rose quartz bangle over and over on her wrist. "It feels like I'm missing part of myself somehow, only I haven't misplaced anything." Lifting her eyes to Ami, she asked, "Doesn't it *ache*?"

Ami absentmindedly rubbed at her chest, ever conscious of the hollowness left there by Gaden's absence. "Yes," she said quietly. "It does."

"How do you bear it?"

"I don't know," she said honestly. "I suppose I do because I have no other choice."

Zhara made a face. "You make it sound so easy." She flopped dramatically atop the pallet. "Sometimes I feel like I can't function for the *yearning*."

Ami shook her head with a smile. "It almost sounds like you like the yearning, though."

Zhara bit her lip. "I suppose it is romantic," she said thoughtfully. "In all the novels I've read, it's always the parts where the lovers cannot be together for some reason that are the most delicious." She sat up. "I suppose that makes me the heroine of my own romance now." She laughed. "Thanks, Ami."

Ami was nonplussed. "You're welcome?"

"What have you been working on?" Zhara asked. Her good humor had returned, and the contrast between her previous mood and her current one sent Ami's head spinning.

"I'm trying to get started on my encyclopedia," Ami said. "But I keep getting tripped up on where to begin."

Zhara looked thoughtful. "What is the most important thing we need to know right now?"

Again she thought of the redheaded spirit's last words before he disappeared. "*Beware the Sleepers,*" she said slowly, "*for they wake.*"

"Do you think the Sleepers have something to do with the waking dreamer sickness?" Zhara asked.

Ami shook her head. "I don't know what the Sleepers are at all." She picked up her stack of notes, riffling through the pages. "I don't think I've ever come across them before."

"What of the waking dreamer sickness?"

Now *that,* Ami had found. "*Waking dreamer* is an old phrase for anti-magician," she said. "I found references to the Moth Demon being able to control the souls of the waking dreamers."

"Any information about how to defeat them?"

"No." Ami frowned. "There's something different about the Moth Demon from the other Lords of Tiyok," she said. "Only I can't quite make out what it is. Demons cannot exist on the physical plane; that's why they need to possess the bodies of magicians or the dead. Pure chaos is incompatible with the order of matter. There was something about the Moth Demon not needing a body, but I don't have that part of the book. That must be in one of the missing fragments of *Songs of Order and Chaos.*"

"And this so-called Paper Wolf hasn't had any luck finding it, according to Yuli." Zhara closed her eyes. "Do you think the northern fragment might have been destroyed?"

Ami fiddled with her brush. "I hope not. For all our sakes."

Upstairs they heard a faint knocking. Zhara and Ami froze, staring at each other in fear. The entire population of Urghud including Tarkhun was at the Grassmoot, and there should have been no one left in the city.

"Should we go see who that is?" Zhara whispered.

Ami pressed a finger to her lips and tiptoed to the wooden ladder leading out of the cellar. She held her brush in her hand, ready to cast a spell if necessary, and pushed the trapdoor ajar. It opened beneath the selling counter of Tarkhun's bookshop, with a full view of anyone who came to the door.

A shadowy figure stood outside, their silhouette

visible through the rice paper panels. They rapped their knuckles on the threshold again, pressing their ear to the door. Ami held her breath while they lingered outside, as though debating whether to enter. After several fraught moments, the figure jimmied the door open a fraction and a small slip of paper fell onto the floor of the bookshop. They stepped back as though surveying their handiwork before their silhouette disappeared.

It was a long time before Ami let out her breath.

Once she was certain the stranger had gone, she pushed the trapdoor open all the way and climbed onto the floor.

"Ami!" Zhara hissed.

"They're gone," she said. "And I think they left a note."

She picked up the slip of paper and unfolded it.

*I have what you are looking for,* the message read. *Meet me at the Hills of the Dead at midnight.*

There was no signature, but Ami recognized the symbol at the bottom of the note. A bisected circle, one half dark with a drop of light, the other light with a drop of dark.

A *taikhut.*

# 11

For such a serious affair, the Grassmoot was surprisingly . . . fun.

The last time Yuli had been to the Tower of Offerings had been for her grandfather's funeral, when the shamans sang the Warlord's soul to the eternal blue skies while offering his corpse to the carrion creatures in a sky burial. Once his bones had been picked clean, the remains were tossed into the ossuary pit—save for the skull, which had been given to the Gommun Kang to bury with the rest of their ancestors at the Hills of the Dead. The tallest structure for miles around, the Tower of Offerings was one of the most sacred sites in the steppes, the place where important leaders and nobles were returned to the cycle of death and rebirth, and where the people of the north gathered for festivals, sporting competitions, and other rituals.

Yuli was surprised and overwhelmed by the number of people assembled at the Grassmoot. Festivals and sporting events were well-attended, but they were nothing compared to the sheer mass of humanity that had arrived, some even from villages as far north as the tundra. Long-lost and distant family members greeted each other with laughter and tears, exchanging gifts, sharing food, dancing and playing music in celebration of reunion. Yuli watched a pair of children give each other matching handmade bracelets with an unexpected twinge. Her fingers went to her own bare wrist, feeling the ghost of turquoise beads against her skin. She didn't wear much jewelry, but she had worn that bracelet faithfully for years until she ripped it off her arm the night Jochi was exiled.

"Yuli-yah," Auncle Mongke reprimanded. "You're letting the banner drop."

With a grunt, Yuli lifted the spear bearing the sigil of the Gommun Kang—a black bear surrounded by thorns on a field of red. The standard wasn't heavy, just unwieldy, but as First Daughter, she was responsible for carrying the flag. She glanced around the clearing, noting the sigils of the other Five Golden Families scattered throughout the crowd—the green horse of the Nuwage, the blue eagle of the Tzorig, and the white spear of the Shulgin. To her surprise, the yellow wolf of the Maltak was nowhere to be seen. The flag of the Golden Horde also flew on a pole beneath the Tower, but there was no war leader on a horse beside the standard-bearer. Yuli could hear the conspiratorial whispers beneath the cheers and singing of the crowd.

*I hear the Grand Kang is ill.*

*Succumbed to the waking dreamer sickness, they say.*

*Can the Grassmoot even be held without her?*

The waking dreamer sickness. The Gommun standard wavered as Yuli thought of the myriad spirits wandering down by the harbor. Ami had said they were the ghosts of the living, disembodied souls untethered from their bodies, and that the waking dreamers were simply empty vessels waiting to be filled by a demon. She shuddered, wanting to shout that the Grand Kang was *not* afflicted with the waking dreamer sickness, that Aunt Görte was merely feeling poorly, and had been for some time now. Jochi's exile had badly affected her health; ever since the loss of her son, she had taken to shutting herself up in her rooms more and more, barely emerging to eat and speak with the other members of her family. Today had been an especially bad day, and no amount of pleading or cajoling had been able to rouse her from her bed.

A sudden ragged chant rose from the assembled, parting to make way for a procession headed toward the Tower of Offerings at the center of the clearing.

*Maltak! Maltak! Maltak!*

Of course the Lady of Wild Things would make a dramatic entrance. She rode at the head of the column on a gleaming black horse, resplendent in a fur-lined gown of brushed white wool, a fur-trimmed vest of gold brocade, and a matching fur hat made from the pelt of a gray wolf. Yuli could feel her grandfather's disdain for pomp and ceremony rise up within her, along with a growing disquiet about the cheers she trailed in her wake. The citizens and refugees of Urghud had also mustered at the Grassmoot, and it was their cries that echoed in the crisp winter air.

*Maltak! Maltak! Maltak!*

Yuli and Auncle Mongke exchanged glances. The other heads of the Five Golden Families congregated beside the Drum of Sorrows beneath the Tower of Offerings looked nervously at one another, clearly taken aback by the wave of support for one of their own. The Lady of Wild Things took her place beside them, her long-lashed eyes lowered demurely as she settled in the line. She allowed the cheers to continue on for several moments, before raising a gloved hand to quiet her followers.

"Welcome, my friends," she said, her clear, sweet voice carrying on the wind. "I thank you all for coming."

At a nod of her head, a member of the Council of Shamans raised an enormous mallet and struck the Drum of Sorrows.

*Boom! Boom! Boom!*

The Grassmoot was about to begin.

What Yuli needed more than anything at the moment was a good nap. The late night she had spent waiting in the harbor for Zhara and Ami to arrive had taken its toll, and she struggled to keep the banner of the Gommun upright as the current supplicant droned on and on. She spied several of the children around her asleep in their parents' arms and wished she were a little girl again. As the First Daughter of the Gommun Kang, Yuli had little to do at the Grassmoot but sit on horseback and look impassive, which was easy enough. The problem was keeping her eyes from rolling toward the back of her head. She always had the best of intentions when it came to these sorts of gatherings—to pay attention, to invest herself in the troubles of those around her, to figure out how to solve their problems. Yuli knew these issues were important, but by the eternal blue skies, none of them were *interesting*.

Stifling another yawn, Yuli surreptitiously wiped at her watering eyes with the back of a mittened hand as the current supplicant at the Grassmoot wildly gesticulated with the drumstick in their hand. It was less a drumstick than a repurposed mace with a mallet tip fashioned from leather and fur, used to strike the enormous Drum of Sorrows situated at the base of the Tower of Offerings whenever someone had a grievance to air.

And there were a lot of people with grievances to air.

Harvest yields, wool yields, trade disputes, hunting ground borders and boundaries: these were all mundane matters to be heard and settled by the heads of the Five Golden Families. There was also the issue of how to handle the scores of refugees arriving by the day, fleeing rumors of abominations, the undead, and the Heralds of Glorious Justice. Although Yuli was not keen on civil war, she thought she might have welcomed a war council to break up the tedium.

"Certainly not," said the leader of the Nuwage Kang. "If we give over a portion of our hunting grounds to the Tzorig, then there won't be enough for anyone to survive the winter."

"Then the Nuwage have done a poor job preparing for hard times," said the Shulgin Kang. "And that is not anyone's fault but your own."

"Offer up your lands then, cousin," the Nuwage Kang returned.

"The nomadic clans in question border your lands, *cousin*," said the Shulgin Kang. "Not mine."

"Cousins, cousins," the Lady of Wild Things said soothingly, stroking a black stone amulet she wore at her throat. "Remember, we, the people of the north, are one. What belongs to one belongs to all."

There was a subconscious straightening of spines of everyone present at the sound of the Lady's voice. The Maltak leader had been called the Lady of Wild Things for as long as Yuli could remember, for it was said the beauty of her voice could charm even the most savage of beasts. Yuli had never found Kho's mother particularly charming, but she couldn't deny the effect the Lady had over a crowd.

Unbidden, Yuli's eyes slid to Kho standing among the Maltak faction with her kang's standard. The only thing Kho had inherited from her mother were her long, dark lashes. The Lady's daughter possessed none of her mother's charisma or ruthlessness; instead, Kho had always been gentle and unfailingly kind. As a child, Yuli thought Kho to be the sort of girl Uncle Bayar had always wanted her to be—humble, clever, with a sort of pleasing grace that had been utterly lacking in his niece. Where Yuli had been rough-and-tumble, Kho had been serene and composed. Where Yuli had been brash and bold, Kho had been sweet and elegant.

*A pair of mismatched fillies,* Obaji used to say. *But nevertheless of the same brood.*

Yuli's hand once again went to her bare wrist where a friendship bracelet used to be. But that had all been a lie. The young woman Kho had become had proven to be just as ruthless as her mother.

"Fine," the Nuwage Kang said grudgingly. "We acquiesce to the Grassmoot's decision."

The Lady of Wild Things looked down at the suppliant kneeling before the Five Golden Families, right fist pressed to their left shoulder. "Have we concluded matters to your satisfaction?"

The supplicant nodded. "Yes, Your Grace."

*Boom! Boom! Boom! Boom!*

A wild-eyed elder with raggedy gray hair and broken teeth grabbed the mace and struck the Drum of Sorrows with all their unexpected might. "A curse!" they cried. "A curse upon the land!"

The heads of the Five Golden Families shifted on their horses, taking in the suppliant's haggard appearance and foreign style of dress without any markers of family or clan.

"State your name and kang," Uncle Bayar said imperiously.

The elder scoffed. "I thought anyone living within

northern borders was permitted to speak at the Grassmoot."

Uncle Bayar's face soured. "Your name and kang," he repeated.

The supplicant looked to the Lady of Wild Things, then straightened their shoulders. "Liu Baichen," they called out. "And I have no kang."

A refugee, Yuli realized. One of the hundreds flooding the city.

The Maltak leader nodded her head graciously at the supplicant. "We welcome Liu Baichen to the Grassmoot," she said. "Speak, and we will listen."

"Listen? Ha." The elder brandished the mace menacingly at the heads of the Five Golden Families. "For months we refugees have been begging you to listen to us about the threats to the empire and the people, but all you lot do is sit around talking of petty matters!" They gesticulated wildly, nearly toppling over from the unwieldy weight of the mace. "Abominations! The undead! Magic has returned to the Morning Realms and every single one of you has turned a blind eye!"

Gasps rose from the gathered. Yuli's heart thundered in her ears.

"Rumors," said the Nuwage Kang uncertainly, glancing around to the others.

"From what I hear," said the Tzorig Kang, "stories of these monsters roaming the land originate from the south and west, where they are allowing magicians to live free." They waved their hand dismissively. "There are no magicians in the north. We need not worry."

"Are you so certain of that?" Liu Baichen's eyes glittered with the fervor of righteousness. "Only last week you let a magician slip through your grasp!"

A tense silence fell over the crowd, every eye drawn to Ogodei. To Yuli's surprise, he looked wan and withdrawn, as though he had been ill. There was none of his usual merriment or malice in his face; instead, his countenance was flat and serious. If it weren't for the wolf helm he wore, she might not have recognized him. "The Huntsmen shall find them," he said quietly. "Never you fear, ancient one."

"Nevertheless," the Tzorig Kang continued, looking unsettled, "it is the Heralds of Glorious Justice who pose the greater threat. Should they claim the imperial city and the Sunburst Throne, chaos will descend on the Morning Realms."

A murmuring susurrus of fear and doubt rose from the audience.

"And what have you been doing to protect us from such chaos?" the refugee demanded. "The Sunburst Throne lies empty, with no heir to take the Warlord's place!"

The murmurs grew louder, the mood turning.

"Who will step forward to guide the Morning Realms to order?" Liu Baichen shouted. "Who will lead us out of the darkness?"

"Maltak! Maltak!" someone yelled from the crowd.

At once the entire assembly broke into cries of support for their own kangs. *Maltak! Tzorig! Nuwage! Shulgin! Gommun!* A cacophony of argument and agreement. The clamor rose to a deafening pitch, and there was the ring of metal as the assembly drew blades.

"Peace! Peace!" the Lady of Wild Things called. Her sonorous voice never quite reached a shout, but the words rang out over the crowd like a bell. The audience quieted immediately, spellbound by her tone. "Friends," she continued, "Liu Baichen has the right of it. I will not deny that chaos threatens the Morning Realms, chaos and civil war. The Heralds harry our people, and magic—that ancient evil—has once again taken root." Her long-lashed gaze swept over the crowd. "But we have been balanced on the knife's edge for longer than many care to acknowledge."

The Nuwage Kang sat up in their saddle. "What do you mean?"

The Lady of Wild Things smiled sweetly. She was not an especially beautiful woman—her features were too long, too sharp, too lupine, and when she smiled, her face took on a terrifying aspect. "Under the watch of the Gommun Kang, the empire has declined, allowing abominations and the undead to roam the land."

"Watch your words, cousin," Uncle Bayar warned. His ordinarily placid bay mare tossed her head anxiously. "Without the Warlord, without the Just War, the Mugung Emperor would still be terrorizing the people of the Morning Realms."

The Lady gave a nod of acknowledgment. "The old bear was mighty in his prime," she said. "But you cannot deny that he started going soft in his twilight years. What of your nephew, Gommun Jochi? He who was exiled instead of executed?"

A sharp intake of breath from the crowd.

"Get my cousin's name out of your mouth," Yuli growled beneath her breath. Beside her, Auncle Mongke laid a restraining hand on her sleeve. "Sending a fourteen-year-old child to the Frozen Wastes with nothing but the clothes on his back was as good as a death sentence."

The words fell into the quiet with a thud, louder than she had intended. Another gasp of shock arose from the crowd, discomfited murmurs following in its wake.

The Lady of Wild Things turned to her, acknowledging Yuli's presence with a nod. "You hear the truth of it from the princess's own lips," the Lady said silkily. "The Gommun Kang are weak. They would protect their own instead of protecting the people of the empire." She stroked the edge of her black stone amulet with her gloved thumb. "A true leader would understand that order is greater than blood."

"What are you saying?" Uncle Bayar asked, his jaw tight.

The Lady of Wild Things lifted her long-lashed eyes to meet the Gommun leader's gaze. "I invoke the Law of Might," she said simply. "The moon has set on the time of the Gommun; now it is for the sun to rise on the time of the Maltak."

*Maltak! Maltak! Maltak!*

At the Lady of Wild Things' proclamation, the shouts of the Maltak Kang and the refugees rose to a deafening roar, drowning out the protests from the others gathered at the Grassmoot.

The Law of Might.

If Obaji had been alive, he might have laughed.

Yuli's grandfather had ever been aware of the Maltak's scheming and conniving, but had called them *soft* for their inability or unwillingness to openly challenge his rule. *A true northerner would take what was theirs by right,* he would say. He despised those who talked out of both sides of their mouth, and for all his blunt, uncomplicated ways, the Warlord was no fool.

The Lady of Wild Things was no fool either.

*Maltak! Maltak! Maltak!*

The other heads of the Five Golden Families stared at one another helplessly, none of them able to speak for the rising tide of approbation from the assembled. The Lady of Wild Things said nothing, merely smiled from atop her shining black horse. She had the power, for she was in control of the audience, and there was nothing any one of them could do about it.

The Grand Kang would have done something about it, Yuli thought. If Aunt Görte were here, she would have grabbed the mace and sounded the Drum of Sorrows for silence. The eldest child of the Gommun had been doughty in her prime, swiftly rising through the ranks of the Golden Horde to win the title of Grand Kang. As was tradition, she had challenged her father, the Warlord, in the Grand Game after his ascension to emperor, handily winning two of the three trials. Obaji had never been more proud of his firstborn. Of all the potential heirs to the Sunburst Throne, Gommun Görte had been considered the strongest candidate.

*Boom! Boom! Boom! Boom!*

The chanting died down as one of the members of the Council of Shamans held up the drumstick for silence. "Friends," they quavered, their voice weak and wavering, "the Law of Might has been invoked. The Lady Maltak declares herself for the Sunburst Throne. Do we have any challengers?"

Again the heads of the Five Golden Families exchanged glances. Yuli silently shouted at her uncle to say something, wishing she could speak with him mind-to-mind without betraying her magic. Of the Warlord's children, he had always been the least audacious, more bookish than brawny, retiring where he should be bold. He was easily cowed by powerful women, having been bullied by his older and younger sisters—and even his niece—his entire life.

The Lady of Wild Things cast her gaze over the crowd, then at each of the heads of the Five Golden Families, her eye lingering on the Nuwage Kang. The leader quailed and seemed to visibly diminish beneath the intensity of her stare.

"I support the Lady Maltak's bid for the Sunburst Throne," the Nuwage Kang said in a small voice. There were gasps from the sea of green.

She next fixed her gaze on the Tzorig Kang.

"I also support the Lady Maltak's bid for the Sunburst Throne," they said.

"I do not!" Uncle Bayar burst out. "The Lady Maltak has no right!"

The Lady of Wild Things tilted her head. "I welcome any challenge to my invocation," she said calmly. "Do you offer me one, cousin?"

He hesitated. Yuli wanted to scream with frustration, to drop the standard of the Gommun Kang and rip the necklace of bear claws off her uncle's neck. *Weak*, the Warlord had always called him.

"The Gommun have kept the empire safe these past twenty years," Uncle Bayar said uncertainly. "And the Gommun will continue to keep the empire safe for the next twenty thousand."

*Gommun! Gommun! Gommun!*

Yuli and her kang raised their voices in approval, but compared to the roars of support for the Lady of Wild Things, they sounded small and pathetic.

"How?" Liu Baichen retorted. "Twenty years after the Just War, magic still threatens the Morning Realms. Under the Gommun's watch, the Heralds of Glorious Justice have flourished and we stand poised for another civil war! What did the Warlord do but place a bandage over a still-bleeding wound?"

"And what does the Lady Maltak intend to do instead?" Uncle Bayar returned. He faced the Lady of Wild Things, chin lifted. "What can you do for the empire that the Gommun did not?"

She inclined her head. "The matter of magic is not an evil that, once defeated, vanishes forever. Your father was proof that unless the problem is destroyed at the root, it will find a way to flourish. No, my friends," she said, her sweet voice keeping the crowd spellbound, "the way to keep us safe is not through force. It is not by cutting the heads of weeds as they grow, but by pulling them out and planting our own seeds instead." The Lady of Wild Things fiddled with her amulet, then looked over at Kho holding the standard of the Maltak Kang and Ogodei standing beside her. "We raise our children with our values so that they grow strong and not weak, united instead of fractured. The Warlord, for all his indomitable will, was an indulgent patriarch. He allowed the other provinces of the Morning Realms to retain their customs, their culture, their ways. They grew up independent, unruly, defiant." She slid a glance toward Yuli. "No, the way forward is to sow our seeds throughout the empire, so that we may cultivate the garden of the future."

The Lady of Wild Things had a way with words that was both captivating and confusing. Yuli struggled against the dulcet tones of her voice, trying to parse out the substance of her words. She could see the enraptured faces of those gathered at the Grassmoot hanging on the Lady's every word, lulled by *how* she was speaking instead of *what* she was saying.

"Speak plain," Uncle Bayar demanded. "The fancy ways of speech you learned abroad mean nothing here."

The Lady smiled. "If the empire is to grow strong, then we must raise the people as our own. Imagine that instead of provinces, we have kangs. Imagine the Maltak, the Nuwage, the Tzorig, the Shulgin, and, yes, the Gommun as heads not just of the Five Golden Families, but of the Middle Kingdom, the southern cities, the Azure Isles, the outermost west, *and* the north?"

Cheers erupted from the crowd once more. *Maltak! Maltak! Maltak!*

"Can it be done?" Uncle Bayar shouted over the noise. "How do you intend to follow through on your promise?"

But his protests were drowned out by the tide of enthusiasm from the assembly. Yuli had never heard such a roar of support, not even at the summer and winter games. She could feel the rumbles of agitation in her chest, the thunder of voices, the thumping of fists, the stamping of feet, a tumult of thousands upon thousands. A chill ran down her spine at the sight of so many mustered and ready to fight. The implications were terrifying. Not just civil war, but total war.

*Boom! Boom! Boom! Boom!* The head shaman furiously struck the Drum of Sorrows for silence. "The Lady Maltak has spoken!" they called. "The Law of Might invoked. What say the Maltak Kang?"

*Maltak! Maltak! Maltak!*

"What say the Nuwage Kang?"

*Maltak! Maltak! Maltak!*

"The Tzorig?" More cheers. "The Shulgin?" Even more cries. "The Gommun?"

To Yuli's surprise, there were a number of ragged voices raised for the Lady of Wild Things even among her own kang, although the relative quiet of their cheers was deafening.

"You forget someone, wise one," Uncle Bayar said to the head shaman. "The Golden Horde."

Silence fell over the proceedings. The Lady Maltak might have the support of the people, but the Golden Horde was the sword arm of the north, and they were honor-bound to follow the Grand Kang. And the Grand Kang was still a Gommun, still the Warlord's daughter.

The Lady of Wild Things looked around the clearing

beneath the Tower of Offerings. "I do not see the Grand Kang here."

Murmurs bubbled through the audience. Yuli shifted uneasily on her feet. She felt strange and unsettled, her spirit quivering and vibrating within her. She tightened her grip on the pole flying the Gommun standard as though she could keep a firm grasp on her ki, to prevent herself from untethering and dissolving.

"The Grand Kang is ill," Uncle Bayar said, stiffening.

The Lady of Wild Things acknowledged the statement with a nod. "I offer my prayers for a swift recovery."

More murmurs of appreciation at her graciousness and generosity. Yuli felt the icy hand of despair wrap its fingers about her neck. A seasoned competitor, she could sense when defeat was nigh. Without the use of force, the Maltak had asserted their dominance at the Grassmoot, and she could do nothing but marvel at the Lady's game.

"The Grand Kang will never ride for you," Uncle Bayar spat out. "And without the Golden Horde, you have no army to march to the imperial city."

"Then perhaps it is time for a new Grand Kang!" Ogodei called. The Huntsmen thumped their fists to their chest in agreement. "Gommun Görte is weak. She rots away in her bed while the Horde grows more sluggish and lazy by the day." He gestured to the flag beside the empty space reserved for the Grand Kang. "A true warrior would be here, in sickness or in health!"

"Maltak Ogodei," the head shaman said to the wolf-helmed warrior. "Are you calling for the Grand Game to be held?"

The words *Grand Game* rang throughout the clearing, echoed by myriad astonished voices. Numbness swept through Yuli, and she forced herself to remain present, remain focused. She felt heavy, leaden, trapped, caged within the prison of her flesh when she yearned to dissipate, find Temur, and look away from what was happening. This was not happening. It could not be happening.

"I do," Ogodei replied. "I call for the Grand Game to be held!"

Excited chatters burst from the crowd.

*Boom! Boom! Boom! Boom!* The head shaman sounded the drum again. "Is the Grassmoot in accord?" they asked.

*Maltak! Maltak! Maltak!* came the answer.

Uncle Bayar went pale.

The head shaman looked to the others in the Council, who each nodded in turn.

"Who will challenge the Grand Kang for the title?" they asked, turning to the assembly. They looked to Ogodei, but Maltak Huntsman was silent. Heads swiveled back and forth as people waited for someone to step forward, to rise to the call.

"I will." The standard of the yellow wolf wavered as Kho stepped forward. Her voice was small but clear. "I will stand for the Maltak."

There was a hum of surprise as those surrounding Kho cleared space around her, directing all eyes toward the plump, long-lashed girl in the center.

"You?" Yuli burst out. She couldn't believe it. Quiet, clever, bookish Kho who had never won a single archery or racing competition in her life? Kho, the university student? Kho, who wasn't even part of the Golden Horde? "By the Great Bear, you can't be serious!"

Silence reigned as she started laughing, but she couldn't help it. It was all too ridiculous, it couldn't be real.

Kho lifted her chin. "Do you have something to say, Gommun Yulana?"

Yuli scoffed. "If you are the best the Maltak have to offer, then I fear for the future of the Golden Horde. I know how many times you've lifted a sword or a bow in your entire life." She shook her head. "You? A warrior?"

Kho's eyes flashed. "I have every right to challenge the Grand Kang."

Yuli rolled her eyes. "You have the right," she agreed. "But do you have the skill?" She turned to the others, seeking out those she knew rode with the Golden Horde. "Will none of you gainsay this folly?"

There was no response. The Grand Game was no lark. The first two trials—the Trial of Strength and the Trial of Wits—were easy enough, but the Trial of the Soul was a grueling race to the Frozen Wastes to retrieve an egg from the rookery of the golden rocs that lived just south of the tundra. This close to winter, it would be brutal.

"No one?" Yuli asked in amazement. "Not a single one of you? You would trust an untried warrior with the leadership of the Horde?"

She had not known how far the Lady of Wild Things' influence could reach.

"*A great general leads not with his sword, but with his mind,*" Kho quoted. "I know how to shoot a bow, Gommun Yulana, but more than that, I know where to aim."

Yuli could not deny that. Kho would have studied the tactics of the greats at university, and the Trial of Wits would test the cleverness of the competitors. Aunt Görte had lost the second trial to the Warlord all those years ago.

"I had thought better of you," Yuli said with disgust. "Of all of you."

More silence.

"Then it is settled," the head shaman said. "The Grand Game will commence on the new moon." They struck the drum again. "Maltak Kho will challenge Gommun Görte for the title."

"Hold a moment," Yuli interrupted. "What if my aunt is still sick?"

The head shaman gave her a hard look. "Then the Game is forfeit and the Horde belongs to Maltak Kho."

Dread spread through Yuli's limbs at this pronouncement. Once more, she had underestimated the Lady of Wild Things' canniness. She thought of her aunt, empty-eyed and listless back at Gommun Manor. Even if she were to recover some measure of her old self by the new moon, she was in no condition to compete. They would either have to forfeit or lose. They were lost either way.

Unless there was another challenger.

Yuli went still. Her spine tingled as though she stood on the edge of a great precipice. She had always been reckless, leaping before she looked, and she felt that same inexorable call toward the great unknown now. She felt disconnected from the moment, almost as though she stood outside herself in spirit form, watching as she handed Auncle Mongke the Gommun standard and walked forward to grab the mace from the head shaman.

*Boom! Boom! Boom! Boom!*

"I challenge Maltak Kho to the Grand Game for the honor of my kang."

Her words drummed the air, and she could see them ripple through the crowd, an ever-expanding circle of shock. But Yuli's gaze never left Kho's as she spoke. For the first time in two years, she allowed herself to study her former friend's face, to take in the changes time had wrought, to compare the softness of her cheeks to the angles of her jaw. There was little of the knobby-kneed girl Yuli had known standing before her—only Kho's eyes, as dark and long-lashed as ever. Kho returned her stare, and for a moment, Yuli felt as she had when they were children, standing in solidarity before their tutor in the classroom, singled out and set apart. The ghost of something like camaraderie fluttered about her heart.

Then Kho closed her eyes and thumped her fist to her shoulder in acknowledgment. Yuli caught a flash of blue on her wrist. A bracelet of turquoise beads. Something like pain twisted her heart and she almost wanted to shout, *I take it back! I take it back!* Once they had stood together on the same side. Now it seemed as though they would be divided forever.

The head shaman took the drumstick back from Yuli. "Any other challengers?" they asked.

There was no response but the sighing of the wind.

"Then I declare the Grand Game open." The head shaman swung the mace against the Drum of Sorrows. "Do you, Gommun Yulana, declare yourself the rightful Grand Kang?"

Yuli stared at Kho. "I do."

"Do you, Maltak Kho, declare yourself the rightful Grand Kang?"

Kho lifted her gaze, and it was as though she were a complete stranger.

"I do."

# 13

Stealing *Songs of Order and Chaos* from Ogodei's quarters had been more difficult than Kho expected.

After the Grassmoot, the majority of the Maltak and the Huntsmen had gone out into the lower city's taverns to celebrate. Tuyaa had tried to convince Kho to join them, but to no avail.

"I'm tired," she demurred. "It has been a long day."

And it had been a long day. Kho wanted nothing more than to go down to the kitchens to make herself a nice filling bowl of stir-fry before climbing up to her bedroom to sleep. The events of the Grassmoot still did not feel quite real, as though they had happened to someone else instead of her. The world was forever changed now with her mother invoking the Law of Might, the balance of power between the Five Golden Families shifted in ways she could not yet begin to comprehend. The time had come for the sun to rise on the time of the Maltak, but Kho wasn't sure she was ready to greet the dawn.

Especially now that she was to compete against Yuli in the Grand Game.

Her mother had not expected anyone to challenge them, a rare miscalculation by the Lady of Wild Things, but to be fair, the First Daughter of the Gommun Kang had never been known to meet anyone's expectations. As a girl, Yuli had been considered flighty, frequently abandoning all duties and responsibilities to do what she pleased. If there was one thing about her former friend Kho knew intimately, it was Yuli's inability to withstand discomfort, to struggle or bear the hard things. If things did not come easy to the princess, then the princess avoided them at all costs, preferring to go riding on the steppes or spend time in pleasurable pursuits.

And the Grand Game was nothing if not hard.

Kho had always envied Yuli her freedom. As the favored grandchild of the Warlord, the princess was constantly being indulged or forgiven her whims. As the First Daughter of the Maltak Kang, Kho was expected to be obedient and loyal and to think of the greater good of her family and bloodline. It felt as though Kho was always having to do the hard thing, the right thing, while Yuli got to do whatever she pleased. She supposed that was why she had cherished every moment spent with the redhead; they had been the only moments she felt like a *girl* and not her mother's heir. The moments they had spent chasing each other through the grass, braiding each other's hair, exchanging tokens of friendship. Kho toyed with the turquoise bracelet about her wrist. Yuli had been Kho's only indulgence, the one decadent thing that was hers and hers alone that no one could take away.

Until Jochi.

Kho wrenched herself out of her bed. The manor was empty and now was the perfect time to sneak up to Ogodei's rooms to retrieve the folio with the *taikhut*.

She had no way to be sure if the bookseller had gotten the message she sent, but she didn't want to fall through on her promise. Besides, she was eager to look through her brother's papers, to see if she could make sense of what he had been studying and why. Tiptoeing upstairs, she reached the third-floor landing and slowly, carefully opened the trapdoor and pulled down the ladder.

His quarters were spotless, every trace of the ink-and-paper-strewn mess she had stumbled upon that morning gone.

Startled, Kho began rummaging through her brother's things—opening desk drawers, cupboards, clothing chests. Had she imagined it? There was no evidence of the writing she had previously discovered, no ink stains, no brushes, nothing. Moreover, the folio with the *taikhut* was also missing, as though it had never existed in the first place. But the image of the symbol of the bisected circle was burned into her mind, as well as the bone-deep certainty that *Songs of Order and Chaos* had been in her brother's possession. Had Ogodei taken his things with him to go celebrate in the streets of Urghud? The idea was absurd, not to mention dangerous, for if the Huntsmen discovered the forbidden writing on his person, they certainly wouldn't hesitate to set him aflame with it, despite their professed love and loyalty for him. Yet Kho could think of no other explanation for the disappearance of the papers.

Of course, there were other hiding places in the manor. As a child, whenever Ogodei wanted to skip out on his lessons, he would frequently hide in the lofts above the stables, where there were a dozen small nooks and crannies a boy of ten could crawl into and disappear. Kho sighed. It seemed as though she would always be chasing after her brother for some reason or another—either to drag him back to his studies or to drag him home after a raucous night out.

Downstairs, the house was dark, the retainers excused from their duties by the Lady of Wild Things to spread Maltak cheer throughout the taverns of Urghud. It had been a long while since Kho had the manor to herself, and for the first time in ages, she felt pressure ease from her shoulders. Without the rest of the kang around, she no longer had to be the First Daughter; she could simply be Kho. Kho, who was not always gracious and humble. Kho, who was not always perfect and poised. Kho, who was not always biddable and obedient. She retrieved her coat and a lantern from her rooms and made her way outside into the frigid air to search the stables.

She spied a flickering light above an empty stall.

"You're writing it all wrong," came an unfamiliar voice. The voice grated at Kho's ear, both high-pitched and low at once, containing two dissonant pitches that clashed and screeched like the scrape of a fingernail over slate. "The order of the strokes is just as important as the characters themselves."

"You do it then," a deeper voice grumbled. Ogodei. He had not gone with the Huntsmen after all.

Kho frowned, extinguishing her lantern and creeping slowly toward the stalls. She could see a pair of legs dangling from the rafters and a candle balanced precariously beside them.

"I would if I could," the voice replied.

There were two figures sitting on the rafters. She recognized her brother straightaway, his features illuminated by the candle beside him. He held a brush in his hand and something large in his lap, which Kho thought might be a saddle. She could not make out the face of the figure beside him, cloaked entirely by shadows.

"Curse this wretched body," the figure said. "There's no chaos in the blood to make use of."

"You're the one who took that ridiculous form," Ogodei said.

"Watch your mouth," they snapped. "I called you here, and I can send you back again."

Ogodei looked chastened as he returned to what he had been doing previously. Kho squinted. It looked as though he were painting something on the underside of the saddle. "I don't know why magicians bother with all this writing," he complained. "It would be so much simpler to manipulate the void directly."

"Spells have their place," the figure said. "It certainly makes it easier for magic to go unnoticed."

Spells? Kho thought of the pages upon pages of writing that had papered her brother's quarters and the open folio of *Songs of Order and Chaos* on his bed. Had he been practicing writing *spells*? But Ogodei merely had the affliction, not the ability to *do* magic. She felt the brush of something deeply, deeply wrong feather down her spine.

"I don't understand this need for subterfuge and secrecy," Ogodei groused. "We have power the humans can't even begin to comprehend."

"Sowing the seeds of chaos takes time," his companion said. "Besides, we don't want to draw the attention of the Guardians of Dawn. You know what happened to my brethren."

Kho straightened. There had been rumors that the Guardians of Dawn, elemental warriors who had fought the Mother of Ten Thousand Demons a millennia before, had been reborn. The refugees had brought with them tales of more than abominations and the undead; they had brought stories of a girl who could turn into flame and another who could command the earth to dance. Yuli's auncle Mongke told the best stories about the Guardians of Dawn, but Kho had always thought of them as just that: stories. She thought of all the horror novels she had read as a little girl—monsters and revenants, ghosts and ganshi—reveling in their thrills and chills. All stories had a kernel of truth buried within them, for in many of these tales the creatures had been defeated by magicians and heroes of legend with powers beyond mortal ken. But Kho had never thought of these stories as *real*, not the way histories were real. If the rumors of the Guardians of Dawn were true, then it would mean that demons were real.

"Weak," Ogodei muttered.

"I can't disagree," the figure said. "Not only weak, but stupid. We must be smarter than them, therefore we must necessarily be more subtle about our plans."

Plans for what? Kho crouched closer, pressing herself against the walls of the stable.

"What was that?"

Kho froze.

"What was what?" Ogodei asked.

"Did you hear something?"

A pause. Kho held her breath.

"Nothing," he said.

"I thought we were alone," the voice said.

"Everyone's gone," Ogodei said impatiently. "Except for the girl. She's asleep in her rooms."

"Are you certain of that?"

Another pause. "I suppose we could go check."

A rustle from above, and then a creak of the rafters as Ogodei shimmied down the posts. Kho carefully crawled back toward the manor, out of sight of the stables. Once inside, she slipped off her shoes and hurried up the stairs to her quarters on the second floor, throwing herself into bed. She could hear the thud of her brother's footsteps following close behind.

The door to her rooms slid open. Kho shut her eyes, trying her best to keep her breathing slow and even.

"See?" Ogodei said. "Asleep."

"Hmm," said his companion. "Perhaps it was nothing then."

"Let's go," her brother said. "We should finish up before the others return."

As they moved toward the door, Kho chanced opening her eyes to see who the figure beside Ogodei had been. They were tall and slim, dressed in flowing robes that obscured any other distinguishing feature about them. As though sensing her gaze, the figure paused at the threshold and half turned to look back at her.

Kho squeezed her eyes shut.

Moments passed, and she was terrified they could hear the thumping of her heart over the silence in the rest of the manor. But presently the door to her rooms slid shut, and she was alone. She could hear their footfalls retreat back down the stairs, back toward the courtyard and the stables, back to whatever illicit activity she had stumbled upon them doing.

Kho lay in bed. She was not going to be able to make the rendezvous at the Hills of the Dead. She told herself there would be other opportunities, and that it was best to go to sleep and try again another day.

But it was a long time before she fell asleep, haunted by the image of a black stone amulet about the figure's neck.

# 14

There were strange lights in the sky over the Hills of the Dead.

Sneaking out of Urghud after nightfall had been no easy feat. In many ways, Urghud was much like Zanhei —a sprawling city located on a harbor, surrounded by walls guarded by a city watch at all times. But Zhara was unfamiliar with its rhythms and rituals, unaware of its hidden corners and secret recesses, and worst of all, utterly at the mercy of the Huntsmen prowling the streets looking for trouble. As the nights grew longer and colder, hardly anyone set foot outside after dark, so their presence would certainly not go unnoticed.

After receiving the note from the Paper Wolf, she and Ami had agonized over how to get to the Hills of the Dead, an ancient necropolis a few hours' ride from Urghud's eastern gate. The Grassmoot had brought with it thousands from all over the steppes to the lands surrounding the northern capital, and the way was thick with people. Tarkhun had said that once they got through the gates no one would question them moving through the throng, as the nomads mostly minded their own business, but it was getting through the gates and back again that would be the greatest obstacle. The Guardians of Dawn's foothold in the north was much smaller than it had been in the south, and there was no one on the watch Tarkhun trusted enough to bribe. Hours and hours were spent trying to plan after the bookseller returned from the Grassmoot, but to no avail. Ami fretted about missing the appointment with the Paper Wolf; the symbol on the message indicated they had found the northern fragment of *Songs of Order and Chaos,* and she was desperate to get her hands on it.

It was Yuli who had given them the solution.

"If you can't go through, then why not over?" She had grinned.

"What does that mean?" Ami had asked.

Yuli had laughed. "You'll fly there on Temur, of course."

The princess had arrived shortly before midnight in spirit form, having been unable to leave Gommun Manor in the wake of the furor caused by the Grassmoot. All the heads of the Five Golden Families had gathered to shout, argue, and negotiate over the day's proceedings, which Zhara gathered were quite significant, although she was ignorant of the political ramifications of it all. The Eagle of the North herself arrived shortly thereafter, landing awkwardly in the yard adjacent to Tarkhun's bookshop.

Although she had interacted with Temur several times before, the magnificence of the enormous bird never failed to take Zhara's breath away. The Eagle was covered with ivory feathers speckled with bronze, silver, and gold that shimmered beneath the starlight, and her two sets of falcon's wings practically glowed with brilliance. The tips of the crest on her head glittered like gems, and her sky-blue eyes were crowned by long pure-white lashes that gave her a demure look.

"It feels almost rude to be riding such a glorious creature," Zhara murmured, stroking Temur's beak. Her white lashes fluttered half-shut in pleasure.

"She's used to it," Yuli said affectionately.

"Sajah barely deigns to offer his back to anyone," Zhara remarked as Temur bent her legs and head to allow the girls to clamber on. From his perch in the loft, the orange cat scowled.

"What do I hold on to?" Ami asked, looking around apprehensively. She sat behind Zhara, an awkward fit, even though Yuli had claimed Temur could easily carry six people.

"You can hold on to Zhara," Yuli advised. "Zhara, just grab a handful of Temur's feathers. I promise it won't hurt her."

Gingerly, Zhara sank her mittens into the plush down of the Eagle's back. Temur was warm and soft, like the most comfortable bed at the end of a long day, and Zhara resisted the urge to press her face into the Eagle's feathers. Without warning, Temur leaped into the air, four wings pumping as the city fell away from them at an alarming rate. Ami yelped and squeezed Zhara's ribs so hard she feared they might break.

*Just like riding a horse!* She could hear Yuli's voice in her head as they soared into the skies.

Too bad the princess couldn't hear her in return, because Zhara would have had some choice words to share.

Mercifully, the flight itself was short, and before long, Zhara and Ami found themselves on solid ground again, although the descent might have been worse than the ascent. Han had once told her he was afraid of heights, and Zhara thought she understood better now why.

"Took you long enough." Yuli's spirit smirked as they landed.

"That took entirely too long," Zhara agreed as she slid bonelessly off Temur's back. She was not looking forward to the journey back.

"That was nothing like riding a horse," Ami groused. Her glasses sat askew on her face, her short, shorn hair a mess from the wind. Temur ruffled her feathers in a huff before taking off for the skies once more.

"No, it's not," Yuli said cheerfully. "I just thought it would make you feel better."

Zhara gazed at the freestanding stone gate that marked the entrance to the Hills of the Dead. It reminded her a bit of the gates surrounding the Temple of the Immortals back in the religious quarter of Zanhei, which marked the transition from the mundane to the sacred. There were no words chiseled into posts or lintels, but the stones had been carved with beautiful reliefs of bears, wolves, eagles, and other animals. Strings of prayer flags were draped across the top, the red, yellow, green, blue, and white fabric flapping in the wind.

"Welcome," Yuli said quietly, "to the Hills of the Dead."

Through the gate, there were mounds upon mounds upon mounds, each the height of a full-grown adult, spread out over the land as far as the eye could see, the tops dusted with a light frost. Set into the earth before each mound was a stone pillar engraved with the names of the dead, painted red, yellow, green, blue, and white for each of the five major kangs of the steppes. There was a faint mist that wreathed everything in gentle haze, and Zhara thought of the spirits of the living lingering down by the harbor.

"Are we alone?" she asked.

"Just us and the dead and their ghosts," Yuli said. "Come, we'll wait for the Paper Wolf with my mother."

She led them down the center path to a modest mound marked GOMMUN TATYA. To Zhara's shock, the princess clambered atop the mound as though climbing a hill looking for a place to picnic before settling her spirit on the frozen grass.

"Yuli," Ami said reproachfully, "show some respect."

The redhead laughed. "You southerners are so serious," she said. "Here in the north, we make cozy with our dead." She patted the ground. "Don't we, Mama?"

Zhara turned around, half expecting to see the ghost of Yuli's mother standing behind them.

Yuli laughed again. "She's not here," she said. "Her soul has been sung to the eternal blue skies."

Ami sat down beside Yuli's spirit atop Gommun Tatya's tomb. "Are ghosts what remain if the souls of the dead aren't sung to the eternal blue skies?"

The redhead nodded. "It's tragic, isn't it?" She gestured to the mist around them. "Those who are lost, those who die alone, those who are without loved ones to give their remains a proper sky burial linger on."

"You can see the ghosts of the dead?" Ami asked in surprise.

"Can't we all?" Yuli gazed into the distance. "There have been ghost stories since time immemorial."

"Oh." Ami sounded disappointed. "I thought it was a special Guardian power."

"To see them as they once were, maybe," Yuli said. "I think most other people experience a feeling, or an emotion, or just the sense that they are not alone."

"You sound as though you are very familiar with ghosts," Zhara said quietly. She sat down on the hillock beside the others, cuddling up to Ami for warmth. She supposed she could have started a fire, but somehow that seemed even more disrespectful than lounging atop someone's grave.

Yuli shrugged. "Life on the steppes can be very harsh," she said. "And death is as much a part of our existence as anything else." She tilted her head back. "See," she said, pointing north. "Those are the souls traveling on to the eternal blue skies."

It was a long while before Zhara could make out faint ribbons of multicolored light streaking across the stars. She gasped. "What is that?"

"The Shimmer," Yuli said.

"The Shimmer?" Ami asked. She peered over the tops of her spectacles. "I don't think I've ever read about that in *Songs of Order and Chaos*."

"Probably because it has nothing to do with demons," Yuli said. "The Shimmer has been a part of our culture forever." She lay down on her back, watching the curtains of color tremble and dance. "The lights are stronger farther north, closer to the Frozen Wastes. When I was little, my mother used to tell me stories of how the Sleepers journeyed to the edge of the world, searching for where the earth met sky."

Ami started. "Beware the Sleepers," she murmured, "for they wake."

Yuli sat up.

"The Sleepers," Zhara said with a frown. "Your cousin mentioned something about them, didn't he?"

"Yes," the redhead said slowly. "He did." She looked from the mist to the Shimmer and back again. "I suppose I didn't make the connection to the legend of the Sleepers. I thought he was talking about the waking dreamers."

So had Zhara. "What is the legend of the Sleepers?"

Yuli bit her lip. "I don't remember much," she admitted. "But for as long as I can recall, we've had this myth about the Sleepers, a group of thirteen shamans who went in search of the source of the Shimmer. Auncle Mongke says they were more likely magicians and not shamans, but back then, they were one and the same. They wanted to find some way to pass through the world of the living into the world of the dead, although I can't remember the reason why. The Shimmer is a bridge of souls, you see, so they thought that if they could follow it all the way to where it originated, they would—I don't know—gain the power of immortality or something. I think it was immortality."

"Hmm," Ami said dubiously. "That sounds very much like how magicians used to summon demons from another realm in order to gain powers."

Yuli looked disturbed. "They wouldn't have," she protested weakly.

"How do you know?" Ami asked. "So much of the history of the magic of your people has been destroyed."

"It's a fairy tale, not history," Yuli said irritably.

"All fairy tales have a kernel of truth," the scrivener replied.

Yuli made a face. "Well, if the Sleepers went in search of immortality or whatever, then they failed. They never returned."

"What happened to them?" Zhara asked. "Why are they called the Sleepers?"

Yuli went silent. "Because," she said after a moment, "legend says that they untethered their souls from their bodies, leaving them lying forever in a state of perpetual sleep."

Zhara went still.

"And what happens when the Sleepers awaken?" Ami asked in a low voice.

Yuli shifted. "I don't remember," she said faintly, her brows knitting together. "I never really paid attention, I guess."

"They were the first waking dreamers," Zhara breathed.

"And we know what happens to waking dreamers when they wake," Ami said grimly.

Zhara closed her eyes. Nurden. The memory of the night they were attacked returned to her with vivid force. The visceral horror of his wrongness assaulting her senses. The darkness of the anti-ki—the demon—within him burning her Guardian vision. The uncanny magic he could summon, magic that seemed to counteract her own Guardian abilities.

"Demons walking around in human bodies." Yuli shuddered. "And there are so many afflicted with the waking dreamer sickness among the refugees."

The enormity of it all pressed on Zhara's lungs, making it difficult to breathe. "All those empty vessels," she whispered. "Just . . . lying there. For what purpose?"

"An army," Ami said quietly.

Zhara's hands went to her mouth in horror.

"A demon army." Yuli sucked in a sharp breath. She looked ill. "What do we do?"

The girls looked at one another, and once again, Zhara felt the overwhelming burden of being a Guardian of Dawn. She, Ami, and Yuli were elemental warriors reborn as ordinary girls to fight the forces of chaos, and there was no one else to whom they could turn. The threat of Tiyok, the Mother of Ten Thousand Demons, was theirs to handle, and theirs alone.

"We continue as planned," she said at last. "We find the northern portal and seal it."

Yuli squirmed. "Yeah . . . about that. I might, uh, have some other obligations to fulfill before we get to sealing the portal."

Zhara raised her brows. "What obligations?"

The redhead sighed. "The Grand Game."

"What's the Grand Game?" Ami asked.

"A competition for the title of the leader of the Golden Horde," Yuli said sheepishly.

"You decided to get into a competition *now*?" Zhara

demanded. "With the threat of the Mother of Ten Thousand Demons looming over heads, is this the best time?"

"Yah," Yuli protested. "I'm not just a Guardian of Dawn, I'm also a princess, you know. I can't just disappear to do whatever I like *all* the time."

Zhara closed her eyes. "Well, what are Ami and I going to do while you go off to do princess duties, or whatever?"

"Well, figuring out *where* the northern portal is might be a start," Yuli said. "Once we get our hands on the next piece of *Songs of Order and Chaos*, I'm sure you'll have plenty to do while I win the Grand Game."

Ami watched the delicate play of light dance across the sky. "Do you think," she said quietly, "that the source of the Shimmer is the location of the northern portal? The Singing Skies?"

The girls held their breath. Far above, they could hear a faint whispering, as though the ghosts traveling along the Shimmer to the eternal blue skies were speaking to one another. The whispers were nearly melodic, rising and falling in pitch, almost like a song.

"The place where the earth meets the sky," Yuli said wonderingly. "The Sleepers believed it was a portal to another realm. Who's to say they were wrong?"

Zhara studied the mist lingering over the other mounds. Ghosts, Yuli and Ami had said, but she was no longer afraid of them. Instead, all she felt was sadness. To be cut off from the cycle of death and rebirth, to continue existing long after all those you had known and loved were gone, seemed like torture of the highest degree. The thought of immortality seemed more like a burden than a gift, and she wondered why so many heroes of myth and legend had gone in search of it. "Is there no way to send these ghosts on to the eternal blue skies now?" she asked. "Can a shaman give them their rites?"

Yuli shook her head. "We would need to know their names," she said. "And those are lost to time and memory."

"What of your cousin?" Ami said gently. "You know his name. The shamans could send him on, couldn't they?"

Yuli stiffened. "We don't know he's dead," she said defensively. "He was exiled, not executed. Jochi could be a disembodied ki, like those of the waking dreamers we saw down by the docks."

Zhara's heart twinged with pity, for Yuli and for the ghosts of the dead as well as the living. "I wish we could save them," she said softly. "There was nothing Ami nor I could do for Nurden's spirit."

Yuli's eyes widened. *"The Guardian of Wind can tether and untether souls from their vessels,"* she murmured.

Zhara gave her a sharp look. "What was that?"

"That's what Jochi told me," Yuli said excitedly. "I can obviously untether my spirit from my own body"—she gestured toward herself, her form slightly blurred around the edges—"but I've never considered whether or not I can do that for others."

Ami sat up straight. "The Guardians of Dawn have power over ki," she marveled. "Of course."

"Do you think you can do it?" Zhara asked the princess. "Send these ghosts on?"

"There are no bodies to return them to," Yuli said. "But I can try."

She rose to her feet and reached a hand out to the mist. Zhara could have sworn the mist formed fingers to reach back. At their touch, a bright white-gold glow formed, illuminating the haze around them. Zhara watched as light spread throughout the Hills of the Dead, as faces formed out of the fog, each bearing a look of relief.

Then their features blurred and dissolved, and Zhara grabbed Ami's hand, watching as the souls dissipated, streaks of multicolored light streaming up to the heavens to join the Shimmer.

"Oh, Yuli," Zhara breathed, tears in her eyes. "It's so beautiful."

The girls watched in awe as one by one, the ghosts of the long-forgotten dead were released. It was as though they were in the middle of the Shimmer itself, surrounded by luminescence. Yuli had called ghosts a feeling or an emotion, and Zhara's sadness transformed into joy as a bridge of light formed to touch the sky.

Before long, the ghosts were gone, and the girls were alone.

"Farewell," Yuli said softly. "Be at peace."

The girls sat in silence for a while, soaking in the emptiness of the Hills of the Dead.

"It feels . . . lonely somehow," Zhara said with some surprise. "But not in a bad way."

Yuli looked down at her still-glowing hands. "I always thought my powers were pretty useless," she admitted. "But now . . . now I know that's not true."

Zhara smiled and wrapped her arms around the redhead's ghost in a hug. Now that she had actually hugged the physical Yuli, she could feel the difference, but she could have sworn she felt the princess's spirit hug back.

Ami glanced around at the deserted mounds. "The Paper Wolf is late," she said worriedly.

Zhara thought of the city watch and the vast throngs of people standing between them and Urghud. "I hope nothing happened to them," she fretted. "If it hadn't been for Temur, we wouldn't have made it to the Hills of the Dead."

Yuli bit her lip. "Let's give them some more time."

"Easy for you to say," Zhara muttered. "You can't feel the cold."

"You can turn yourself into living flame," Yuli said. "You shouldn't be able to feel the cold either."

Zhara made a face, but removed her mittens, allowing a lotus blossom of fire to bloom in her hands. She and Ami huddled around it as they settled down to wait, watching as the lights of the Shimmer faded with the rosy glow of dawn.

But the Paper Wolf never came.

# 15

Although Yuli would never admit it, she was excited for the Grand Game.

She had always loved competing in the youth games every summer and winter, pitting her skills against others her age and showing off her talents at archery and fencing. Of course, it didn't hurt that she usually won these challenges, but more than that, it was the air of drama surrounding the events that fueled her passion. She felt a familiar frisson of anticipation race up her spine, the same tingling sensation that accompanied each festival.

After all, what was the Grand Game but a giant festival?

It was easier to think of the upcoming competition in this manner than what it truly was, which was a game with the highest stakes for which Yuli had ever played. Nothing less than the fate of the entire Golden Horde was in her hands, and with it, the potential outcome of the civil war on all of the Morning Realms. If Yuli thought too much about what she had gotten herself into, she would become paralyzed by doubt, and she was nothing if not well-versed in fleeing from uncomfortable feelings. And it was easier to think of the Grand Game than it was to think of the scourge of waking dreamers and the potential army to be raised by the Moth Demon. As the Guardian of Wind, she had a responsibility to bring balance to the world, but the thought of that was an even greater discomfort than the stakes of the empire, so Yuli did what she did best in times like these: exercise.

Just outside the eastern gates of Urghud was a vast plain on which a temporary arena was set up as a practice ring. Flat, featureless, and full of shrubby grass that was readily cleared, it was maintained throughout the year for anyone's use. The Grand Game itself would take place at the Tower of Offerings, and laborers and volunteers were preparing the grounds—leveling the field and hauling in cartloads of sand brought in from the shores off the Bay of Dragons to the southeast—but there were already crowds gathered around the practice ring, placing wagers on the substance and outcome of the three trials. The only trial of which anyone could be certain was the Trial of the Soul, the final contest, which was a race to recover a golden roq egg from the rookery near the southern edge of the Frozen Wastes. Historically, both the Trial of Strength and the Trial of Wits were not determined until shortly before the day of the event itself, and could include anything from archery to sword-lance, a history exam to a recitation of poetry.

She hoped the Trial of Strength would be archery.

Yuli strode out onto the practice field where the targets had been set up, past the crowd of onlookers who studied her with great interest. She couldn't resist the urge to strut and preen a little, especially before a gaggle of girls she recognized from her school days. She gave them a wave and a wink, and a few of them tittered in response. Kho had always hated it when she flirted with other girls, and Yuli used to tease her about it, asking if she was jealous. Kho had never given her a straight answer, and Yuli never pressed her on it, mostly because such questions were dangerous. There was friendship, and there was something more, and Yuli had been too afraid of losing friendship to ask for more.

Not that it mattered now.

Yuli walked up to the line of chalk that marked the distance from the targets, then unslung her short recurve bow from her shoulder. If archery was chosen for the Trial of Strength, the competition would comprise three different challenges: one stationary, one from a moving horse, and a free chase on horseback through the steppes, where a moving target would toss several thatched balls into the air with circles drawn in various colors to indicate the number of points scored when the arrow hit. Removing the arrow string from the pouch about her waist, Yuli efficiently strung her bow, then drew back, testing the tension. Satisfied, she removed an arrow from the quiver at her hip, took aim, and loosed.

*Thwack!*

A bit high.

Adjusting her aim, she loosed a second arrow. Then a third. And a fourth.

*Thwack! Thwack! Thwack!*

Squinting, Yuli lowered her bow and checked her target. All four arrows were clustered neatly in the center ring. She smiled to herself. Not bad for a warm-up.

Presently, she noticed that her crowd of admirers had grown. The giggling girls were now joined by a large group of children. The people of the steppes began learning martial arts at a young age, so she was unsurprised to find herself surrounded by younger generations whispering and making sounds of appreciation every time she confidently struck her target.

But what she hadn't expected was someone else her age standing among them, watching her every move like a hawk.

Kho.

Feeling curiously naked, Yuli walked down the field to retrieve her arrows. She should have expected her competition to show up to the practice field but had forgotten—or perhaps chosen to forget—who that competition would be. Out of the corner of her eye, she watched as Kho walked up to the chalk line, fitting an arrow to her own bow.

*Zzzzt!*

The arrow went wide and short. Kho fitted another arrow to her string and tried again.

*Zzzzt!*

Again, the arrow fell short. Yuli could see the girl's stance was all wrong: her feet too close together, her elbow too low, her release not timed with her breath. She also thought the bow might be too small for her, as though the last time Kho had even touched one was when she was a child and she had not accounted for the change in draw strength that might be necessary with a change in height and weight. Kho grunted in frustration and adjusted her stance, this time pointing higher and loosing faster, without taking the time to properly aim.

*Zzzz-thump!* It was the flat of the arrow that struck the top edge of the target and bounced off.

Yuli couldn't take it any longer. Incompetence was one thing, but unsafe form was another. "Hoi!" she called. "Do you even know how to use that thing?"

Kho shot her a glare as she drew close, her entire body turning with the arrow still nocked on the string.

"Yah!" Yuli shouted, gesturing frantically for her to lower her bow. "Watch it! What if you accidentally shoot someone?"

Fury boiled up within Yuli at the prospect. There were

children around, and the last thing any of them needed was for anyone to get hurt. Or get the wrong ideas about the correct way to do archery. She marched over to Kho and took the bow from her hands.

"What are you doing?" Kho demanded.

"Firstly," Yuli said, "you're not getting the range you want because this bow is made for a child." She handed Kho her own bow. "Secondly, you're standing all wrong."

Kho lifted a brow, but accepted the weapon nonetheless. "Oh?"

"You need the proper stance before you do anything," Yuli said. "Don't you remember what Mistress Khing used to say?"

"Don't remind me," Kho muttered. "*A solid foundation is what empires are built on,*" she said in a cracked voice, imitating their old archery teacher perfectly.

Yuli gave her a half smile. Kho had always had the gift of mimicry. Her impression of the Warlord had been downright uncanny; she had even managed to get his throat-clearing harrumphs down. Then she remembered herself. "Stand slightly wider than hip width apart, knees loose, slightly more balanced on your toes," she ordered.

"Say please."

Yuli glared at her, but Kho tilted her chin, a hint of her old insouciant twinkle in her dark, long-lashed eyes. Despite everything, despite Jochi and the ancient rivalry between their two kangs, the ghost of their lost warmth flickered between them. "Please."

Kho did as she was bid, but Yuli rolled her eyes.

"Wider," she commanded. "Your balance is still off."

Kho made the adjustments without comment.

"Now, when you draw the bow—"

"I know how to draw a bow," Kho snapped. She hooked her thumb into the string, and pulled up and back in one smooth motion and made to release.

"Wait, wait, wait, wait!" Yuli cried. "Remember, no dry firing the bow!"

Kho relaxed and made a guilty face. "I forgot."

"How long has it been since you were last on the practice field?"

Kho furrowed her brow. "Three years, I think?"

"Not since your dismal performance at the Endless Night Championships when we were thirteen, eh?"

She glowered at Yuli. "Yes." She held out a hand. "Hand me an arrow."

"Say please."

Kho merely gave her a look before she nonchalantly pulled an arrow out of the quiver on Yuli's right hip. The casual intimacy of the gesture made something shiver inside Yuli. Kho nocked it to her bow, drew back, and loosed.

The arrow sailed over the target.

"Better," Yuli said.

Kho pulled an arrow from her own quiver and tried again. This time the arrow struck the target on the top right side of the outermost ring.

"Keep your elbow level," Yuli said. She lightly touched her fingers to Kho's arm, gently guiding her to the right angle. Her skin tingled where it touched the other girl's sleeve.

The arrow hit closer to the center this time. Kho tried again, her aim still a little off to the right.

"Try opening up your release a bit," Yuli suggested.

"What does that mean?"

Yuli came around to stand behind her. She hesitated, then just barely wrapped her left hand around Kho's as the other girl stood ready to fire. Something fluttered in her stomach when she realized she could see over the top of Kho's head. Hadn't it been only yesterday when their eyes had been level with one another? She was suddenly aware of the distance between them—both physically in the moment and emotionally in their relationship. There had been a time when it had been nothing to stand this close to her best friend. Now everything was fraught.

"When you let go," Yuli said, appalled to hear her own voice trembling slightly, "try twisting your aiming arm to the left. Just a little. Just enough to give yourself breathing room." She demonstrated by carefully maneuvering her own body so that Kho's movements followed hers, her right shoulder touching Kho's back, the front of her thigh to Kho's hip. The other girl sucked in a sharp breath, but whether it was from surprise or understanding, Yuli wasn't sure.

Kho loosed. This time the arrow thudded even closer to the middle. Yuli stepped back.

"Why are you helping me?" Kho asked, and Yuli wasn't sure, but she thought she heard the barest tremor in the other girl's voice.

Yuli cleared her throat. "Because I don't want you accidentally killing anyone at the Trial of Strength," she said, forcing humor back into her tone. She felt strange and unsettled, suddenly too aware of her body, how her muscles and tendons were connected, how her skin sat upon her bones. Ordinarily, if Yuli thought too hard about her corporeal self, she felt uncomfortably itchy with the need to vacate the prison of her flesh, but there was an aching sort of pleasure to this awareness now that she had never experienced before.

Kho fired again. Even closer this time. "And what if I win?"

"The Trial of Strength?" Yuli scoffed. "Unlikely."

"You never know."

"I do know," Yuli said. "I've got five Championships and you have none."

"I'm a quick learner."

And so Kho had been. The brightest in their class.

"So you'll take the Trial of Wits." Yuli shrugged. "And it will be up to the Trial of the Soul to see who will come out on top. I mean," she said quickly, feeling a blush heat her cheeks, "who will win."

Kho's dark gaze briefly touched hers before darting away again. The corners of her lips quirked for a moment before her expression sobered. "Yuli," she said softly, and something both hurt and healed within her to hear her affectionate name from her old best friend once more. "Why are you even competing in the Grand Game?"

"Why are you?" she returned.

Kho's face was unreadable as she fitted another arrow to her bow. "Because I want what is best for the Maltak Kang." The arrow went wide.

"You stumbled on that release," Yuli remarked. "Next time, breathe out as you let go." Kho fired off another shot. "And you didn't answer me."

"I thought I just did."

"I asked why *you* were competing in the Grand Game," Yuli said. "Not why your mother wants you to."

Kho said nothing, shooting another arrow. "I am the First Daughter of the Maltak Kang," she said. "My mother's wishes are my own."

Yuli was acutely conscious of the distance between them again, every inch a mile. "Do you even have a mind of your own?" she asked.

"I do." Another shot. "But unlike you, I don't have the freedom to do as I please."

"I'm not as free as you think," Yuli said.

"No?" Another shot. "Then pray tell, Gommun Yulana, what keeps you caged?"

The secret of her magic rose in her throat, the truth of her real identity as the Guardian of Wind. "I have responsibilities too" was all she said.

"You?" Kho said, laughing in disbelief. "I don't believe it."

Yuli crossed her arms. "And why is that so difficult to believe?"

"Because you never take anything seriously," Kho said. "You never have."

Yuli blinked. There had been no malice in Kho's tone, yet the words still stung. All her years fleeing responsibility, fleeing accountability, and fleeing anything that caused her discomfort caught up to her in that moment, and she was overcome by the sharp, sickly sweet sensation of shame. She stiffened, steeling herself against the feeling.

"I am the First Daughter of the Gommun Kang," she said. "I take the honor of my family name very seriously."

Kho scoffed. "You've never cared about that."

"I have always cared about honor," Yuli said coldly. "And if you knew me at all, you would not be questioning it."

Kho was silent. "It was a miracle we were ever friends," she said after a moment. "Wasn't it?"

For some reason, that hurt more than anything else Kho had said. "Maybe," Yuli said quietly. "But I don't take miracles for granted."

Kho looked startled at that. "Yuli," she said, "I—I don't—back then, I—" She cut herself off, frustrated with the words she could not voice. "I'm sorry," she said at last.

Yuli was perplexed. "For what?"

"For Jochi."

And just like that, the present moment caught up with Yuli, a dash of cold reality far more bracing than the bitterest winds from the tundra. "Don't," she said, her voice brittle.

"I just . . . I wanted to tell you—"

"Don't!"

Kho was agitated. "I never meant to—"

"I don't care what you *meant!*" Yuli said furiously. "You can tell me whatever you want, Maltak Kho, but that doesn't change what *happened.*" She looked away. "You betrayed my cousin to your father, the Falconer. You are the reason he's exiled. You are the reason he might be *dead*."

Kho said nothing for a long moment. "I thought," she said in a small voice, "I was doing the right thing."

"No." Yuli's voice was hard. "You were doing what *your mother* said was the right thing."

Kho stiffened. "I'm not my mother's lackey."

Yuli snorted. "Are you not?"

Kho crossed her arms. "You don't know me."

"No, I don't," Yuli agreed. "Not anymore."

They stared at each other for a long while, and years of words unsaid weighed down the air between them. Yuli had plenty of things she wanted to say to Kho—many of them unflattering or unkind—but she kept her mouth shut, lest the words that had been sitting on the tip of her tongue their entire conversation fell out.

*I miss you.*

Yuli had never lacked for casual companions. She had been a sociable and gregarious child, quick to form connections with others. Playing was easy, especially for someone who didn't mind getting a little dirty or sweaty with the others. But friendship . . . true friendship was hard. It was harder to find someone who wanted to be with her in the quiet as well as the fun. People wanted to laugh with Yuli; they did not want to cry with her.

Kho had cried with her. Kho had raged with her. Kho had been there through all the highs and lows of emotion, and had never wavered.

Until Jochi.

"Here," Kho said, handing Yuli back her bow. "I can manage my own practice from now on. Thank you for your help, but it's not necessary."

Yuli grabbed her weapon. "You're welcome," she said shortly. "Good luck at the Trial. You're going to need it."

Kho lifted her chin. "You too."

# 16

It would be sword-lance for the Trial of Strength.

Yuli had been a little disappointed that she would not be competing in her best event, but she was confident she could at least outperform Kho.

The opening ceremony of the Grand Game had started at high noon, a ritual of prayer led by the Council of Shamans, after which the spectators had milled around the field beneath the Tower of Offerings, partaking of the food from vendors scattered throughout the clearing. Yuli could smell the deep-fried fats, garlic, onion, spices, and sugar from where she stood with her mare, Sartai, in the holding pen beside the arena, wishing she were out there instead. She could be waiting in line at the stand of an elder making treats out of caramelized sugar, pressing shapes into the softened cookie for the children to try to carve out with sharpened twigs. She thought of all the times she and Kho had done the very same thing at celebrations and holidays, how they had teased each other when the cookies eventually broke and crumbled, obliterating the shapes.

But she would *not* think about Kho.

Yuli was feeling a bit out of sorts as she waited for the Trial of Strength to begin; the day had begun much earlier than she was used to. There were many things Princess Yulana did not appreciate, and on the top of that list was being rudely awakened at a godsforsaken hour for a purifying bath in freezing cold water. Then there had been the offering to her ancestors at the Hills of the Dead, the ritual gifts of white foods—dumplings, sponge bread, and noodles—left for the deceased Gommun along with the appropriate prayers. She couldn't help but remember the last time she had been to the necropolis outside the city, and had to stop herself from growling at Auncle Mongke that there wasn't anyone to make these offerings to. Not anymore, at least. She could have used a few more hours to rest; she had been up later than she intended reading the first installment of *The Maiden Who Was Loved by Death*. Yuli often couldn't sleep the night before a big event, so she thought a few chapters from Prince Rice Cake's favorite book would put her right out. Instead, she had finished the entire thing and was dying for the next book, hating herself a little for it. The story was dreadful—full of feelings and no action—but at least it had been eminently readable. She didn't know whether she thought better or worse of Han for loving it.

Adding to her troubles was her horse, Sartai, in a skittish mood. The mare pulled at her lead, digging in her hooves and rolling her eyes at everything that crossed her path.

"Shh, girl, shh," Yuli soothed, stroking her neck, but Sartai was in no mood to be handled. Yuli had double-, then triple-checked her saddle and other fittings before the start of the event, but it was not a burr or scratch that seemed to be troubling her horse; it was nerves. The hostlers on either side of Yuli were equally distressed, and she just wished everyone could *calm down*. Sartai was her best horse, her most responsive, and her most attentive, and she needed the mare to be focused. Sword-lance was quite dangerous, as it required agility, accuracy, and complete trust in one's mount. Sartai had competed in several other bouts of sword-lance before with perfect composure, so Yuli couldn't quite understand what was wrong.

But perhaps she was simply responding to Yuli's own uneasy state of mind.

Despite her confidence in the event, her gut churned with nausea. She settled, then resettled herself on her saddle, trying to find the right seat. Everything had felt off since they got Sartai fitted for the first trial. The connection Yuli usually felt with her mount seemed muted, awkward, uncomfortable, as though they were strangers meeting for the first time. All the signals and understanding that had been built between horse and rider seemed to have vanished overnight, and Yuli had been momentarily overcome with doubt, wondering if she should switch out Sartai for a different mount, even if another horse was less experienced in sword-lance. But the instant she pressed her forehead to Sartai's nose, she felt that connection again, knew that Sartai was her very best girl, and berated herself for even thinking of replacing her with another for this event.

But as she waited to enter the arena, Yuli was overcome with doubt once more.

Yuli stared out onto the field, surrounded on all sides by a mass of shouting, roaring spectators. Despite knowing that she likely wouldn't be able to find them, she couldn't help looking for Zhara and Ami, who had risked leaving Tarkhun's bookshop simply to support her in the event. Uncle Bayar and Aunt Görte were seated on the central thrust platform on the right side, and the

Lady of Wild Things and Ogodei were on the opposite side, while the judges—one from each of the Five Golden Families—were seated behind barriers on the ground.

"The contestants may enter the field!" came the crier's shout, their voice amplified by the speaking trumpet.

Yuli clicked her tongue and shifted her hips, urging Sartai forward. The mare tossed her head a few times before reluctantly stepping into the arena. On the opposite end, Kho rode forward on her own horse, her small form made even smaller by the distance. The field was divided into six lanes—three for each contestant—in which five iron rings the size of a human hand lay, each one marked by a small flag planted in the ground. The aim of sword-lance was to pick up as many of these rings as possible with a flexible bamboo pike while running down the lanes without dismounting one's horse. There were thirty rings in total, and the maximum number of points possible was fifteen. One of the Gommun hostlers handed Yuli the pike, while on the other side, a Maltak handler did the same for Kho.

"The contestants may salute each other!"

Yuli lifted her weapon with her right hand to the cheers of the crowd. Kho made a mirroring gesture, and the spectators broke out into competing chants.

*Maltak! Maltak! Maltak!*

*Gommun! Gommun! Gommun!*

Sartai whickered plaintively.

Yuli glanced to Aunt Görte, but to her surprise, her aunt was not looking down at the proceedings but straight across at the platform where the Maltak Kang sat. The Lady of Wild Things was surrounded by a few retainers, as well as her son, Ogodei. Ogodei, too, had his gaze fixed forward—staring at Aunt Görte. There was something about the quality of their gazes that made the hairs on the back of Yuli's neck stand on end, a similarity that was not of the features but of the expression. Her sense of unease deepened.

Sartai tossed her head and stamped her feet.

"Shh, shh," Yuli soothed again, more to herself than to her horse.

"At the sound of the gong, let the Game commence!"

High above in the crier's tower, the announcer picked up a mallet with a flourish. Yuli tensed, feeling the solid weight of Sartai between her legs, letting the mare grow still with anticipation.

*Gong!*

"Hyah!"

Yuli and Sartai sprang from their side of the arena, followed half a moment later by Kho and her mount. Gripping Sartai tight between her knees, Yuli leveled her pike and leaned down toward the right to pick up the first of her iron rings as they charged down the rightmost lane.

One.

A roar of approval from the crowd.

Leaning down again, Yuli picked up another.

Three.

Another. Four.

Another. Five.

She slowed Sartai down as they reached the other end of the arena, settling back onto her saddle and readjusting the balance of her pike with the new weight of the rings. There was a sigh of disappointment as she rounded her horse to face the other direction; Kho had missed one of her marks. Handlers rushed onto the field to clear the flags of the claimed rings and straighten the ones that had been missed. There were twenty-one rings left on the field, with five on Yuli's pike, four on Kho's.

Once the lanes were clear, Yuli readied Sartai for another charge, but the mare was being difficult. Sartai kept shaking her head and snorting, whinnying and signaling discomfort.

"Whoa, whoa," Yuli said, tensing her knees and trying to bring her horse back in line. But Sartai—ordinarily so obedient—was only growing more and more agitated. If Yuli dismounted now to settle her down, she would be disqualified. "Come . . . on . . ." she said through gritted teeth.

A good horse and well-trained, Sartai stilled, although she was starting to show the whites of her eyes, her ears flicking to the left, then to the right. Something prickled at the side of Yuli's face, and she looked up to find Ogodei staring down at her with such intensity that it made her skin crawl. His face was blank, impassive, but his eyes were wholly black, eager, and his mouth was moving, as though whispering to himself. The world seemed to still and slow down, and a high-pitched ringing started in her head. Above the shouts of the crowd, Yuli could swear she could hear a voice muttering something in a language she did not know that grated at her soul.

She shook her head, breaking the spell, and the moment returned in a whoosh. On the other side of the arena, Kho was preparing her second charge. Cursing herself for being distracted and wasting time, Yuli leaned over her saddle and clicked her tongue, urging Sartai into a run.

*Clink!* Yuli picked up another ring. Six.

*Clink!* Seven.

There was the thunder of hooves as Kho rattled past, trailing groans of disapproval in her wake. She had missed her fifth and seventh rings.

*Clink!* Yuli scored another. Eight. She thought she could still hear eldritch murmuring tickling her ears.

Sartai stumbled.

Startled, Yuli grabbed the mare's mane, nearly

dropping her pike in the process. The strange whispers grew louder, not in Yuli's ears, but inside her head, drowning out the rest of the commotion. Yuli felt even more removed from her horse than before.

Then Sartai began to scream.

The horse reared and bucked, nearly succeeding in throwing Yuli from her seat. Yuli gasped and grabbed Sartai's reins—which she rarely needed to use—trying to guide her mount around, but Sartai kept bucking. Yuli rose up in her stirrups, muscles burning as all around her, cries of excitement and confusion swelled.

"Sartai!"

She had to bring her horse back under control. She had to stay her seat. If she was thrown, she would be disqualified. She would lose the Trial of Strength. If she lost the Trial of Strength, she had no hope of winning the Grand Game. If she lost the Grand Game, the Morning Realms would be lost. Sartai kept swishing her tail and bucking, fighting Yuli with all her might. Yuli guided Sartai around, trying to urge her forward, to reach the other end of the run and regroup. Sartai spun in a circle, trying to bolt, but Yuli pulled back on the reins, preventing the horse from lowering her head for a charge. Her saddle began sliding to the right, coming loose, and Yuli started to slide with it, her foot tangled in the straps.

Behind her, a wave of cheers. Kho had reached the end of her run and was turning around for the last pass.

There was nothing else for it. Muttering an apology to Sartai beneath her breath, Yuli placed her free hand on the mare's neck, grabbing her mane and rolling forward to free her left leg from the stirrup. Spooked, Sartai reared, but Yuli was prepared, keeping her grip on the horse's mane and letting the saddle slip beneath her. If she could just get her seat back without the blanket and the saddle between herself and the horse, she could try to finish this event bareback. Sartai reared again and Yuli inched herself up onto the mare's shoulders, gripping tight with her left leg and reaching for the clasps beneath her. When all four hooves touched the ground again, Yuli had managed to get the saddle undone and kick herself free. The Gommun hostlers ran forward, grabbing the seat and clearing it off the field.

The instant she was in direct contact with Sartai, all discomfort vanished. The connection between horse and rider was restored and the mare immediately ceased her agitation. Miraculously, throughout all this, Yuli had managed to keep hold of her pike. She was not disqualified. Yet.

She managed to get to the end of the lane and turned Sartai around with her legs. "Good girl," she said, patting Sartai's neck. The mare flicked her ears back at the sound of her voice, dancing lightly as though to ask where she had been. "Let's try this again, lah?"

The handlers had cleared all the markers from the lane. Yuli had missed the last two, and now had eight rings on her pike. She didn't know how many Kho had managed to pick up on the last charge, but judging by the volume of the shouting from the spectators, she suspected their scores were close. Yuli threaded her fingers through the lock of hair at the base of Sartai's neck, wondering if she could even finish the event. She had never performed sword-lance bareback; she had always relied on the saddle and stirrups for the right leverage to lean down and pick up the rings; without them, she would have to rely on the strength of her legs alone, with one hand on Sartai's neck for balance. The muscles were already trembling in her thighs.

Yuli took in a steadying breath. She trusted her horse. Her horse trusted her. She could do it. *They* could do it.

Across the field, she locked eyes with Kho, who

had waited for Yuli to collect herself in a show of sportsmanship before starting her last run. Kho lifted her pike in salute. Yuli returned it. Another roar shook the arena as the crowd shouted their approval. Northerners always did love a good show. The girls stared at each other for several long moments as understanding passed wordlessly between them.

They would start their last charge at the same time.

Kho lowered the tip of her pike and Yuli quickly counted the rings as they slid down the length of the shaft. Eight. The two girls were tied. Yuli lowered her own weapon and nodded. Kho would take the lead, Yuli would follow half a breath later.

"Hyah!"

Kho urged her mount onward with her hips, and Yuli clicked her tongue. Sartai took off, picking up speed as Yuli came up to the first marker. Gripping tight with her left leg, she leaned forward and down, the tip of her pike pointed straight at the first ring.

*Clink!* Nine.

Cheers erupted.

*Clink!* Ten.

The first two in the final lane were easily scored, but Yuli was dangerously close to slipping off and had to miss the third ring to regain her seat. Boos burst forth from the crowd as Yuli repositioned herself on Sartai's back, her left leg shaking as she pressed her heel into Sartai's ribs for balance. She leaned down again as she approached the last two rings. Timing was crucial; if she lowered her pike too late, then she would miss.

*Clink!* Eleven.

Last one left. Sweat slicked her palm where she gripped Sartai's mane, and she hitched up her right leg for support against the mare's flank. Hang on just a little bit more, just a little while longer . . .

*Clink!* Twelve.

With a sigh of relief, Yuli righted herself on Sartai's back again, riding comfortably to the end of the lane. Turning her horse around, she raised her pike above her head, showing her prizes to the crowd. The audience screamed, *Gommun! Gommun! Gommun!* On the other side of the field, Kho had come to the end of her ride as well.

"And now, the counting of the rings!" the crier's voice came from the tower.

Yuli and Kho both turned their mounts and rode to the judges sitting behind the barrier.

"The Gommun shall count first!"

Yuli handed her pike to the attendant, who presented the weapon to the judges with both hands. The Nuwage judge began sliding the rings off one by one, presenting each to the crowd and counting aloud.

"Twelve!" the crier proclaimed.

*Gommun! Gommun! Gommun!*

"Now the Maltak!"

Kho presented her staff to the attendant, and this time it was the Tzorig judge who did the counting. Yuli held her breath as she kept track of the number of rings falling to the table.

Eight, nine, ten . . .

"Eleven!" the crier yelled.

Yuli closed her eyes as the wave of sound rushed over her.

*Gommun! Gommun! Gommun!*

Beside her, she could feel the hostlers and handlers of her kang jostling and cheering her win, but instead of elation, what Yuli felt was exhaustion. She had come so close to losing. While Yuli, like any other competitive person, hated to lose, for the first time in her athletic career, she felt the weight and significance of what loss would mean. Not merely a loss of pride, but a loss of the empire to total war. She hated these stakes, and for the briefest moment, she entertained the idea of quitting, of abdicating responsibility, so she would not be accountable if she were to fail.

Yuli opened her eyes. She felt the touch of someone's gaze atop her head and lifted her chin to the viewing platform above where the judges sat. To where the Maltak Kang had sat, watching the entire event. She met the Lady of Wild Things' eyes, and the Lady tilted her head in acknowledgment of her victory, the gesture surprisingly gracious. Yuli returned the acknowledgment by thumping her right fist to her left shoulder.

"Good game," Kho said softly, and despite her loss, there was a genuine smile on her face.

"You too," Yuli said, and she meant it. The other girl had far outperformed her expectations.

"The Trial of Wits next," Kho said.

Yuli nodded. "I know."

Kho grinned. "Good luck," she said. "You're going to need it."

Again, the words *I miss you* lingered on the tip of Yuli's tongue, but she swallowed them down. "You too," she managed.

With one last rueful smile, Kho turned her horse and cantered to the other side of the field, returning to the horse pens, leaving Yuli suddenly aching for the taste of caramelized sugar cookies.

Sartai's saddle had been cursed.

It had taken Ami a long time to find the spell, and an even longer time to decipher the strange characters inked into the underside. She had recognized the Language of Flowers straightaway, but not the glyphs themselves. They were odd combinations of various radicals and morphemes she had never seen put together before, and while she could usually puzzle out the meaning of characters she did not know from the context around them, she was at a loss with the string of nonsense before her.

But there was power in the characters. Ami could sense it, even if she could not make sense of the meaning.

Beside her in the cellar, Zhara was diligently working at transcribing Ami's notes into the encyclopedia, dutifully indexing the information and topics with page numbers in the master journal. Ami had seen the futility of trying to keep everything perfectly neat—they were missing half the original text, after all—but at least the knowledge would be organized. She didn't often think about what life would look like after—if—they managed to defeat the Mother of Ten Thousand Demons, but when she did, she thought wistfully of a little house by the canal, surrounded by books, tea, plants, and Gaden, where she could finally write a definitive reference book on *Songs of Order and Chaos.*

"Zhara," Ami said, "can I see what we have on curses?"

Zhara looked up from her work, a spot of ink on her nose. "There's not a lot, or I haven't gotten to all of it yet," she said, turning to the master journal for page numbers. "Why?"

"There's something . . . off about this spell," Ami said, pointing to the characters written on the saddle.

Zhara flinched when Ami showed the glyphs to her. "You think it's some sort of hex?"

"Yes," Ami said seriously. "I know there's something about cursed objects in *Songs of Order and Chaos.*"

Zhara flipped through the pages. "Here," she said, handing Ami her journal. "There's a passage about ancient magicians summoning spirits into inanimate vessels."

"No, that's not it," Ami said with frustration. "Let me have the notes."

Zhara happily relinquished the loose sheets to the scrivener. "I remember Mihoon telling me about cursed objects once," she said thoughtfully. "There's an entire black market for enchanted objects in the Azure Isles."

"*Qin bound the demon into a black stone, which he wore around his neck as he rode into battle*—no, that's not it." Ami harrumphed, pushing up her spectacles and pinching the bridge of her nose. "Maybe something about words of power."

Zhara gingerly took the saddle from Ami and ran her fingers lightly over the black ink. She shuddered. "It feels . . . dark. Like my magic gets muffled whenever I get close. It feels like when I got attacked by the demon possessing Nurden."

Ami went still. She remembered the first time she had ever touched a plant blighted by a demonic infection, how her magic had gone numb from the contact. There was ki and anti-ki. Order and chaos. Magicians were those capable of manipulating the void through reason, through writing, through intention and control, but demons . . . demons were beings made purely of the void. They had magic of their own, a sort of chaos magic. But without a vessel, they had no way to direct it in the physical world.

"Zhara," she said quietly, "can I see the saddle?" She took back the equipment and studied not the characters but the power radiating off them. All magicians left traces of their ki whenever they cast a spell, a signature, an imprint of their soul in the enchantment they could perform.

There was no ki in these characters. It was the opposite of ki. Anti-ki.

Ami dropped the saddle to the floor and recoiled in horror.

"What?" Zhara asked in alarm. "What is it?"

She thought of the terrifying battle with Nurden all those weeks ago, of the strange, uncanny magic he was able to wield. He had been a waking dreamer possessed by a demon, and that demon had somehow been able to make use of its chaos magic *in that body*. There were waking dreamers all over Urghud. Potential vessels for a demon army . . . all of whom would be able to wield magic.

"A demon cast the spell on that saddle," Ami said hoarsely.

Zhara went ashen. "Are you sure?"

Ami nodded.

"The Moth Demon?"

Ami frowned. "I don't know. But I think the waking dreamer problem has gotten even more urgent."

The cellar door suddenly opened. "There's a letter for you, Zhara," Tarkhun said, coming down the stairs.

Zhara startled, then recovered. "For me?" she asked, voice cracking. "From whom?"

With a shrug, the bookseller dropped a bamboo tube carved with her name on the desk before her. Bemused, she popped the wax cap off one end and reached inside to fish out the message. She brought the paper to her nose.

"It smells of perfume," she said in surprise.

"A love note?" Tarkhun teased.

"From Han?" Ami asked.

Blushing, Zhara unrolled the note and read aloud, "*Write the answer to reveal the message.*"

"What does that mean?" Tarkhun asked.

"An encryption spell!" Ami said excitedly. "I've heard of those before. The letters are written according to a cipher, to key to which is provided in the form of a riddle or a poem. When you have the answer, you write it onto the note itself, which will rearrange the words into something only the recipient is supposed to read." She craned her neck, trying to catch a glimpse of the message. "What does it say?"

Zhara studied the paper before her. "*More potent than rice wine or brandy is your love, only I'm not allergic to it. The only thing sweeter than your kiss is my name on your lips.*"

Tarkhun made a face. "If that's either a riddle or a poem, it fails at being both."

"That definitely sounds like my cousin wrote it," Ami said drily. She stared at Zhara curiously. "Are you crying?"

"No." Zhara hastily wiped at her cheeks. "There's just something in my eye, is all."

Ami never could understand why people lied when the truth was so obvious, but she held her tongue. "Do you know the answer?" she asked instead.

Zhara nodded with a watery chuckle. "Plum blossom." She dipped her brush in the inkwell and wrote it on the page.

Nothing happened.

"Oh," Zhara said with dismay. "Have I ruined it?"

"Could the answer be something else?" Tarkhun asked.

"I don't think so," Zhara said. "It's a joke between my"—she blushed again—"between Han and me. He claimed he was allergic to alcohol and that it turned him bright red. I used to call him Master Plum Blossom, because he turned that exact shade whenever I teased him." Her smile wavered. "I'm certain that's the key."

"Here," Ami said gently, taking the message and the brush from Zhara's hands. With swift, sure strokes, she wrote the character for *plum blossom* in the Language of Flowers, the lines glowing a faint green-gold.

Everyone held their breath as the letters rearranged themselves, with even more letters emerging from the paper itself. A page full of words written by a rounded, childlike, but well-educated hand formed, dense lines crowded with information.

"It *is* from Han," Zhara said delightedly. She scanned the message, not even bothering to hide her tears this time.

"What does it say?" Ami asked, but Tarkhun gave her a gentle nudge.

"Shush," he said. "Let the girl read first."

Ami waited patiently while Zhara finished the letter and handed it over.

"You can read it," Zhara said. "There's nothing too personal."

Eagerly, Ami read.

*My* ~~dear sweet~~ *Zhara—*
*I'm sorry it's taken this long to write. I've started this letter over a thousand times, trying to figure out how to even address you. The letters Little Flame and Lord Death exchange in* The Maiden Who Was Loved by

Death *are beautiful and romantic and poetic, but I'm no fey lord of the otherworld with a gilded tongue. What even is a gilded tongue anyway? Why would anyone want to coat their tongue with gold? You would never be able to taste anything but metal again, not to mention I can't imagine it's very healthy.*

*I really want to start writing this letter over again, but Xu tells me that I should just get on with it, and that you will still like me even if my literary skills leave something to be desired. Writing letters is harder than writing poetry; there are so many more words and so many more opportunities to get them wrong. I hope you liked my riddle, by the way. I spent a long time on it, and I think it's pretty good.*

Ami snorted.

*Gaden, Okonwe, and I arrived in Zanhei safely, along with the Bangtan Brothers and Crackle. I missed my father's funeral, but Anyang has been serving as regent in my absence. He's grown so much since I saw him last and is almost as tall as me now. I guess I can't call him my little brother anymore. My coronation went as planned, and I'm officially prince of Zanhei now. Being prince isn't all that different from being the Royal Heir, except for the robes, which are a lot heavier and much more uncomfortable. The crown too. I hate it. It's got this beaded curtain that hangs in front of my face and gets in the way whenever I'm trying to read proclamations and other things that need my seal that Xu shoves in front of me. Xu is my Chancellor now, although they tried to refuse the appointment. Bad memories, I guess, but I don't think I would be able to govern without them. They're the one who paid attention during our lessons on history, current affairs,* and philosophy, after all, and I find they're a lot more helpful than a bunch of wispy-bearded tutors counseling me at every turn. Xu misses you, by the way. They send you their love.

As promised, one of the first things I did as prince was open up my city to magician refugees fleeing other parts of the Morning Realms, and I've been trying my best to get the other princes of the south to agree. Magic has been openly practiced here ever since we defeated the Frog Demon this past summer, and there have been no outbreaks of abomination since. People are still cautious, but the school the Guardians of Dawn established before we left is flourishing. Jiyi officially left Wisteria House and hasn't written a single poem since she started teaching the rudiments of the Language of Flowers to students. I asked her if she missed the old poetry parties at the teahouse and she said no. I think she's lying, though. Jiyi, I know you're reading this. You can tell the student who's going to enchant this message that you don't miss writing, but I know better. Pleased to meet you, by the way, my fine student. Do take care with this letter. I hope you know you've got my heart in your hands.

The Heralds of Glorious Justice continue their march on the imperial city. After speaking with Gaden, I've sent word to Pang Lok and the Heralds of Glorious Justice that Zanhei's resources are at their disposal to help oust the Falconer and the Kestrels from the capital. Gaden doesn't seem keen on a reunion or reconciliation with their old companions, but they say that beggars can't be choosers when it comes to civil war. Their presence has caused something of a stir here in the south, as people have been speculating endlessly about their identity. Some rumors get closer to the truth than others, but we have neither confirmed nor denied anything. I *asked Gaden what they would do if Pang Lok and the Heralds proclaim them the lost Mugung heir and they said they don't know. I didn't have the heart to say that their claiming the Sunburst Throne might be the answer to all our problems and give the south and the west a unified cause to rally around. But I respect their wish to keep anonymous. I wouldn't want to be the next emperor either. It's bad enough having to be a prince.*

*Oh, Gaden also sends their love. They miss everyone, but especially you, Ami.*

To her horror, Ami found her own eyes smarting with tears.

"Is everything all right?" Zhara asked with concern.

"Yes," she said, and it was true. "I'm fine."

*We've received word from our contacts in the north that someone called the Lady of Wild Things has put herself forth as the Warlord's heir and intends to claim the imperial city for herself come spring, provided she can garner the support of the Golden Horde. We don't have the numbers to fight the infamous northern warriors, but Okonwe has gone back to Kalantze to convince the Right Hand of the Qirin Tulku to see if we can't ally with the Free Peoples of the West. The outermost west escaped the worst of the Just War twenty years ago, and Gaden fears that the Right Hand will simply look to the protection of the Gunung Mountains and the Zanqi Plateau to deter any invasion. But we need more than warriors if we are to fight the northern forces; we will need magicians and their knowledge. So much was lost during the purges; we can barely teach the children here how to control their powers, much less harness them. We hope Okonwe can at least bring back some texts from the library at Kalantze; if you should come across anything we could use in your search for the northern fragment of Songs of Order and Chaos, that would be much appreciated.*

*Meanwhile, Xu says we should look east to the Azure Isles to see if we can't form an alliance with the Baron Flotilla. Officially, the Fleet Queen was loyal to the Warlord during the Just War, but there are rumors of a challenge to her rule. Her niece, Min Suhwa, who was spirited away and hidden somewhere when she was just a baby. No one knows where Min Suhwa is, or whether she's still alive, but Xu thinks if she could rally the navy, she would be someone whose favor we should court, as she is the rightful Marquess of the Azure Isles. The Bangtan Brothers are eager to play ambassador for us; we may send them abroad to search for this elusive heir. They also give you their love, by the way.*

*More soon. Write me back when you can. Everyone else has sent you their love, so it's my turn now, I guess. Wherever you go, whatever you do, know that you carry my heart with you. I miss you all dreadfully and will count down the days until we are all reunited.*

There was a knock on the door to the bookshop. Tarkhun glanced up through the cellar entrance with surprise. "We're closed," he said. "Who would be knocking at this hour?"

"Could it be the Huntsmen?" Zhara asked worriedly.

"I'll go check," he said. "In the meanwhile, shut this door tight behind me and seal the cracks with a spell for silence. I'd do it myself, but"—he showed his hands apologetically—"I have the affliction but not the ability."

And then he was gone. Ami set down the letter and pulled out her brush to do as the bookseller asked, wiping away her tears as she did so.

"Did someone die?" came a voice from the corner.

Ami whirled around to see Yuli standing in the cellar in spirit form. "Why is everyone crying?"

"No one died." Zhara laughed, rubbing at her eyes. "We just got a letter from Han."

"Subjected you to some of his poetry, did he?" Yuli asked sympathetically. "I would cry too."

Zhara laughed again and gave Yuli a light punch.

"I probably deserved that," Yuli said ruefully, rubbing at her arm. "Anyway, what news from Prince Rice Cake?"

Ami handed Yuli Han's letter. The princess scanned the message, but with laughter instead of tears.

"Oh, Han," she said, returning the note to Zhara. "You know, we might have been able to make a decent go at marriage after all, he and I."

Zhara punched Yuli again, a little harder this time, but the redhead merely grinned and winked.

There was another knock, this time on the cellar door. Yuli flickered out of sight as Ami and Zhara held their breath, wondering if it was a Huntsman.

"It's Tarkhun," the bookseller's muffled voice came through. "You'd best come up. We've got another message from the Paper Wolf."

# 18

The wind smelled of burnt metal.

Yuli wandered through the streets of Urghud to meet up with Zhara, Ami, and Tarkhun at the northern gates to the city. She had left before the arrival of the Paper Wolf's message, so she was surprised by the jingling of the bell at her window an hour or so later, when Sajah had shown up in cat form with a note tied around his collar. The three of them would meet her and Temur at the northern gates, where the Eagle would bear them all to the Tower of Offerings to finally meet the Paper Wolf.

It would have been easier to simply spirit-walk to the agreed-upon rendezvous, but Yuli was in an anxious mood. Ami's note had relayed her findings about a demon sabotaging her at the Trial of Strength, not to mention leaving her body empty of ki no longer seemed like a safe idea. She didn't know if demons could possess the body of the Guardian of Wind, but if what Ami had discovered about them being able to wield chaos magic through human vessels was true, she didn't want to risk it.

So she was stuck in her physical form as she wended her way through the revelers enjoying themselves in the taverns and teahouses of Urghud. The festival atmosphere from the Trial of Strength had spread to the city, and refugee and resident alike were recounting the events for those who hadn't been able to attend, as well as placing wagers on the outcome of the next Trial. Odds were on Maltak Kho winning the Trial of Wits next week, but opinions were more divided on the Trial of the Soul.

"Gommun Yulana, hands down!" she could hear a bettor shout. "The princess has won five Championships in a row!"

"The Maltak girl is a capable horsewoman," returned their companion. "The odds are longer, but the reward would be much greater if she won!"

People hailed her as they stumbled past, evidence of a good time visible in their shambling gaits and the pungent, yeasty scent of fermented mare's milk wafting from their breath. Yuli kept a hood over her red hair, but she didn't think anyone would recognize her in their inebriated states. More than once she spied a member of the city watch among the crowds, drinking and gambling and throwing cards with everyone else.

"So much for protecting Urghud from the Heralds of Glorious Justice," she muttered under her breath.

The wind had picked up, damp and cold. It had the feel of snow, and the skies overhead were heavy with clouds. But that burnt-metal smell persisted, and Yuli found herself with the beginnings of a headache. Her mood was taking a sour turn, and she felt cramped and uncomfortable in her own skin. She wanted to be home in her own bed. She wanted to go spirit-walking. She wanted to do anything but be present and miserable. She nearly tripped over someone passed out in the middle of the street, their bowl of spilled mare's milk already icing a little.

"Hoi," she said irritably, nudging them with the tip of her boot. "Get inside lest you freeze to death."

They did not move.

More and more bodies littered the street as she drew closer to the northern wall, the alleyways thick with fog. The hairs rose on the back of her neck as she thought about the night Zhara and Ami arrived in the city, the harbor wreathed with the mist of ghosts.

The ghosts of the living dead.

Ahead, a figure stood in the middle of the street, their hands raised in warning. In the weak light of the torches and lanterns, she thought she could glimpse a hint of red in their curls.

"Jochi?" she breathed.

Her cousin's form solidified, as though her calling his name was a summons from another world. His mouth worked frantically, and although she could not hear him, she could clearly read his lips.

*Go back. Go back.*

"Yuli?" a voice called from the fog.

"Zhara?"

The Guardian of Fire materialized out of the mist, her wavy hair wild about her face. She held the crystal from Mount Llangposa aloft in her hand, and Jochi vanished as soon as its rays of light touched his form. "There's something wrong with Tarkhun!"

The bookseller sat on the ground, back propped against the outer wall of the city and breathing hard. In the rosy-gold glow of Zhara's crystal, Tarkhun looked drawn and pale, an unhealthy grayish pallor to his features. "I can't—I can't—" he gasped, puffs of visible breath hazy before his face.

"What happened?" Yuli demanded.

"I don't know," Zhara said. "He just collapsed!"

Tarkhun's eyes rolled back into his head, and he

exhaled a long sigh, a stream of mist pouring from his mouth.

Ami clapped her hands over her mouth in horror. "His ki," she choked out. "It—"

Yuli removed her mitten and touched her fingers to Tarkhun's neck. The instant she felt his skin, she was immediately overcome with a sense of wrongness. Something sticky, tar-like, only it wasn't physical; it was as though Tarkhun's ki were coated in some sort of oily substance. The burnt-metal stink was even stronger now, and Yuli felt infected by it.

But it was the shrinking of his essence that was the most troubling.

Like water leaking from a hole in a jar, she could feel the bookseller's ki getting smaller and smaller, dwindling, disappearing, dissipating. She didn't know how to hold on to it, how to grasp it with her own spirit to keep it from vanishing between her fingers.

"His breath," Ami said. "His ki—"

Without thinking, Yuli reached out to touch the breath he exhaled. At once her mind was overwhelmed by a rush of images, scattered scenes from memories and experiences and emotions, and she cried out, falling to the ground.

"Yuli!" Zhara cried.

She had touched a spirit not her own with her physical body. It had been entirely unlike the ghosts she had sent on from the Hills of the Dead. There were no boundaries, no discreteness, no sense of identity, of self—it was all an ocean of spirit and she was afraid of drowning. There was a constant screaming in her mind in a voice that was not hers, and she thought she might go mad with it.

"Yuli!" Ami knelt beside her, shaking her urgently. "It's the waking dreamer sickness!"

She froze, paralyzed with sudden fear. The wind rose

up all around them, a tuneless melody that whistled and shrieked within the mind. "What do we do?" she rasped.

"Help me," Zhara said, wrapping one of Tarkhun's arms around her shoulder. "We need to get him back to the bookshop. We'll figure it out from there."

Yuli was bigger and stronger than the other girls, so she crouched on the ground and offered her back. "Get him up here," she ordered. "I'll carry him."

Zhara and Ami hoisted the bookseller onto Yuli's back. The skin of his bare cheek brushed the nape of her neck as his head flopped forward and she flinched. Although he was no longer filled with himself, the emptiness within Tarkhun had weight. He suddenly felt heavy in her arms and she nearly staggered beneath him.

Tarkhun gasped.

On Yuli's back, he jerked and twitched, causing her to drop him back on the ground. The bookseller spasmed, his limbs curling and uncurling disjointedly. His fingers grasped at Yuli's leg and even through the layers of clothing between them, she could feel a howling darkness lurking within him.

*Guardian of Wind, there you are . . .*

"Demon!" Ami cried out, her spectacles flashing in the moonlight.

Yuli kicked out with her foot, catching Tarkhun beneath the chin. He went flying, but caught himself in midair, his body twisting like a cat's to land on all fours. There was a burst of brightness as Zhara went up in flames, transforming into her Guardian form. Beside her, Ami's form rippled as she also claimed her Guardian powers—her skin aglow with a green-gold light, her hair a sudden rich auburn threaded with flowers. A wave of lightheadedness passed over Yuli as her physical eyes tried to reconcile what she was seeing with the truth of who her friends were: the Guardian of Fire and the

Guardian of Wood. They appeared now in the flesh the way they had always appeared to Yuli when she saw them in her spirit form—as beings of pure elemental power.

Tarkhun hissed when he saw them appear, turning to run down the street.

"No you don't!" Ami thrust out her arm and clenched her hand into a fist, dragging the bookseller back toward her as though he weighed no more than a feather. But Tarkhun twisted out of her magical grasp, breaking the Guardian of Wood's control without a thought. A dark corona of black wreathed the bookseller, an inverse glow like the glow of a magician's power.

Anti-ki.

"I can't hold on!" Ami reached out again, but the demon within Tarkhun evaded her magical grasp, countering with a blast of its own power. Darkness swirled and the Guardian of Wood crumpled, falling to the ground. Zhara ran up behind the waking dreamer and grabbed his arm with her burning hands, blocking another burst of power, transmuting the anti-ki into a shower of flower petals.

"Turn him back!" Ami shouted.

"I can't!" Zhara said in a panic. "He's still human!"

Yuli cast about for something to do, feeling spectacularly useless in the fight. Her grasp of her own Guardian powers was limited to what she could do to her own ki, not to anyone else. With a roar, Yuli leaped onto Tarkhun's back; if she could not do anything with her gifts, then at least she could be another obstacle for the demon to fight.

An agonized howling filled her mind, as the abyss within the bookseller raged at her touch. The shock of the maelstrom of absence within him shook Yuli to the soul, and for the briefest moment, she felt as though her spirit had been knocked from her body, that all-too-familiar rush of freedom enveloping her ethereal senses.

Her eyes—her ki—saw the waking dreamer for what it truly was: darkness made corporeal. Without stopping to think of what she was doing, Yuli pressed her palm onto the demon's chest, but pushed part of her spirit into the body—the vessel—itself, piercing the abyss with her own white-gold glow. Tarkhun shrieked as the demon within writhed in pain, wrenching himself free of her touch.

Yuli gasped and fell backward.

"Yuli!" Zhara's eyes, glowing with the light of her power, were wide with something like awe.

She stared at her palms in shock. A ghostly pair of hands, wreathed in a white-gold light, traced her physical fingers like a shadow, only bright instead of dark. She had somehow managed to partially disembody herself without fully untethering her soul from her body. She felt strange, half exposed, half protected, experiencing both the ethereal and physical worlds at the same time. It was like the feel of an arctic breeze through sweat-soaked clothes, welcome and dangerous all at once.

"Yuli." Ami reached a hand out to her. "Your Guardian form . . . it's . . ."

In the reflection of the girl's glasses, Yuli could see herself, her spirit swirling around her like a tempest, blurring her shape.

Her Guardian form. Until this moment, she had not known how to hold her two selves together—her body and her spirit. She had always thought her Guardian form was simply her ghost untethered from her physical vessel, but she knew now that wasn't true. She was both physical and ethereal at once.

"Zhara!" Ami's warning cry came too late as another waking dreamer attacked the Guardian of Fire from behind, leaping atop the girl to wrap their fingers about her neck.

All around them, shadows began moving and writhing

as the people collapsed on the street got to their feet. They hadn't been drunk; they had been emptied of their ki.

Only now they were filled again with demons.

Zhara struggled with the waking dreamer on her back. Too far for Yuli to grab, so she reached out with part of her spirit once more. An arrow of white-gold light flew straight into the demon's back, and they seized, their nerveless fingers sliding from Zhara's neck as they collapsed to the ground.

"Look out!" Ami shouted at her.

Whirling around, Yuli fashioned a bow and arrow from her spirit and fired into the darkness rushing toward her. The ganshi fell, the demon within dissipating, leaving the body an empty husk. In quick succession, she fired more spirit arrows into their attackers, and one by one, they tumbled to the ground, waking dreamers once more.

All except one.

Tarkhun.

"Well," the bookseller said, and his voice was simultaneously deep and shrill, as though two voices spoke at once at different pitches. "If it isn't the legendary Guardians of Dawn."

*Guardian of Wind, there you are.*

Yuli immediately conjured another arrow aimed straight at the bookseller's face.

"Wait!" Ami cried, holding out her hand. "Before you banish the demon, let's ask them a few questions."

Yuli loosened the draw on her bow, lowering the point of the spirit arrow to the ground. "Go ahead."

"What is your purpose in being here?" Ami asked.

Tarkhun laughed. "What we've always wanted," they said. "Chaos. To pave the way for our Mother to return."

"Why the bodies of anti-magicians?" Ami pressed, looking at the fallen figures all around them. "The waking dreamers?"

"Ah." Tarkhun smiled. "That is the genius of our master, the Moth Demon. It turns out that your so-called anti-magicians are uniquely suited to hosting me and my brethren due to their connection to the void."

"But they can't use magic, nor be affected by it," said Zhara.

"*They* can't," the demon said. "But *we* can. Anywhere there is anti-ki, so we can be."

"Who is the Moth Demon?" Yuli demanded.

Tarkhun met her gaze. "That I will not tell you."

Yuli lifted her bow again. "Then say farewell to this realm."

"No!" The bookseller fell to his knees. "Have I not been a good little demon, Guardian of Wind? Spare me and I shall be your pet. I shall do your bidding. I shall help you win the Trial of Wits!"

"Don't," Ami murmured under her breath. "Deals with demons always end badly. It's how we ended up with cursed objects."

"One last chance," Yuli said, pulling the arrow back. "Tell me who the Moth Demon is and I might consider sparing you."

Zhara sucked in a sharp breath. "Yuli—"

Tarkhun hesitated, his mouth falling open as Yuli released her arrow. It struck him straight in the chest and dissipated throughout his body. The demon gave a scream of shock and rage, the shrillness of their voice scraping at Yuli's ears, before he crumpled and fell to the ground.

The bookseller lay still in the middle of the street.

"They weren't going to tell me anyway," Yuli said quietly, vanishing the bow and pulling her power back beneath her skin.

"What did they mean," Ami murmured, "when they said, *Anywhere there is anti-ki, so we can be?*"

"Just another mystery to solve once we find more of *Songs of Order and Chaos*." An immeasurable exhaustion overcame Yuli in that moment, and she wanted nothing more than to lie down with the other waking dreamers in the street.

"We can't meet with the Paper Wolf tonight," Zhara said grimly. "We have to help these poor souls."

She meant the fallen bodies, but Yuli in her Guardian form could see the disembodied ghosts of the living hovering all around them. Now that the demons had been banished, the mist was coalescing into discrete figures. She watched as heads, then arms, then torsos, then legs, then finally features materialized out of the fog. The ghosts surrounded them with expressions of fear and panic, their mouths opening and closing with silent pleas for help. "How?" she asked.

Ami considered the unconscious waking dreamers. "I can move their bodies," she said. "But their souls . . . their spirits, the essence of what makes them who they are, are gone. Without them, they're just . . . empty."

"What do we do?" Yuli whispered.

"You are the Guardian of Wind," Ami said. "Can you . . . guide their spirits back to their vessels?"

Yuli looked down at her hands, then at the nearest ghost. A youth, not much older than her. A student at the university, perhaps, out on the streets for a night of revelry after the Trial of Strength before running afoul of . . . whatever had happened. She held out her hand to the spirit, who trepidatiously took it in their own. Although she felt nothing but air in her palm, her soul wrapped itself around the ghost.

Images flooded her mind. The library at the university. Another student their age laughing. Kisses stolen between the stacks. A parent's disapproval. Yuli stared into the ghost's eyes, memorizing their features and looking for their echo among the waking dreamers at her feet. "Do you know where you are?" she asked softly.

The ghost nodded and drifted toward one of the bodies.

The ghost who had taken her hand stood before the figure of a young person wearing the long-eared hat of a university student. Yuli tried to guide the ghost into their body, but no matter how hard they both tried, the spirit simply passed through flesh without sinking in.

"Yuli," Ami said quietly, "instead of forcing it, why don't you simply . . . be the conduit?"

"Conduit?"

"Bridge," Ami said. "Maybe . . . allow the spirit to pass through you into the vessel."

She supposed it couldn't hurt. Yuli took the student's physical hand in hers, concentrating on the emptiness within the body and imagining the ghost in her other hand flowing through her back to its home.

The spirit merged with her, and for a moment, it was as though she were porous—no longer skin and muscle and bones but paper. She was the student and the student was her, and Yuli felt herself panicking at the loss of boundaries between herself and another person. But the sensation was brief, and within moments, the ghost was reunited with themself.

The student gasped and sat up.

"Thank you," they croaked. "Thank you, thank you, thank you, Your Highness."

In that moment, she was overcome with a spasm of fear about the student knowing her true identity, that the Gommun princess was the Guardian of Wind and a magician.

"I will pray to the ancestors that you win the Grand Game," the student continued. "You are the leader we need in this time of crisis."

Yuli blinked in surprise. "Thank you," she said quietly. "For your support."

The student gripped her hand tightly in their own. "You must win," they repeated. "For all of us."

One by one, Yuli returned the other ghosts to their bodies, and each time, that feeling of *being* someone else unsettled her. Although she tried not to, she fought against the intrusion, struggling to hold on to her sense of self. At last, almost every single ghost was returned to their original vessel.

She turned to Tarkhun. "Here," she said, holding out her hand to the pale shade of the bookseller. "Time to go home."

"There's one more ghost," Zhara said quietly, pointing to a lone figure drifting in the street ahead of them.

But there were no more bodies lying the street. Yuli squinted before she recognized her cousin's red hair in the flickering of the torches around them.

"Jochi," Yuli said quietly.

Her cousin inclined his head in acknowledgment. She held her hand to his and he slid his against hers. Like the ghosts at the Hills of the Dead, he felt insubstantial, barely there.

"Where is your body?" she asked. "Where is home?"

Her cousin gave her a sad smile. *I am home.*

An epiphany was struggling to flutter to the surface of her mind, but Yuli forced it back down. "What do you need?" she asked. "Why are you here?"

His eyes were solemn as he held her gaze. *The Sleepers have awoken,* he said. *And soon they will attack.*

The Guardians of Dawn never came.

Kho had waited as long as she could at the Tower of Offerings, but the night had grown too cold and the hour too late for her to stay out. She had pretended to go out to join the revelry on the streets following the Trial of Strength but had headed straight for the rendezvous from Maltak Manor.

Her stomach rumbled. She had stolen some dumplings from the kitchen before she left but not enough to quell the constant gnawing hunger that seemed to claw at her bones. Kho was hungry all the time these days for reasons she could not quite understand, her body one constant, insatiable churn of *need* that nothing but food could fulfill. Her shape over the past few years had changed quite a bit; it was evident in the tightness of her gowns across the bust and hips, and in the way certain gazes around town lingered on her curves with an altogether different sort of hunger.

She hated it.

The image of Yuli during the Trial of Strength rose up in her mind. Yuli had always had an athletic grace about her—long-limbed, broad-shouldered, and narrow-hipped, almost boyish in her form and figure. Muscles rippled beneath her freckled skin when she moved in a way that reminded Kho of a snow leopard's prowl, all predatory poise and power. Unlike Kho, Yuli had never seemed to have an awkward period; she was as shapely now as she had been as a girl. Kho, on the other hand, had been sticks and bones for the longest time, gangly and gawky and never quite strong enough. She had always envied Yuli that unconscious elegance; it made her stomach roil in a way that had nothing to do with wanting food. It *was* want, but of a different kind. If Kho thought about it too hard, it made her anxious, so she tried not to think about it at all.

The majority of the household was still out drinking and dining in the streets when she came home from the Tower of Offerings, but to her surprise, there was light still on in her brother's quarters on the top floor. Ogodei had gone out with the Huntsmen, but it appeared that he, too, had returned home early. A prickle of apprehension crawled up her spine. There had been a change in her brother ever since she dragged him home that night she had found him unconscious at the Eagle's Nest. At first she had thought it had been a return of one of his darker moods, but after an initial bout of gloom, he had resumed his previous activities with the Huntsmen. Yet he wasn't fully back to his usual insouciant, reckless self; there had frequently been an unusual . . . impassivity to his interactions with his sister and his cadre that had gone unremarked by the others, but that Kho couldn't help but notice. A deadpan response to a joke. A slightly too long pause before laughter. Gibes that would have riled him and made him defensive before now seemed to glance off him without effect. Sometimes it was though her brother had been replaced by a stranger, his responses just ever so slightly askew.

And then there was the matter of the secret writings in the Language of Flowers she had discovered in his quarters.

All trace of the treasonous materials had disappeared; Kho had sneaked into his rooms more than once since she first found *Songs of Order and Chaos* on his bed but had been unable to recover any scrap of evidence of his dabbling in magic. The other hiding places in the stable loft, beneath a cornerstone in the kitchen, and in the family vault had similarly yielded nothing, leaving her to wonder if she had simply imagined it all.

*I don't know why magicians bother with all this writing. It would be so much simpler to manipulate the void directly.*

*Spells have their place.*

She had not imagined the night she had come across him and his mysterious companion in the stables. The night she had found him . . . casting a spell? She had not been able to confront Ogodei about that night—or anything else—since, and the pressure of keeping that secret had been growing like dread in her chest.

Could her brother do magic now? How? Or had he always been a magician?

And if he were a magician, what was she to do?

The ghost of Jochi rose up in her mind. She had been taught to act for the greater good, and since birth, she had been told that magicians were dangerous to the people of the empire. To act for the greater good was to do the right thing, even if it meant it was hard.

Betraying Jochi had been the hardest thing she had ever done in her life.

Except she was no longer sure it had been the right thing.

The guilt she felt over Jochi's death had only increased with time. She had known of the consequences of telling Ogodei about her suspicions, but what she had not anticipated was her brother telling their father about their friend's treason without her. She had wanted to talk things through with her brother, to ask him what they should do, to alleviate her turmoil and doubt, but Ogodei had wanted the Falconer's approval. It had been the first time she had gone to someone other than Yuli with her troubles, and she wasn't sure which betrayal the princess had felt more keenly.

She was in the wrong and had been trying to make up for it ever since. Jochi's sentencing was the first time she understood that magicians weren't a faceless horde of enemies but whole human beings with entire lives and loves. Jochi hadn't been an enemy; he had been a friend. Although he had received a stay of execution, his exile had been tantamount to a death sentence, and the horror of being directly accountable for someone's death had never left Kho. Her work as the Paper Wolf had been her way of making reparations; she could never make up for the loss of one life, but she could do her part to save the lives of others, in whatever small way she could.

It was her way of threading the needle between doing the right thing and acting for greater good.

Kho wondered if her brother was also suffering the same moral crisis.

She quietly climbed the stairs to the third-floor landing beneath Ogodei's quarters. The trapdoor was closed as it ever was, but there was a time when it had always been open to her. She reached up to knock and announce her presence when she was stopped by the sounds of a conversation filtering through the floorboards.

"—should happen if she loses the Trial of Wits?"

It was the same grating voice she had heard speaking to her brother in the stables the previous week.

"She's clever," Ogodei said. "Cleverer than the princess, at any rate. It is the Trial of the Soul we should be concerned about."

"I have a plan for the Trial of the Soul," his companion said. "But I feel uneasy at leaving the Trial of Wits to chance."

"You always have plans within plans. You must know what we would do if we should lose the Golden Horde."

A pause. "The Baron Flotilla," the grating voice said.

"I thought the Fleet Queen had already promised her allegiance."

"That was contingent upon killing the girl."

Kho brought a hand to her mouth to stifle her gasp of horror. Whomever her brother was conversing with was speaking of murder.

Ogodei was silent. "You're sending me to the Azure Isles," he said after a long moment.

"Yes," his companion said simply. "Are you or are you not a Huntsman?"

Another pause. "What is the proof of death the Fleet Queen requires?" Ogodei asked.

"Her heart. A curiously barbaric practice for a human, but I am not one to judge."

All the hairs stood on the back of Kho's neck. Whatever Ogodei was talking to, it was not human. She thought of the stories Yuli's auncle Mongke used to tell them of fairies and demons, ganshi and ghosts, and of the hapless fools who made bargains with creatures of the otherworld for beauty, riches, or power. She had believed supernatural creatures were nothing more than myth, but with the return of monsters and revenants to the Morning Realms, she was no longer certain.

"When do I leave?" Ogodei asked his companion. "The

waters are not safe to travel until the spring thaw, and that is months away."

"We can wait," the fairy? demon? ganshi? ghost? entity? replied. "We'll see about the outcome of the Grand Game first. Whether we win or lose changes nothing but the timing of your task."

Another long pause. "Understood," Ogodei said at last. "Good."

A long silence followed thereafter, and the entity did not speak again. There was a rustling sound, as though someone were gathering papers together, and then footsteps headed toward the trapdoor.

Light flooded the third-floor landing as the door fell open with a *bang!*

"Mimi!" Ogodei said in surprise. "I thought you had gone out with the others."

"I—I got tired," Kho stammered. She squinted against the brightness, trying to make out her brother's shape against the light. He carried a leather folio in his arms, and to her astonishment, their mother's black stone amulet dangled from his wrist. She tried to look into his quarters for his companion, but she couldn't see anyone.

He narrowed his eyes. "What are you doing here?"

"I—I saw the light in your rooms and thought you might also be awake."

He peered at her. "So you wandered up here for a bit of a chat?"

Kho nodded. "Your door used to always be open to me, gogo."

Again, that strange impassivity crossed his face, flattening his expression into one she could not read. But a moment later he broke into a smile. "Well, I'm feeling a bit peckish, so I'm going down to the kitchens to see what I can scrounge up. Care to join me?"

Kho shook her head, even as her stomach pinched

with hunger. "I just wanted to wish you a good night."

Blankness settled over his face. "Oh," he said after a moment. "Well, good night, mimi."

"Good night, gogo."

Ogodei disappeared down the stairs. Kho waited for a long while on the landing, wondering if the entity would make an appearance. But as moments passed and no one descended the ladder, she decided to take a look around her brother's quarters for herself.

"Hullo?" she asked as she climbed into his rooms. "Is anyone there?"

Nothing but her echo replied.

# 20

Yuli hadn't known what to expect from the Trial of Wits, but what she certainly hadn't expected was a public spectacle.

The Trial of Strength and the Trial of the Soul were physical challenges and would necessarily draw a large audience, which was why those events were held at the Tower of Offerings. But the Trial of Wits was a mental challenge, so she had assumed it would be something like an exam administered to her by a tutor, sequestered somewhere away in a room at the university. Instead, there was a makeshift stage built by the Council of Shamans in the town square where penny philosophers and petty prophets often preached to whoever would listen. It was the largest open space in the city of Urghud itself, where the greatest number of people could gather and observe whatever performance or pronouncements were to be made.

The fact that a crowd was going to be party to Yuli's humiliation made her want to disappear.

She knew she was going to lose the Trial of Wits, and she hated it. She took things rather personally whenever she didn't win. Yuli had been that way ever since she was a child—not one of her most attractive traits, she knew—but she couldn't help it. Many things came naturally and easily to Yuli, so she had grown accustomed to being the best at whatever she tried her hand at. On the playing field, at least. Running, racing, archery, fencing, sparring—she picked up new skills.

Academics, on the other hand, were a different story.

She had never been an especially gifted student. Uncle Bayar used to despair of her lackadaisical attitude toward her education, but the truth was Yuli simply could not bring herself to feign interest in her studies. Her auncle Mongke had tried to tutor her as best they could, engaging her interest in history and philosophy through stories and other tricks, but if subjects didn't come easy, then she didn't find them worth the effort. The truth was Yuli hated trying—she hated the tedium, the labor, and the inevitable feeling of failure that followed when she didn't succeed straightaway.

If there was one thing she hated more than losing, it was being made a fool.

*You never take anything seriously.*

Kho took everything seriously, which was why Yuli supposed the other girl was such a good student. She had admired that about her best friend once—not Kho's academic performance, but her unflinching and unfailing sense of honor in all things. The Gommun watchword was *honor,* and while Yuli never quite lived up to her uncle's expectations of it, she had always adhered to their principles in her own way. To her, honor was obligation—not the superficial or shallow promises people made to one another but a deep and abiding connection to which she was faithful. Kho had always taken their friendship seriously, so Yuli had always assumed she would honor it.

How wrong she had been. In the end, Maltak *loyalty* had won over Gommun *honor*.

As with all the other events of the Grand Game, the Trial of Wits was to begin at high noon. Before the start of the Trial, she and Kho had been given quarters in the university itself to prepare, although what they were supposed to prepare for, she had no idea. Auncle Mongke had suggested meditating, but Yuli hated sitting in stillness almost as much as she hated losing. She hated boredom and tried her hardest to avoid it whenever possible. If she had thought about it properly, she would have brought the next volume of *The Maiden Who Was Loved by Death* in order to pass the time while the Council of Shamans finished setting up the stage outside. Auncle Mongke, being on the Council of Shamans and one of the judges, had not been allowed to stay with her. A part of Yuli was tempted to find Temur, to see if she could use the Eagle of the North's eyes to spy on the proceedings, but she didn't think her celestial companion would appreciate Yuli taking advantage of their connection for less than honorable reasons.

Presently, the jingle of bells outside her room announced the presence of a shamanic acolyte who had come to escort her to the Trial. Yuli followed them across the university courtyard, through the gates, and out into the square where spectators were gathered. Not nearly as many in the audience as there had been for the Trials of Strength, but far more than Yuli had anticipated. The acolyte indicated she wait behind the makeshift stage, and soon enough, she was joined by Kho, led by her own acolyte escort, to her left. Seated in the front row before the stage were the heads of the Five Golden Families.

The girls' gazes met. Kho's soft lips parted, then shut. "Good luck" was all she said.

Yuli frowned. "Are you making fun of me?"

Kho blinked. "I'm merely wishing my opponent good luck. I thought it was a sporting thing to do."

Once again, Yuli felt the wriggle of shame squirm in her stomach. Perhaps this was merely a tactic by Kho to unsettle her and make her perform worse, which was *not* a particularly sporting thing to do. But Yuli merely nodded, accepting Kho's best wishes and offered some of her own. "Good luck to you too."

On either side of the stage stood two shamans dressed in ceremonial black, red, and blue, each positioned behind a large drum that came up to their waist. Their hands, covered by long, trailing sleeves that fluttered to the ground, held wooden sticks poised above their heads, the strings of bells that hung from their hats jingling faintly in the wind. The sun was high overhead, another clear early winter's day in Urghud.

At a nod from the crier in the center, the two shamans began striking a rhythmic beat. Yuli felt the sound of it thump behind her ribs, slow and steady despite the racing of her heart.

"The Trial of Wits begins!" the crier shouted into the speaking trumpet. "Let the contestants approach the stage!"

At the acolytes' direction, Kho and Yuli walked forward, with Kho ascending the stage from the right, Yuli from the left. Once Yuli climbed to the platform, she saw that two low scholar's desks had been placed facing each other, with a large silk blanket between them. On the desks were laid sheets of paper, a dish of water, an inkstone, a well, and a brush. That must be the poetry part of the competition, Yuli reasoned. On the blanket was a curious set of objects—a candle, a bundle of grass, a prism, a mirror, a mask, a flute, and a sword. Riddles indeed, as she had no idea what on earth they were for.

"The two contestants shall acknowledge each other

before taking their seats before the Council of Shamans."

Yuli raised her right fist to thump her left shoulder. Kho mirrored the gesture, then both girls sat down at their scholar's desks. Their judges, a shaman from each of the Five Golden Families, sat on a large fur hide on the ground before the stage, clad in the pointed black hats with long tails that marked them as members of the Council. Yuli spied Auncle Mongke on the far right side, directly across from Kho. Their face was unreadable.

Another shaman ascended the platform, carrying a large scroll half the size of their body. On either side of the stage, the drumbeats stopped.

"The contestants shall listen to five riddles," the crier announced.

The shaman unrolled the scroll, the bottom of which fell to the platform at their feet. Written in a big, bold, and legible hand were the five riddles, laid out in a poem. The shaman cleared their throat and read aloud:

> *I am a knife that cuts the wind,*
> *    yet I bend to your every whim.*
> *I draw with no ink, I sing with no tune.*
> *All shapes and features I can boast,*
> *    no flesh, no bones, no blood, no ghost.*
> *I am lighter than a feather yet no one can hold*
> *    me for long, not even the very strong.*
> *I am not a bridge, yet I span the air,*
> *    my beauty is beyond compare.*

Yuli glanced at Kho, who was watching the shaman intently. Her dark, long-lashed eyes were bright, eager, and already Yuli could see her mind at work.

"You have heard the riddles," the crier said. "Now behold, you find the answers before you."

The shaman gestured to the blanket, then stepped

back. Yuli was mystified, and she instinctively looked to Auncle Mongke for some sort of hint. But the Gommun shaman's expression was schooled into careful blankness; she would find no help from them. She shouldn't have expected it; Auncle Mongke might have been the greatest and best keeper of her magic secrets, but they were also Gommun to the core—ruled by honor. Yuli sighed and turned to the blanket between her and Kho, wondering what the objects had to do with any of the riddles.

"The contestants will now write a poem based on the answers to the riddles," the crier continued.

Yuli stared blankly at the objects laid out before her, then looked to the scroll with the riddles written in a clear hand. There were five riddles, meaning there were five answers, but there were seven objects on the blanket. She felt stupid, slow, confused as to what was being asked of her. The fear of humiliation creeped up the back of her neck, her entire body flushed with embarrassment. This was not going to be a gracious defeat. Yuli picked up the brush on her desk, contemplating the dish of water and block of ink. Well, at least she knew how to make ink, even if she didn't know what to write with it. She decided she wasn't going to overthink the answers or the poem; if she was going to fail, then she wasn't going to give anything but the barest minimum of effort. She studied the scroll a while longer, then wrote down her answers—sword, flute, mask, grass, and candle.

Across the stage, Kho was writing swiftly, making notes to herself as her gaze flitted from blanket to desk, blanket to desk. Yuli tried to follow the path of her eyes, reminded of the times she had been tempted to cheat during exams. But Yuli, like Auncle Mongke, was Gommun through and through. She would rather fail honestly than win by deceit. That honor was what separated their kang from the Maltak. So she took her (most likely) incorrect answers and arranged them as best she could into a rudimentary poem.

> *Sword, the knife that cuts the wind*
> *A voiceless flute sings with no tune*
> *A mask becomes all features*
> *While the grass floats lighter than a feather*
> *A beacon in the air,*
> > *the candle bridges night and day*

She finished ahead of Kho and set down her brush, trying her best not to feel silly. No one expected her to win the Trial of Wits anyway; it would all come down to the Trial of the Soul before the winter solstice. Yuli had more confidence in her ability to win the next Trial. It wouldn't be easy—even as little girls, Kho had been a competent rider, but Yuli had always been just that little bit better, winning three races out of five.

"Have the contestants finished writing their poems?" the crier asked after Kho had finally set down her brush.

They both nodded.

"Then would the Gommun stand up and recite their work for the judges?"

Awkwardly, Yuli shuffled to her feet. Holding her sheet of paper before her, she recited her poem for the Council of Shamans in a voice that did not carry, unable to bear looking at any of them. The poem was terrible, and the answers were wrong, but the judges said nothing, merely nodding their heads in acknowledgment once she had finished.

"Would the Maltak stand up and recite their work for the judges?"

Yuli wished she had simply been dismissed after her own dismal work. She never liked to linger long when she knew she had failed; it was why she often finished her exams so early as a child—there was no point in dwelling and overthinking. She had either gotten the answers right, or she had gotten them wrong. No amount of stewing was going to change that.

Kho elegantly rose to stand in one smooth motion. Holding her poem out before her, she began to recite in a gentle voice:

> *Green, the fleet-footed Nuwage horse*
> *that tramples the blades of grass*
> *Red, the blood of the Gommun bear,*
> *the sword of the north*
> *Yellow, the eyes of the Maltak wolf,*
> *mirrored by the sun*
> *Blue, the eagle of the Tzorig,*
> *and white, the spear of the Shulgin*
> *Flies through the eternal blue skies*
> *on the breath of wind*
> *Colors all, one heart,*
> *a rainbow born of a prism*

Although she already knew the outcome of this Trial, Yuli's heart fell when she heard Kho's poem read aloud. She looked to the riddles written on the scroll, then at the objects on the blanket. Grass, sword, mirror, breath— likely represented by either the candle or the flute, and rainbow—the prism. Of course. When arranged in such an order, Yuli felt like an even bigger fool than before. Already the Council of Shamans was humming their approval and murmuring among themselves. She felt pinned by the knowledge of her loss, wishing she could just slink away and not face the outcome. More than anything, she loathed the ceremony of this whole affair, the public nature of it, but the shame of walking away now would be greater than the pity and scorn on the audience's faces.

"And now the judges will take the time to deliberate." One by one, the Council of Shamans rose to their feet and shuffled to the side, but the result was clear: Kho would win.

"Congratulations," Yuli murmured to the girl sitting across from her.

"I haven't won yet," said Kho.

Yuli scoffed. "Don't lie. Your poem was clearly superior to mine. Your answers were correct, for one thing."

Kho inclined her head in acknowledgment. "Thank you," she said quietly.

Yuli didn't know whether she hated it more that Kho didn't gloat. If her opponent had been smug in her victory, then Yuli could have borne the coming shame with spite. But this graciousness only amplified her defeat and made her discomfort that much worse.

"The Council has made their decision," said the Shulgin shaman.

Yuli held her breath.

"We declare the Maltak the winner of the Trial of Wits."

Applause burst forth from the audience, and Yuli consoled herself with the thought that the sound of cheers for her Trial of Strength win was infinitely better than the polite clapping of hands. Kho clapped her right fist to her left shoulder as she accepted her win, while someone began chanting *Maltak! Maltak! Maltak!* Ogodei.

Kho met Yuli's gaze. To her surprise, there was no triumph in the other girl's long-lashed eyes. Instead, there was something akin to worry as Kho slid her glance to her brother sitting beside the Lady of Wild Things in the front row.

"Yuli," she began, then paused. She bit her lip. "Good luck at the Trial of the Soul," she finished.

Yuli was taken aback. For some reason, she had thought Kho would say something else.

"You too," she said softly. "You too."

# 21

*I have a plan for the Trial of the Soul.*

Kho couldn't get those words out of her mind throughout the entire Trial of Wits, and she had been afraid she would lose the contest due to the distraction. The conversation she had heard between Ogodei and the mysterious entity echoed around and around in her thoughts in the days leading up to the Trial, and she almost begged her mother to call off the entire Grand Game. There was something bigger than politics at work in the steppes, something beyond the mortal ken. She thought she understood better now the Warlord's fears about magic and magicians; it was not the power they held but the uncanniness they carried with them that was so terrifying.

But on the morning of the Trial, the Lady of Wild Things had raised a toast to her daughter before the entire kang.

"May the First Daughter carry with her the blessings of the ancestors as we head into this next Trial," she said, the black stone amulet back around her neck. "And may she win in the name of the greater good."

The greater good. Kho felt the suffocating weight of her position as heir settle over her throat, choking back the words she had wanted to say.

*I no longer know what the greater good is, Mother.*

Kho had asked once what would happen if she lost the Grand Game, if they lost the support of the Golden Horde in her mother's bid for the Sunburst Throne. The Lady of Wild Things had spoken of the Azurean navy, and of a favor to be owed. Back then, she had believed the right thing to do was to compete in the Grand Game, to abide by her loyalty to the kang. But the mysterious entity in Ogodei's rooms had also spoken of the Baron Flotilla and of her brother traveling to the Azure Isles in the spring, and now she was no longer certain of what the right thing was. There was the civil war, as well as the potential murder of a girl across the Strait and the existence of supernatural forces in the world, and Kho didn't know what to do. She was lost and confused and wanted nothing more than to turn to someone to pour out her thoughts, her worries, her fears.

She had no one.

Kho had never given much thought to her loneliness, but she felt her isolation as an even bigger burden than her position as First Daughter. At the Trial of Wits, she had thought of saying something to Yuli, of warning the princess of some sabotage to come, but Kho didn't know where to start. She didn't even know how to untangle the knots of worry from her own mind, and she felt strangled by her thoughts.

So she had grasped for the only thing that made sense: going through with the Trial of Wits as planned. Perhaps winning would clarify her path.

It had not.

Afterward, she had declined to join the Huntsmen in celebrating her victory with them down at the Eagle's Nest, although she regretted it a little when she found herself alone in the manor with nothing but her anxiety to keep her company. She wished she could be more like her brother or her former best friend, able to shuck off concerns like unwanted layers of clothing. The only way Kho had ever been able to escape her dread had been to bury herself in work, just as she had at the Trial of Wits, and again at the university archives.

The archives.

She thought of the underground organization with whom she had been exchanging messages in the past weeks. For two years she had been passing them whatever she could find on magic and its history, and if there was anyone who could possibly help her smooth out her dilemma about Ogodei, the entity, her mother, and Yuli, she thought it might be them. She laughed at her own desperation; she was so lonely she was reaching out to a complete stranger for help.

But a complete stranger was better than no one.

A measure of calm overcame her now that she had direction. Purpose. Kho got up from her bed and began gathering her sneaking-around clothes: a pair of her brother's old leather leggings and a drab brown jacket, as well as a carved wooden mask of a wolf's head. She knew the bookseller down at the end of the Street of the Spear was part of the organization; she would make her way there in the hopes that they would be able to help her.

But how would they know to trust her? She imagined turning up at the bookshop claiming to be the Paper Wolf with nothing to show for it. A secret organization of magician sympathizers was certain to be wary of anyone appearing and proclaiming knowledge of magic without some proof.

*Songs of Order and Chaos.*

She needed to find it. The Paper Wolf had been promising the text for weeks, and if she showed up with the folio in her hands, surely that would be proof of her pure intentions. She had last seen the folio in her brother's possession the night she overheard him talking to that entity in the stables, so she knew she hadn't imagined it.

There was one hiding place of Ogodei's she hadn't yet thought to check.

If there was one place in the Maltak Manor that her brother was loathe to enter, it was the library. And what better place to hide a book than among other books? Years ago, she had stumbled upon Ogodei's stash of illustrated stories of *The Adventures of the Pirate Baron* behind their family's genealogy accounts; what more perfect place to store a forbidden book than behind dull records no one had touched in generations?

Her hunch was proven correct.

She found the leather folio stamped with the *taikhut* where she thought it would be, along with several volumes of Huang Jiyi's more salacious poetry. She replaced those with a shudder, wishing she had not seen them. Stuffing *Songs of Order and Chaos* into her rucksack, she slipped her wolf mask over her face and stole out the back gate of Maltak Manor.

Outside, the streets were surprisingly quiet, empty of revelers save for the already drunk sleeping on the ground. There was an odd mist that wreathed everything despite the cold, and Kho's skin broke out into gooseflesh. There was a faint singing—celebrants, she assumed—their voices carrying from the taverns and other eateries down in the central business district. The wind whistled, a high, keening sound that practically had a voice of its own, and it made her shiver, thinking of that invisible entity in her brother's rooms.

Ahead, a lone figure walked among the slumped-over bodies, and with a start, Kho realized that the singing was coming from them. Drunk? The fact that they were wandering the streets alone was unusual; normally revelers traveled in groups, but the stranger did not seem inebriated or otherwise indisposed. In fact, their walk was slow, deliberate, focused, light, and almost preternaturally smooth.

"Hullo?" Kho called out. "Are you all right, friend?"

The figure did not stop, although the singing grew louder. Kho did not recognize the melody or the language; the words were odd, and the tone even odder—dissonant and doubled, as though two voices were singing at once.

The bodies slumped on the ground twitched.

"Are you all right?" Kho knelt beside the nearest figure, gently turning them over. No smell of alcohol or sick. Their eyes were glazed, staring half open into nothing, and if it weren't for the gentle rise and fall of their chest, Kho would have thought them dead. "Friend?"

No response.

Kho looked down the street at the other bodies. Running to the next, she placed her hand on their shoulder, trying to shake them awake. "Hullo?"

Again, no response. Their head lolled back, boneless and limp. Like the other person on the ground, their eyes were half open and heavy lidded, their breaths slow and shallow. A cold, pricking sensation crawled down Kho's arms, her body telling her something before her mind caught up. She had seen this stillness before, down by the harbor in the refugee settlement.

This person was afflicted with the waking dreamer sickness.

"Hoi!" she called after the singing figure in the street. "Hoi! Go get help! These people are sick!"

The figure paused in their singing. "Are they?"

Something about the quality of their voice scratched at Kho's ears, and there was a thick, clotted sound to their words that made her want to clear her throat.

"We have to get them inside before they freeze to death out here!"

A cracked cackle of a laugh from the figure. "Hot or cold, it matters not to these poor souls. Not anymore." They lifted a hand, running it through the wreathing mist. The high-pitched keening intensified, and Kho clapped her hands over her ears, but the sound was somehow not in her body; it was in her very spirit.

"Please," Kho said through gritted teeth. "They'll die."

"Death?" The figure kept their back to her, and she could not see their face, although she thought she recognized their voice somehow. "No, not death. But in a very real sense, neither are they alive anymore. Empty vessels, waiting for chaos to fill them."

Kho frowned. "Who are you?"

The figure paused as the clouds parted overhead, revealing a nearly full moon. The stranger turned around slowly, their features coming into view piece by piece. Kho sucked in a sharp breath.

"Gogo?"

Her eyes must be playing tricks on her. Surely Ogodei was down at the Eagle's Nest with Tuyaa and the rest of his cadre. But the moonlight did not lie, and as the pale beams brought the stranger's face out of shadow, the face of her brother was revealed to Kho.

"Gogo, what are you doing here?"

Again that infinitesimal pause, that hesitation before he spoke. "Mimi?"

"Yes, it's me!" she said in frustration. "I asked you what you were doing out here."

"I could ask the same of you." He tilted his head to an uncanny angle. "You shouldn't be here."

There was a strange, dreamlike quality to the air. Kho surreptitiously pinched herself. The sharpness of the pain grounded her, kept her present in the moment. "Why not?" she returned. "I have just as much right to be celebrating my triumph as anyone else."

A slow smile spread across her brother's face. It hung off his jowls, as though it were only loosely affixed to his jaw. "Of course," he said. "But you shouldn't be *here*, mimi. The streets are filled with sleepers, and they will soon wake."

Ogodei opened his mouth, and once again the sound of singing filled the air. But no cloud of breath escaped his body, no sign that he was alive. All around them, the bodies on the ground jerked and seized in time with the beat, as though they were all having the same convulsive fit at once. Then, as one, the bodies rose from the ground as though drawn up by the invisible strings of some unseen puppetmaster. Alive. Awake.

"Ah," Ogodei said, and there was something like regret in his voice. "I wish you hadn't seen that."

"Gogo, what is wrong with you?"

He laughed and Kho resisted the urge to clap her hands over her ears. "With me? Nothing. With your brother? Everything."

At once Kho was struck by a powerful blow to the stomach, sending her flying against the low stone wall lining the street. But none of the people surrounding her had been close enough to land a strike, and none of them held any ranged weapons in their hands. Kho struggled to get to her feet when she felt another blow to her jaw, knocking her back down to the ground. She raised a hand to steady the wolf's-head mask on her face, but the carving had not moved, and she felt no lingering pain on her cheek where she thought she had been struck.

"Your death will be an unfortunate waste," Ogodei

said. "But I'm afraid there's nothing for it. My master has plans within plans, and should we lose the Golden Horde, we at least have other options to fall back on."

Another blow, once again to the stomach, and Kho curled up around the pain. But it wasn't a physical pain, or at least it felt nothing like the accidental hits she had taken when play-fighting with other children when she was a little girl. This pain was somehow within her flesh but not of it, running along the pathways of her body in a way that felt invasive and violating all at once.

Magic.

Kho gave a choked scream as her throat began to close, cutting off her breath. There was no invisible hand, no feeling of pressure about her neck, yet she couldn't draw breath, couldn't force her lungs and muscles to move, to function. Spots burst on the edges of her vision, as she struggled to keep conscious. Blackness hovered about her head as she thrashed and thrashed, trying to shout, trying to make noise, trying to bring precious air back into her body.

There was a sudden bright blaze of light before her. Kho blinked, trying to make sense of what she was seeing—three figures, human-shaped but not human. One seemingly made of fire, another shimmering with flowers in their hair, and yet another whose silhouette blurred and shifted like snowdrifts in the wind.

"Halt, demon!" came a ringing voice from the tallest figure. "I order you to halt!"

Then Kho knew no more.

# 22

A somber mood had fallen over Tarkhun's bookshop in the wake of Yuli's defeat at the Trial of Wits.

Silence reigned as Zhara and Ami worked at their own tasks, listening to the cheers and cries of the celebrants outside. Ami carefully transcribed her notes into her encyclopedia, highlighting passages about the Singing Skies and the Moth Demon, while Zhara, with Sajah dozing in her lap, sorted through the various messages passed to their safe house from the other cells of the Guardians of Dawn. Tarkhun, still recovering from his brush with the waking dreamer sickness, had retired early to his bed in the loft above the store. Ami had pestered him with questions for days after the attack about his experiences until Zhara finally told her to stop.

"People are not walking encyclopedias," she said gently. "And healing from trauma takes time."

Afterward, Ami had retreated into her work on the encyclopedia. Zhara had the sense that she had hurt the scrivener's feelings, but did not know how to apologize for it. Ami rebuffed all her helpful overtures, saying it was quicker and faster for her to organize her own notes on *Songs of Order and Chaos*. Feeling spectacularly useless, Zhara had decided to go through all the correspondence Tarkhun had received from the Guardians of Dawn for something to do. Perhaps she would find something useful to give to Ami as a peace offering.

Most messages were what Zhara had been expecting: tasks or requests to fulfill or pass on to other members of the mutual aid society. There were magicians in need of smuggling from their homes to safety, pleas for expertise or second opinions on a matter of spell craft, and even more mundane questions on more basic matters, such as weather conditions for farming and planting. Zhara had not known until she discovered the Guardians of Dawn just how deep and communal this well of magic went— that the study of magic was a living tapestry to which all those who practiced contributed threads of knowledge. More than texts, it was other people who kept the practice of magic alive. To her delight, she found another bamboo tube with her name on it that she thought might be a letter from Han, but it was one with the seal of the music academy in Jingxi that stopped her in her tracks.

Suzhan.

Zhara had not heard from her sister in months, and the tube looked worn and battered, as though passed from hand to hand to hand as it traveled all over the Morning Realms on her trail. Guilt settled over Zhara's shoulders like a shawl; she had not been any place long enough for her sister's words to reach her. There had been a time when they had been each other's best and only confidantes, back when they had no one else but each other. But in the time since she had learned she was the Guardian of Fire, Zhara had found friends—even family—outside those with whom she had been raised.

She sincerely hoped her sister had found the same at the academy.

Uncapping the message, she pulled out the rolled-up piece of paper inside and began to read.

*Dearest nene,*

*Thank you so much for your letter. It's good to hear your voice again, even if your words are read aloud to me by someone else. Your adventures make for good stories to share at bedtime, and the other students here loved reading your tale about the Beauty and the Beast aloud to one another. They say that you might almost be as good a writer as Jae Hyun, the author of The Girl Whose Lover Died and those other romance serials you love so much. Not that I can tell, but I wanted to make sure to pass along their compliments to you.*

Zhara smiled to herself. Suzhan had never been much for love stories. Sajah curled his paws around the bamboo tube and gnawed at the open end.

*Of my own life here at the Academy, there is much to do but little of which to write. My days are filled with practice, practice, practice, and while my tutor sings my praises daily (sometimes literally), they also despair of the years I spent languishing in bad habits. They are transcribing my letter to you now, so you know it must be the truth. Sometimes it's hard feeling so behind the other students in my year, but what I lack in experience, I make up for in hard work. Every year, the Academy puts on a showcase for all the noble patrons and courtiers from the various southern provinces, and for my diligence, I have been rewarded with a solo performance at the winter solstice festival. My friends tell me it is a great honor, and I am grateful for their confidence.*

Suzhan had always had a talent for the zither, a talent that Zhara had been unable to financially support while still living under the Second Wife's roof back in Zanhei. A profound sorrow and regret overcame Zhara at the life she and her sister ought to have had—loving and supportive instead of divisive and abusive—but a small glow of pride and satisfaction warmed her heart to know that Suzhan was thriving now.

> *I know that there is little you can say of the work you are doing now, and I will not ask. Nevertheless, I am grateful for the stories you do choose to tell me, for it assures me that you are still, well, you, nene. I once called you an incurable romantic, and you accused me of making it sound like a disease. But I am wiser now in the ways of art, and I know that romance is your music. So don't stop. Keep writing me stories. Tell me more of this Beauty and her mysterious Beast, but when you can, tell me of the little girl who slept among the ashes and cinders of her stepmother's hearth and of her prince in disguise. What of their fairy-tale ending, nene? I miss you. Write again when you can.*

Zhara folded up the missive and set it aside, feeling the tears well up along her lower lashes. What of the little cinder girl and her prince indeed? They were separated now, with demons, abominations, undead, waking dreamers, and an entire potential civil war between them. Beauty and her Beast were also divided, with the fate of the empire potentially lying entirely in the Beast's hands. They were both in the part of the romance novel where the lovers were apart, yearning for the other but being unable to touch. A few weeks ago, she had thought it romantic. But as the days went on, the yearning had grown painful, and she wasn't sure if she had the fortitude to withstand it. A tear dropped onto Sajah's golden fur, and the cat turned his face up to give her a disgusted look.

"Oh shush," she said quietly. "I know you miss Han too."

The cat sniffed, then began washing his whiskers.

"*Anywhere there is anti-ki, so we can be,*" Ami muttered.

Zhara lifted her head. "What was that?"

"Cursed objects," the scrivener continued, ignoring her. "It always comes down to cursed objects."

"*Qin bound the demon into a black stone, which he wore around his neck as he rode into battle.*" Ami set down her notes and looked at Zhara, blinking owlishly. Or not quite at Zhara, more like through her, as though she weren't even there. The scrivener sometimes got so lost in her thoughts that she acted as though the rest of the world did not exist. "A demon talisman," Ami said to no one in particular. Her eyes suddenly came into focus. "A demon talisman!"

"Yes?" Zhara asked carefully. "What about a demon talisman?"

In response, Ami dug into the neck of her tunic, pulling out a crystal necklace on a chain. "*Anywhere there is anti-ki, so we can be,*" she repeated excitedly, as though Zhara could understand. "Don't you see?"

Zhara blinked in confusion. "What's all this about?" She was grateful that the scrivener was speaking to her again at least, even if she couldn't make heads or tails of it.

"Hmm? Oh." Ami picked up her notes. "I was reading up on the Moth Demon again, and remember what I said about the Moth Demon not needing a body?"

Zhara didn't, but she didn't interrupt.

"I was wondering how that was possible, and then I remembered us talking about cursed objects after the Trial of Strength. What if the Moth Demon isn't a person but an *object*?"

Zhara sucked in a sharp breath. "Can that even be done?"

"Think of the Star of Radiance," Ami said. "For years it was contained in various vessels before Gaden came into possession of it. If one drop of will from every living person in the Morning Realms can be contained in a gem, then it stands to reason that a greater demon can possess one as well, providing the vessel had the right properties."

Zhara frowned. "I'm not sure I understand, but go on."

Ami lifted her crystal before her face. "Order and chaos exist in balance. These crystals from Mount Llangposa are made of magic but are neither dark nor light on their own. It is our power"—the stone brightened in the scrivener's hand—"that makes them glow, and the presence of demons that makes them go dim. They are magic made material, vessels primed for possession."

Understanding dawned on Zhara. "You think that maybe the Moth Demon, like the Star of Radiance, is contained in a gem."

"Or some other talisman," Ami said. "Something made of magic. Or chaos. They're one and the same, really." She returned the crystal to its usual place at her throat. "Magicians can manipulate the void with spells, while demons are beings made entirely of the void. What is magic but chaos governed by reason? That's what the demon possessing Tarkhun's body meant by *anywhere there is anti-ki, so can we be*. Ki is order. Anti-ki is chaos. Anywhere there is magic, so can they be."

"That doesn't narrow our search for the Moth Demon down at all," Zhara said ruefully.

"No, it doesn't," Ami said cheerfully. "But it did answer a question that had been bothering me for a while."

Outside, the wind had begun to rise, whistling through the minuscule cracks in the doorways and windows of the bookshop with the sound of a hollow flute. Zhara shuddered. The inside of the bookshop was warm enough, but she could feel the wind cut straight through her bones.

*Mrrrrow,* Sajah growled as his ears twitched, his fur standing on end.

"What is it?" It was a moment before Zhara noticed that the shouts of the revelers had died down and a heavy silence reigned.

No, not silence. The wind continued its eerie whistling, filling the night with a discordant song. Then came a sharp scream, cut short with a choke.

Ami rose to her feet. "What was that?"

Zhara rushed to the window and slid the shutters aside. A blast of flurries swirled inside, melting as soon as they came in contact with the heat. There were bodies scattered on the ground just below the window, covered in a light dusting of snow, but a lone figure walked slowly through the storm. The light in Ami's crystal flickered and grew dim, like a candle being buffeted by a breeze.

Demon.

Yuli was plagued by restless dreams.

She had never been an easy sleeper. As a child, she frequently suffered strange bouts of paralysis in the middle of the night, where her mind remained awake while her body refused to move. The first time it had happened to her, she thought she had died, that death was eternal helpless consciousness and that she was doomed to exist forever aware with no escape. She had lived in terror of falling asleep for weeks afterward, forcing herself to stay up until she involuntarily collapsed from exhaustion.

It turned out that it had been the first time she untethered her spirit.

She didn't know what was happening to her then. Yuli had already known she was a magician, and she feared her nighttime spells were precursors to her transforming into a monster. Auncle Mongke was the only person who knew her secret, but even with all their shaman knowledge, they had no idea how to help. It wasn't until she met Temur in a dream that she began to understand she was learning to spirit-walk. The Eagle of the North had come to her like a heavenly maiden from a fairy tale, gently filling her mind with images, showing her visions of her ki floating above her sleeping form and teaching her how to travel the spirit realm.

Temur came to her now.

In her dreams, Yuli was flying just below the clouds above the city of Urghud. A light snow was falling, gently coating the rooftops with a dusting of white. People flowed through the streets and alleyways, celebrating the first snowfall of winter with laughter and dancing, gathering up handfuls of it to bring inside to mix with sweetened milk for a treat. Things appeared not as they were in the physical world but as their essence when Yuli traveled the spirit realm in dreams. She did not see brick and stone and dirt; she saw form and shape. She did not see the rats and vermin in their lairs; she saw the pinpricks of life. And she did not see vague silhouettes and shadows of people she did not know; she saw their souls.

One soul stood out.

Jochi.

Unlike the others, Yuli could make out every detail of his ghost clearly through Temur's eyes. The deep red of his curly hair, the freckles scattered across his tan skin. When they were children, people had thought they were twins; their eyes, their hair, and their height mirrored each other. As though sensing the Eagle's gaze, Jochi lifted his head toward the skies, and Yuli felt a jolt in her physical body as his eyes met hers through the spirit realm.

*They are coming!* She could not hear his voice, but she understood his words. *Hurry!*

Pools of darkness began spreading around him, blooming across the snow like black bloodstains. The darkness hurt, burning her spirit vision like a too-bright light, leaving hazy afterimages like smoke.

*Jochi!* she screamed in her mind. *Jochi, run!*

She could feel a pull on her spirit, and Temur flapped her wings, struggling against the current that tried to drag her down. The Eagle cried out, and ribbons of light burst through the black on the ground. She soared back up again, pumping all four wings to take her higher, higher, and higher above the clouds.

*No!* Yuli thought. *Take us back! We need to help him!*

But Temur did not turn around. Instead she flew back toward Gommun Manor, toward where Yuli's sleeping body lay in bed.

Yuli woke with a gasp.

Throwing off her covers, she ran to her windows and slid the shutters open, letting in drifts of snow and ice. In the distance, she could spy a sinuous shadow slithering its way through the skies in her direction. She had to help. She had to get to Jochi and fight off the demonic menace blossoming in the streets. Rushing to her wardrobe, Yuli grabbed the first things that came to hand—a pair of thick woolen leggings, loose trousers, and a long, padded tunic. She didn't bother with a sash, shoving feet into socks and then her boots as Temur came winging up to her window. She clambered over the ledge and leaped onto the Eagle's back, threading her fingers through feathers as they sped off to where Yuli's cousin was besieged by demons.

The world looked different through her physical eyes, but she could sense the same dark pull on her spirit, pointing them toward a spot in the lower city, near Tarkhun's bookshop. The streets were dark, the light of the moon and stars obscured by storm clouds, and then suddenly—a burst of searing light. Yuli threw her arm over her face to shield against the brightness, but she could recognize that column of fire anywhere.

"There!" she pointed as Temur dove.

Dark forms crawled out of the shadows, surrounding Zhara and Ami with malicious glee. The girls were aglow in their Guardian forms—Zhara wreathed with flame and Ami a vision in flowers—but they struggled against the newly awakened waking dreamers, who deflected their attacks with a swirl of demonic magic. Beside them, the Lion of the South and the Unicorn of the West roared and reared, their sharp claws and hooves driving back the hordes.

Atop Temur's back, Yuli reached for her own Guardian form, freeing her spirit from its bounds but remaining centered in her body. She conjured a spirit bow and arrows, taking aim at the waking dreamer who wrapped tendrils of darkness around Ami's neck. She loosed her shot, and her aim was true, lodging straight in the middle of the waking dreamer's back. The arrow dissipated into their body, flooding their entire vessel with white-gold light. The demon within shrieked with pain as it shriveled to nothing, cast back to Tiyok from whence it came.

"Yuli!" Zhara cried as she and Temur landed on the ground. "So good of you to finally show up!"

"A girl needs her beauty sleep." Yuli leaped off the Eagle's back, another spirit arrow nocked to her bow. She loosed it at the nearest waking dreamer, who crumpled to the ground as their demon left their body. "Watch out!"

Zhara awkwardly deflected a flying shard of stone with her enchanted blade while Ami threw up a wall of earth. The wall rippled, then splashed to the ground, transformed into water by another waking dreamer. They clenched their fist as the water puddled around the girls' feet, freezing instantly. Zhara melted the ice with a wave of her hand, ducking as another stone whizzed past. There was a roar and a crackle of lightning, causing an explosion of rubble that came tumbling down on the demon-possessed bodies.

"Over there!" Ami gestured. "The leader is over there!"

The world warped and rippled, distorting Yuli's perception as waves of anti-ki washed over her. Before them, a figure made entirely of the abyss ran down in the middle of the street.

"Halt, demon!" she called toward the fleeing figure. "I order you to halt!"

The demon paused and turned. With her Guardian eyes, Yuli could make nothing of their features through the depthless void that infected their entire being; they were a shadow made real. This demon was nothing like the other waking dreamers, whose chaotic parasites were small and weak from being newly called into their hosts. This demon stood assured in their magic, comfortable in their human skin.

"So, Guardians of Dawn," they said, and their voice clawed at her insides, "we finally meet."

Yuli swiftly fired an arrow, but the demon easily cast it aside with a swirl of dark magic.

"How quaint," they sneered. "Little girls and their little toys. I had heard much about you, but you are merely children, scarcely grown into your powers."

"Who are you?" Yuli rasped. "Are you the Moth Demon?"

The demon laughed, stone scraping against stone. "I'm flattered you think so highly of my abilities, but I am merely my master's loyal servant, called into this vessel to pave the way for their ascension."

"Tell us who the Moth Demon is," Zhara demanded, brandishing her blade. "And we shall go easy on you."

"Easy on me?" The demon laughed again, and although they had no face, Yuli could have sworn she saw the glint of a sharp-toothed grin. "No, children, it is you who will wish I had gone easy on *you*."

The demon lifted their arms and the ground rumbled

and shook as a pair of hulking, monstrous forms rose up from the snow. Shards of ice ran in spines down their backs, tusks grown from stone, and two house-sized boars stood before them, their eyes black with oily malice.

"Chaos magic!" Ami gasped.

The beasts lowered their heads and charged, and the girls threw themselves out of the way, barely avoiding being trampled underfoot. The boars trailed wrongness in their wake, ribbons of emptiness that scored deep lines of destruction into the surrounding buildings. Yuli threw up a spirit shield, protecting herself and the others from the dark lashes of power. Recovering, the girls scrambled to their feet, bracing themselves as the creatures turned around for another run.

A liquid cry and Temur dove from the sky, dragging her claws across their backs, shattering their spines. The boars stumbled, surprised by this unexpected angle of attack. Sajah stood on his hind legs, his mane a corona of fire about his head, and grabbed the tusks of the nearest boar, wrestling its nose to the ground and leaving scorch marks on its frozen hide. Rinqi lowered her own head and charged at the other, driving the tip of her horn deep into its side. It roared and wrenched itself free, shaking off its pain and tossing the Unicorn aside.

"Rinqi!" Ami cried.

But there was no time to tend to her as the boar reared and stampeded in their direction. Ami clapped her hands to the ground, sending deep fissures through the earth. The creature stumbled, its legs caught in the cracks, but within a blink, its form blurred and melted before dissolving into a mass of rats. The rodents escaped the crevices in a river of writhing bodies and wriggling tails, flooding the street with squeaks and gnashing teeth. Zhara blasted them with fire, but there were too many, as more and more rats crawled over the smoking piles of charred fur and flesh, congealing and coalescing into a hideous monster that lurched and lumbered toward them.

"An abomination!" Yuli shouted. "Zhara, turn it back!"

"She can't!" Ami shouted back. "It's not a magician! It's pure chaos magic!"

Yuli unslung her bow and fired spirit arrow after spirit arrow into the monster. The demonic creature roared as her weapons left glowing craters in its flesh, which did not heal.

"Ki against anti-ki!" Ami gasped. "Yuli, your powers! Your weapons can counteract the chaos!"

Yuli rolled and dove out of the way as the monster raised a squirming arm and brought it down where she had just been standing. She nocked another spirit arrow to her bow and fired straight at the pooling, oily wells that she hoped were its eyes. Her aim was true and the creature shrieked in pain as she took out a chunk of its face. Howling with rage, the monster reared, swinging blindly, hobbled without its sight. It stumbled forward and tripped over a piece of rubble, shattering into a thousand rats once more.

Zhara pulled up a wall of fire, creating a temporary barrier between themselves and the chaos creatures, but the rodents pushed through the flames, the smell of roasted meat rising in the air. "Sajah!" she called out. "Drive them this way! Ami!" She turned to the Guardian of Wood. "Block off the other end of the street!"

At the other end of the street, the Lion grappled with the boar, throwing his massive body against the monster, sending it skidding toward Zhara as Ami raised piles of boulders behind it.

"Yuli," the Guardian of Fire said, "if we keep them contained, do you think you could find some way to destroy them?"

"I don't know." Yuli was exhausted, but the exhaustion was not in her bones; it was in her spirit. "We would need a big weapon of some sort, and I don't know if I have the strength to conjure that much power."

Zhara surveyed the scene before her. "A net," she said after a moment. "Do you think you can create a net to trap them in?"

Yuli hesitated. It was easy to conceive of her power as bolts to fire against an enemy, but a net was stretching the limits of her imagination. "Yes," she replied, although she was still not entirely sure.

"Hurry!" Zhara gritted out, and Yuli could feel the heat of the flaming wall intensify as the chaos creatures thudded and crashed against the fire.

Clambering up a wall onto the nearest rooftop, Yuli looked down at the proceedings. Zhara and Ami had managed to keep the monsters close together with their barriers, preventing them from breaking loose. Taking a deep breath, Yuli fitted another spirit arrow to her bow and aimed high above them, loosing the bolt with a breath. The arrow soared toward the creatures, and Yuli imagined it changing shape in flight, growing larger, wider, flatter, a blanket of white-gold settling over horrors. The monsters seethed and shrieked as anti-ki met ki with a hiss like melting water over ice. Gesturing with her hands, Yuli molded her blanket into a dome that contained the chaos creatures, trapping them inside a bubble of light.

"Now what?" she yelled, wincing as the monsters struck the dome. She could feel their attacks against her spirit shield, not as a physical pain but as a slow draining of will. It felt like the end of a race, when things became as much a mental challenge as a physical one. She flickered between determination and fatigue with each blow. How much longer would she be able to withstand the onslaught?

Zhara's eyes darted from Yuli to the creatures, brow furrowed in thought. Then she picked up a handful of snow and crushed it in her palm. Her gaze met Yuli's, and even without a mind-to-mind connection, she understood.

Yuli focused her attention back on the creatures struggling to escape the dome. She was greater than chaos. Stronger than it. Bringing her palms together, she began shrinking the dome, crushing the monsters inside as they screamed and thrashed. Smaller and smaller, until the dome was the size of a boulder, a rock, an egg. She grit her teeth, she was in the last stretch, she was so close, she had to dig deep. Smaller and smaller, the egg was now a pebble, pinprick, and then finally, with a release of pressure that popped her ears, the chaos creatures were gone.

She collapsed.

"Yuli!" Zhara ran to her side, warm hands propping her up. "You did it!"

She was thoughtless, blank. Yuli stared off into space before her, too tired to even blink. With a gentle flap of her wings, Temur landed on the street beside her, nudging her enormous feathery head beneath her arm. The Eagle laid her head on Yuli's stomach, looking up at her with sky-blue eyes, and Yuli felt a measure of peace come over her.

Ami came running up behind them. "The demon," she said grimly. "They're gone."

The street was empty, with only the scattered bodies of waking dreamers littering the ground. The walls and buildings around them had also been completely destroyed. The Unicorn of the West gently picked her way through the rubble, the light of her healing horn spreading its glow over the destruction. Cracks vanished, holes disappeared, as, little by little, Rinqi set the area to rights.

"Who were they?" Yuli asked. "The demon." She ached all over, but the pain was in her mind, not her flesh. She felt like a limp washrag, utterly wrung out.

"It doesn't matter." Zhara gently helped Yuli to her feet. "They're gone, and it's pointless to go searching now. Let's go back to the safe house and regroup."

"Zhara! Yuli!" Ami called. "Over here!"

The girls rushed over to where the Guardian of Wood knelt beside a crumpled body in a wolf mask. Ami held a leather folio in her hands, stamped with a strange symbol on the cover that Yuli had never seen before.

"*Songs of Order and Chaos*," Zhara breathed.

"I think they must be the Paper Wolf," Ami said, lightly touching the wolf mask. "They must have been trying to get it to us when they were caught in the middle of that demon attack."

"Are they alive?" Yuli asked.

The figure gave a soft moan.

"We need to get them back to Tarkhun's shop immediately," Zhara said.

Yuli looked around at the fallen bodies. "What of the other waking dreamers?" she asked.

Ami glanced at the mist that had begun to gather around them. "Their ghosts are returning," she said softly. "I don't think they're going anywhere."

"We can return them to their bodies later," Zhara said.

Yuli groaned. "And by *we*, you really mean *me*."

"Well, you're the Guardian of Wind."

"Come on," Ami said, trying to lift the Paper Wolf. "Help me get them inside."

With a sigh, Yuli bent down and scooped up the figure in her arms. The Paper Wolf's hand flopped to the side, and something slid from their wrist to land in the snow. Zhara picked it up.

"What is that?" Ami asked.

"A bracelet of some sort," she said. "Made of turquoise beads and white tassels."

Yuli went still. She knew that bracelet. She had worn its twin around her own wrist for years.

Kho was the Paper Wolf.

# 24

Kho awoke to the scratching of pencil against paper.

She was in some sort of cellar or dungeon, lying on a pallet of furs and straw. Her lungs ached and her head hurt, the pain worsening as she tried to recall where she was and how she had gotten there. The last thing she could recall was sneaking out of Maltak Manor with *Songs of Order and Chaos,* only to run into . . .

Kho sat up with a gasp, immediately feeling for the wolf mask on her face. Her cheeks were bare.

"Don't worry," came a voice from the middle of the room. A slim, short-haired figure in spectacles sat at a low writing desk, scribbling furiously at a pile of pages. Some sort of clerk or scrivener? They held up the leather folio stamped with a *taikhut* without bothering to look up from their own work. "The book is safe."

"Who are you?" Kho demanded. "Where am I?"

The scrivener set the folio down and blinked owlishly at her over the tops of their glasses. "I'm Li Ami," they said matter-of-factly. "And you're in the safe house of the

Guardians of Dawn."

Kho sat up straighter on her pallet. "The Guardians of Dawn?" she asked in confusion, thinking of the fairy tales Yuli's auncle Mongke used to tell her. "The elemental warriors who defeated the Mother of Ten Thousand Demons?"

"No, the magical mutual-aid society." Li Ami furrowed their brows. "Although I suppose that does also include me, Zhara, and Yuli, the actual Guardians of Dawn."

Kho's head whirled. Images of fallen bodies on the ground twitching in time to her brother's song mingled with the vision she had had of three figures standing before her—one surrounded by flames, one dressed in flowers, and the other shimmering and translucent. Her headache was growing worse, and she pinched the bridge of her nose.

"I—" she began, but found she was at a loss for words. "I'm . . . confused." She felt the seams of her world unraveling as her mind tried to sort through and rearrange what Li Ami was telling her. Fairy tales were real? And if the Guardians of Dawn were real, then that would mean demons and chaos and monsters were—

"Confused about what?" Li Ami tilted their head.

Kho closed her eyes. "Everything." Suddenly all she wanted to do was lie down, slip back into the blissful arms of unconsciousness, and wake up in her own bed to discover this was all a bad dream. But memories of dark bodies rising from the ground and the feel of invisible blows against her ribs kept surfacing in her mind, more terrifying than nightmares.

A pause. "I can try my best to answer any questions you have."

Where to begin? Kho opened her eyes, taking in her surroundings more fully. The room where she found herself seemed more like a stock cellar than a dungeon, surrounded on all sides by sacks of grain and other foodstuffs, along with shelves of books and a writing desk in the center. Kho glimpsed a few of the titles she had managed to salvage and pass on from the university archives, and a measure of calm overcame her. Despite the overwhelming amount of new information she was trying to process, there was a connection here to her previous life. A bond of trust, even if it had come behind a mask. Whatever else this so-called magical mutual-aid society might be, Kho was in safe hands.

"What happened? How did I get here?"

Li Ami pursed her lips. "We found you passed out on the street outside this bookshop with *Songs of Order and Chaos* by your side. As for how you got there, I'm afraid you'll have to tell me."

*The streets are filled with sleepers, and they will soon wake.*

Kho shook her brother's voice loose from her head. "I'm . . . not sure." She remembered discovering *Songs of Order and Chaos* in Ogodei's hiding place in the library at home, wanting to bring it to this secret organization because . . . because she needed someone to talk to. To sort out and make sense of her tangle of thoughts, about the invisible stranger in her brother's room, about her brother's strange behavior and his . . . magic. Then the uncanny encounter on the street, the people afflicted with the waking dreamer sickness coming to life as Ogodei sang—her mind went in circles and she needed to stop thinking or she was going to vomit. "Is there . . . may I have a drink of water?"

The scrivener's face was unreadable as they got to their feet and crossed to the corner of the room to dip a wooden cup into a clay cistern. They were neither friendly nor hostile, and Kho couldn't help but feel awkward and unsure in their presence, feeling both as though she were an unwanted burden and an honored guest. Li Ami handed her the drink, which was icy and hard to swallow but restored some of her composure.

"Thank you," she said.

The scrivener said nothing, merely sat and waited for her to speak.

Kho took another sip. "I"—her voice cracked—"I suppose you're wondering who I am."

Again, Li Ami said nothing.

"My name," Kho said softly, "is Maltak Kho."

The scrivener merely blinked. Kho felt slightly unmoored, feeling a bit as though she were speaking to a brick wall. There was no recognition in Li Ami's eyes, but neither was there confusion or censure or surprise. Only a sense of waiting, as though the scrivener were a blank page to be written on with Kho's words.

"I . . . am the First Daughter of the Maltak Kang?" she faltered.

A slight wrinkle appeared between Li Ami's brows. "I'm afraid I don't know much about northern politics."

Kho felt wrong-footed and off-balance. Perhaps she shouldn't have started with who she was. Perhaps she should have started with her misgivings about Ogodei, about the strange happenings she had witnessed before . . . before she lost consciousness.

"I think my brother might be a magician," she blurted out.

At last a flicker of emotion, something akin to relief, crossed the scrivener's face. "Is that why you wanted to join the Guardians of Dawn?" they asked. "To help your brother?"

"No, I mean, yes, I mean—I don't know." Kho hated feeling so tongue-tied. "My brother has the Taint. There are many other people in Urghud and beyond with the Taint, so I had never given it much thought. He has the affliction but not the ability, as we say." She was babbling and she hated it, but she didn't know what else to say. "But one day . . . one day I came across evidence of him writing in what I think was the Language of Flowers, and that's when I found *that*." She nodded toward the leather folio. "*Songs of Order and Chaos.*"

Li Ami looked interested. "Did you know what it was?"

"Not at first." Kho shook her head. "All I had heard from my contact was that you all—the Guardians of Dawn —were in search of a folio with a particular symbol."

"The *taikhut*," the scrivener supplied.

"Yes. I had heard of *Songs of Order and Chaos,* but I never expected to find it in my brother's possession."

Li Ami studied her through her spectacles. "Is that what made you think he was a magician?"

"I wasn't sure what to think," Kho admitted. "I thought . . . I thought that perhaps my brother, like me, had been trying to make amends for a wrong we did someone years ago. It's why I became the Paper Wolf, you see. Because of me, a magician—a *person*—died. If I could not wash their blood off my hands, then I would do what I could to make sure the blood of others would not stain them further."

The scrivener remained quiet, but unlike before, their silence now seemed patient. Kind.

"I thought—hoped—my brother felt the same," Kho whispered. "But then . . . then. . . ." She trailed off. How could she possibly explain what she had witnessed without seeming as though she had lost all grip on sanity? "I don't know why I'm telling you this," she muttered.

Li Ami blinked again. "What happened to your brother?" they asked.

Kho paused. Her mind skittered away from the preceding events like roaches before a fire, and she didn't want to examine the confrontation she had had with Ogodei. Or with not-Ogodei.

*Gogo, what is wrong with you?*

*With me? Nothing. With your brother? Everything.*

"Can"—she swallowed—"can someone who cannot do magic suddenly develop the ability?"

The scrivener stilled. "Yes," they said quietly. "When their empty vessel is possessed by a demon."

The bluntness of their response took Kho aback. "What?"

Li Ami tapped their lower lip. "There's a lot about demons we don't know," they said. "It's why the Guardians of Dawn reached out to the Paper Wolf for *Songs of Order and Chaos.* But we are discovering that demons can do more than corrupt magicians into monsters; they can possess the bodies of the undead, as well as take control of anti-magicians. This waking dreamer sickness plaguing the people is a demonic infection, leaving behind bodies empty of ki that are ripe for demons to inhabit."

Kho burst into tears.

The scrivener squirmed, looking both guilty and horrified. "Er," they began. "Is everything all right?"

Kho did not reply, wrapping her arms around her knees and burying her face. The building waves of terror and exhaustion of the past several weeks had finally broken, and she was in very real danger of drowning. She had come to the Guardians of Dawn in the hopes that they would rescue her from being swept out to sea. She hadn't realized until this moment that she had hoped that they would save her—that they would offer her comfort, take the burden of responsibility from her shoulders, tell her everything would be all right. What to do about Ogodei. The Grand Game. Her position as First Daughter of the Maltak Kang.

But instead, they had made everything worse.

Beside her, she could hear Li Ami get to their feet and walk to the cistern again. Kho saw a soft green-gold glow out of the corner of her eye—magic, Kho realized with some awe—and presently the scrivener returned with a cup of hot water.

"We don't have any tea," they said apologetically. "But I thought that maybe something warm would help."

Despite Li Ami's awkwardness, there was something incredibly kind in the gesture that loosened the knot about Kho's heart. "Thank you," she said hoarsely, accepting the drink. She wrapped her hands around the cup, feeling the heat seep into her fingers. The storm had subsided, and she could think clearly again.

"I'm sorry," the scrivener said. "I didn't mean to upset you. I know I can be a bit . . . much."

Unexpectedly, Kho laughed, choking a little on her hot water. Li Ami looked mortified, but Kho set down her cup and smiled. "It's all right," she said softly. "It's not you . . . it's just . . ."

"Your brother is possessed by a demon." This time, the bluntness of the scrivener's tone did not rattle her.

"Yes," Kho whispered. "I think so."

The hot water had fortified her enough to finally face what had happened to her before waking up in the Guardians of Dawn safe house. The inhuman laughter. The strangely discordant voice. The ever-so-slight change in his personality. Ogodei had not been the brother she had known for a while now. There was some peace in knowing that she had not lost her mind, but in the wake of such an epiphany came grief.

"I'm sorry," Li Ami said again, seeing the tears roll down her cheeks.

"How do I get him back?" Kho wiped at her eyes, thinking of the stories the shaman Mongke had told her and Yuli of demons and the Guardians of Dawn. In their stories, the Guardian of Fire was the cure for abomination, but Ogodei was not an abomination. He was a hollowed-out husk of himself, filled with an eldritch parasite. She tried to remember what the other elemental warriors could do, but could recall nothing except for the Guardian of Water's ability to change reality itself.

"If we find your brother's soul, Yuli can return him to his body," Li Ami said.

Kho nearly dropped her cup in astonishment. "Yuli? Gommun Yulana?"

The scrivener nodded. "The Guardian of Wind can tether and untether souls from their vessels."

Numbness spread through Kho's body, and she noticed dispassionately that her hands were shaking. The revelation that Ogodei was possessed by a demon had been a blow, but the knowledge that Yuli—*her* Yuli—was not the person she thought she had known her entire life was devastating. With her brother, she had sensed for a while now that something was wrong, that he was not the reckless, impetuous boy with whom she had grown up, but to know that Yuli was not just a magician but a legendary elemental warrior of old . . . it was as though she had just discovered that the sun rose in the west, that everything she had been told about the natural world had been a lie. Kho had mourned the loss of their friendship, but now she was unsure if there even had been a friendship to begin with, if she had simply loved someone who did not exist.

"Maltak Kho?" Li Ami said. "You've gone pale."

Kho set down her cup and brought her hands to her mouth. "Yuli . . . is the Guardian of Wind?" she choked out.

The scrivener frowned. "Yes. There are more of us, you know—Guardians of Dawn, that is. Zhara is the Guardian of Fire, and I'm the Guardian of Wood. We haven't found the Guardian of Water yet, but we can only assume they have also been reborn to bring balance to the world."

Kho heard Li Ami's words but did not comprehend them, her mind snagged on a single word, a single thought, a single name. *Yuli. Yuli. Yuli.*

"I understand it's a lot to take in," the scrivener continued uncertainly. Their eyes were worried, darting from Kho's wan face to her trembling fingers. "The existence of demons, elemental warriors, and all that. But now that we have this fragment of *Songs of Order and Chaos,* we will have a better understanding of how to bring balance to the world."

Kho nodded, trying to center herself back in her body, to the present moment. Ogodei. Demons. The waking dreamer sickness. These were things she could understand, even if they frightened her. "How will the Guardians of Dawn bring balance to the world?" she rasped out. "How will you stop this demonic infection?"

"By stopping it at its source, either by sealing the demon portal at the Singing Skies or by defeating the Moth Demon."

Kho struggled to stay focused. "The Moth Demon?"

"One of the Lords of Tiyok. We believe the Moth Demon is hiding somewhere in the north, possibly contained in some sort of talisman."

Kho frowned. "A talisman?" She could feel the tides of dread rising once more and fought to stay afloat.

Li Ami held out a crystal strung on a chain about her neck. "Something like this," they said, laying the stone on her palm. It began to give off a soft green-gold light. "This is a magic stone that glows at our touch but goes dark in the presence of demons. Greater demons usually need magicians to possess, but there aren't many magicians in the north. It's far more likely the demon possessed a magic stone and is somehow working through whoever is carrying it."

Kho's heart dropped to her feet. "A stone that goes

dark in the presence of demons," she murmured, and she could feel herself losing the battle against drowning.

The scrivener nodded. "It would likely be solid black," they said. "The void is . . . the void is a sort of emptiness that nothing can escape." They looked down at the crystal. "It seems silly to ask, but you wouldn't happen to have seen something like that?"

Kho closed her eyes. She had. She had seen something like that every day.

Hanging around her mother's neck.

# 25

It had been a long, long time since Yuli had gone riding on the steppes.

The Trial of the Soul was to be a race to the golden roq rookery and back, but she wasn't out on the grasslands with Sartai to practice for the Grand Game. No, she was out there to run away from her thoughts, to flee her body in a way she hadn't indulged in since she discovered she could spirit-walk. Untethering her soul allowed her to disassociate from the uncomfortable feelings she carried in her body like dread or shame or embarrassment, but what it could not do was quiet her racing mind.

Only sweat and the burn of her thigh muscles as she clung to Sartai's back could do that.

Yuli was careful not to overtire her mare, but she couldn't resist the urge to encourage her mount faster and faster across the plains in bursts of speed that felt both cleansing and cathartic. Flying on Temur's back was exhilarating, but nothing could compare to the rush of excitement tinged with fear that came with racing so close to the ground. The instant her mind wandered would be the instant Sartai faltered, so for the moment, she let herself become one with the mare, release all her thoughts to leave nothing but the scent of wind and grass and the vast, vast emptiness of the steppes. Yuli had been riding since she could walk, but the sheer power of a horse was still a force to be reckoned with and respected. If she wasn't wholly in her body, if she wasn't present and aware of her surroundings, if she wasn't connected to her horse, one wrong step could send them both tumbling to their doom with broken legs and broken necks.

But by the Great Bear if that edge of danger didn't feel invigorating.

Presently, Sartai began to grow tired and Yuli let her slow to a walk. She released the reins and sat back in the saddle, allowing the mare take the lead, snuffling among the tall, frozen grasses for something to eat. The ever-present herds of sheep and yak had already moved south for better grazing this time of year, so she and Sartai were completely and utterly alone. Yuli tilted her head to look up at the skies, heavy with snow-laden clouds. Another storm was brewing; she could smell ice on the wind.

"Come on, girl." Yuli clicked her tongue after she judged the mare had eaten enough. "Let's go."

But Sartai ignored her, shaking her head and blowing out a frustrated breath.

"Fine," Yuli sighed. She let the mare graze some more, feeling her muscles relax. She was loose, easier in her skin than she had been that morning, her mind clear of anything except the scent of wind, the grass, and the vast, vast emptiness of steppes. She was tired, but it was a good tired now instead of the bone-deep exhaustion she had felt the previous night when she had stumbled home after chasing down errant ghosts to return to the bodies of waking dreamers. She had slept the entire day after that, causing an uproar in Gommun Manor as the household believed that she had succumbed to the waking dreamer sickness. There were reports that the waking dreamer sickness had now spread to even the affluent parts of Urghud, in the households of the Five Golden Families themselves.

They hadn't been able to wake Aunt Görte either.

Uncle Bayar had chased Yuli away from Aunt Görte's quarters, saying the current Grand Kang would be attended to by the Council of Shamans. She had wanted to shout back that there was no cure for the waking dreamer sickness, that only the defeat of the Moth Demon could bring these sleepers back to life, but she had been too tired, too overwhelmed, and too drained to resist. The Trial of the Soul was the following day, and Yuli felt suffocated by the weight of all the responsibilities she bore. The fate of the Golden Horde, and her role in the coming civil war. The bodies of the waking dreamers, an army just waiting to be raised by the Moth Demon. The closing of the portal at the Singing Skies, the place where the earth meets sky. She was the First Daughter of the Gommun Kang, a challenger in the Grand Game, the Guardian of Wind, and she was only seventeen, not yet the age of majority. For all her power, she was still just a girl, not even fully grown. For once, she would have liked to be Yuli again—just Yuli.

She fingered the turquoise bracelet on her wrist.

Yuli didn't know what to feel about Kho keeping it all those years, despite everything. The realization that her former best friend was the Paper Wolf should have been the most shocking discovery, but it had been the cherishing of this small trinket that had affected Yuli the most. The formerly white tassels were a dirty gray-brown now, battered and worn as though Kho had never taken it off. Yuli remembered making the bracelet for her when they had been twelve, sitting together in a gem merchant's shop and choosing the beads. Kho's wrist had been smaller than hers even then, and the beads dug against her skin now. But Yuli wore the bracelet anyway, finally allowing herself to feel what she hadn't dared let herself feel for the past two years.

Longing.

She had friends—Zhara and Ami—but in many ways they were more her comrades-in-arms than intimate companions, united by the need to save the world. Sometimes she wondered what her relationship with them would be like if it weren't for the Mother of Ten Thousand Demons. What would it be like to simply *be* together, the way she and Kho used to sit in silence, lying on their backs in the grass in summer, holding hands and watching the stars?

Yuli looked down at the bracelet. Could she imagine herself holding hands with Zhara and Ami? No. In their own ways, they belonged to other people—Zhara to Han, Ami to Gaden. Kho had been *hers*—completely, utterly, and wholly *hers* in a way that no one else was or would ever be. She loved her friends, but she belonged to Kho the way this turquoise bracelet belonged to her.

Thunder rumbled in the distance. Yuli glanced up at the cloudy skies in confusion but saw no flickers of lightning.

Then she saw the other rider racing across the steppe.

She recognized the horse before she recognized the rider—a buckskin with black legs and mane. Altan, Kho's gelding, named for the pale gold sheen of his coat. For a moment, Yuli considered turning Sartai around and heading back toward Urghud, but the turquoise beads on her wrist made her reconsider. Her mare had finished eating, so she urged Sartai into a gallop, heading to intercept Altan.

Within moments, Yuli drew up beside Kho, but neither girl said a word. Instead, they exchanged glances and rode on in silence, racing each other as they once had when they were little girls. Their worries, troubles, and concerns streamed past them like the frozen wind, and for the first time in a long time, Yuli felt communion with someone else that did not require speech or even mind-to-mind connection; their presence was enough. *They* were enough.

Presently, the horses began to tire and the girls slowed them to a walk. Still they did not speak, but the air between them thickened with the weight of all the things unsaid. Jochi. The Paper Wolf. Magic. Secrets. Betrayal. Yuli sat astride Sartai, keeping pace with Altan, the muffled thud of the horses' hooves the only sound aside from the rising wind. Snow was flurrying in earnest now, catching on Yuli's lashes.

"You should have worn a hat," Kho said, reaching up to brush the snowflakes from the end of Yuli's auburn braid. The casual intimacy of the gesture twisted Yuli's stomach. "You'll catch a cold."

Yuli did not answer, merely pulling the collar of her overcoat tighter over her throat. Kho's eyes caught on the turquoise bracelet on her wrist.

"You found it," she said softly.

"I did," Yuli said hoarsely. "You kept it."

"I did."

More silence, but the mood had shifted—less tense, more comfortable. Yuli looked away, unable to bear the expression in Kho's long-lashed eyes. Hope, regret, anger, betrayal . . . affection. It was the affection that hurt her the most.

"Why?" was all she managed.

Why did Kho keep the bracelet? Why did she betray Jochi? Why did she become the Paper Wolf?

"Because," Kho said softly, "I was trying to do the right thing."

It answered so much and so little. "Help me understand," Yuli said. "You betray my cousin to the Falconer. Then you join a secret society of magician allies. Then you challenge my aunt to the Grand Game in a bid to help your mother claim the Sunburst Throne, knowing full well your mother intends to go even further than my grandfather in a crusade against magic."

"I don't know!" Kho burst out. Altan shifted uneasily beneath her. "What I have done, I have always done in the name of the greater good, which I believed to be the right thing."

"The greater good," Yuli scoffed. "You were always your mother's lackey. You have always done what *she* believes to be for the greater good."

Kho's eyes flashed. "I didn't intend to betray Jochi," she said furiously. "When I discovered he was a magician, I didn't go running to my father. I went to Ogodei. We were *friends*, Yuli, all four of us. I didn't know what to do. We had been raised with the belief that magic was the ruination of the empire, but Jochi was no monster. He was no danger to any of us. I went to Ogodei because he was my big brother, because for once I wanted to put down the burden of being First Daughter and let someone else make the hard decisions. That was my mistake. *He* went to the Falconer, not me."

Yuli went still.

"You don't know what it's like," Kho continued, "to live with the guilt of your friend's death. You don't know what it's like being my mother's heir, to have known since childhood that the honor and well-being of your kang sit on your shoulders. You've only been your kang's heir since Jochi was exiled, Yuli. For most of our lives, it was your cousin who bore responsibility for the Gommun

Kang's future. He would have understood, and he did." Kho turned her head away. "And now he's gone."

Yuli sucked in a sharp breath. "Why didn't you tell me?" she whispered.

"Would you have listened?" Kho crossed her arms. "You had already decided I was the enemy. I didn't just lose Jochi that day; I lost *you*."

And she had. Yuli had broken her matching turquoise bracelet that night. "You should have trusted me," she said quietly.

"Should I have?" Kho gave a bitter laugh. "You've never trusted *me*, have you? You are a magician and I never knew. Fourteen years, Yuli! You are the Guardian of Wind and I never knew."

Yuli closed her eyes. Shame and remorse rose within her, and her spirit shivered, wanting to escape. Kho did not know—could not have known—how much she had longed to tell her. But as much grace as she had been given as a child, she had still been beholden to Auncle Mongke, who had impressed upon both her and Jochi the importance of keeping secret, keeping safe.

Kho softened. "I understand why you couldn't tell me," she said gently. "It must have been difficult, carrying that secret for so long. But I won't deny that it hurt, Yuli. It *still* hurts."

Yuli could feel the burn of tears rise up in her throat. "Oh, Kho," she said tremulously. "I'm sorry."

"No." Kho shook her head. "I'm sorry."

Those words unleashed something in her, a tide of yearning and affection and love. Yuli dismounted Sartai just as Kho jumped down from her own horse and the girls embraced, two years of distance and distrust erased with a single touch. Kho felt different in her arms, both larger and smaller than she remembered, softer now than she was as a coltish young girl. Yuli pressed her lips to

Kho's forehead and was overwhelmed by the faint scent of her pine and amber soap, familiar and foreign at once. The top of her head only came up to Yuli's chin, and her friend was tucked perfectly into the crevices of her body, fitted together like two pieces of a puzzle. It felt right to hold Kho like this, in a way she had never had the courage to before, and she cupped Kho's face in her hands as she drew back, wiping away her tears.

Kho stilled in her grasp, blinking those long lashes up at her. Without thinking, Yuli tilted her head and pressed her lips to Kho's.

The world held its breath, and even the wind seemed to have stilled for this moment. Kho stiffened in surprise, then softened, her lips pressing back, hesitant, shy. Yuli trembled, devastated by the rush of hope and fear that swept through her. She had kissed girls before, but none of them had felt like this—like holding something precious and precarious in her hands. She dared not move, scarcely dared to breathe, terrified if she did something wrong, she would startle Kho into running away. Into regret.

After a moment, they ended their kiss. Kho's lashes fluttered as she brought her hands up to her lips, as though she could hold on to the feel of Yuli's mouth against hers. "Yuli," she murmured, "I didn't . . ." She trailed off.

Yuli's heart was thrumming so fast, she thought it would burst from her chest. "Yes?" she whispered.

"I didn't come here for this." Kho reached up to rest her hand on Yuli's cheek.

"Do you regret it?"

"No." Then, "I don't know. This is all—this is all so much."

Yuli broke away, ears burning. "Oh," she said in a small voice.

"Don't." Kho grabbed her wrist. "Don't pull away. Don't leave me again."

Yuli stilled.

"It's just . . . I don't know. There's so much at stake. There are demons loose in the world, and you're the Guardian of Wind. Civil war is brewing, and I'm still your opponent in the Grand Game."

"You care about that?" Yuli laughed in disbelief. "After everything else?"

Kho looked pained. "I want to do the right thing."

"Then defy your mother and join me." Yuli ran her fingers through Kho's silken black hair, knotted by wind and horse riding. "Tell her you want to forfeit the Game. Help me find the Moth Demon and restore balance to the world."

Kho parted her lips. "Yuli, I . . ." She trailed off, looking both uncertain and afraid.

"Please." Yuli had never begged anyone before, and the agony of it was as pleasurable as it was shameful. She would get on her knees if it meant having Kho at her side. "Please."

Kho closed her eyes. "I don't know," she said. "I don't know what to do."

"Are you afraid?"

"Yes," she said honestly. "But I'm more afraid for you than for me."

"Why?"

"Because," Kho said, "there are foul plans afoot. I would feel better if you did not compete in the Trial of the Soul tomorrow."

Yuli was nonplussed. "Are you still trying to win the Grand Game?"

"No," Kho said. "I think I'm trying to save your life."

Yuli frowned. "And what of the Golden Horde?" she asked. "What of the Lady of Wild Things' ambitions for the Sunburst Throne? If you win, then it means we ride to war."

Kho bit her lip. "I don't know," she repeated. "I have to think."

"Kho—"

"I have to think."

And then she was gone, leaving Yuli alone on the steppes with a racing mind and an aching heart.

*Beware the Sleepers, for they wake.*

Urghud was thick with the ghosts of the living.

They wandered, homeless and without anchor, gathering as mist in nooks and crannies, mouthing *help me, help me* to the wide awake. But they were chased away by a wave of the hand, passed through as though they were not there, invisible to all those who loved them. The ghosts were nothing but the impression of unease, the hint of dread, the unexplained anxiety in the mind, and those who were awake sensed the disquiet in the air. The city was tense, as though holding its breath for a disaster that hovered on the edge. The clouds above dark and ominous and heavy with snow.

A storm was brewing.

But it would not be snow that fell.

Like drifts that accumulated over time, the numbers of waking dreamers throughout Urghud had swollen and grown over the past several weeks. The fabric of the universe had grown threadbare, patchworked with holes.

Jochi could sense the emptiness that lurked beneath the veneer of sleep, but he was voiceless, powerless to warn the living of what was to come. A demon crouched in their lair in the middle of the city, unraveling the world one strand of ki at a time to build their cocoon of power. And it was nearly time for them to emerge from their chrysalis.

*Beware the Sleepers, for they wake.*

Far to the north, at the place where the earth met sky, a group of thirteen dreamers rose from their eternally icy beds. Shamans and generals they had been, leaders in a bygone age, and they were waiting. Waiting for word, waiting for the signal they were to march south to lead the hordes of chaos into battle, waiting for the moment their Mother emerged at last, ready to devour the world. The void was growing, the forces that held the bonds of matter loosening. Unrest and pandemonium rippled beneath the empire, shaking its foundations and feeding the abyss. The spirits that held the portal shut were weakening and soon the Sleepers would descend. Soon.

*Beware the Sleepers, for they wake.*

Jochi could feel the darkness around him tremble as the wind picked up. Residents of Urghud shivered and pulled their collars up about their ears, but they could not hear the words entwined in the melody. A singing voice called to the demons of the abyss, summoning them into their vessels to rise up against those who were awake.

*Rise, my friends. Rise.*

Down by the harbor, the refugees opened their eyes. In their pallets and beds, the citizens of Urghud opened their eyes. In the teahouses and taverns of the city, the sleeping stable hand, the drunken dicer, and the tired traveler opened their eyes. One by one, the hordes of chaos were summoned, crushing windpipes, stomping ribs, and trailing shadows that growled and snarled in their wake. Their master had called, and they had answered. High above, drops of darkness slipped through the holes of the world, falling onto the roofs of Urghud as black snow coated the city in a blanket of uncanny magic. Creatures formed out of the mist as the ghosts of the living were transformed by demonic power, monstrous forms with too many eyes and limbs and teeth.

And upstairs, in her room at Gommun Manor, Aunt Görte opened her eyes.

*Rise, my friends, and attack.*

# 27

Kho could not sleep for the whispering.

It was the night before the Trial of the Soul, and it had been threatening to snow for days. Kho never could sleep very well the night before a big event or a storm. The pressure in her head was too thick for rest, and the thrumming of her heart too loud for peaceful dreams.

*I have a plan for the Trial of the Soul.*

She didn't know whether the whispering was in her mind or in her ears. The wind whistled through the cracks in her window, bringing with it the scent of ice and despair, but she could have sworn there were voices downstairs, conversing with words too muffled to understand.

She should not have come home. She should not have pretended that all was well to her mother and her household, not when Ogodei was possessed by a demon and the Guardians of Dawn had been reborn. The world had changed irrevocably, and Kho was no longer certain of her place in it or what to do. Magic and monsters, demons and death—she was only an ordinary girl, with no power of her own.

But she had to know.

The first thing she had done when she returned from riding on the steppes was look for the Lady of Wild Things, to speak with her mother about potentially forfeiting the Grand Game. Kho didn't know what the consequences would be—of her request, of the succession crisis, of the civil war—but she knew it was the right thing. When Yuli had begged her to join in fighting the Moth Demon, Kho understood for the first time that the stakes of her moral decisions had always been small. What was the honor of her kang compared to the end of the world? If her becoming the Paper Wolf had been her small act of protest in the face of the magician genocide, then refusing to uphold her duty as First Daughter would be her first *true* act of rebellion. Her first act as who she truly was, not as the heir to her mother's legacy. As Kho.

But her words died in her throat at the sight of the black stone amulet about the Lady of Wild Things' neck.

*Greater demons usually need magicians to possess, but there aren't many magicians in the north. It's far more likely the demon possessed a magic stone and is somehow working through whoever is carrying it.*

Kho had never given much thought to the talisman around her mother's neck. The Lady of Wild Things owned many pieces of jewelry, some gifted to her by nobles from the Azure Isles, others heirlooms passed down through the generations. The black stone amulet had been a constant in her mother's wardrobe, as much as the necklace of wolf fangs that denoted the Lady as head of the Maltak. Just another part of the Maltak regalia, as ceremonial as it was decorative.

But what if it were a demonic talisman?

"Where have you been?" her mother had asked, as sweet-voiced as ever.

"Riding," Kho had replied. "I needed to clear my head."

"Of course," the Lady said, inclining her head graciously. "Tomorrow you will win the Trial of the Soul and will be anointed Grand Kang. It is a big change, and you must be prepared."

*I have a plan for the Trial of the Soul.*

"Mother," Kho said cautiously, "how do you know I will win the Trial of the Soul?"

The Lady of Wild Things only smiled. "I have faith in you, my daughter."

And with that, Kho had gone to bed, citing the need for rest.

Snow was coming down in earnest now. Kho could see the shadows of flakes drift down past the paper paneling of her windows, but her headache had not lessened. She had spent hours mulling, considering, and agonizing over what to do, lying in bed with the covers pulled up to her chin. Teacher Alani had once told her she thought too long, too hard, and too deeply about things, that sometimes answers were simple, not complex. Her entire life, Kho had contemplated every outcome, every conclusion, every consequence of her actions, weighing the effects of her decisions against potential hurt, harm, or benefit. The greater good. Everything in the name of the greater good. Jochi. The Grand Game. The Paper Wolf. Ogodei.

That her brother was possessed by a demon should have upset her more, but in the wake of her initial grief had come relief. There was nothing Kho could do to save him, nothing save help the Guardians of Dawn defeat the Moth Demon. It was not her brother who had changed, but a demon who had changed him. A demon who had tried to kill her in the streets of Urghud that night she stole *Songs of Order and Chaos.* Her brother—her real brother—was out there somewhere, and the Guardian of Wind could tether his wayward soul back to his body once the true danger had been destroyed.

The Moth Demon.

Contained inside a demon talisman.

The whispering had grown louder, and Kho thought she could make out the occasional word here and there.

"—foolish of you."

"—the girl—live."

"—played—hand. Now—attack tonight."

Kho rose from her bed and tiptoed to her door, sliding it open a crack. The voices grew louder, and she thought she recognized the grating, discordant voice of the mysterious stranger from her brother's rooms.

"What was I supposed to have done?" It was Ogodei, or the demon who wore his skin. "Convince her it was all some sort of bad dream? Charm is not my talent; it's yours. Besides, after tonight it won't matter."

Kho quietly retrieved a fur-lined robe and wrapped it about her body, slipping her feet into warm socks. She slid the door open all the way and silently crept downstairs. She thought the voices were coming from the library.

"It's messy," the voice complained. "I would have preferred to do this without all the fuss."

"I hate all this hiding and sneaking around," Ogodei replied. "That way, we can draw those pesky Guardians of Dawn out into the open, only this time, we'll have an entire army at our backs."

"At Gommun Görte's back," the voice corrected. "You will not be leading them."

"I won't?" Ogodei sounded disappointed. "You know how I love a bit of chaos."

"For our plan to work, the people of Urghud must see that it is the former Grand Kang who leads the horde of demons, not one of the Maltak. They will denounce the

Gommun and rally to my cause. You will rally the Golden Horde in the Maltak name."

*My cause.* All the hairs stood up on Kho's neck as her stomach sank with dread. She hovered on the stairs, too afraid of peering around the corner to confirm her deepest fears and suspicions.

"And what of the girl? I thought she was to take the title of Grand Kang."

"She will," the voice said. "Once the Gommun have fallen, the people will declare her the victor of the Grand Game by default."

"And what of me?"

"You are still headed to the Azure Isles."

"You still want me to hunt down Min Suhwa?"

"Yes," the voice said. "We can no longer wait for spring. If we are to take over Urghud and begin our march on the imperial city, we need all the allies we can muster as soon as possible."

"Understood." Ogodei sounded resigned.

"Good. And remember, the Fleet Queen wants the girl's heart in a box."

"Barbaric," Ogodei said, but sounded rather impressed. "I hear and obey."

The sound of footsteps as the demon in her brother's body exited the library. Kho held her breath, listening for the mysterious stranger to emerge, but there was no sound. She descended the last few steps, one foot in front of the other, striving for silence. As she rounded the corner, she saw the golden glow of lantern light spilling into the corridor from the open doors of the library and the shadow of a figure cast on the opposite wall. Someone tall and slim.

The Lady of Wild Things looked up as Kho approached.

"Kho-yah," she said in surprise. Her voice was roughened with the edge of sleep, but still dulcet, still pleasing to the ear. "What are you still doing awake?"

The black stone amulet about her neck did not glint in the light.

A stone that went dark in the presence of demons.

"Who are you?" Kho asked hoarsely, her gaze fixed on the amulet.

The Lady frowned. "Is everything all right?"

"Who are you?" Kho repeated.

"I'm your mother," the Lady said, and the concern in her eyes made Kho doubt her convictions. Standing before her was the woman who had soothed her brow when she was sick, had sang her to sleep every night when she was little. Surely no demon could feign genuine worry like this. "Are you sure everything is all right?"

Kho shook her head. "I heard you talking to Ogodei," she said. "I heard it all."

The Lady of Wild Things lifted her brows. "Heard what?"

"About your plans for Gommun Görte," she said. "And the assassination of Min Suhwa."

"Ah." Her mother smoothly rose to her feet from the floor where she had been sitting before a writing desk. "Well, I did say we had a plan should we lose the Grand Game."

"You said you had faith in me," Kho said. "That I would win the Grand Game."

The Lady of Wild Things nodded. "And so I did. But for every plan to succeed, one must have dozens of contingencies."

"*I have a plan for the Trial of the Soul,*" Kho said quietly. "I know. I heard you. You were conspiring with Ogodei since the start. I heard you in the stables, casting a spell on the saddle that nearly cost Yuli the Trial of Strength. You called the demon into my brother, and you have been orchestrating everything since."

Her mother went still.

*The Moth Demon is hiding somewhere in the north, possibly contained in some sort of talisman.*

"I know who you are," Kho whispered. "You are the Moth Demon."

A slow smile spread across the Lady's face. "Clever girl," she said, and the doubled voice of the mysterious stranger emerged. Now that Kho was standing before her mother, she could hear the grating tones echo from the amulet itself, twinned with the higher, sweeter voice of the Lady of Wild Things. "Perhaps your brother was right to have tried to kill you after all."

At once Kho lunged for the talisman around her mother's neck, but she was tossed aside by an invisible hand. She went crashing into the shelves of the library, bringing a cascade of texts down about her head.

"Mother," Kho rasped. "Mother, please. You can do it. You can fight the Moth Demon. You can return to yourself."

"Can she?" The Lady of Wild Things' mouth did not move, but the words rang in the room. "Clever as you are, you clearly know so little about demons."

The shadows writhed about Kho, taking on a life of their own. Tendrils of darkness reached for her, wrapping around her neck.

"Let her go," Kho choked out. "Set her free."

"Your mother willingly made this bargain with me," the amulet continued. "Although she might not have known it when she found me."

"How"—Kho coughed—"where—"

"At the Singing Skies, of course." There was no expression on the Lady's face as she advanced on her daughter, but her dark eyes reflected malice. "There was a time your people pilgrimaged to the place where the earth meets sky. Before the Warlord, before the Just War. Your mother had been an intrepid explorer in her youth, and she had heard the legend of the Sleepers. Ambitious even then, she was determined to discover their final resting place, or to see if they had truly discovered the secret of immortality and to claim it for herself. She found me instead."

Stars burst at the edges of Kho's vision. She grasped for the shadow tendrils, but her hands slipped through air; there was nothing to hold on to. Nothing to do to relieve the pressure about her throat.

"You humans," the amulet said with amusement. "Always searching for power you do not have. Your mother was not the first, nor would she be the last. The Sleepers went in search of immortality and they found it, of sorts, their souls trapped forever on the ice, protecting your world from Tiyok. Your mother went in search of glory, and she also found it, of sorts. I granted her the power of persuasion, of charm, and the ability to convince people to her whims with words alone."

Kho struggled to breathe, kicking out futilely against the crushing of her windpipe. She reached for something—anything—she could use as a weapon, to strike out against the demon about her mother's neck. Her fingers brushed a heavy scholar's stone, a gift from one of the barons of the Azure Isles, a weighty ornament for contemplation and meditation. Wrapping her hand around its base, she hurled it with all her might at the Lady of Wild Things.

It struck her mother in the shins, and the tendrils about Kho's throat loosened. Sucking in deep breaths, Kho crawled toward the Lady, grabbing her skirts and hauling herself to her feet. Her mother's hands beat uselessly at her shoulders, as though the demon controlling her had no idea how to move her limbs effectively. Kho grabbed the amulet at her mother's neck, screaming at the sudden pain that jolted through her. Black ice flooded her veins, the cold stabbing every part of her body. Distantly, she could hear the rest of the household come awake, shouts of concern filtering in from the courtyard and the kitchens.

"Don't!" the amulet cried. "Remove me and your mother dies!"

Kho paused.

"It takes tremendous will and a pure soul to resist the power of a greater demon," the amulet said. "Your mother gave her ki to me in order to wield my power."

Kho stared at her mother's face, blank and lifeless, with no spark of love to light her long-lashed eyes. "The Guardians of Dawn can return her soul," she said uncertainly.

The amulet barked, an odd sound that Kho realized was meant to be laughter. "Her soul is gone," the amulet said. "I've devoured it."

Rage, sorrow, and despair filled Kho at those words. To defeat the Moth Demon, she would have to take the necklace. But to take the necklace was to lose her mother.

She had to do the right thing.

There was a ringing sound as a fist slammed into the side of her skull. With shock, Kho realized the Lady of Wild Things had swung at her and, a moment later, raised her fist for another blow. Kho ducked, instinctively wrapping her arms around her mother's hips, trapping her legs. She could feel the strikes rain down on her back and Kho dug in her heels, ramming the Lady of Wild Things against the wall. There was a crack as the back of the Lady's head struck the edge of a bookcase, but her mother managed to free her knee, bringing it up to connect with Kho's face. Kho stumbled back as the Lady kicked her in the rib cage, and threw up her arms to block the next blow. She had never been especially good at sparring, but she had had years of practice at the youth competitions. The Lady raised her leg for another kick, but Kho stepped in to block, reaching up to yank the amulet from her mother's neck.

The Lady crumpled to the floor.

"Mother," Kho croaked. "Mama."

The Lady of Wild Things lay prone, her arms and legs splayed at awkward angles. Her long-lashed eyes were still open, but there was no life in them. There hadn't been, not for a very long time.

Kho sat on the library floor as the shouts of the household drew ever closer. She had to run. She had to get to Tarkhun's bookshop at the end of the Street of the Spear. But she could do nothing but clutch the amulet to her chest and sob and sob and sob, mourning the loss of her mother she had never known.

She had done the right thing, and it had been the hardest decision she had ever made in her life.

# 28

Zhara wished Ami would come to bed.

The Guardian of Wood sat at her writing desk in the middle of the cellar, furiously translating the new pages from *Songs of Order and Chaos*. The cellar was freezing, and Sajah's furry bulk in Lion form was not enough to keep Zhara warm. She marveled at the scrivener's ability to ignore the world around her when she was in a period of intense focus; it was as though neither cold nor hunger nor fatigue could touch her.

"What's so urgent that it can't wait until morning?" Zhara yawned.

"Hmm?" Ami raised her head from her work with a distracted look on her face.

"There's nothing in those pages that won't be there tomorrow," Zhara said. "It's cold; let's go to sleep and try again when it's warmer."

"It's snowing," Ami said, pushing her spectacles up her nose. "I doubt it will be much warmer tomorrow."

Zhara sighed. Sometimes Ami's singular way of thinking baffled her.

"Besides," the scrivener continued, "I think I have some confirmation that the source of the Shimmer is the Singing Skies."

Zhara sat up in her pallet. Sajah rumbled a sleepy protest. "Is there any information on where it is exactly?"

"There's no map," Ami said. "But it appears to be about a week's journey north of a town called Darun."

For the first time in a long time, Zhara felt a sense of clarity in what step they should take next. Ever since they arrived in Urghud, they had been pulled in several different directions—from Yuli's participation in the Grand Game to the waking dreamer sickness and the Sleepers to the implication that the Moth Demon was not possessing someone but *something*. "We should tell Yuli," she said. "And make preparations to leave as soon as the Trial of the Soul is over."

"And if Yuli loses?" Ami asked.

Exhaustion fell over Zhara's shoulders like a cloak. She might have been the Guardian of Fire, and the others might have looked to her to make decisions, but she was also just a seventeen-year-old girl. "One step at a time," she said, repeating the words Bohyun used to say when she was traveling with the Bangtan Brothers. "Whether the Morning Realms fall into civil war is out of our hands. But what we can do is defeat each of the Lords of Tiyok to prevent the return of the Mother of Ten Thousand Demons."

Ami tapped her chin thoughtfully. "There's still one Lord of Tiyok left after we defeat the Moth Demon."

Zhara appreciated that Ami had said *after* they defeated the Moth Demon, not *if*. "And one more Guardian of Dawn," she said quietly. It had been the three of them for so long—Zhara, Ami, and Yuli—that she sometimes forgot there was a fourth.

"The Guardian of Water," Ami said. "They who defeated the last Lord of Tiyok."

"Who is the last Lord of Tiyok?"

Ami grimaced. "The Ancient One."

Zhara racked her brain trying to recall the stories of the Guardians of Dawn she had heard. The Bangtan Brothers had performed the Sunburst Cycle in Zanhei every year, but the narrative always took place after all the greater demons had been banished and the Sunburst Warrior was facing off against Tiyok herself, sealing her away in her underground lair with the power of the Star of Radiance. "What is the Ancient One's power?" she asked.

"I don't know," Ami said. "If it's in this section of *Songs of Order and Chaos,* I haven't gotten to it yet. I've mostly been looking for information about demonic talismans." She gave a rueful look at her pile of journals. "My encyclopedia is such a mess."

"Have you made any progress?"

"No," Ami said with frustration. "There is a story about a warrior named Qin in a time before the Morning Realms were united harnessing the power of the Mother of Ten Thousand Demons to conquer the independent kingdoms, but nothing about a talisman."

Zhara shuddered. "How does one harness the power of the Mother of Ten Thousand Demons without succumbing to abomination or worse?"

Ami looked troubled. *"The power of Tiyok is greater than her Lords,"* she quoted. "We know greater demons can possess magicians without turning them into abominations, and we also know that at least one of them can possess objects to manipulate others. But like the Lords of Tiyok, it would seem she needs a vessel in order to enter this world."

Zhara thought of her encounter with the Frog Demon,

of how he said he would offer his Mother the perfect vessel—her, the Guardian of Fire—to possess. Ami had told her how the Locust Demon had captured Gaden with the intent to sacrifice them as the perfect vessel. She thought of all the empty bodies scattered throughout Urghud, each one a potential host for a demon . . . or *the* demon of demons, Tiyok herself.

"We need to seal that northern portal," Zhara murmured. "As soon as possible."

"Agreed," Ami said. "And the eastern portal at the Lake of Illusion after that."

Zhara frowned. Each of the portals had been opened at the resting place of the Four Celestial Beasts—the Lion of the South, the Unicorn of the West, the Eagle of the North, and the Dragon of the East. Each thus far had been tied to a place of legend or myth from a different region of the empire—Mount Zanhei in the south, the Root of the World in the west, and the source of the Shimmer in the north. "Do you think," she said carefully, "that the location of the final portal is in the Azure Isles?"

Ami picked at her lower lip. "More than likely," she said. "After we seal the portal at the Singing Skies, that's likely where we need to go next."

"What about the Guardian of Water? Surely we need them too."

Ami tilted her head. "I can write my father and ask him to cast star charts for the potential birth dates and places of the Guardian of Water. He knew I was the Guardian of Wood when he cast mine when I was born."

It seemed like an unnecessarily complicated gesture, but Zhara decided not to remark upon it. "One step at a time," she said again. "Let's speak with Tarkhun about arranging transportation to Darun on the morrow."

*Thud!*

The muffled sound of a body falling to the floor above

them. Sajah's hackles rose, and he gave a low rumble of warning.

"What was that?" Ami whispered.

"I'll go check," Zhara whispered back. She pulled the crystal from Mount Llangposa out from beneath her shirt and held it aloft as she climbed the ladder leading out of the cellar. She pushed the trapdoor open a crack, peering into the darkness. "Tarkhun?"

The light in her crystal immediately dimmed.

Demons.

It was then Zhara noticed the ringing sounds of what sounded like a pitched battle. Metal clanged against stone, and there were shouts and cries of both fury and fear. The reddish light of flames filtered in through the paper panels of the sliding doors, and shadows clashed and writhed. She pushed open the trapdoor fully and climbed out onto the ground floor of the bookshop, recoiling in horror as she nearly tripped over a body.

"Tarkhun?"

It appeared as though the bookseller had fallen from his sleeping loft above the shop, but when she turned him over, she was horrified to find his eyes half open, his face frozen in a rictus of agony. Zhara frantically placed her fingers on his neck, searching for a pulse. There was none.

The light in her crystal went dark entirely.

*Bang! Bang! Bang!*

"Open up!" came a panicked voice. "Is anyone here? It's the Paper Wolf!"

The pressure against Zhara's ears was nigh unbearable, but Ami pushed her out of the way. "Let them in," she said.

"Please," came the voice again. "I need your help. I have your talisman!"

Ami rushed to the door and slid it open, letting in a blast of snow, ash, and cold air. On the other side stood a figure so bundled in furs that Zhara could not make out any of their features. They stumbled inside and without taking the time to dust off the snow from their coat reached into their sash and pulled out a silk-wrapped bundle.

"What's going on?" Zhara demanded. "What's happening outside?"

"I don't know," the Paper Wolf gasped, "but the streets are overrun with demons and shadow monsters."

Zhara thought of the chaos creatures she and the others had fought the night they found the Paper Wolf lying unconscious in the snow. "The waking dreamers," she breathed. "They've risen."

The Paper Wolf nodded. Without the mask, they looked young and frightened, not much older than Zhara herself. "They're being led by the old Grand Kang," the Paper Wolf said. "And my brother is rallying the people against the Gommun, calling them traitors to the north." They looked around. "Is Yuli here?"

Ami shook her head. "She's back at Gommun Manor."

The Paper Wolf looked panicked. "We have to get to her!"

"Hold a moment," Zhara said. "I know you said you are the Paper Wolf, but how do we know we can trust you?"

They bit their lip and unwrapped the silken bundle in their hands. At once Zhara felt as though the room were sucked of air. In the middle of the Paper Wolf's mittened palm was a black stone amulet. She felt the presence of anti-ki radiating from the talisman and felt sick.

"What is this?" she breathed.

The Paper Wolf exchanged glances with Ami. "The Moth Demon," they whispered.

Zhara recoiled. "What?"

The Paper Wolf swiftly covered the amulet up again. "Do you trust me now?"

Zhara nodded. "Ami," she said, "can we destroy it? Will that stop the fighting outside?"

"I tried that already," the Paper Wolf said grimly. "With a hammer, with a knife, and even with fire. The only thing I could think of to do was come here."

"We have to get to the northern portal," Ami said. "Straightaway. It's possible the only way to destroy it is at the source."

Zhara glanced at the shadows outside the bookshop, then at Tarkhun on the floor. "We have to get to Yuli first." She turned to the Paper Wolf. "Do you know where Gommun Manor is?"

They nodded. "I'm not sure I can go out there again," they said weakly. "There are things . . . there are things human eyes were never meant to behold."

"We will protect you," Zhara said. "My name is Zhara, by the way. Jin Zhara."

"Kho," the Paper Wolf replied. "Maltak Kho."

Zhara was taken aback. "You're Yuli's challenger at the Grand Game! The First Daughter of the Maltak Kang."

"Was." Kho grimaced. "The Grand Game is over, and we have all lost. I'm coming with you to destroy the Moth Demon."

Ami reached a hand out to Kho. "Welcome," she said softly, "to the Guardians of Dawn."

# 29

The night was lit by a strange orange glow when Yuli awoke to the sound of chanting.

In her dreams, there had been the thunder of hoofbeats as she raced across the steppes, pursued by the shadow of a winged creature she could not see, no matter how much she turned around. The wind whooshed and whistled past her head as bile rose up in her throat—sharp, sweet, and sour all at once. Her fingers fumbled with the bow slung on her shoulder, and she could not seem to grasp a single arrow from the quiver at her waist, moving slowly, oh so slowly, while the invisible assailant above her swooped ever closer. Somewhere beyond the edges of the plains, there was the smell of smoke, making her retch.

Then Temur appeared in her sleep, her beak open in a liquid cry. The dream shattered and Yuli awoke with a gasp.

And coughed.

It took her a moment to gain her bearings, her heart still pounding with anxiety as the last remnants of the nightmare faded away, leaving the memory of dread lingering in its wake. She had almost caught a glimpse of her winged pursuer in her sleep, but the image broke apart when she tried to grasp at it, leaving only the recollection of a deep, dark black hole in the sky.

Yuli rubbed her eyes. Her room was hazy, and her throat was scratchy, as though she had fallen asleep beside a bonfire. In the distance, she could hear the throb and thrum of voices but was unable to make out the words.

"Yuli!" Auncle Mongke burst into her quarters, barefoot and dressed only in a simple night shift. "You have to go. Now!"

"What," she croaked, "what is going on?"

The shaman looked grim. "The city is overrun with monsters and the waking dreamers, with your aunt Görte at the head."

"*What?*" The last vestiges of sleep fell sharply away from Yuli as she threw aside her covers. The floor was icy as she leaped out of bed, and she hissed in shock as her feet touched the ground. "What do you mean, Aunt Görte is at their head?"

Auncle Mongke pulled open Yuli's cupboards, roughly tossing their niece's clothes and outerwear onto the bed. "She wasn't in her bed when the attacks began," they said in a low voice. "The city watch brought news of pandemonium down by the docks to your uncle Bayar, but their reports were . . . incoherent. Incomprehensible. Stories of beasts made of shadow, of dreamers rising from their beds to slay their loved ones . . . all commanded by your aunt. Once the leader of the Golden Horde, now the leader of a dark one. Bayar and I went up to her rooms, but her bed was empty. She was gone."

The waking dreamer sickness. The abyss had awoken in the Grand Kang, and now she was possessed by a demon.

*There are foul plans afoot.* Yuli thought of her conversation with Kho on the steppes, when she had tried to convince—beg—her friend to join her. Kho was about to warn her of something to come. She ran to the windows and threw open the shutters as snow and ash fluttered inside. In the distance, a false dawn glimmered behind the buildings, billowing clouds of smoke mingling with the heavy skies. Shadowy shapes ran through the snow, hideous and inhuman, snarling as they swiped and snapped at the hapless citizenry on the streets.

Chaos creatures.

Urghud was under attack.

"We have to do something," she said, yanking on a pair of socks and trousers over her silk underwear. "We have to help!"

The shaman shook their head. "No," they said determinedly. "You have to go. Find the Guardian of Fire and the Guardian of Wood and get out of the city."

"And abandon everyone to demons?"

"You have no choice." Auncle Mongke tossed a rucksack filled with supplies at her feet. "More than half of Urghud is under the Moth Demon's thrall, and you are overmatched. Your only hope now is to get to safety and regroup. There is a ship waiting for you down in the harbor that will bear you to Arkhevet."

"What about you?"

They did not reply straightaway and Yuli knew her auncle would not be joining her. Amid the clash of weapons and screaming outside, she could hear distant voices chanting:

*Maltak! Maltak! Maltak!*

"Come with me," Yuli pleaded.

The shaman shook their head. "Someone has to stay and help the survivors get out of Urghud. I will rally with the other members of the Guardians of Dawn."

"Let me help then! I can banish demons with my powers!"

"No." Auncle Mongke's voice was firm. "You are the Guardian of Wind. You and your friends are all that stand between us and ten thousand years of chaos. You must find a way to seal the demon portals and defeat the Lords of Tiyok."

"I can't just leave you here."

"You must." The shaman reached up and tucked a lock of auburn hair behind Yuli's ear. "Once you have defeated the Moth Demon, we can start to rebuild here. Until then, someone must defend our home."

Tears stung Yuli's eyes. Aside from Jochi, Auncle Mongke was the family member she had loved most, had relied and depended upon to survive. They had been both mother and father to her ever since her own parents died, the one person she could fully, truly, wholly trust. They were the first person to know of her magic, to know of her true identity as the Guardian of Wind. They had introduced her and her cousin to a secret society of magicians and their allies, had taught them how to keep safe. Auncle Mongke had been Yuli's first and best champion, and it had nothing to do with the strength of their arms.

Outside the chanting grew louder.

*Maltak! Maltak! Maltak!*

"What's happening?" Yuli asked. "Why are they chanting the Maltak name?"

"Maltak Ogodei has rallied the Golden Horde to fight the demons and your aunt Görte," the shaman said. "They've declared the Gommun Kang anathema and traitors to the north for harboring a magician in our midst. They march toward Gommun Manor even now."

Yuli closed her eyes. This must be the Lady of Wild Things' doing. "What of Kho?"

"I don't know what happened to the girl."

Fear shot through Yuli as she thought of their exchange out on the steppes. What if the Lady of Wild Things had discovered her own daughter's treachery? What if Kho was lying somewhere in Maltak Manor, her neck broken, having no longer proven useful to her own mother? No, she couldn't think about that. Kho was clever. Kho would find some way to escape.

"Get to your friends and make your way down to the docks," Auncle Mongke said, sliding the doors to Yuli's room open. "Sartai is ready for you in the stables. The ship's captain is named Rhul, and he'll be leaving within the hour. You cannot miss it; there will be no other way out of the city tonight."

Having finished getting dressed, Yuli hoisted the rucksack over her shoulder.

*Maltak! Maltak! Maltak!*

"Go," Auncle Mongke said, their voice low. "Now. You don't have much time."

But Yuli took the moment to throw her arms around the shaman, crushing them in her embrace. "Stay safe," she whispered into their hair. "I will come back. I will."

Auncle Mongke held Yuli's face in their palms. "Don't look back," they said softly. "If we survive the night, I will find you. We will meet again soon." They thumped their right fist to their left shoulder. "Honor to the Great Bear."

Yuli returned the gesture. "Honor to the Great Bear," she whispered.

And then she slipped into the night.

Torches lit the night as the mob of demons advanced on Gommun Manor. The entire castle was in disarray, the servants and retainers having already fled through the city gates toward the steppes. The stable doors had been opened, the horses running rampant through the streets of Urghud, their panicked whinnies and cries audible above the shouts of the crowd. Sartai was in her stall, rearing and screaming in panic.

"Shh, girl, shh," Yuli soothed, grabbing the mare's halter to calm her down. There was no time to saddle her up, so she grabbed Sartai's mane at the base of her neck and hauled herself onto her back. Snow had begun falling in earnest now, but the drifts on the ground were so thoroughly mixed with ash that the piles were gray and black with soot underfoot.

She closed her eyes and found Temur circling the skies above. Yuli could feel Temur's worry and panic for her and the others as their minds connected. Through the Eagle's eyes, Yuli could see Urghud burning, warriors on horseback hacking away at shadow monsters with blades, waking dreamers drawing on chaos magic and inflicting damage and destruction to people and property alike. A crackle of lightning, then an explosion. In the middle of it all, Yuli spied a fiery lion carrying two girls on his back—Zhara and Kho—accompanied by a unicorn and Ami. The relief that flooded her was short-lived; the girls were surrounded by creatures of darkness, which Zhara blasted out of the way with her flames.

"We've got to go, girl," Yuli murmured to Sartai and the mare tossed her head anxiously. She urged her mount out into the courtyard and made ready to run.

It was pandemonium in Gommun Manor, the guards shouting conflicting orders at one another as they tried to rally their defenses. Yuli had never seen such panic and disorder in the ranks; the Gommun took pride in their martial prowess, and it shamed her to see their discipline fall apart in the middle of an ambush. Twenty years of relative peace, and her kang had grown soft.

*Maltak! Maltak! Maltak!*

The guards were gathered around the main entrance gate, forming defensive lines with pikes against the bang and bam of the battering ram. Archers from the towers fired into the mob below to shouts and cries of pain. Yuli scanned the courtyard, noting that the eastern gate was unmanned and undefended. She dismounted Sartai and ran to the gate, digging in her heels and pulling the enormous wooden door open.

Just outside, a handful of Maltak bearing torches were advancing toward the unprotected eastern side. They hadn't yet caught sight of her or the chink in the defenses; she would have to make her escape swift and silent.

Too late. A shout rose from one of the advance scouts and they began rushing the gate. Yuli whistled for Sartai. As frightened as she was, the mare responded instantly, galloping straight toward the egress. As she ran past, Yuli leaped and grabbed onto the horse's mane, hauling herself onto Sartai's back.

"To the eastern gate!" Yuli cried behind to the Gommun guard as she barreled through the mob gathering outside, trampling a few unfortunate attackers beneath Sartai's hooves. But she didn't have time to think, no time to regret or wonder at any injuries, as she urged her mount ever faster down the narrow streets of the northern capital city toward the lower city where Zhara and the others were embroiled in battle.

That flight through Urghud was nothing like any of the races or competitions she had ever participated in before. The course was not set, the obstacles unexpected, and safety was an afterthought. More than once she had to sharply veer to the left or right, galloping down a narrow alley that she wasn't sure wouldn't stop in a dead end, leaping over barrels and sacks of spilled grain, praying Sartai wouldn't slip. It was one thing to let her mount run free, to ride without a saddle as they went in straight lines over the grasses; it was another to actively *ride*, to be responsible for both her horse and her own well-being. The citizens of Urghud paid her little heed as she rode past; many other families were running from their homes, while scavengers and opportunists looted what was left behind. There was no escaping the terror rising in Yuli's throat, no time or place to dissociate and go spirit-walking; she had to be *here*, to be present. She pushed down the panic that threatened to overwhelm her, focusing on the feel of Sartai's muscles between her legs, the balance of her body atop her mount.

"To me, my friends!" In the distance she spied a figure standing atop a fallen building, rallying people with their blade. Another flash of lightning from Sajah's horns, and in the flickering light, Yuli caught a glimpse of the old Grand Kang's face. "Destroy them! Destroy them all!"

Aunt Görte.

Sartai nearly faltered as she sensed her rider's hesitation. Yuli wrenched her mind away from her demon-possessed aunt, focusing on the task at hand. She couldn't stop. She had to go on, to continue, to move forward. The only way to save Aunt Görte—to save them all—would be to seal the northern portal at the Singing Skies with the other Guardians of Dawn. But a part of her cried out as she and Sartai galloped away, wishing she could turn around and do something.

Ahead, the shadows crawled.

The night was no longer mere darkness; it was the void come to life. The gloom had shape and weight, a presence that was as much physical as it was spiritual. Claws and fangs appeared out of every corner and Sartai leaped and jumped over monsters that attacked them from the abyss. They were surrounded. Yuli summoned a spirit bow, ready to take a stand.

Another roar, and another flash of lightning. Sartai reared with surprise as the ground before them exploded, sending the chaos creatures scattering everywhere.

"Zhara! Ami! Kho!"

"Yuli!" Zhara cried. She struck out inexpertly with her enchanted blade, slicing ineffectually at the hide of the nearest monster.

"This way!" Yuli gestured. "Toward the docks! We have to leave Urghud now!"

A creature flew from the roof and Yuli immediately shot at the thing with a spirit arrow. The shadow dissolved, leaving behind nothing but the echo of a shrieking scream. The girls fought their way through the city streets toward the harbor, making their way toward the lone ship standing in the quay. A figure hailed them from the bow. Captain Rhul.

"Hoi!" they called. "Over here!"

Yuli raced Sartai down the dock toward the gangplank, but the mare shied away from the ship, her eyes white. Yuli dismounted, pulling the horse up the causeway by the halter, whispering a mixture of pleas and curses at the animal. "Come on," she gritted out. "Come on!"

Sartai resisted, but Kho came to her aid, coaxing the mare aboard with gentle words. The others followed suit, boarding swiftly. The captain called out orders to the crew and the ship set sail.

Gathered on the docks were more shadow creatures, snarling and growling as they paced along the shore. Ami gestured with her hands and a ripple went through the harbor, crumpling the wooden planks and sending the chaos creatures into the frozen water. A few broke the surface and began swimming toward the boat. Zhara threw out her hand over the surface, transforming the ice into stone, trapping the monsters in rock. Yuli aimed her spirit arrows at the heads snapping and baring their teeth at the retreating ship, sending them back to Tiyok one by one.

Silence reigned.

"We're in the clear," Zhara said, breathing hard. "I think that's the last of them."

The sounds of battle were muffled in the distance, the shouts and cries fading as they drifted farther and farther from Urghud. Yuli stood at the stern, watching the city in which she had grown up, the city she had called home, burn down.

Kho came up to stand beside her. "We'll be back," she said softly. "We'll save them. My brother, your aunt, everyone. We'll save them all. We will."

Zhara and Ami joined them as the snow continued to fall, offering nothing but their presence as comfort.

Urghud had fallen.

# PART

## THE SLEEPERS

Kho had never been on a boat before.

Despite living on the shores of the Sweet Sea, the source of the Infinite River and the Dragon's Beard tributary into the Bay of Dragons, Kho had never once set foot on the deck of a ship, although she had seen many come and go from Urghud's harbor. In fact, she had never been more than a few days' ride from Urghud by horse; when comparing herself to her companions, she felt very provincial indeed.

Once they had set sail, Ami asked the captain to redirect their course and bear them up the Bitter Tears to a small port city at the southernmost edge of the Frozen Wastes called Darun.

"Absolutely not," Captain Rhul said. "The Gommun shaman paid me for a passage to Arkhevet, so it is to Arkhevet we will go."

"But the source of the Singing Skies is in the tundra," Ami said in frustration. "And Darun is the closest place on the map."

"All the more reason not to take you girls up there," the captain replied. "You're not outfitted for such extreme weather. It will be death for you. Only fools would dare venture up there this time of year."

"This is of the utmost importance," Ami said. "It is a matter of life and death!"

"And so it is," the captain said remorselessly. "It would be the death of you all."

"Captain," Kho said, coming to Ami's aid. "The Maltak will soon discover that I have escaped and will give chase. What is the first place you think they will go? Arkhevet is the nearest port city, and it would only make sense that I will have fled there. But they would not think that we would have gone to Darun. As you say, only fools would dare go."

The captain hesitated. "I promised your auncle I would keep you alive, Your Highness," they said to Yuli.

"And so you shall," Yuli said. "By taking us where the Maltak would not expect us to flee."

They shook their head. "I am going to regret this," they murmured, then directed the sailors to change course.

The ship would sail the Sweet Sea for four days before reaching the Bitter Tears, the icy glacier rivers that fed the enormous inland lake, then another day to reach Darun up one of the tributaries. The plan was to outfit themselves in Darun; the townsfolk there would hopefully be able to supply them with the equipment, food, and furs they needed to survive on the tundra. Kho couldn't help but be a little worried; although she was experienced camping out on the steppes in the middle of winter, even the hardiest of northerners avoided the harsh tundra until the spring.

"What are the Singing Skies?" Kho had asked Ami. "And why is it so important we go there?"

The scrivener fiddled with her spectacles, which

constantly fogged from the cold. "The place where the earth meets sky," she said. "In your stories, it's the source of the Shimmer, where the Sleepers journeyed all those years ago to find immortality. It's also where we believe a portal to Tiyok has been opened, allowing the Moth Demon to enter this world. If we seal the portal, we should be able to defeat them and save Urghud."

"The Shimmer," Kho breathed. She looked to the skies overhead. The storm had passed and the heavens were clear, and to the north, a faint band of color danced above the horizon. She thought of what the Moth Demon had said about her own mother journeying to the final resting place of the Sleepers. "So the stories are real."

"All stories are real," Ami said matter-of-factly. "The fact that the Guardians of Dawn exist proves it. Zhara, Yuli, and I are real, aren't we?"

Kho stole a glance at where Yuli was teaching Zhara how to wield her enchanted blade on the deck. The redhead was running the Guardian of Fire through her paces, showing her the proper stance and the proper parries and assigning drills to work in the muscle memory.

"Who taught you to hold a sword?" Yuli complained. "A dancing bear?"

"Han taught me," Zhara said, somewhat defensively. "On our journeys in the outermost west."

"As I said, a dancing bear?"

Kho smiled as she recalled all the times Yuli had done the very same thing for her, going over the forms and correcting the tiniest mistakes in posture. Kho had never been as hopeless as Yuli claimed; in fact, she had basked in the sunshine of Yuli's attention, reveling in the thrill of the princess's singular focus.

Over the next four days, the novelty of sailing on a ship would wear off quickly for Kho.

The vessel was small, for one thing. She had never

realized how much she had taken for granted the great expanse around Urghud and her freedom to escape and ride on her horses whenever she wished. She felt the sorriest for Sartai, who had clearly never been on a boat either. Just two steppe creatures, trapped on a tiny wooden contraption with nowhere to go. Yuli had offered to let Kho take Temur for a ride in order to stretch her legs, but she had the sneaking suspicion she would like being surrounded by nothing but air even less than being surrounded by nothing but water.

By day, the temperatures were much more tolerable, and the girls spent as much time above deck as possible, soaking in the weak winter sunlight. Zhara and Yuli practiced their unusual Guardian powers, and at first Kho had enjoyed watching them transform into living wind and flame, transfixed by both the beauty and the uncanny nature of their magic. Zhara apparently had the ability to transform the essence of things, so she would frequently demonstrate by turning various objects around the ship to gold, much to the captain's delight. They considered it payment for their unexpected detour to the southernmost tip of the treacherous Frozen Wastes.

Yuli, on the other hand, liked to practice spirit archery, as she called it. She could conjure a bow and arrow made entirely of a white-gold light, and she would take aim at the various birds and fish surrounding their ship, crowing in victory whenever she scored a hit. The weapons never brought in any game or meat; they were made entirely of spirit, she said, and dangerous only against ghosts and demons.

While the other two Guardians of Dawn showed off their skills for Kho, Ami spent the vast majority of her time with her nose in her journals, translating and cross-referencing from her notes to *Songs of Order and Chaos*.

Kho assisted the scrivener where she could; although she could not read the Language of Flowers—much less the archaic form Ami was struggling to translate—she could at least index the content of Ami's journals. It reminded her of the work she did for Teacher Alani at the university archives, and brought a measure of peace amid all the changes.

"Are you looking for anything in particular?" Kho had asked.

"Anything on the Moth Demon or demonic talismans," Ami had instructed her. "I could have sworn I read a story in there ages ago about a demonic talisman and how to destroy it, but I can't remember it now. This," she said, pinching her nose to stave off a headache, "is why it's important to have an encyclopedia."

Kho thought of the black stone amulet, safely wrapped and stowed away with the rest of their bags belowdecks. She had not dared look upon it since the night she took it from her mother's neck, afraid of the voice contained therein. She shook her head and returned to Ami's journals. The scrivener might have a neat hand, but the information itself was disorganized and messy. "It would be easier to find the information," she said mildly, "if everything was written in order."

"I wish." Ami blew out a frustrated breath. "But I don't even have the source material in order." She showed Kho the *taikhut* symbol on the corner of each of the pages in the fragments, which fit together like a puzzle. "For the longest time, I only had pieces. It was like trying to see the whole of the night sky for the stars."

On the second day of travel, Kho finally found something of interest. "Here." She beckoned to Ami. "I'm not sure if it's entirely relevant, but there's something here about the nature of enchanted vessels."

"What does it say?" Ami pushed her glasses up her

nose, blowing out a frustrated breath when they clouded over again.

*"The principle of balance is not one of victory and defeat but of harmony,"* Kho read aloud. *"Neither order nor chaos can be destroyed by the other, not in man, not in nature, and not in the whole of the cosmos. There is no shadow without light, and no light without night with which to compare. To persuade a spirit to leave an enchanted vessel, one must offer it an equivalent exchange."*

Ami frowned. "What does that mean? That we have to offer the Moth Demon a soul to entrap in the stone?" Her hand went to the crystal at her throat. "That's horrifying."

"I don't know." Kho thought of all the disembodied spirits of the waking dreamers wandering without bodies. "But that's just persuading the demon to leave the vessel itself. It says nothing about banishment."

Ami looked thoughtful. "We can seal the cracks between this world and Tiyok," she said. "But true banishment, that's something only the Star of Radiance can do."

"The Star of Radiance?" Kho asked. "But I thought that was lost."

The scrivener shook her head. "No, the Star of Radiance is alive and well."

Kho raised her brows. "You speak of it as though it is a living thing."

"It is," Ami said matter-of-factly. "The Star of Radiance is the lost Mugung heir."

"You mean Princess Weifeng survived?" Kho was astonished. "The rumors are true?"

"Their name is Gaden," Ami said sternly. "And yes, they survived. They were smuggled out of the palace when they were a baby and raised in the outermost west."

Kho fell silent. She thought of Ogodei's belief that the Mugung heir was still alive, back when he was still her brother and not a demon. "Will Gaden claim the

Sunburst Throne?" she asked in a quiet voice. "They are the rightful heir, after all."

Ami was silent for a long while. "I don't know," she said at last. "Gaden has always said that they never wanted to rule. That the Star of Radiance had been abused and perverted from its true purpose, which was to give the Sunburst Warrior the power to seal Tiyok away in her chaos void. They always spoke of returning the power to the people; after all, it was the people of the Morning Realms who gifted the Sunburst Warrior one drop of will to form this awesome weapon."

"If this Gaden doesn't want to rule, then who do they think should sit on the Sunburst Throne?"

Ami worried her lower lip between her teeth. "I don't think they believe anyone should sit on the Sunburst Throne." Her eyes grew soft. *"Power concentrated in the hands of too few leads to strife,* they said. Look at what happened to their grandfather, the last Mugung Emperor. To the Warlord. An empire is only as strong as its emperor, only as just, and just as corrupt."

"So you believe the provinces should be independent," Kho said.

Ami blinked. "Perhaps," she said. "I suppose I've never given it much thought before. But we were sovereign kingdoms and principalities, duchies, and marquisates before the coming of the Sunburst Warrior. We were united by a common enemy. Perhaps it's time to return to the old ways."

Kho said nothing. The future was still too far distant to even conceive of what it would look like. There was still the northern portal to seal, the Moth Demon to defeat, to say nothing of the civil war. "I wonder," she said softly, "what the future of the Morning Realms will hold."

"One step at a time," Ami said. "One step at a time."

# 31

Yuli thought she understood now why the Shimmer was also called the Singing Skies.

She sat at the bow of the ship bearing them ever northward up the Bitter Tears to the port of Darun, looking at the dance of red, green, yellow, white, and blue ribbons across the night sky. The world was silent save for the gentle lap of waves against the boat, but beyond and above that was the gentle whisper and crackle of the multicolored lights streaking overhead. The voice of the Shimmer was ethereal, inhuman, almost like the singing of the demons, only somehow sweeter. It made a whispering sound, and she could have sworn she could almost make out words, a chorus of conversation held by strangers on the other side of a wall. She thought of when she and Kho were little girls, when they would lie back on the grass of the steppes for as long as they could stand the cold, watching the interplay of light in the sky. Yuli had always wondered what it would be like to spirit-walk amid the Shimmer, what it would be like to be free and unfettered amid the shining curtains, but Kho was terrified of the immensity of the heavens. It gave her vertigo, she claimed, and she thought she could feel the tilt of the earth beneath her so that she was no longer sure whether she was looking up or down into infinity.

*Hold my hand,* she would whisper to Yuli. *Hold me fast to the ground.*

And Yuli would interlace her fingers with Kho's to keep her right beside her, but in truth, it had always been the feel of Kho's skin against hers that kept Yuli tethered to her own body. She never felt the urge to dissipate and disappear when Kho was by her side.

She knew she ought to head down belowdecks soon; it was the sort of brilliant cold that allowed the stars to shine their brightest, the sort of cold that crystallized people into a complacent sleep and death. If Yuli were more reckless, she would have gone spirit-walking, seeking out Temur to ride through the Shimmer and feel the voices of the heavens within her soul. But Auncle Mongke was not here to watch over her body now; she had to be the one to take care of herself.

"There you are." Yuli turned around to see Kho standing on the deck, huddled beneath a fur blanket thrown over her coat. "The others were wondering when you would come down."

"In a bit," Yuli said thickly, her lips stiff.

Kho sat down beside her, letting her feet dangle off the edge of the bow, just like Yuli's. "It'll be warmer with two," she said, offering her blanket to snuggle under. Yuli accepted the blanket gratefully, pulling the fur up and around her face to protect it against the wind.

"Star-watching?" Kho asked.

"A little," Yuli said. "But I don't know them very well."

"I could have brought Ami out here," Kho said jokingly. "She's an astrologer's daughter."

Yuli shook her head, feeling just warm enough to laugh now. "I prefer your company."

"I do remember a few stars and constellations, if you want a half-hearted catalog." With a mittened hand Kho pointed straight ahead. "The pole star, and the Immortal Dragon that circles it."

Yuli studied the seven stars of the Immortal Dragon, each of which governed a mansion of Reason, according to the star worshippers of the south. She was aware of their faith in the southern provinces; she had had to study it in preparation for her engagement to Prince Rice Cake. A chuckle rose in her throat at the thought of having to marry Han now. She studied Kho, comparing her friend's face to his. Han was a good-looking boy, but there was nothing about his beauty that moved her. Not like the girl sitting beside her.

Kho met her gaze. "What?"

"Nothing." Yuli flushed. The rush of blood to her frozen cheeks was almost painful in the cold.

"And there . . ." Kho pointed. "The watcher of our people, the Eagle of the North. And the brightest star within it, the eye."

"Temur," Yuli murmured. The name of the star, and the name of the celestial companion of the Guardian of Wind.

Kho raised a brow. "I thought you said you didn't know the stars very well."

"I don't," Yuli said. "But Temur . . . I know Temur very well." She glanced back up at the sky where what appeared like a wisp of cloud snaked its way through the constellation. The Eagle of the North herself, returned from wherever she had been flying free among the Shimmer.

Kho fell silent. "When your auncle Mongke told us stories about the Guardians of Dawn and their celestial companions," she said after a moment, "it never even crossed my mind that the stories were not only true but real." She hugged her knees to her chest. "The Lion of the South and the Guardian of Fire. Zhara. The Unicorn of the West and the Guardian of Wood. Ami. The Eagle of the North and the Guardian of Wind"—she lifted her eyes to Yuli's—"you."

Yuli said nothing.

"How long have you known?" Kho asked softly, and beneath her words Yuli thought she could hear another question: *How long have you kept this secret from me?*

"I was ten years old when I went spirit-walking for the first time," Yuli said quietly.

"Ten," Kho breathed. "That long?"

Seven years, although they had not been friends the entire time. "I thought I was dying at first," Yuli said. "I would wake up in the middle of the night, unable to move. Sometimes I would hear things, or see things. That was when Temur came to me for the first time." She smiled. "I thought she was a demon at first. I kept thinking of those tales you liked to tell me from all those horror books you read about beautiful women who would suck out your soul while you slept."

Kho lifted her gaze toward the constellations. "I'm not sure of your taste in women if you thought a four-winged raptor chimera was the pinnacle of feminine beauty."

Yuli blinked in surprise, then threw back her head in a laugh. "Those beautiful women were shape-shifters too, if I recall."

"I'm surprised you remembered," Kho said. "You never cared much for books or stories."

"Ah, but I care very much about beautiful women."

Kho ducked her head, and although it was too dim to tell, Yuli thought the other girl's cheeks darkened in a blush. Yuli grinned.

"Is that when you discovered you were a magician?" Kho asked.

Yuli's face fell. "No," she whispered. "I've known that for as long as I can recall."

Kho said nothing. "I don't know what to feel," she said at last. "It feels silly to say that I feel betrayed. You had good reason to keep that hidden, not the least of which was because of your own grandfather, the Warlord." Her hand went to the wolf-fang pendant at her throat. "It's just that . . . I was supposed to be the person who knew you best. I was the one who had cataloged and categorized every expression and emotion of your face, the one who understood their meaning." She bit her lip. "You were mine, Gommun Yulana," she said in a low voice.

Something twisted in Yuli's chest at those words. "And you were mine," she replied.

"Until Jochi."

There was nothing she could say to gainsay that. "Until Jochi," Yuli agreed. The shade of her cousin hovered beneath them, present in memory if not in spirit. She would never forget the day the Falconer arrived at the Gommun Manor to arrest Jochi, a frightened boy of fourteen, with charges of treason.

"You were once an open book to me," Kho said softly. "But ever since Jochi, you have been a language I once knew but have since lost. Oh, Yuli." Her voice broke. "Will you ever forgive me?"

Yuli was quiet for a long moment. The truth was, she had forgiven Kho that moment on the steppes when she took her face in her hands and kissed her. "It wasn't your fault," she said. "It was Ogodei."

"I'm still responsible," Kho whispered. "I am First Daughter of the Maltak Kang. I should have known the right thing to do instead of relying on someone else to tell me."

Yuli laughed. "Oh, Kho," she said. "Always taking things so seriously."

Kho gave her a watery smile. "Someone has to, of the two of us."

They sat in silence for a while, listening to the whisper of the Shimmer overhead.

"I should have gone to you first," Kho said after a while. "I should have known. I should have protected us, because you had been what was most precious to me. Instead I was, as you once said, my mother's lackey." She gave a humorless laugh. "How selfish of me."

Yuli shook her head. "Your heart has always been pure and true," she said. "But I didn't want to believe it then. It was easier not to believe it, to think the worst of you."

"Why?" Kho asked.

"Because it made losing you hurt that much less."

A soft intake of breath. Kho's face was so close Yuli could see the lights of the Shimmer reflected in the other girl's dark, long-lashed eyes. Between them was a gravity almost too strong to resist, but Yuli thought of the very first kiss they had shared that day on the steppes, of how Kho had pulled away and hesitated. But there was no hesitation on Kho's face now as the other girl pressed ever closer, her lips softly parted.

"Kho," Yuli began, but stopped at the feel of the other girl's mouth on hers.

Even through the numbness of the cold, Yuli was aware of every sensation. It was nothing like the kiss on the steppes. This kiss was gentle and exploratory; it was asking and granting permission. Yuli closed her eyes and leaned into Kho's embrace, her mittened hand coming up to gently cup the other's girl's cheek. She could feel the feathery brush of Kho's lashes against her nose, ticklish, like the touch of snowflakes during winter's first storm. Of all things, it made her want to giggle. She thought she could understand Zhara's blushes better now.

They both pulled away at the same time, and Yuli lifted

her arm to wrap around Kho's shoulders, but the other girl stopped her with a touch. Slowly, deliberately, Kho removed her left mitten, then worked her fingers against Yuli's mitten, revealing her skin to the elements. Kho's skin was warm atop her own, and Yuli automatically turned her palm over, lacing their fingers together as they had when they were little girls. Kho tilted her head up to the heavens with a smile, and Yuli suddenly understood. Smiling too, she lay back on the deck, Kho snuggled beside her, as the two of them watched the Shimmer stream by, hands clasped together, for as long as they could stand the cold.

# 32

They arrived at Darun the following day, just before dawn.

Zhara was the first to wake. A lifetime of getting up before the others in order to prepare breakfast was ingrained in her bones, and she still found herself jolting out of bed most mornings in a cold sweat, thinking she had overslept. Once the fog of dreams had lifted, it didn't take long for her to regain her bearings, but as she lay curled up in her hammock aboard the ship, Zhara tried to make sense of the strange, persistent feeling of dread that lingered.

Then she realized that the boat had stopped.

And Sajah was gone.

It was more than the chill his absence left behind that troubled her; it was the fact that he had roused himself from sleep to go investigate. Like all cats, big or small, the Lion of the South was eminently lazy; something must be terribly wrong. The other girls were still asleep—Ami with her head pillowed against Rinqi's flank, Yuli and Kho on the floor in a pile of furs. The Unicorn of the West lifted her head as Zhara climbed out of her hammock, the light in her horn pulsing faintly with concern, but did not rouse herself. Pressing a fingertip to her lips, Zhara pulled on her boots and grabbed a blanket to wrap about herself as she headed up onto the deck.

The blast of cold that greeted her as soon as she headed outside was so intense it made her eyes instantly water and the world blur with tears. Zhara pulled the blanket over her head, hiding her face in the furs until the ice had melted from her lashes. Everything was utterly silent and still, with not even the gentle lap of water rocking against the hull of the boat. The whisper of the Shimmer overhead was louder than ever, and Zhara swore she could almost make out words in the sound.

*Beware, beware.*

Zhara took a cautious step out onto the deck. A thick rime of ice had coated every surface of the ship during the night, and she was careful not to slip as she made her way toward the lone figure standing guard—Sajah, in his Lion form, watching the skies intently. His stubby silver horns and ruff crackled with lightning, and his flaming peacock's tail swished back and forth uneasily as he stared out into the open.

No, not the open.

A harbor.

"Sajah?" Zhara asked thickly, her lips stiff and numb. The Lion's ears twitched at the sound of her voice, but he kept his golden gaze fixed on the port ahead. "Where is everyone?"

There were no sailors out on deck, no one working the sails and oars to guide their ship into the quay. The waterways of the Bitter Tears were flat and glassy, and no breeze stirred the fur on Sajah's back, yet the boat moved silently, inexorably toward Darun, the movement so smooth and slow that she had not thought they were moving at all. It was then Zhara noticed the ripple of mist billowing along the sides of their vessel, pushing them toward town.

Ghosts.

Overhead, the shadow of a four-winged bird cut across the Shimmer as Temur drifted down to land on the deck beside Sajah. The Eagle's blue eyes glowed with a white light, and she opened her beak to let out a melodic trill, the song a warning. Behind Zhara, the door to the cabin belowdecks opened, and out stepped Yuli, her own eyes glowing.

"Temur?" she said in a voice still cracked with sleep. The redhead raised a hand to her head, shaking it as though to dislodge the dreams still fogging her mind. "What is it, girl?"

The Eagle of the North trilled again, and Yuli closed her eyes. Zhara knew that the Guardian of Wind and her celestial companion could communicate mind-to-mind and wondered what Temur had encountered on her flight across the Frozen Wastes.

"Warriors," Yuli murmured, her eyes still closed. "Wearing ancient armor. Five . . . six . . . ten . . . thirteen." She opened her eyes. "Attacking a town. Attacking *this* town." Her eyes widened. "The Sleepers."

"*The north will fall should the Sleepers rise again.*" Zhara turned to find Kho standing on deck with a still-groggy Ami by her side. "Why would they attack Darun?"

"The better question would be *Why have they risen?*" Yuli said grimly.

Ami rubbed at the ice crystals forming on her lashes. "The actual question should be *How?*"

"Let's wake the captain and the rest of the crew," Zhara said. "I don't like the idea of just drifting into dock."

But the sailors were not asleep.

Zhara found the captain at the stern, slumped over the jib of the ship, frozen solid to the touch. There was an unnatural stillness to their face, and although their eyes were closed and they looked peaceful, she knew in that instant they were dead.

"Yuli!" she cried out in a cracked voice. "Ami! Kho!"

The other crew had seemingly suffered the same fate.

"What have I done?" Yuli buried her face in her hands. "I convinced them to come north and led them straight to their deaths."

Rinqi emerged from belowdecks, the light of her horn glowing with worry.

"Can you heal them?" Zhara asked the Unicorn.

The Unicorn blew a soft breath over the captain, then slowly shook her head.

"What about you, Ami?" Zhara turned to the Guardian of Wood. "Your gift is over life itself."

Ami looked troubled. "I can grant life where there is none," she said quietly. "But I have never raised anyone from the dead. Even if I did . . . without their spirits, what good would it do? They would simply be like the undead we encountered in the lands of the Qirin Tulku— mindless and soulless."

Three pairs of eyes turned to Yuli.

"No." Yuli paled, the freckles scattered across her nose and cheeks standing out in stark contrast like a windburn. "That would be . . . a violation."

Zhara looked to the mists surrounding the ship. In the fog, she thought she could see the faces of the captain and the crew. Even in death, they were pushing the girls onward to their destination.

"Perhaps you could ask them," Zhara said softly. "What they would like to happen to their ghosts."

As if they heard her words, a wisp of mist curled up on the deck, forming the shape of the captain. They gazed solemnly at the girls and Yuli reached a hand out to them.

"I'm so sorry," the redhead said, her voice breaking. "I'm so, so sorry."

The captain gave her a rueful smile and took her hand in their own.

*I promised your auncle I would keep you alive, Your Highness.*

Zhara heard their words not with her ears but with her soul.

"Shall I—shall I bring you back?"

The captain's ghost shook their head. *Once we bring you to shore, release us to the eternal blue skies.*

The ship made its slow, inexorable entry into the one-pier harbor of Darun. The entire town was similarly wreathed in ghosts, but a single, solitary figure stood out amid the desolation.

A redheaded youth, twin to the Guardian of Wind, standing onshore.

"Jochi," Yuli breathed.

The waters were still as the boat pulled into dock, but without crew to tie them to a post, they had to make their way to shore carefully. Zhara and Ami, having grown up around the canals of Zanhei, were the most familiar with watercraft and disembarked first, holding the ship steady as Yuli and Kho carefully lowered Rinqi to the pier, followed by Sartai, then Sajah. The spirit of Yuli's cousin beckoned as they assembled on the pier, a silent gesture to follow.

Darun was a ghost town.

As the foursome made their way through town, which was little more than a collection of ger along the shores of the Sweet Sea, they wandered through the wreckage and aftermath of an attack. It was difficult to tell how long ago the skirmish had taken place; the frigid air had preserved the bodies and overlaid the entire town with a thick rime of ice. The inhabitants could have died two weeks ago. They could have died yesterday. The air was hushed, muffled, heavy—not even the hint of a breeze ruffled a single strand of fur or feather on Sajah, Rinqi, Sartai, or Temur. Zhara had hoped to purchase equipment, supplies, or even a guide once they arrived in Darun, but now they were faced with the prospect of nothing. No way to survive the journey into the Frozen Wastes.

"What are we going to do now?" Ami whispered, looking around at the ruined tents and bodies.

Yuli glanced at Jochi, who continued to beckon them forward. "We'll have to scavenge what she can," she said determinedly. "Kho and I will do our best to gather what we need."

"Yuli," Kho said softly, "neither of us have ever ventured out onto the tundra."

"But we know how to survive out here," Yuli said. "We'll have to do our best, or die trying."

Zhara studied the carnage around them and held her tongue. The possibility of dying was much closer and much more real than she was comfortable with.

The spirit of Jochi continued beckoning, leading them deeper into town where there were a few slightly permanent-looking residences—short, squat buildings built of stone and wood. They seemed to have survived the battle mostly unscathed, and the girls broke the ice coating the doors and pushed their way inside the nearest one. Inside were stores and stores and stores of food— wheat, barley meal, dried meats—an entire long winter's worth. The next building was filled with furs, boots, and other gear. While Zhara and Ami gathered provisions, Kho and Yuli ventured into other parts of Darun for a small tent to dismantle and fuel for fires.

The sun had begun to rise in earnest, brightening the oppressive darkness around Darun but deepening its sense of eerie stillness. No noise, no bustle of humanity, nothing but the girls and the ghosts, who swirled around the proceedings, occasionally coalescing into eyes, lips, faces, before dissipating back into mist. The last vestiges of the Shimmer were scarcely visible; soon they would be hidden by the light of day.

"How will we get to the Singing Skies?" Zhara asked. "If we follow the path of the Shimmer, we will have to travel at night."

"We can't travel at night," Kho said. "We'll die of exposure."

The ghost of the ship captain materialized beside the girls and gestured toward Yuli. When she touched their hand, his words filled their minds.

*Release us*, they said. *Release us and we shall guide you.*

The spirit bow and arrow shone in Yuli's hands, the light of her power like that of a star in the early-morning light. Taking aim, she loosed her weapon, and an ethereal bolt struck the ghost in the chest. Their eyes closed as they gave what seemed like an almost audible sigh of relief, a whisper like the swishing noises of the Shimmer above. Their entire being was flooded with a rainbow glow, which intensified as the edges of their silhouette blurred and dissolved, leaving behind nothing but a trail of colors as they drifted into the sky.

The trail pointed north. Temur leaped from the ground in a whoosh of air, following the ghost across the heavens.

Yuli turned to the mist around them. "Will you guide us?" she asked the ghosts. "Will you help us get to the source of the Shimmer?"

Again, that whispering sound. Zhara's hair stood on end—not from fear but from awe. And this time, she could make out the words.

*We shall.*

# 33

The journey to the Singing Skies passed by in a dream.

Ami had never known such brutal cold in her life, not even atop the Zanqi Plateau, where she had spent the past two winters. It was the sort of chill that seemed to slow down and narrow every aspect of life to the breath that seared in and out of her lungs, the steady thump of blood pounding in her ears. The cold had moved beyond bitter into unrelenting; there was no change, no shift, no getting used to it. It was a numbness that had become all-encompassing, affecting not only her body but her mind as well.

It was a killing cold.

They had been on the Frozen Wastes for hours. Or days. Ami could no longer tell.

Yuli and Kho led the way, allowing frequent rests, but never allowing them to stay still for long. At night, the girls huddled together with their companion beasts—and Sartai—in a single tent, surrounded by the warmth of Sajah's flickering fur. They slept in shifts, conscious of one another's breathing, ever aware of the high-pitched whisper-song of the *Shimmer* and the river of souls traveling ever northward overhead. Eating had become a chore, more necessity than pleasure. Although she was constantly hungry, Ami didn't have the appetite to eat the same bland meals over and over and over again. It was worse than the tsampa she had had to endure while traveling across the outermost west to Mount Llangposa; at least they had run into other travelers and encampments for a brief respite from the dullness of road rations. She had thought the pastures and rolling hills of the Zanqi Plateau were isolated, but it was nothing compared to the absolute emptiness of the Frozen Wastes. Nothing but endless fields of snow and ice, with occasional dunes and drifts pushed about the howling winds.

Even the celestial companions seemed to struggle, with Rinqi's breath coming hard and labored, Sajah's padded footfalls becoming plodding and heavy. The Lion of the South kept them all alive more times than they could count with his constant flickering flames, but even those started to look weak the longer they traversed across the tundra. Only Temur seemed unaffected.

The only figure untouched by the strain was the ghost of Yuli's cousin. The spirit had wandered the wilds for a long time now, and guided them to easier paths across the terrain. The constant flare of souls joining the Shimmer was their compass during the daylight hours, shorter and shorter now with each passing sunrise and sunset. More than once, Ami wondered at the futility of their endeavors; the journey to the Root of the World had been difficult, but hardship had a different meaning here. Here was the endless nothing of ice and snow, no variance in landscape, no game, no signs of life. There had been passages in *Songs of Order and Chaos* about a land of the dead, where forgotten ghosts lingered for all eternity. Back in warmer climes and easier times, she had merely thought of them as fanciful stories. But now she knew all those stories were true.

And then there was the amulet.

The effect the demonic stone had on all of them was pronounced, but none more so than Kho. She was not a Guardian of Dawn; she was a mere mortal, with only the strength of her will to protect her from its influence. Ami, Zhara, and Yuli all took turns carrying the stone, and each of them felt a dampening of their powers whenever the pendant came in contact with their skin. It was not unlike the fatigue and exhaustion of pushing their labored muscles through the pain, only it was not physical; it was spiritual. It was the feeling that the world had somehow become muted, dull, as though someone had placed an invisible blanket over their senses, even though their eyes, ears, noses, mouths, and hands worked the same as before.

Ami bore the brunt of carrying the amulet. Zhara's fire, like Sajah's, was the most crucial to keep them alive on the snow, while Yuli's powers kept the ghosts guiding them ever onward to the Singing Skies. She drew strength from the light of Rinqi's healing horn, but even the Unicorn was flagging as they made their way north. Sometimes Ami wondered if they would be trudging toward the Singing Skies forever, whether they had, in fact, died already and had become like the spirits above leading the way.

But the singing of the Shimmer grew ever louder.

They were getting closer.

And behind them, a contingent of Maltak forces were in pursuit.

One night, as they were huddled around a fire, having forced down yet another dry, tasteless meal of jerky and barley meal, Temur returned from one of her many scouting journeys, her eyes aglow with what she had seen and witnessed.

"A force of twenty," Yuli said, her own eyes glowing as her mind connected with her companion's. "Wearing the colors of the yellow wolf."

"The Huntsmen." Kho closed her eyes. "It must be the amulet."

The girls looked to Ami, who brought her hand up to cover the pendant.

"We need to destroy it," Zhara said wearily.

The cold had not affected the stone nor turned it brittle; instead, it only seemed to grow in power the nearer they drew to the Singing Skies. Ami did not know if it was simply her tiredness, but the amulet was heavier than before, and sometimes she found it difficult to get up and get going for the weight about her neck.

"Be my guest," Yuli said, equally weary. "I barely have the strength to lift my head, let alone lift a mallet to try to crush that thing."

"Something tells me it won't be as easy as simply striking it with a hammer," Ami said quietly. "In *Songs of Order and Chaos,* the first demonic amulet was destroyed by the Star of Radiance." She thought of Gaden down south with Han and Okonwe. Missing them had been an ever-present emotion since they parted, but she was swamped by a sudden wave of longing that threatened to drown her. She wanted to lie down and feel their arms around her and sleep for days.

"Can we just . . . leave it here?" Kho asked.

Yuli opened her mouth, then closed it again, leaning back against Sajah's bulk with a groan. "Even if it were to get lost in the snow and ice, once spring comes, someone is bound to find it. I don't think the Moth Demon"—she glared at the amulet—"is defeated that easily."

"One step at a time," Zhara said softly. "First we get

to the portal and seal it. Then we'll deal with the amulet."

And then, on the fifth day, they arrived at the Singing Skies, just as twilight was beginning to settle over the Frozen Wastes. The Shimmer had been growing brighter and brighter, visible even while the sun was out, the only sign they were reaching their destination. All the ghosts—save one, Jochi—were gone now, having joined the streaming bridge of colors overhead.

It was Jochi who showed them the way.

The Shimmer arced overhead like a rainbow, and it seemed as though they would never find its end. Ahead, there had been a smudge of gray hills covered in snow, which Jochi had insisted they cross. At a different time, a different season, a different life, Ami wouldn't have found it so difficult to climb. She was past tiredness now, to a point of numbness where words like *weariness* no longer had meaning. But she had summited Mount Llangposa, the tallest peak in the Zanqi Plateau; she could do this.

They crested the hills and came upon a vast circular basin, unremarkable save for one thing:

A ring of darkness in its center, out of which a column of multicolored light reached into the heavens.

The source of the Shimmer.

The Singing Skies.

"We're here," said Yuli, and the relief in her voice made Ami suddenly aware of every ache in her body, and the last bit of distance between them and the entrance to the ring of darkness felt insurmountable. Yet they did it, one step at a time, until at last, they had arrived.

"Well," Kho said. "Of all things, I didn't expect the entrance to the Singing Skies to simply be . . . a hole in the ground."

Ami would have laughed if she had the energy. The ground beneath the show was a glassy black, like obsidian, and Ami was reminded of the lava vents that surrounded the ruins of Old Changxi down south, only without the belching smoke and molten rock.

Zhara knelt and placed her hand on the ground. "The earth is made of that demonic stone," she said quietly. "It's all around us."

Ami shuddered. Anti-ki material. She reached for the pendant around her neck.

"How do we close this portal?" Yuli asked, leaning over the edge of the pit into the earth. The hole fell away into nothing; it was impossible to tell just how deep it went for the darkness ringing its mouth. "Do we just . . . cover it with earth? It can't possibly be that simple."

Ami thought of the roots of the Pillar, of the nothing that ate at the death in its branches. "Demon portals are holes in the fabric of the universe," she said. "When I—we—sealed the one in the outermost west, we had to use our gifts to transform anti-ki into ki and sew up the breach."

Yuli tilted her head at Zhara. "Can you do that here?"

With a frown, Zhara removed her mitten and placed it against the bare black rock. Her usual rosy-gold glow seemed pale and weak as it touched the ground. "I don't know if it's because I'm exhausted or if there's simply . . . too much anti-ki," she said at last.

"There are three Guardians of Dawn," Kho pointed out. "Perhaps you can work together."

Yuli continued to stare down into the physical abyss. "Do we need to enter the pit itself?" Beside her, the ghost of Jochi was shaking his head. Yuli looked to her cousin. "Do you know how we can seal the portal?"

The ghost nodded. The princess reached out to take his hand in hers and his words touched their minds.

*The portal is not on the physical plane,* he said. *It is in the spirit world.*

"Spirit world?" Ami looked to Yuli. "Does that mean only the Guardian of Wind can go?"

*Anyone can enter the spirit world,* Jochi said. *But most of us can do it only in dreams or death.*

Death. Yuli started to cry. It was the first confirmation that her cousin had indeed perished during his exile on the Frozen Wastes. The tears froze as they dripped down her face to her collar, forming a necklace of ice around her neck. Kho covered her mouth, her own eyes glistening.

"Oh, Jochi," Kho said. "I'm sorry. I'm so sorry."

The ghost only gave her a wavering smile.

"How does Yuli get to the spirit world?" Ami asked.

Jochi turned to his cousin. *Follow me,* he said to Yuli. *Come with me to the eternal blue skies.*

"What will"—Yuli swallowed—"what will happen to you?"

*I will return to the cauldron of consciousness at the center of the universe to be reborn.*

"And what will happen to me?"

Again, his only response was to give an enigmatic smile.

Yuli bit her lip, then looked to Temur. "Will you come with me?"

The Eagle of the North bobbed her head up and down in a nod. With a leap, she took off into the sky, circling the column of light before diving in and disappearing.

Yuli looked back at the other girls. Zhara's eyes were shining. The redhead smiled.

"Be sure to destroy that amulet for me," she said. "I'll be right back."

And with that, she untethered her soul, leaving her body behind, and walked into the column of light, hand in hand with her cousin for the last time.

# 34

Falling through the Shimmer in her spirit form was not unlike swimming, or at least as Yuli's ethereal senses perceived it. The swirl of ki around her seemed to have *form* and *weight,* if not exactly sound or sight or smell or taste or touch. Jochi was gone and she was drowning in sensation, but not the physical kind, and if it weren't for the presence of Temur in the Shimmer with her, Yuli would have been lost, the edges of her self dissolved utterly in the sea of souls around her, streaming on their way to the eternal blue skies. It was hard to remember who she was, who *Yuli* was, against the onslaught of images and memory and emotions that swirled around her. She had always cherished the freedom of being incorporeal, of being boundaryless, but in that space where neither time nor place had meaning, she struggled to maintain her identity in the maelstrom of the infinite. She was Yuli, she reminded herself, even as her self frayed and fell away. She was bold, brash, avoidant, flirty, a poor friend, a good friend, and—and—and—

She felt—sensed—the presence of Temur beside her, within her, as her, and bit by bit, piece by piece, Yuli gathered the disparate parts of herself. In lieu of a body, she built a self out of memories. Of the first time she met Zhara on the streets of Zanhei, the rose-gold ki of her wrapped around her own spirit like a flame. The glint of Ami's spectacles in the candlelight as she hunched over her journals filled with notes on *Songs of Order and Chaos*. Sartai's scent after a long ride on the steppes. The ache in her muscles after practicing her archery on the practice field. The feel of Kho's lips against her own, soft and gentle.

And all around her was music.

A part of Yuli understood that she was not *hearing*, not with her ears, but that she was experiencing the environment around her through something her mind interpreted as sound. She understood better now why the source of the Shimmer was called the Singing Skies; here, the whisper-crackle she had heard while sailing up the Sweet Sea to Darun was a choir of several thousand voices or more, each croon and serenade a different melody, a different tune. The sound quivered and vibrated through her spirit, as though her soul were the string of an instrument, made to echo and resound. She thought of musicians playing at festivals, the tambour and the drum, the fiddle and the flute, and suddenly she was dancing, the memory of her body moving in rhythm further grounding her sense of self. The world around her began to reorder itself, assembling itself into proper structures, and something like sight and sound and smell and taste and touch returned.

But threaded through these sensations was a discordant note, a sour taste, a rotten smell, a slimy feeling. Through the joy and wonder and freedom of the flow of souls around her was something dark, something that trailed dread and anxiety and fear in its wake.

Yuli opened her eyes.

She had no true eyes to see, but her mind was finally able to grasp and encompass the sensations surrounding her, within her, translating the ethereal world into something resembling the physical one. She let go of trying to understand and merely allowed herself to experience and be present, and as she did, her environment resolved into some semblance of a chamber. Yuli stood in a large circular room, the biggest room she had ever seen in her entire life, taller than twenty people and just as wide. It reminded her somewhat of the Temple of the Immortals she had seen in the south—a courtyard surrounded by twelve columns and open to the air. On the ground beneath her feet was a circumscribed twelve-pointed star carved into the flagstone, and at each of the points was a glowing figure bound with black ropes. Yuli blinked and to her spirit eyes, the glowing figures were clad in what appeared to be ancient armor, trapped by slithering snakes of depthless black that writhed and wriggled beneath their feet, dripping pools of ink that swirled toward a hole in the center of the star. Straddling the pit was a thirteenth glowing figure, wrestling with wisps of darkness that escaped from the abyss.

The Sleepers.

She could only be looking at their souls, locked in an eternal battle with the demons that escaped through the portal.

The source of the demonic infection in the north.

Yuli felt Temur's presence all around her and saw that the Eagle of the North had gathered herself into her familiar four-winged shape, her feathers wrapped around Yuli's spirit in a protective embrace, shielding her from the storm of darkness that whirled from the pit in the middle of the temple. It was as though Yuli herself had grown wings, the two of them melded together into a single entity.

The figure straddling the pit lifted their head and their eyes met, which Yuli felt as a connection between their souls.

"Who are you?"

The words brushed across her mind like the touch of a feather, instantaneous understanding formed not from language but from pure sensation.

"I am the Guardian of Wind," Yuli replied, sending images of a winged warrior made of tempest winds, wielding a bow and arrow.

"You are twenty years too late, Guardian of Wind," the figure replied. "The power of the Moth Demon was carried away from here and is now loose in the physical world."

The amulet.

"My friends and I have brought it back," Yuli said. "And we mean to destroy and seal this portal."

"Seal this portal?" The Sleeper laughed, and Yuli experienced it as a series of fizzing pops and bubbles in her spirit. "You?"

"Do you not believe me capable?" Without thinking, Yuli conjured up a spirit bow and a quiver of arrows, striking at a formless mass of emptiness that crawled out of the pit. The chamber shuddered, and for a brief moment, the image in her mind of the temple dissipated into a blur of light and color before reforming back into the colonnaded courtyard.

The figure never paused in wrestling the wriggling demons and merely laughed again. "You do not know what you ask, Guardian of Wind. To seal the portal is not a matter of power but of sacrifice."

"I am willing to make any sacrifice necessary!"

The Sleeper scoffed. "Spoken like someone who has never had to make a hard decision in their life."

*You never take anything seriously.*

A surge of irritation rippled through Yuli, scattering her sense of self like a stone breaking the surface of a still pond. "You don't know me."

At that, the figure of the Sleeper shivered, its edges blurring and shifting, its shape transforming into another as a second pair of arms emerged, then another, then two feathery appendages sprouted from the head as the eyes bulged and moved toward each side of the head. The figure hunched over as its shoulders rippled, growing, bursting, as a pair of quivery wings emerged from its back. The laughter that bubbled throughout Yuli changed, becoming sharp, needlelike, scratchy.

"Oh, but I do," said the Sleeper in a voice that sounded dissonant, doubled, discordant. "I know you very well, my ancient enemy. You, who flee before trouble; you, who fly away from any difficulty."

Yuli struggled to hold on to her edges, to maintain her identity, her sense of wholeness and discreteness. For she recognized the figure at the center of the twelve-pointed star, although she had never met them before in this life as Yuli.

The Moth Demon.

Another laugh, and the figure blurred again, resuming the form of the Sleeper.

"This is what you face in order to seal the portal to Tiyok," they said. "Fighting for your existence at every moment, to contain the emptiness that is chaos with the fullness of yourself. What is your power compared to the sacrifice of your soul?"

"The amulet," Yuli said. "The demonic talisman, the physical manifestation of the Moth Demon on the physical plane. Would destroying that banish this Lord of Tiyok and seal the portal?"

The Moth Demon reemerged with another laugh. "No, Guardian of Wind. Only by banishing me could you destroy that amulet. Any attempts your little friends make will prove futile."

"What of the Star of Radiance?"

A ripple of hesitation from the monstrosity at the center of the chamber. "You have not that power."

No, but she knew who had. But Gaden was far out of reach, along with Han and their other allies.

Yuli was alone.

"How do I banish you?"

The Sleeper emerged once more. "You must take my place and stand guard against the pit for all eternity."

The hard decision. Perhaps the hardest decision she would ever face in her life.

"Is there no other way?"

"Do you know why the Singing Skies is where the souls return to the cauldron of the universe?" the Sleeper asked. "The cauldron births both order and chaos, ki and anti-ki. They destroy and create each other in the same moment, and neither can exist without the other. That is balance."

"A constant battle between order and chaos?" Yuli asked. "That doesn't sound like peace to me."

"Peace?" The Sleeper scoffed. "Balance is not *peace*. Balance is not stasis. It is fluid and ever-changing. Balance requires constant maintenance, constant vigilance, constant diligence. It is not a war that is fought once and then won forever. Not even real-life wars are won forever."

Yuli thought of the Lady of Wild Things' plan to advance against the imperial city, at the head of yet another anti-magic crusade. Doubt crawled in, weighing down her soul.

"The opposite of anti-ki is ki," the Sleeper continued. "The only way to seal the darkness away is to become one with chaos. A soul must be sacrificed to keep balance."

# 35

The amulet called to Kho.

It had a voice, and it sang to her from the black depths of the stone. Soft, sweet, charismatic, charming, it did not sound at all like what she thought a demon would sound like. She thought of the screech of iron over slate, the high-pitched keening shriek of a whistling arrow, the screams of raptor birds circling the steppes. She had thought a demon would contain all that and more, but instead the voice was gentle. Melodious.

It was the voice of her mother.

*Kho-yah, Kho,* the Lady of Wild Things sang.

No. She shook her head. Not her mother. A demon. A curtain of sorrow fell over her shoulders as she realized that she might never have heard the true voice of the Lady of Wild Things in her entire life. Her mother had carried the amulet for as long as Kho could remember, so long that the demon had poisoned her soul. How much of the Lady of Wild Things' ambition had been hers? Kho's mother had always lived by the motto of the Maltak

Kang—*for the greater good*—her work and her advocacy always in service of order and the Morning Realms.

But how much of that had simply been a demon working toward chaos? Undermining good intentions, perverting them to a darker cause? It chilled Kho to think how easily the idea *for the greater good* had been twisted and corrupted in the wrong hands, how close she had come to doing the wrong thing for the right reasons. She had wanted peace for the Morning Realms, and had thought order was the solution. But what was order at the cost of strife and oppression? Of genocide? One could not forget the human cost. She must not forget the human cost.

Zhara and Ami were conversing in low tones about how to best break and shatter the talisman. A spasm of regret twinged Kho's heart at the thought of destroying such a beautiful piece of jewelry—a demon amulet was so unusual, so unique, it would be a pity to—

She wrenched herself back from the thought with a glare at the stone. Throughout the journey from Darun to the Singing Skies, she had had time to disentangle her thoughts from that of the demon contained within the amulet, although it had taken some time to recognize which ideas were her own and which belonged to an outside influence. It had gotten easier once she understood what parts of her had come from her mother and what parts had come from the books she'd read, the teachers who'd taught her, her brother, her friends. Yuli. Jochi's presence on their trek north had kept her grounded, the knowledge that what had been done to him was wrong. That the ideology with which she had been raised was wrong. She held on to that sense of personal justice, for it reminded her that she was her own person with her own moral compass even amid the concept of *the greater good.*

"I can try to strike it with an enchanted blade," Zhara was saying.

"Will that be enough?" Ami asked.

"I may not possess the Star of Radiance," the Guardian of Fire said, somewhat huffily, "but I'm no slouch either."

"I feel like destroying this is not just a matter of physical force," Ami said.

"Well, if you have any better ideas—"

Kho looked to Yuli's body, lying on a pile of furs with her head resting against a saddlebag. The Lion of the South wrapped his furry bulk around her to keep her vessel warm while her spirit was away. Kho would have thought that the body of someone who had gone spirit-walking would look as though it were sleeping, but the quality of Yuli's stillness was not that of sleep. If it weren't for the rise and fall of her chest and the faint clouds of mist wafting before her face, Kho could have almost believed she was dead. A sudden rush of pain racked her heart at the thought; they had only just found their way back to each other after years apart, after years of misunderstanding and distrust, and had found a new connection that made her chest ache with a different sort of pain. To have found someone, then to lose them—she didn't know if she could bear that.

"Come back to me," Kho whispered to Yuli, unsure if the princess could hear her in the spirit world. She hoped so. She was reminded of sitting beside some of the waking dreamers on her missions of mercy with the Lady of Wild Things. Sometimes speaking with them reminded Kho of writing letters to someone, of putting truth out into the ether with no guarantee of a reply. The waiting space between them was the perfect place to spill secrets, for there would never be any judgments, any shame, any ridicule.

"Come back to me," Kho said again. "Remember that

you are mine, and I am yours." She sat down beside Yuli's body and wrapped her mitten around the other girl's hand.

There was a faint vibration to the ground when she sat down. At first she thought it was simply the hum of the Shimmer, the chorus of souls that poured out of the ground and from the sky. Whenever the demon in the amulet pressed too closely on her mind, she found that focusing on the harmonic cacophony of whisper-singing that streamed from the Shimmer cut through the spell the Moth Demon tried to cast in her mind.

But the hum was not in the air. Beside her, the Lion gave a low rumble, and Sartai flicked her ears forward and back nervously.

With a frown, Kho got to her feet and peered over the edge of the pit. A loose pebble tumbled over the lip and into the emptiness. No echo returned.

*Thwap!*

Zhara had taken the amulet and smashed it against the rocks surrounding the pit. Ami clapped her hands over her ears and Kho winced at the sound, which had somehow deafened her—not her physical senses but her mind. There was a ringing sound somewhere in her head that made it hard to think, but through the pain, she felt the vibrations beneath her feet clearly. The thrum wasn't constant; more rhythmic, like the beat of a drum or the gait of a horse.

The ground started shaking.

"Do you feel that?" Ami asked.

Suddenly, a hand broke through the snow beneath their feet. Kho shrieked and rolled away as the hand was followed by an arm, a shoulder, a torso. A wizened, leathery face followed, the flesh long since withered beneath mummified skin, the eyes rotted and gone. A faint jingle filled the air and to Kho's horror, she saw the head of the creature before her wore the long-eared cap of a shaman.

"Sleepers!" Kho cried.

*Punch! Smash! Thud!*

More and more hands broke through the ground beneath their feet as thirteen mummified corpses—centuries old—clawed their way out of the ice. Sajah leaped to his feet with a roar, tossing Yuli's body aside like a rag doll as he swiped an enormous paw at the nearest Sleeper. Sartai reared and screamed, her hooves striking out at the closest head. A hand grabbed one of the mare's hind legs and she bucked, bolting away from the danger as fast as she could run. Nearby, Rinqi swung her head left and right, catching a few more Sleepers with her horn before lowering her head to charge.

"Ami!" Zhara went up in a blaze of flame, a girl made of fire. She pulled the blade from the scabbard on her back, its keen edges rippling with rosy-gold light.

"Kho!" Ami cried. "The amulet!" She tossed the talisman and Kho caught it with her mittened hand. "Find some way to destroy it!"

And with that, her own silhouette rippled and blurred, revealing the form of another figure beneath—one with skin tinted with spring green and auburn hair laced with impossible flowers. Ami knelt down and pressed her hand to the earth, which trembled and shook. Ice, snow, and dirt shuddered underfoot, as the ground gathered itself into crude human shapes, an army of makeshift soldiers.

A clap of thunder, and then a bolt of lightning came down from the clear sky, blasting one of the Sleepers into pieces, which immediately disintegrated into dust, leaving nothing but a haze of darkness where the body used to be. Sajah threw back his head and roared, the rounded silver horns atop his head crackling with energy.

*Zzzzzzthunk!* An arrow thudded into the ground beside Kho.

"The amulet!" Ami shouted. "Destroy the amulet!"

"I need cover!" she gasped.

In that instant, a wall of fire went up around her, encircling her in a barrier of flames.

*Ssssshisss!* Bits of ash floated about Kho's head as any arrow or projectile instantly went up in a blaze of char, disintegrating upon contact with her shield.

"I can't hold it for long!" Zhara ground out. "Hurry!"

Casting about for something to smash the amulet with, Kho found a granite rock the size of her head. Grabbing it, she hefted it high and drove it down onto the pendant.

*Crack!*

A flash of negative light, a dark streak of lightning, and the stone in Kho's hands fell apart, crumbled to dirt. The amulet lay on the ground, whole and undamaged, smoking a little from impact.

"Kho!" Zhara cried as the barrier of flame vanished.

Through the steam and smoke, she could make out the silhouettes of armored warriors advancing, the soft crunch of icy snow beneath their mounts loud in her ears.

The Maltak Kang had arrived.

# 36

*A soul must be sacrificed to keep balance.*

"There must be another way," Yuli said determinedly. "It wasn't until twenty years ago, before the Just War, that the Moth Demon appeared on earth. The portal must have closed before then."

"Closed?" The central Sleeper shook their head. "No, Guardian of Wind. This portal has been open ever since Qin the Warrior journeyed to the Singing Skies to make a bargain with the Mother of Demons and the Lords of Tiyok a thousand years ago."

Yuli was taken aback. "But . . . he was defeated. The demon talisman he wore was destroyed by the Sunburst Warrior and the Star of Radiance."

The Sleeper scoffed. "The amulet might have been destroyed, but demonic influence was still leaking into the world. Why do you think the Sleepers journeyed here all those years ago?"

She sucked in a sharp breath, or she would have if she'd had a body. Even though Yuli existed solely on an ethereal level, she couldn't help but act and think and move as though she were still entwined with the physical world. She realized then that the body was just as important as the spirit, that both were inherent to the human experience.

"The thirteen of you came," and her mental voice quavered, "to harness the power of the Shimmer."

"Is that what they say of our sacrifice?" the Sleeper asked in dismay. "No, me and my brethren came here to stop the spread of a demonic plague across our land, one that turned magicians into monsters and brought the dead back to life."

The cycle of order and chaos once again. Was there no end to this eternal battle? Yuli could feel the futility of it all press against her, weighing her spirit down with doubt, pushing her toward resignation and indifference. Was there even a point in fighting?

*I want to do the right thing.*

The right thing. The right thing would be to save the Morning Realms. It was what Kho would do, for the greater good. Yuli drew strength from her thoughts of Kho, of her surety, her purpose, and her unwavering sense of justice. Kho was the compass by which she set her heart, and she would do whatever it took to live up to being worthy of her.

Even if it meant doing the hard thing.

"What happened twenty years ago?" she asked. "How is it that the Lady of Wild Things was in possession of the Moth Demon amulet?"

"We have no concept of time," the Sleeper said. "Twenty years or twenty days, it is all the same to us."

"There was another human who came here before me."

The Sleeper writhed, and for the briefest moment, Yuli saw the face of the Moth Demon once more. "There have been many humans who have come here before you."

"Many?" Yuli was shocked. "What happened to them?"

"Consumed by the chaos," came the reply. "The magicians transformed into monsters, the non-magical dead, their bodies hosts for the demons until time and the tundra killed them all, returning the demons to the void."

"But one survived."

Uncertainty flickered across the Sleeper's expression. "There was one," they said at last, "who journeyed here for"—they sneered—"a game. A game of power."

The Grand Game. Yuli tried to remember what her aunt Görte had told her of the Trial of the Soul all those years ago. She and Kho were supposed to have raced to the rookery of the golden roqs at the southern edge of the tundra to steal an egg. Aunt Görte had won the title of Grand Kang for having triumphed at the Trial of Strength and the Trial of Wits, but lost the Trial of the Soul . . .

. . . to the Lady of Wild Things. The year the roqs did not come to roost.

"They stole," the Sleeper said, "a piece of the Singing Skies. One of the crystals that form the heart of this very pit."

Did the Lady of Wild Things know what she had carried with her from the Singing Skies? Or had she been an unwitting stooge in the machinations of demons for the past twenty years? Intentions didn't matter; what happened was the consequence of that action.

And that consequence was a soul to hold back the chaos.

"You sacrificed your spirits," Yuli said. "All thirteen of you. But you said only one was needed."

"We did not know," the Sleeper said. "When my brethren and I came, we were trapped by the demons here, who have fed on us for the past thousand years. We may have given ourselves to hold the chaos back, but we are also the reason the portal cannot be sealed. Not completely. Our life, our essence, our ki gives the demons strength, even as we fight them with our very existence."

. An idea formed in Yuli's head. "If I release the other twelve, will that weaken the demons?"

The central Sleeper hesitated. "Perhaps," they said reluctantly. "Perhaps without a source of energy, they will dissipate back into the void."

Within her, she could feel the brush of Temur's doubt like feathers against skin.

"Perhaps," the Sleeper continued, "if my brethren are freed, we can combine our energies and fight the Moth Demon together."

Again, that stir of doubt and hesitation from Temur.

Another hard decision. Yuli wished someone could make it for her, but she was here. She would have to be responsible, no matter the outcome.

"I'm sorry, Temur," she murmured, and lifted her bow to aim it at the slithering black snakes that coiled around the soul of the Sleeper directly to her left. She fired.

The arrow struck the darkness, which dissipated with a shrill squeal and made Yuli want to clap her hands over her ears.

"Yes!" The central Sleeper looked astonished. "Now come to me, my sibling! Help me! Lend me your strength so that we may subdue the chaos!"

The newly freed spirit looked from Yuli to the figure in the middle, then flowed toward the middle, arms outstretched. The figures merged, and the resulting Sleeper seemed bigger, even more powerful than before.

"I think it's working," the Sleeper gasped. "Quick, release the others!"

In swift succession, Yuli fired at demonic chains that bound the other eleven, as one by one, they slipped toward the center of the room to join the super-Sleeper. The robes of the shaman disappeared and the figure clad itself in armor, sprouting multiple arms, each brandishing a weapon.

"Yes!" The super-Sleeper roared and Yuli felt the entire chamber shiver and shake. Laughter rippled throughout the cavern, and she felt herself unravel at the sound, the edges of her identity shredded and frayed.

The face of the super-Sleeper grew shapeless, formless, indistinct, and emerging from its cheeks was an enormous pair of black, black eyes. From its head sprouted two antennae and several pairs of arms merged to form wings.

"Ah, Guardian of Wind," said the Moth Demon. "How easily fooled you are."

Where the twelve Sleepers had been were now holes in the fabric of the ethereal world, through which thousands upon thousands of monstrous snakes crawled through.

"The strength of the other twelve fuels me," the Moth Demon said. "And now . . . prepare to be devoured."

# 37

In the distance came the thunder of hooves and the ululating howls of the Maltak battle cry. Barreling toward them was a force of twenty warriors, each one an expert archer and marksman, loosing arrow after arrow at Kho and the others.

"Zhara!" Kho gasped, throwing herself at the Guardian of Fire as an array of arrows thudded into the ground where she had been standing just a moment before. Zhara rolled away as another cloud of arrows rained down, pulling up a shield of fire to cover them both. The missiles disintegrated into ash instantly upon contact. To their left, Ami raised a wall of rock, the arrows harmlessly glancing off the hard face.

But Yuli . . . Yuli's body was out in the open and unprotected, lying face down in the ice.

A roar and another lightning strike, and the ground exploded where the bolt came down amid the herd. The horses reared and scattered, running in a panic for the edges of the basin as Sajah sent bolt after bolt after bolt against the Maltak. Taking advantage of the break in the volley, Kho dove for Yuli, hooking her hands beneath the girl's shoulders and bodily hauling her behind Ami's fortification. The redhead was heavy with muscle, and her dead weight was difficult to shift, but Kho dug in her heels and dragged with all her might, pulling them to safety just as another arrow came whistling down.

"The amulet!" Ami's glasses were askew, fogged with the effort of creating her snow-and-ice soldiers. "Do you still have the amulet?"

"No." She had left it lying in the snow, still smoking from her last attempt to break it. "I think we have more pressing problems to deal with at the moment!"

"The amulet is the most important thing!" With effort, Ami closed her eyes and created a ripple of earth, bringing the pendant toward them.

Zhara ran to their side, breathing hard. Her fire shields were lasting for shorter and shorter periods of time, and it was clear she was exhausted. "Here," she said, handing her blazing sword to Kho. "Try to destroy the pendant with this."

"What about the Sleepers and the Maltak?" Kho asked.

"Ami and I will deal with them," Zhara said through gritted teeth. "But we can't forget what we came here to do: defeat the Moth Demon and seal the portal. Yuli is doing her part. We have to do ours." She raised another wall of fire, which lasted only a moment before sputtering out. "We have a greater goal."

*The greater good.* Kho grabbed the amulet and threw it on the ground, holding Zhara's flaming blade with the point facing down. The sword wasn't heavy, but she hoped speed and accuracy would be enough to do what was necessary. Lifting the weapon above her head, Kho drove it down onto the stone.

Yuli gasped as the sword struck the pendant.

"Yuli!" Kho cried.

The amulet remained unscathed, without even a scratch on its glassy surface. But blood began seeping through an invisible wound on the princess's chest, as though striking the pendant had done damage to her instead. The Unicorn of the West galloped toward them, lowering the tip of her glowing horn against the wound.

Yuli's body spasmed and twitched, and for the briefest moments, she opened her eyes. "Help . . . me . . ."

And then she was gone again.

Kho crawled to the pit and leaned over the edge. The Shimmer streamed up and to the heavens, seeming to originate from somewhere deep beneath the earth. If Yuli needed help, if she was struggling, someone had to be with her.

She threw the amulet around her neck and jumped.

# 38

Kho had never known such darkness.

The ground fell off into a steep slope, which Kho rolled down, trying her best to protect her head as she was bumped and tossed about on the loose scree. Pebbles and rocks clattered down in a shower of rain beside her, and for the briefest moment, Kho was terrified there would be no end to the fall, that she would be tumbling forever toward a bottomless pit straight into Tiyok.

*Thump!*

The breath was knocked from her as her body landed with a thud at the base of the slope. She lay there on her back in the stillness, staring at the streaming lights of the Shimmer snaking overhead. The hole through which she had fallen seemed impossibly small, no more than the size of her hand as she lifted it to her face. The light that reached the bottom of the pit was thin and wavering, like starlight through water, barely penetrating the depths of black surrounding her. Beyond the circle of light shining down on her, there was nothing but shadows. She reached her hand into the darkness, sucking a sharp breath at how completely it was swallowed up by the nothing.

It wasn't a complete absence of light, not the way she imagined being trapped in a burial mound on the Hills of the Dead would be. No, it was that the darkness had *presence*, like a person breathing over her shoulder. Kho had the distinct feeling she was not alone underground, but it was not the existence of ghosts or even demons on the other side of that ethereal veil that frightened her; it was something greater and even more unfathomable. Uncanny. Wrong.

Chaos.

As a little girl, Kho had liked to imagine herself as a heroine in one of the spooky tales she loved to read, liked to imagine what she would do in a situation like this. She had never considered herself particularly brave, but she was comfortable with discomfort in a way others were not, thrilling at chills and reveling in sensations of unsettlement. She might not have been the doughtiest or mightiest warrior, but she was calm, rational, and able to maintain composure even in the face of unimaginable pressure.

But she wondered if this was perhaps as much of a fantasy as the fairy stories children liked to tell each other on the playing field.

She was not just afraid of the dark; she was terrified.

"Yuli!" Kho called into the nothing. There was no reply, not even an echo. "Yuli!"

The amulet.

With a start, she patted herself down, feeling for the amulet around her neck. She didn't know whether to be relieved or dismayed that the stone was intact. To her, the pendant almost seemed to have a life of its own. A part of Kho balked at the thought of destroying it, did it not have the right to exist, just like the magicians—

She wrenched her thoughts away from the demon's influence. It was getting harder and harder to recognize when the pendant's power was warping her feelings; it was becoming better at manipulating her beliefs for its own survival. She thought she understood better how her mother had succumbed to it.

Presently, Kho's eyes adjusted to the dimness around her. The lights of the Shimmer pouring in from the hole above her head cast strange shadows about her, illuminating enormous columns of clear, mirror-blue ice that reflected bits and pieces of her body back at her. An eye, a hand, the hint of a scared expression, and Kho tried to hold on to the knowledge that she was alone, that the people she caught glimpses of were simply herself, fractured and frightened.

"Yuli!" she called again.

She did not know what she expected. Yuli's body was lying still and unmoving on the ice of the tundra above, but the knowledge that her spirit was *somewhere* down in the depths beneath the Singing Skies made her reach out nonetheless, hoping for a response. Yuli was battling demons somewhere on the ethereal plane, she needed help, but now that Kho was underground, she realized she had no way of reaching her. She could not untether her ki from her body, she could not disappear into the Shimmer.

Kho took in the cavernous space around her. Although it seemed to be some sort of natural chamber underground, there was a sense of orderliness, of structure about it. As though it had been *built* rather than formed by the whims of nature. The columns of ice soared toward the ceiling, regularly spaced, and the chamber was almost perfectly circular, the walls studded with smooth, glassy black stones similar to the pendant she wore around her neck. She thought of the illustrations of the temples and places of worship of the desert peoples west of the Dzungri basin she had seen in her library books, with their glass mosaic walls forming incredible tableaus from history, and Kho had the sense that these stones had been arranged with a purpose. To her untrained eye, they reminded her of a script, spelling eldritch spells out of rock. She shuddered.

In the center of the chamber was a flat-topped structure, waist-high, reminding her of the altar slab at the top of the Tower of Offerings. The pedestal was caught in the beam of light streaming down from the hole above her, every last part of it brightly illuminated and clear as day in the murky dark of the underground temple in which she stood. The same strange script was carved into the surface, and for a moment, she wished she had paper and charcoal with which to make some rubbings to bring back to Ami. The scrivener was good at languages; she would have delighted at this.

If they survived, that is.

However, there was a symbol in the middle of the pedestal that she did recognize. A circle, bisected by a vertical line: the sign against the evil eye. Now that she was familiar with it, the symbol reminded her of a cruder, simpler *taikhut,* but without the light and dark halves. The symbol was carved deeply into the surface of the pedestal, and when Kho studied it again, she thought that it looked like it was meant to hold some sort of vessel or chalice. Some sort of offering.

She fingered the amulet around her neck. An offering. It was the exact size of the stone in her hand, almost as though it were meant to receive it—

Slowly, almost as though she were standing outside herself and watching herself move, Kho pulled the amulet over her head and laid the stone in the carving.

All went dark.

The light of the Shimmer above suddenly disappeared, and the blackness was so absolute she cried out in terror. But then, just as quickly as it had gone away, the light returned, and for a moment, Kho wondered if she had just imagined it, if the fear that pulsed through her had simply snapped her mind.

There was the flicker of movement out of the corner of her eye.

Kho whirled around, thinking she would merely catch her reflection in the column beside her, but to her astonishment, she saw the figure within the ice, writhing and wrestling with what looked like a black snake wrapped around its body. They wore the long, hand-covering sleeves of a shaman, and she saw the long-eared, bell-laden cap on their head.

A Sleeper.

The soul of a Sleeper, trapped in the column of ice.

Whirling around, she counted the other columns—twelve in all—each containing a Sleeper's spirit. Where was the thirteenth? And where was Yuli?

Then she saw them. High above her head, floating above the pedestal in the center as though trapped in the shaft of light coming down from the Shimmer, were Yuli and the final Sleeper, whose form shifted back and forth between human and something more insect-like.

The Moth Demon.

# 39

The Moth Demon advanced on Yuli, brandishing a blade made of darkness in four of its arms.

"You've lost, Guardian of Wind," the demon said. "By releasing the other Sleepers, you've broken the last bits of protection holding my mother back."

"You tricked me!" Yuli held out her bow before her, then imagined it in the shape of a sword. She had fought hand-to-hand multiple times before, but never against an opponent with four blades. She imagined a shield in her other arm; this would be a defensive fight, no matter what.

"Of course," the Moth Demon said. "I am a creature of chaos, after all."

Within her, Temur stirred and stretched her claws, which curled around Yuli's ribs like her own extra set of arms. Each golden talon was the length of a dagger, and just as sharp. She was reminded that she was not alone, no matter how she felt. The Moth Demon advanced, and Yuli's head whirled as she tried to keep track of its many arms.

*Breathe.*

She had no body and no lungs, but the words of her old fencing master returned to her, the image of his pockmarked face and long mustache wavering before her. Reality and memory were difficult to separate in the spirit realm, and it was as though he truly stood before her in that moment.

*Breathe, still the mind.*

Calm settled over Yuli. All fights were a game of anticipation and reaction, and the combatant who did not allow themselves to be overcome with emotion always had the upper hand. Yuli extended her senses to encompass the whole of the chamber, the columns now writhing with demon snakes, the ribbons of darkness that slithered toward the pit beneath the Moth Demon. An arm twitched, and Yuli threw up her blade as the sword swung down, countering it. She pulled in her shield arm to guard her side as another arm cut in from the left, as one of Temur's talons raked across the Moth Demon's eyes. Yuli felt both divided and whole, aware of the Eagle of the North fighting with her, protecting her, as she focused on the Moth Demon's attacks. Left, right, left, there was no connection between her mind and her body, and she moved faster than thought without the weight of flesh to hinder her.

"You cannot win," the Moth Demon hissed. "Even if you destroy me, the Mother of Ten Thousand Demons shall return and cover the Morning Realms with ten thousand years of darkness!"

Temur was sending Yuli an image as she fought of driving the point of her spirit blade into the heart of the Moth Demon so that it shattered into pieces. It fought erratically, with no strategy or thought to its own defense, and while that made keeping herself ahead of its assault difficult, it also left it vulnerable if Yuli could just find and take the opportunity. The shattered demon in Yuli's mind fell into thirteen pieces, and she understood that Temur was telling her to split the super-Sleeper back into individuals.

The blades of darkness were a blur before Yuli, and again and again and again the Moth Demon parried her attacks. She could not get an opening, not from this distance. Yuli leaped back, feeling Temur's wings beating as they carried her away from the sphere of engagement. Transforming the sword in her hand back into a bow and the shield into an arrow, she swiftly nocked her missile to the string and drew.

There. The opening.

She fired, and the arrow flew straight and true, right into the heart of the Moth Demon.

Cracks formed in the creature, fissures glowing with white-gold light as Yuli imagined the arrow splitting into twelve, separating and cleaving and carving the thirteen individual spirits away. The Moth Demon shrieked, then burst.

Everything disappeared.

For the length of a blink or a breath, the spirit world fell away, but time had no meaning on the ethereal plane. The moment was both as long as eternity and as brief as a thought, but the overwhelming tide of chaos briefly threw Yuli's spirit from that plane of existence and she thought she found herself in a similar chamber, only the columns were made of ice and the walls were studded with black gems.

Then the spirit world returned.

The thirteen Sleepers were back at the points of the twelve-pointed star on the floor, with the central Sleeper standing on the other side of the Moth Demon.

But there was another figure in the room.

A short, curvy figure with long-lashed dark eyes, her form hazy and transparent, as though seen through a veil.

Kho.

"Yuli!"

She felt her name down in her soul, and she was filled with warmth. "How?"

"The amulet—" Kho said, but her voice was faint, as though heard from another room. She pointed at a dark spot in the Moth Demon's abdomen. "—in the chamber— the real world—"

The Moth Demon whirled to face the interloper, then laughed. "Oh, this is rich," it said. "Your little lover come to help you save the world?"

Kho moved to Yuli's side, lacing her fingers through hers. "Yes."

To Yuli's shock, she *felt* the other girl's hand, as though she had skin and muscle and bone. She reveled in the sensation, and promised herself she would cherish every moment in her own body when they returned to the physical world.

The form of the Moth Demon shifted, and the Sleeper appeared once more. "The amulet!" they cried, pointing to the hole in their abdomen. "Strike it! Destroy it!"

Yuli swiftly drew up her bow, then hesitated. What if it was another trick?

"Hurry!" the Sleeper called before they were swallowed up by the Moth Demon once more.

"The amulet," Kho said quietly, "lies in the center of the chamber. We can't destroy it in the physical realm, but if you destroy the demon here, maybe we can neutralize its power."

The Moth Demon curled around the spot in its middle and Yuli realized that it was trying to protect itself. It was vulnerable, and the presence of the amulet nearby in the real world was its weakness.

She pulled back on her bow, but there was no opening. The Moth Demon was condensing, collapsing, cocooning into a protective shell, but it seemed to be fighting itself, struggling with an invisible assailant.

The central Sleeper emerged once more. They spread their arms open wide, exposing their belly to Yuli. "Now!"

Yuli fired.

The arrow sailed through the chamber, straight into the hole at the center of the Moth Demon. An unbearable whine filled the cavern as the Moth Demon began to glow with a white-gold light before bursting into a shower of stars.

All was still for a moment, for eternity.

The central Sleeper was gone, as was the demon with which it had fought for over a thousand years, but the pit in the center of the chamber remained open. Darkness poured down the walls of the spirit temple, flooding the floor as the spirits of the other twelve shamans cried out.

"The Mother of Ten Thousand Demons is free!"

# 40

When Kho disappeared over the edge of the pit, she had taken the amulet with her.

Ami leaped and tried to grab the back of the girl's coat as she tumbled into the darkness, but it was too late. Kho was gone, and all around them the Maltak Kang were swarming and the mummified corpses of the Sleepers were attacking.

"Zhara!" Ami shouted. "The amulet!"

The Guardian of Fire was grappling with a Sleeper corpse, her flames sputtering in and out as she struggled to maintain her Guardian form. "A little busy at the moment!" she choked out.

One of the snow soldiers barreled into the Sleeper, shattering into drifts upon contact. Ami felt her mind flagging and felt spectacularly useless. Snow was a poor defense against any attack, and ice only a little bit better, but anything more solid was so far below she could scarcely sense its ki. She wished she had learned to fight at least a little from her cousin Han, but there was no time for regrets now.

The mummy attacking Zhara went up in flames at last and the Guardian of Fire rolled away, drawing in deep, labored breaths. Sajah roared and swiped at the attackers with his paws, while Rinqi kept the Sleepers at bay by striking at them with her sharp hooves. Between the four of them, they had managed to destroy all but two of the Sleepers, but that still left the force of riders bearing down on them with bows and arrows.

"What do we do?" Ami asked. "The amulet is in the portal. Do we follow them down? What about the Maltak?"

Zhara pushed her ice-and-sweat-laden hair out of her face. She looked haggard, her brown skin gray with fatigue, and Ami felt guilty at placing the burden of such decisions on her friend's shoulders. "I don't know," Zhara said. "I don't know."

The Guardian of Fire's glow had winked out entirely, and Ami knew she was near collapsing. "Come on," Ami said, placing Zhara's arm around her shoulders. Arrows thudded into the snow all around them, and with effort, Ami dug deep with her power, reaching down, down, down, and grabbed the frozen earth, willing a wall to rise.

The ground shook.

Fissures cracked through the snow, opening deep chasms in the ground. Jagged edges of ice shot up, spearing several of the Maltak and causing their horses to stumble.

"Ami," Zhara said, sounding impressed, "I didn't know you had that in you."

"That wasn't me!" The earth was shaking even harder now, and behind her, rocks began tumbling down into the pit. The ground crumbled and fell away as the portal widened, swallowing the remains of the Sleepers as well as their supplies. Yuli's body slid down the opening hill, falling toward the bottom. "Run!"

The girls stumbled over their feet as they raced across

the snow, trying to outrun the collapsing snow behind them, heedless of the arrows flying in front of their faces.

"Yuli—Kho—the amulet—" Zhara gasped.

"Not now!" Ami half dragged, half carried Zhara as the Guardian of Fire moved sluggishly, exhaustion overcoming even her instinct for survival. Sajah and Rinqi rushed to their sides. Ami helped Zhara climb onto the Lion's back before mounting the Unicorn. "We have to get out of here!"

The celestial companions took off, covering wide swaths of ground with each stride. All around them, the Maltak warriors were in disarray, shouting in alarm as the earth broke and crumpled beneath their horses' hooves. One by one by one, they were each swallowed up by the fissures and chasms that opened beneath them, falling away into the pit.

"We're not going to make it," Zhara said, watching the basin open up into a yawning hole behind them. Ahead, the gray ridge of the low hills that circled the plain seemed to grow no closer. "We're not going to make it!"

Ami's mind spun. She could do it. She could command the earth to move and stop. She just needed time, a bit of breathing space, a moment to gather herself together. "Rinqi," she said into the Unicorn's ear. "Help me."

The Unicorn knew what to do. Whirling around, she reared and drove her hoof down into the snow. Waves of ice and dirt rippled from where her foot met the ground, disrupting the progression of decay. Ami slid off Rinqi's back and laid her own atop the earth, reaching deep into the cracks with her power, filling them with ki.

The basin shuddered, then went still.

Through her Guardian senses, the image of an enormous temple—now in ruins—came to Ami. Enormous columns of ice had fallen, and scattered throughout the land, the dying light of the Maltak warriors who had come in pursuit. She pressed farther, searching for Kho, for Yuli. She found both.

"The others—" Zhara croaked.

"Alive," Ami said.

Zhara fell to the ground in a dead faint.

The portal to the demon realm was open.

"Put us back!" the remaining Sleepers cried. "We must hold the demons back!"

Yuli glanced helplessly at the swirling mass of darkness in the middle of the spirit cavern. She had done this. She had broken the lock by releasing the Sleepers. She had had to make the hard decision, and she had made the wrong choice.

But there was one thing she could do to make it right.

The cavern was beginning to warp, the images blurring and scattering like sand sculptures blown about by a malicious wind. The darkness at the center howled, and she could feel the inexorable pull toward chaos and the void.

*You cannot defeat me, Guardian of Wind,* said the Mother of Ten Thousand Demons, and Yuli felt laughter all around her. *A soul is the lock, and you have not the courage to make that sacrifice.*

"A net!" Kho cried. "Use your spirit arrows to create a net over the pit!"

Yuli fired across from her, imagining a thick rope of her soul flying over the darkness, but the line disappeared into nothing as her spirit arrow found no purchase.

"Use us!" the Sleeper on the other side cried. They held out their hands and bared their chest, presenting a target. "Let us help you!"

No time to think, no time to hesitate. Yuli fired again, and this time, when the arrow struck the Sleeper, she felt resistance on the other end of the line. No, not resistance. Connection. Flooding through the line came memories—a squalling baby, a smiling parent and grandparent, a dark room filled with burning cones of incense—before Yuli gathered herself together and remembered who she was, separate from the other. Turning around, she imagined the rope that connected her to the Sleeper passing through her to another arrow in her hand. She fired that into the Sleeper across the way. The line held, with Yuli herself as the anchor in the middle.

Again and again and again and again, she turned and fired, slowly but surely creating a net of pure ki that the Mother of Ten Thousand Demons could not cross. The void screamed and shrieked its rage, but could not pass. Yuli felt every reverberation of that scream across her soul, and she felt herself grow ragged at the edges, fracturing, disintegrating. She had to hold on. She had to anchor herself to the darkness somehow. Around her, the twelve Sleepers were also dissolving, their essences devoured by the dark maelstrom that swirled up from below.

"Yuli!" Kho cried.

The feel of Kho's words across her mind solidified her sense of self. She was Gommun Yulana. She was the Guardian of Wind. She could do this. She could make the hard decision and do the right thing.

The bow in her hand blurred, then resolved itself into a sword. Yuli turned the point on herself, preparing to drive it home, to use the blade to turn the lock on her soul and close the portal.

"What are you doing?" Kho shouted.

"I'm sacrificing myself," she shouted back.

"You can't!" Swifter than thought, the image of Kho appeared at Yuli's side. "Zhara, Ami, they need you. *We* need you! You are the Guardian of Wind, we can't lose you to the darkness before the war is done!"

"I have," Yuli gritted out, "to do the right thing."

Kho wavered, flickering in and out in surprise.

"You told me once that I could never make the hard decisions," Yuli said, although sound and volume had no meaning in the spirit realm. Their minds were connected, and the words were soft. "I'm making it now. For the greater good."

Kho grasped Yuli's face between her hands and pressed a kiss to her lips. Without the barrier of their bodies between, the touch was more deep, more intimate, more vulnerable than anything Yuli had ever experienced. "I love you," Kho murmured, and although there were no tears on the ethereal plane, her eyes glimmered. Her hands slid to the blade in Yuli's hands. "You are mine."

"What—" Yuli began, but it was too late.

Kho drove the sword into her own soul.

# 42

There was a blast of light and time held its breath.

Zhara struggled against the brightness, swimming back up from unconsciousness. The light called to her, but she resisted, feeling the leaden weight of exhaustion pull at her mind. Through her closed lids, the light had grown almost unbearable, but it did not hurt; it instead filled her with warmth.

Then it was gone as soon as it had come, leaving her colder than she had ever been.

Was this death? The last thing she could recall was the basin surrounding the source of the Shimmer collapsing around an ever-widening pit. The image of Rinqi rearing and striking the ground returned to her, then that of Ami with her hand pressed to the earth. Kho—Yuli—

Zhara opened her eyes with a groan.

She was not dead; the dead would not feel so tired.

"Shh, shh." Ami hovered above her, her silhouette doubled and blurred before resolving into a single image. "It's all right. It's over."

There was a slight pressure at her chest, and Zhara looked down to see Rinqi gently laying the tip of her horn against her coat. The cold receded from her body, and she felt as though she were being flooded with liquid sunshine, and she almost moaned in relief. Fatigue washed away, and she felt more alert, able to access her powers once more. She sat up.

"My thanks, friend," Zhara said to the Unicorn, patting Rinqi on the snout. The Unicorn blinked in acknowledgment, her long lashes sweeping up and down. Zhara looked around at the landscape, broken and uneven where there had been smooth expanse before. The aftermath of their battle was gone, swallowed up by the earth.

"Kho and Yuli are still in the pit," Ami said. "Something must have happened because for a moment the Shimmer faltered and broke and apart before an explosion of light came from below."

"Is the portal closed?" Zhara asked.

Ami nodded. "I can't sense the void beneath the ground anymore."

"And Kho and Yuli?"

The scrivener said, "Alive but . . . something's wrong. I could sense Yuli, but Kho . . . something has happened to Kho."

A long crack stretched from the pit—if it could be called that now—to where the girls stood, a gentle slope leading all the way down. "We should go after them," Zhara said, following this makeshift road with her eyes. In the distance, she could just make out the tops of broken ice columns jutting out of the ground, and smooth expanses of wall, like a chamber of sorts.

"I don't think there's any danger," Ami said. "Not anymore. Best watch our step."

The girls mounted their companion beasts and began the long, slow trek down into the chamber underground.

Zhara hoped that Sartai was all right; the mare had fled at the first sign of battle, and she thought that she had gotten past the destruction radius. Sajah picked his way on padded paws, his footfalls silent and sure amid the loose scree and shale. Behind them, Ami rode Rinqi, light and fleet-footed as she followed the Lion of the South.

Zhara thought she could hear the distant sounds of crying as they drew close. She was afraid of what she and Ami would find down in the ruins, whether it was Yuli's or Kho's broken bodies or worse. She held on to the knowledge that both were alive, that no matter what else, they had all survived the battle together.

"Kho," came a broken voice from the crater. "Kho."

It was Yuli.

Zhara came upon the princess with her arms wrapped around the limp form of the Maltak girl, the two of them gently embraced by Temur's four wings. Kho's eyes were half open and staring into nothing, and for one heart-stopping moment, Zhara thought she was dead. But the breath that clouded before her face belonged to that of a living person, and Zhara knew in that moment that she had fallen into a waking dream.

"Yuli," she said softly, putting a hand on the redhead's shoulder. "Yuli."

"Kho," Yuli said again, oblivious to Zhara's touch. "Wake up. Kho, come on."

Rinqi lowered her horn to the girl's chest, but to no avail. They stood in the ruins of what appeared to be an ancient temple surrounded by black stones radiating with anti-ki.

"Is the—is the Moth Demon gone?" Ami asked.

Yuli did not answer, but continued to weep. Zhara looked around and spied the amulet lying just a few feet away, and walked over to pick it up. She could feel the chaotic nature of it thrumming through the stone, just as she could feel it among the other black crystals scattered in pieces around them, but it was no longer heavy, empty of the demon's presence. The surface remained smooth and unblemished, however, and it looked exactly the same as it had before.

Ami knelt beside Yuli. "What happened?" she asked gently.

"Kho sacrificed her soul to seal the portal," Yuli choked out. "Her ghost is still trapped in the spirit world, holding back the darkness."

Sorrow squeezed Zhara's heart, but the pain she felt was nothing compared to the grief on Yuli's face. "Is there any way to save her?"

"I don't know." Tears streamed down Yuli's cheeks, too hot to freeze. "It was supposed to be my decision to make," she said. "Not hers. It was supposed to be me."

Zhara wrapped her hand around the amulet. "I'm sorry," she said quietly. "I'm so, so sorry."

"Come," said Ami. "There's nothing more we can do for her here. Let's get back to Darun and find some way to get help."

"What help?" Yuli rasped. "If the Guardians of Dawn can't save her—if *we* can't save her, what can be done?"

"I haven't finished translating this fragment of *Songs of Order and Chaos* yet," Ami said. "And remember, the last piece is yet to be found. There will be a way to rescue Kho. I promise."

Zhara raised her brows in surprise. Ami was an eminently truthful person, even when it hurt more to be honest than to lie. But by the determined look on the Guardian of Wood's face, she knew that Ami believed there was a way to save her. That she had to believe there was a way.

"Come on," Zhara said softly. "Let's go. It's over."

The way back was in some ways easier and in others harder. Yuli had gone spirit-walking to Arkhevet to ask for help from the Guardians of Dawn, and Temur had left in order to guide their rescue party. Zhara went looking for their tent and furs in the ruins of the temple, while Ami scavenged the corpses of the Maltak for food and other supplies. It was best they stayed close to where they were while their rescuers came looking, but until then, they had to find some way to survive. Ami wanted to move to more stable ground, so they had taken up the slow, arduous process of moving everyone out of the broken basin.

Sajah bore the burden of carrying the two waking dreamers while they waited for Yuli's spirit to return, and Rinqi carried what few things they had managed to collect—the remnants of their tent, the furs, and some packs of dried food. Ami had also collected some bows and arrows from the Maltak, in the hopes that Yuli could go hunting for game—if not, they would have to go hungry while they waited.

"A week," Yuli said when she came back several hours later. "It will take a week for them to get here."

In the meantime, Zhara decided to set up a more permanent shelter. Ami created a house out of ice, which Zhara then transformed into one of wood and stone, changing the structure agonizingly slowly, bit by bit. Her powers had not yet returned to full strength, and she felt as though she were working with a strained muscle— push too hard and she might injure herself past repair. But once she was done, they could at least keep warm and sleep comfortably until the search party arrived.

The following day, Sartai found them.

Yuli was overjoyed at the return of her mare, and their reunion brought tears to Zhara's eyes. The princess still carried so much grief, but the relieving of that burden, if just for a moment, was something they all needed.

The following day, Kho was gone.

How it had happened, no one knew. The night before there had been a storm, and the girls had fallen asleep huddled around the fire, with Sartai and Sajah and Rinqi and Temur curled around them for warmth. For the first time in a long time, Zhara had slept well, untroubled by dreams or dread. They were on the other side of an ordeal now, and she only had hope to look forward to in the immediate future. Someone was coming to rescue them, they would go somewhere safe, they would be warm and rested and fed and ready to face whatever challenges came next.

Zhara had woken early, as was her wont. Sometimes their little shelter could grow quite stuffy with the heat of so many bodies, so in the morning she would step outside for fresh air.

It was then she noticed the footsteps in the freshly fallen snow.

A single set of prints, leading directly south, as far as her eyes could see.

Rushing back inside, heedless of who she accidentally jostled awake, Zhara tried to account for everyone, but everyone was present. Yuli, Ami, Temur, Rinqi, Sajah, and Sartai. No one was missing.

And then she realized she had forgotten about Kho.

How could she have forgotten about Kho?

Temur immediately went searching for the missing Maltak girl, while the others scoured the nearby areas as much as they dared, but it was as though Kho had simply vanished into the ether.

As had the amulet.

No one had noticed its absence. At first. But as the days went on with no sign of Kho, and the search party approaching, the girls had had to look ahead to the future. It was only in the process of gathering all their things that Zhara realized that more than the Maltak girl had gone missing.

"Do you think . . ." Ami hadn't been able to finish the question.

Zhara had no answer. The talisman had been empty of the presence of the Moth Demon, but it had still been an artifact of anti-ki, vulnerable to demonic energy. Yuli had sworn the portal was closed, but there was no telling if a stray demon had escaped.

They would have to wait.

On the day the search party arrived, Yuli stood apart from the others, overlooking the pit to the underground temple.

"I don't sense the void," the redhead said quietly. "It's gone."

Zhara looked down at the ruins, creepy now in an ordinary way instead of an uncanny one. "Perhaps Kho's spirit returned and she was able to walk away."

Yuli shook her head. "No. I still feel her here. Her strength, her loyalty, her"—her voice cracked—"steadfast desire to do the right thing. She's protecting us, Bubbles. She's holding back the void."

Zhara said nothing.

"Whatever that thing was that walked away," Yuli said, "it wasn't Kho. It was a demon, I'm sure of it."

Zhara rested her hand on the princess's shoulder. "We can still save her," she said. "We know what to do now."

The princess closed her eyes. "There's no saving Kho until we defeat the Mother of Ten Thousand Demons."

"Then we will defeat the Mother of Ten Thousand Demons," Zhara said simply.

Yuli cast one last look at the pit, as though to say farewell. Then she turned to the rising sun, toward the next demon portal in the east. "We will win," she said softly. "For Kho."

# EPILOGUE

The last time Yuli had been in the imperial city, it had been to say farewell to her dying grandfather. She thought she had known grief then, the overwhelming agony of loss mingled with affection and sorrow and regret.

But that was nothing compared to the pain she felt now.

After the destruction of the portal at the Singing Skies and the forfeiture of the Grand Game by both the Gommun and Maltak contestants, the Five Golden Families were in disarray. The Gommun Kang were revealed to be magician sympathizers and traitors, scattered to the four winds, and the Lady of Wild Things was dead. The other heads of the Nuwage, Tzorig, and Shulgin could not come to an agreement over the leadership of the north, and it had fallen to the Council of Shamans to govern until the Falconer had returned to Urghud to claim supremacy of the Maltak. There were reports he and his Kestrels had purged the people of any pro-magic sentiment, installing himself as Grand Kang and uniting the northerners against the southern and western factions of the Morning Realms.

The north was lost.

Yuli had lost.

The Morning Realms were officially at civil war.

She wanted to disappear.

Yuli had never known shame like this. She had lost competitions before, but the stakes had been small, manageable, and ultimately insignificant. Now, not only were there hundreds of thousands of lives within the empire in danger, the entire world as she knew it was vulnerable to the return of the Mother of Ten Thousand Demons.

Tiyok.

They were facing chaos, in more ways than one.

There was still the Conclave ahead, where the heads of the provinces would officially come together to swear fealty to the next Sunburst Emperor, but no one expected there would be any accord. The southern and western provinces had declared their independence, advocating for sovereign rule of their lands. No one could be sure of the Azure Isles' allegiance; the Fleet Queen had brought their navy to the Warlord's side during the Just War, but the isles had long been fractious, fighting imperial rule and their own internal power struggles for as long as anyone could remember. The last Marquess had been the rightful ruler of the Azure Isles before she was murdered by her sister, the Fleet Queen. The last Marquess had been a magician, but the Fleet Queen was not, and the conflict between the sisters had seemingly been a precursor to the events of the Just War.

Han, Gaden, and the former Right Hand of the Qirin Tulku had sent their own emissaries to Kasong to meet with the Fleet Queen, but the condition of her alliance had been the assassination of her niece, the potential heir to the Azure Isles. No one knew the whereabouts of the last Marquess's daughter; the girl had been smuggled out of the capital when she was but a babe.

"Like me," Gaden had said. They shook their head. "All children are to those in power are pawns in their political games."

Although they had been born in the imperial city, they were even less familiar with it than Yuli. Yuli had spent a few winters there when her grandfather had been the Gommun Emperor, although she had ever preferred the steppes to the grandeur of the empire's capital. Gaden had grown up on the Zanqi Plateau under the tutelage of the late Qirin Tulku, and still felt more kinship with the Free Peoples of the West than anyone else in the Morning Realms.

Even though they were the last scion of the Mugung Dynasty.

Even though they possessed the Star of Radiance.

To the rest of the Morning Realms, Gaden *was* the heart of the empire.

If anyone could end the civil war, it was Gaden. If they wanted, they could simply compel everyone in the Morning Realms to do their will, as their ancestors had done in the past. It was what the Heralds of Glorious Justice wanted them to do.

"I will not exchange one form of tyranny for another," Gaden had said in one of their many arguments with Pang Lok, the leader of the Heralds.

"But you could bring *peace*," Pang Lok had said in despair.

"At what cost?" Gaden returned. "And by whose consent?"

"The people!" the warrior said with frustration. "After all, the people of the Morning Realms gifted the Sunburst Warrior with one drop of will each a millennia ago!"

"To seal the Mother of Ten Thousand Demons back into her realm!" Gaden pinched the bridge of their nose. "Not to rule but to defeat chaos!"

Yuli had heard several iterations of this debate, which never resolved and merely went in circles. There were those who believed Gaden should take the Sunburst Throne and restore the Mugung Dynasty, but there were still others in the alliance who believed that each province had the right to decide its own fate. There was even disagreement among the leaders of the southern city-states over the use and regulation of magic. Han, along with a contingent of younger leaders, believed in freedom for magicians, but the older generations were more cautious, the memories of when abominations wreaked havoc on the land fresher in their minds.

"Have we not learned from the mistakes and calamities of the Just War?" Han had addressed the alliance in assembly last week. "It is not just the horrific loss of life but the loss of knowledge that has harmed us all irreparably. We cannot treat abominations and the undead with mere force; these are magical problems that require magical solutions!"

"You've grown up, Prince Rice Cake," Yuli had said afterward, impressed.

"I have?" Han straightened, puffing out his chest. "Xu doesn't think so, but I swear I'm taller than I was this time last year."

She laughed. "Never change, my friend."

The machinery of war continued apace in the imperial city, with the empire's foundries churning out hundreds of weapons by the day. Recruiters from the Heralds were traveling all over the Morning Realms in search of able-bodied people to prepare for the coming battles, and it was the sight of all the glory seekers coming into the capital that made Yuli understand for the first time the true scale of this civil war.

And how very young she and her friends actually were.

"It's frightening, isn't it?" Zhara came to stand beside Yuli in her quarters overlooking the courtyards filled to the brim with people preparing for conflict.

"Terrifying," Yuli murmured. "And the war isn't even our focus."

If there was any comfort Yuli could take from the events of the past several weeks, it was that she and her friends had managed to defeat the Moth Demon and seal the demon portal at the Singing Skies. But there was still one portal left to close, one more Guardian of Dawn to find, and the last of the Lords of Tiyok to defeat.

And then there was the matter of Kho.

When Yuli woke up the morning after the battle of the Shimmer to discover her best friend gone, she hadn't known what to think. None of the other waking dreamers had woken up; their ghosts were still untethered from their vessels. All those anti-magicians were still at risk of demonic corruption, and Yuli did not have the time to rescue them one by one.

That was another failure she would have to face.

But facing that failure was infinitely better than facing the prospect that Kho had possibly been possessed by something even greater than the lesser demons or a Lord of Tiyok.

"Kho isn't a magician," Ami had tried to comfort her. "She's not vulnerable in that way."

"Isn't she?" Yuli had asked. "Lesser demons can possess magicians and turn them into abominations. They can possess the dead and turn them into revenants. They can possess waking dreamers and turn them into mindless thralls. The Lords of Tiyok can walk among us in human guise. Who is to say that the one force greater than them all could . . . could—"

"Don't." Zhara placed a hand on Yuli's shoulder. "It does no good to dwell on that."

"How can I not?" Yuli clenched her fists. "What other explanation is there?"

Neither Ami nor Zhara could answer the question. Only those with a connection to the void—either through magic or through death—could be manipulated by demons, but when it came to the embodiment of chaos itself . . . the Mother of Ten Thousand Demons could possess powers of which none of them could possibly conceive. Even if they had all four fragments of *Songs of Order and Chaos,* there was so much of Tiyok they did not know.

"It does no good to dwell on that," Zhara repeated. "Focus only on what we can control. On the war we have the power to fight."

Yuli closed her eyes. "The last demon portal. At the Lake of Illusion in the east."

"Yes," Ami said. "Somewhere in the Azure Isles."

Yuli opened her eyes and contemplated the troops gathering outside her window once more. "We could have gone with the Bangtan Brothers to the Azure Isles to search for the last Guardian of Dawn."

"They have their own journey to fulfill," Zhara said. "Finding Min Suhwa."

"Where do we even begin?" Yuli asked.

"My father has sent us a letter," Ami said. "Studying some of the maps in the library at Kalantze. Based on his research, he thinks the eastern portal is the crater lake located at the top of Mount Changgun."

It was a start. Although Yuli remained heartbroken, the firm prospect of having something to do lifted her spirits immensely. She started at the knock on the doors to her quarters, then they slid open to reveal Han and Gaden.

"We've received word that the north has declared their

candidate for the Sunburst Throne," Han said. "Our scouts say they march toward the imperial city even now."

Yuli rose to her feet. "The Falconer?"

Gaden shook their head. "No," they said grimly. "Maltak Kho."

It had been two years to the day since any of the Bangtan Brothers set foot on the Azure Isles when their ship finally arrived in the port of Kasong.

The passage from the Sweet Sea, down the Dragon's Beard into the Bay of Dragons, and across the Azure Strait had been uneventful, despite the threat of winter storms that constantly blew down from the Frozen Wastes to the north. They had been traveling by boat for several days before Alyosha, the keenest-eyed of them all, claimed he could see the snow-topped mountains of their homeland from the prow of their ship.

It wasn't possible, of course, but the Brothers frequently indulged their odd little bird, whose pure and childlike way of seeing the world was a source of both delight and puzzlement to the others. They had passed much of the time on board playing his games, elaborating on what they could spy from the decks—people dancing in the streets, tigers and bears prowling the slopes outside the cities, and even dragons frolicking in the clouds above Mount Changgun. They were good at passing time together, the Bangtan Brothers; they had been traveling more or less constantly for the past five years.

The life of a traveling performer was both more exciting and more tedious than most people liked to believe. There were the glamour and thrill of each performance, each stop in a different city, a different town, a different audience, but there were also the interminably long stretches of road and river between each location. There were only so many times one could practice a dance, run lines in a play, or even write new material; there were many more hours when they were too tired or too unfocused or too unmotivated to work. It was in those moments that the Brothers had learned to play—not just games, but with the mundanity of life between each performance. Sungho kept a running tally of favors and chores exchanged and owed, Bohyun and Mihoon made sure the boys were kept healthy and fed, and the Choi brothers ensured that no one was ever bored with their constant gamboling and roughhousing.

But it was up to Junseo, their leader, to keep the bigger picture in mind.

He had been the first to join the Guardians of Dawn five years ago, when he had been just a boy. A gifted magician, he'd had the advantage of a private tutor to foster his education in the Language of Flowers and the development of his powers, and it had also been his idea to create a performance troupe of magicians who could travel the length of the Morning Realms without suspicion. Because he was the first, he was named the leader, even though he was not the eldest. Because he was the leader, he sometimes felt himself at a distance from the others, even if he knew the boys never intended him to feel that way.

"What are you looking forward to eating the most when we get home?" Bohyun asked the others as their ship pulled into the harbor.

"Black bean sauce noodles," Taeri said immediately.

"Deep-fried pork and sweet sauce," Yoochun offered.

"Spicy seafood stew," said Mihoon.

"I want a cup of broth and fish cake from the street vendors," Alyosha said.

"You are all so dull and predictable," Bohyun said with disgust. "We can get any and all of those things elsewhere in the Morning Realms."

Junseo tried to remember the last time he had had a meal prepared Azurean style, made by loving hands and shared communally around a low table in a home. He tried to remember his mother and father, both working for the Guardians of Dawn, maintaining a safe house north of Kasong, but when he thought of *home*, the first images that came to mind were those nights spent camping on the road beside their covered wagon, with Mihoon making a simple pot of fermented chili paste stew filled with quick-fried noodle, supplemented by spicy pickled cabbage and whatever fish or game Bohyun and Yoochun could catch. It made him a little melancholy that he could measure the distance between himself and the Azure Isles now not just by leagues but by memory.

"We'll spend the first night eating our way through Kasong," Junseo promised the others. "It may be the last time we'll have hot food like that for a while."

A collective groan rose from the Bangtan Brothers, and it tugged at Junseo's heart to remind them of the task ahead. It was easier, sometimes, to put one foot in front of the other and not think of the destination when they were walking and riding behind their nag, Cloud, but coming back to the Azure Isles felt more like an ending than a beginning. They were back to where they began, and it was natural for the mind to start looking ahead to the future, beyond the civil war hanging over their heads, beyond the threat of the Mother of Ten Thousand Demons. Would the Bangtan Brothers still continue performing once their duties to the Guardians of Dawn had been fulfilled? For the longest time, Junseo had not let himself think of what life would look like on the other side of this conflict. Too much hope made the present appear too hard and uncertain.

"Where do we even begin looking for this Min Suhwa?" Sungho asked. "And how would we even go about protecting her until this war is over?"

The lost princess. The daughter of the last Marquess of the Azure Isles, before the current Fleet Queen murdered her sister and allied with the Warlord during the Just War. Just a footnote in the annals, barely even named. Min Suhwa could be anyone. Anywhere.

"We find the Maltak Huntsman, that's where we'll begin," Junseo said. "He seems to believe she's hidden somewhere in the convents of the priestesses of Do in the mountains to the north."

"The death nuns?" Bohyun shivered. "They're creepy."

Junseo thought of the veiled, white-robed sisters present at every birth and death across the Morning Realms, who also presided over every ritual and festival in the Azure Isles. Their convents were hospices and infirmaries, and it was said the priestesses knew as many ways to heal a person as they knew to kill them. Orphans and other unwanted children were often left at their doorstep to be reared until the age of twelve, after which they were apprenticed into their communities if they didn't dedicate themselves to the order.

"They're not creepy," Alyosha protested. The Choi brothers had been raised in a convent of the Way, until they ran away to join the Guardians of Dawn. "They're beautiful. They also dance and sing."

Sword dances were often part of the rituals of the Azure Isles, and Junseo remembered watching the priestesses of Do put on a performance during a festival when he was a little boy.

"I don't know," Bohyun muttered. "I like my beauty with a little less edge, if you ask me."

"Even if we do find this Min Suhwa," Mihoon said, "how will we protect her? Where will we take her?"

Six pairs of eyes turned to look at Junseo, and once again, he felt the weight of leadership on his shoulders. "One step at a time," he said. "First we deal with the Maltak Huntsman. Then we will figure out where to go. What to do. In the meantime," he said with a smile, "we'll do what we do best."

Sungho grinned back. "Brothers, let's put on a show!"

Junseo beckoned to the members, and the boys gathered in a circle, each putting his hand into the middle.

"Bangtan, Bangtan, Bang-Bangtan!"

# ACKNOWLEDGMENTS

Writing a book is hard, but writing acknowledgments to said book is even harder.

That said, I would be remiss if I didn't thank all those who supported me through the journey of writing the Guardians of Dawn series. If I miss a name, I'm sorry; there are so many people who have touched this book along the way, and my mind is like a sieve.

First, to my editor, Eileen Rothschild: for being unfailingly patient and understanding, thank you. Thanks also to Char Dreyer, for keeping everything on the rails!

Next, to my agent, Katelyn Detweiler: for being my first and best champion, I am eternally grateful. And all the wonderful people at Jill Grinberg Literary—Denise Page, Sam Farkas, et al.

To the marketing, publicity, production, and sales departments at Wednesday Books and St. Martin's Publishing Group, thank you for championing my titles.

To the Ca$h Money Coven: They say that every group of friends has a weird chat name, and ours is no exception. Thanks so much for keeping me grounded and sane and also listening to my ADHD wittering.

To my family, for believing in me and pushing me to pursue this strange business of publishing, I can say only that I'm blessed. And loved.

To Bear, White-Harp, Castor, and Pollux: I love you and you and you and you.

# ABOUT THE AUTHOR

S. JAE-JONES (JJ) is an artist, an adrenaline junkie, and the *New York Times* bestselling author of the Wintersong duology and the Guardians of Dawn series. Born and raised in Los Angeles, she now lives on the wrong coast, where she can't believe she has to deal with winter every year. When not writing, JJ can be found working toward her next black belt degree, being run ragged by her twin dogs, Castor and Pollux, or indulging in her favorite hobby—collecting more hobbies.